AT LOVE'S COMMAND

HANGER'S HORSEMEN · 1

AT LOVE'S COMMAND

KAREN WITEMEYER

BETHANYHOUSE

a division of Baker Publishing Group
Minneapolis, Minnesota

© 2020 by Karen Witemeyer

Published by Bethany House Publishers
11400 Hampshire Avenue South
Bloomington, Minnesota 55438
www.bethanyhouse.com

Bethany House Publishers is a division of
Baker Publishing Group, Grand Rapids, Michigan

Printed in the United States of America

Library of Congress Cataloging-in-Publication Data
Names: Witemeyer, Karen, author.
Title: At love's command : a novel / Karen Witemeyer.
Description: Bloomington, Minnesota : Bethany House Publishers, [2020] |Series:
    Hanger's horsemen ; 1
Identifiers: LCCN 2019055577 | ISBN 9780764232077 (trade paperback) |
    ISBN 9780764236273 (cloth) | ISBN 9781493425099 (ebook)
Subjects: GSAFD: Western stories
Classification: LCC PS3623.I864 A8 2020 | DDC 813/.6—dc23
LC record available at https://lccn.loc.gov/2019055577

Scripture quotations are from the King James Version of the Bible.

This is a work of fiction. Names, characters, incidents, and dialogues are products of
the author's imagination and are not to be construed as real. Any resemblance to actual
events or persons, living or dead, is entirely coincidental.

Cover design by Dan Thornberg, Design Source Creative Services

Author is represented by the Books & Such Literary Agency.

Baker Publishing Group publications use paper produced from sustainable forestry
practices and post-consumer waste whenever possible.

21 22 23 24 25 26 27   8 7 6 5 4 3 2

The LORD also will be a refuge for the oppressed,
a refuge in times of trouble.
And they that know thy name will put their trust
in thee: for thou, LORD, hast not forsaken them
that seek thee.

—Psalm 9:9–10

For my favorite hero.
Horsemen aren't the only champions
who can save the day.
Whether you are rescuing me from
creepy-crawly invaders, malfunctioning
computers, or villainous piles of laundry,
you are always there when I need you.
Thanks, love.

PROLOGUE

WOUNDED KNEE CREEK, SOUTH DAKOTA
PINE RIDGE INDIAN RESERVATION
DECEMBER 29, 1890

According to the Good Book, there was a time for war and a time for peace. Captain Matthew Hanger of the 7th Cavalry prayed this was a time for peace even as he fit his finger to the trigger of his Remington Army revolver and studied the Lakota Sioux warriors on the other side of the ravine. Matt was sick of war. Sick of training men only to watch them fall on the battlefield. Sick of politicians proclaiming policy without concern for the men sent to enforce it. Sick of right and wrong blurring into a muddy, indecipherable mess until he no longer knew on which side he stood.

He supposed he should be thankful to still be alive after thirteen years of frontier fighting, but he hadn't felt alive since the day he found his parents and baby sister murdered by a raiding party. He'd been five, too young to fight back yet old enough to have his soul hollowed out like the family farmhouse, scorched from within until only a husk remained.

"You think they'll surrender their weapons, Cap?" The low voice of Corporal Luke Davenport cut through the cold winter air.

"I pray they do."

Three companies of dismounted soldiers had entered the Lakota camp and were in the process of surrounding Chief Big Foot's warriors—a contingent that looked to be about a hundred and twenty men, many wrapped in blankets due to the snowy conditions. Matt's company, still mounted, had been ordered to the ridge south of the camp to guard against any attempt by the Lakota to escape.

A low chant carried on the wind. Matt tensed. The Lakota Ghost Dance rituals spooked some of the younger troopers. *Keep your heads,* he silently urged as the men searching the camp for weapons carried out their orders.

The chanting grew louder. A Sioux holy man began to dance, weaving through the younger warriors. Nervous murmurs sounded in the ranks behind Matt.

"Steady, boys." He raised his voice just enough to carry to the troopers under his command. "Don't let them rattle you. Focus on the mission."

The Lakota had been rounded up yesterday near Porcupine Butte. Big Foot had been compliant. But something was different today. Matt could feel it as surely as he could feel the winter wind against his neck.

"Got a verse for me, Preach?" Matt asked.

Corporal Davenport had been with him for nearly a decade. They'd come up through the ranks together. Luke was deadly in hand-to-hand combat—the best swordsman Matt had ever seen—yet Matt had come to rely on him for more than having his back. Luke was a walking repository of Scripture. Always had a verse at the ready. And those verses kept Matt grounded.

If ever there was a time for grounding, it was now.

"'For thou hast girded me with strength unto the battle,'" the corporal murmured, "Psalm 18:39."

Matt let the words sink in. He'd heard Luke quote that one before. It was good for putting a military man in a confident frame of mind before charging an enemy, but less than reassuring when one hoped for peaceful compliance. It lent an ominous tension to the knot already twisting in Matt's gut.

Colonel Forsyth ordered the Lakota to turn over their rifles, his men moving among the warriors and effectively separating them out from the camp where the women and children remained. The older men complied, but the younger braves clung to their blankets as if they had nothing to turn over, their faces stoic masks that brought the hair up on the back of Matt's neck.

All the while, the medicine man kept chanting. Kept dancing.

Matt sat higher in the saddle. His knees tightened around Phineas. His blood bay gelding's ears pricked, and his head lowered in readiness. Matt scanned the entire party of Lakota. No visible weapons among them. Yet the troopers searching the camp had only turned up a handful of rifles.

Something was off.

Movement below sharpened Matt's focus. A Lakota dropped his blanket. Sun glinted off metal. A shot cracked.

From which side? It didn't matter. Purgatory had erupted. "Charge!"

Matt voiced the shout, then signaled Mark Wallace, his

trumpeter, to sound the advance. The bugle called. Horses surged forward. Guns blazed.

More than a dozen troopers in the camp already lay fallen. Twice as many Lakota sprawled unmoving in the snow beside them.

The cavalry's sentinels and scouts sprinted for the protection of the mounted line. Matt urged Phineas forward, his only thought to protect their men. He laid down cover fire, taking down an armed Lakota running for the ravine and another who had stopped to take aim at a retreating trooper.

Behind him, the Hotchkiss artillery boomed. The force of the blasts from the four light mountain guns reverberated through Matt's torso. He leaned low in the saddle, decreasing his target size so as not to fall victim to the crossfire.

Catching a glimpse of a familiar face, Matt steered Phineas to intercept a retreating trooper. Jonah Brooks, a buffalo soldier with the 10th Cavalry, had served with Matt on numerous reconnaissance missions when stealth had been required. He had a talent for making himself invisible and could hit a dime dead-center from five hundred yards. Too valuable an asset to lose in this mess. Plus, he was a friend.

Matt holstered his Remington and yanked his left boot from the stirrup. Slowing Phineas just enough to make a clean snatch, he leaned sideways and offered his arm. "Jonah! Grab hold!"

The black man didn't hesitate. He locked onto Matt's wrist and swung his body upward as Matt leaned away to counterbalance his weight. Jonah got a toe in the stirrup and fought his way onto Phineas's back behind the saddle.

A hand thumped Matt's shoulder. "I'm good, Cap!"

Matt turned Phineas and headed for the edge of the ravine. The Hotchkiss guns had started a panic among the Lakota.

Women and children bolted out of the camp, seeking escape through the ravine alongside their men. But mixing with the warriors only made them targets.

"Protect our retreat!" Matt yelled to his men. Preach turned in his saddle at his call and met his gaze. "But watch your fire! We have innocents in the field." Matt pointed to a woman with a toddler in her arms racing toward the ravine.

Preach nodded and started shouting to the troops under his command. Making war on a trained enemy was one thing, but cutting down women and children . . . neither of them wanted any part of that.

"Preach!" Matt called. "Once the men are clear, block the Lakota's escape."

His corporal tapped his cap brim with the barrel of his revolver, showing he'd heard. Matt trusted him to see to the duty while he got Jonah to safety. Phineas couldn't carry two for long, so Matt headed for a rise to the west of the ravine and called out to the other dismounted troops to rally behind the hill. The Hotchkiss guns were firing too close to the line. The troops were in as much danger from their own artillery as they were from the Lakota. In fact, most of the Lakota were fleeing now, no longer an active threat.

Yet bullets continued to fly. Mortar shells continued to explode. Indians continued to die.

Protect your men. Complete your objective. Ignore the rest.

Matt clenched his jaw and hardened his heart. *Focus on what's within your control.* He couldn't control the artillery. Couldn't stop the panicked flight of innocents into the line of fire. But he could get his men to a protected position and reorganize the troops to halt the enemy's flight.

Once atop the rise, Matt reined Phineas in, and Jonah slid to the ground. "Take my rifle," Matt ordered as he slid his Springfield from its scabbard and shoved it toward Jonah, who'd been left with only his side arm. "You can do more good watching our backs from a distance with this than following us to the ravine with only your Peacemaker."

Jonah said nothing, just gave a sharp nod and grabbed the rifle.

Matt felt better for his men already. Jonah with a single-load Springfield could take down more enemy combatants than half the troopers bouncing around on horseback combined. And his bullets would find the right targets, not fly haphazardly toward anything that moved.

Spotting the gray horse of his trumpeter, Matt signaled to Wallace and instructed him to organize the dismounted men and have them cover the ravine while Matt joined Preach on the west end to contain those trying to flee.

"It's a mess, Cap." Preach strode forward to give his report as Matt slid from the saddle. "There's a group huddled in a cut bank a few yards in. Women and children, mostly. But it'd be suicide to try to get to them with all the cross-fire."

Matt nodded, taking in the chaos of the Lakota camp. His gaze hesitated on the blue coats of fallen soldiers. He scanned the scene as he scoured his brain for a plan that would enable him to accomplish his objective while minimizing casualties.

Indians poured into the ravine, seeking refuge from the barrage of guns and artillery. Some were armed warriors. Others were innocents. Yet with the dirt and blood and constant stirring of bodies, it was nearly impossible to tell them apart.

A handful of warriors had started scaling the ravine. "There!" Matt pointed at the men he'd spotted. "Focus your efforts on keeping those warriors contained. If they crest the ridge, they'll have a clean shot on our boys. I'll see what I can do about the band at the cut bank."

"Got it." Luke gave a sharp nod as Matt turned to address his self-assigned mission. "Hey, Cap?"

Matt turned back. "Yeah?"

"Some of them females have guns. Saw one covered in blood holding a cavalry revolver. Must've stolen it from a fallen trooper. Keep your guard up."

"Always, Corporal." If a woman took up arms and stood beside her man in a fight, she opened herself up to the consequences. But a man of honor protected the weaker sex to the best of his ability in all circumstances. Even in war.

Especially in war.

Ducking behind Phineas, Matt reloaded his Remington, then hunched low and jogged along the edge of the ravine, away from the most concentrated gunfire. He couldn't allow the women and children to escape, but he could take them into custody and move them to a more sheltered position.

Signaling a handful of his men to fall in behind him, Matt circled around to the shallow end of the ravine and began the march into Hades. The constant barrage of cavalry fire into the ravine had turned the Lakota's escape route into a mass grave. The sides of the ravine had hidden the full extent of the destruction when he'd been above, but now nothing spared Matt from the horror of the scores of dead and dying littering the ravine floor.

Blood and gunpowder filled his nostrils, but he marched on. It was what a commander did. Showed no fear. No revulsion. Only confidence and strength. So his men would follow.

Catching sight of the cut bank, he veered to the left. He ordered his men to guard the mouth of the ravine and only to fire if fired upon. Then he strode forward, gun in hand.

A bullet's high-pitched whine tickled his ear as it raced past to slam into the earth two feet to his right. Another pinged off a rock ledge in front of him.

He could see them now. Five of them. Kids, mostly.

An old woman met his gaze and straightened. Not in fear, but in resignation. Pride straightened her shoulders and lifted her chin, even as she moved to shield the children. Matt pointed the barrel of his Remington toward the sky and held his left hand palm-out in an effort to reassure her that he meant no harm. Then he gestured for her to come to him.

She refused to move, just stared at him.

A sudden motion from behind the woman, however, flared Matt's instincts. A half-grown boy lurched around his protector, a revolver in his hand.

Matt didn't hesitate. He lowered his barrel and fired. The kid fired too, his shot going wide as Matt's bullet lodged in the youth's shoulder. Matt rushed forward, needing to secure the weapon. A second child cried out as the boy crumpled to the ground. Matt lunged for him and wrapped his fingers around the gun still in the kid's hand. With a quick twist, the gun fell free. Matt tucked it into his belt, then yanked a handkerchief from his pocket and pressed it against the boy's wound. The kid would need a doctor to remove the bullet and sew him up, but he'd survive.

If they got out of this ravine.

"Captain! Artillery is on the move," one of his men called. "We gotta retreat."

Matt jerked his attention to the canyon wall behind him. Sure enough, one of the Hotchkiss guns was being wheeled into place near the ravine's edge. No one would survive the cannon fire at this range.

He turned back to the old woman. "Come." He gestured urgently and pointed at the mountain gun. "We must leave. Now."

She ignored him. Well, that wasn't precisely true. She ignored his order, not him. Him, she impaled with a look of hatred as she herded the other children back toward the camp. Into the line of fire. As if she'd rather die with her people than follow him.

The boy Matt was tending flailed. He kicked out at Matt and rolled away, leaving Matt's bloodied handkerchief in the snow behind him.

"Wait!" Matt grabbed for the boy, desperate to save at least one, but the kid scrambled rashly after his kin, only to be hit full in the chest by a bullet. He flew backward from the force of the hit.

"No!" Matt charged after him, but a hand locked on his arm from behind.

"You can't save him, Matt." Preach's voice.

When had his corporal come into the ravine? Wasn't he supposed to be guarding the line? No, the line had been overtaken by the Hotchkiss gun.

Matt struggled. He had to get those kids out. Before it was too late.

But Luke only tightened his hold. Dragged him backward.

The boy didn't move. Blood soaked through his coat as the truth soaked into Matt's mind. He was dead. Beyond saving. But what about the others?

Matt scanned the ravine for the old woman and her charges as Luke dragged him away. He spotted her right as the cannon boomed.

"Captain? Can you hear me?"

Matt roused slowly. His head throbbed. His ears rang. His cheek stung. Why did his cheek sting?

He eased his eyes open just in time to see Wallace's open hand swinging in for a slap. His trumpeter's palm connected sharply with Matt's jaw. Matt's head lolled sideways.

Mystery of the stinging cheek solved.

Matt groaned. "I'd like to keep my teeth in my head, if you don't mind."

"Thank God." Wallace slid an arm beneath Matt's shoulders and helped him sit up. "Apologies, Captain Hanger. You've been out for quite a spell. We were getting worried."

That was when it hit him. The quiet. No gunfire. No cannons.

His senses sharpened. "Luke?"

"Here, Cap." Preach's head popped into Matt's field of vision, followed by Jonah's. "It's over."

Over?

As if they'd read his mind, his men braced his arms and helped him to his feet. Dizziness assailed him at the jarring movement, but it was the sight that met his eyes that made his knees buckle. He'd seen death before, but never on this scale. Never so one-sided.

Scores of Lakota lay dead in the ravine. Maybe hundreds. He swallowed hard as his gaze landed on a face he recognized. The old woman. The children scattered around her. Nothing more than lifeless heaps in the snow.

Why? This was supposed to be a simple weapon confiscation. An escort to the reservation. How had it turned into a bloodbath?

Bile burned the back of Matt's throat. He'd joined the cavalry to protect settlers, people like his family. His task had been to bring justice and order to the frontier. This wasn't justice.

"God forgive us," he murmured.

They'd just participated in a massacre.

ONE

Purgatory Springs, Texas
May 1893

They've got us pinned down, Captain."

Matt Hanger braced his back against the wall of the line shack he and Wallace had taken shelter behind and reloaded his Remington. Gunfire peppered the air as the gang of rustlers they'd been hired to eradicate closed in on their position. Matt's former trumpeter returned fire from the opposite side of the ramshackle building while Matt dumped his spent casings and plucked fresh cartridges from his belt.

"Hold the line a little longer, Wallace," Matt ordered, his voice firm. Mark was a good soldier. A mite reckless from time to time, but a man who could be counted on when a situation deteriorated. Like this one.

Preach and the ranchers who'd hired them needed more time if they were going to drive the stolen cattle back to the Circle D before the rustlers discovered they'd been hornswoggled. It fell to Matt and Wallace to keep the gang distracted.

Sliding a sixth bullet into the cylinder, Matt turned back to the fight, aimed, and shot the hat from a rustler who'd taken advantage of the reloading lull to dash through the trees on Matt's side of the shed in an effort to gain a tactical advantage.

The rustler yelped and scurried back to the oak guarding his compatriot.

After mustering out of the army following the disaster at Wounded Knee, Matt and the others had made a pact against the use of deadly force. They might be mercenaries after a fashion, but they made it clear to the people who hired them that killing was off the table.

Using hats for target practice, however . . . well, that kept a man's skill honed.

"Jonah will be in position soon," Matt said as Wallace retreated behind the shed to reload. "We just gotta hold them off for a few more minutes."

Easier said than done when the enemy outnumbered them six to two.

A shot splintered the wood inches from Matt's face. He jerked back to a covered position and cast a quick glance at Wallace to ensure the kid was all right. His head was down, eyes locked on fingers busy shoving bullets into chambers. A good way to ensure speed, yet he sacrificed awareness of his surroundings.

The sight immediately put Matt on edge. He scanned the trees on his partner's side of the shed. Caught a movement. Fired.

A howl echoed as the rustler fell. Wallace's head came up, as did his weapon. He glanced at the fallen man, then turned to Matt, a smile of thanks on his face. That smile immediately hardened. He lunged forward, gun drawn.

"Get down!" he yelled as he shoved Matt out of the way and fired.

A second shot echoed nearly simultaneously. Mark grunted and fell backward.

"Wallace!" Matt scrambled to a better position. He had to protect his man.

Rustlers encroached from both sides. Matt dragged Wallace against the shed wall and crouched down in front of him. He fired at a movement on his right. Then swiveled and fired to his left.

Only two shots left.

God, I could use some help here.

Like a trumpet blast from heaven, a rifle reported from behind the shed. Two shots. One echoed from the left. The other from the right.

"Throw down your weapons," a deep voice boomed. "We've got you surrounded."

Jonah. Thank God. Jonah had been an answer to Matt's prayers more than once during their time together, but never had there been more on the line than today. They had a man down. The youngest of the crew.

"How bad, Wallace?" Matt didn't take his eyes off the trees. He'd put one rustler down with a shot to the leg, but the outlaw could still pose a threat. He was fairly sure Wallace had at least winged his man, but there was too much cover for him to know for sure.

"Shoulder shot, Captain. My gun arm's useless, but I don't think I'm headed to the pearly gates just yet."

The strain in the kid's voice belied the lightness of his words.

Another shot rang out, this time from the opposite direction. A cry echoed in the trees, followed by a soft thud as something heavy hit the dirt. Hopefully a gun.

"The man told ya to drop yer weapons." Preach's voice. He must have circled back after the ranchers got the cattle clear of the box canyon where the rustlers had stashed them. "Better do as he says and come out with yer hands in the air. I ain't exactly the patient sort."

One by one, the rustlers emerged, hands raised. One fellow only lifted a single arm, holding the other pressed against his left side where a bullet had creased him. Another two came out as a pair. The one carrying Matt's bullet in his leg limped and leaned heavily on his partner for support.

Keeping his gaze and his gun trained on the rustlers, Matt stood, shifted left, and backed up until his spine hit the shed wall. Then he slid down the wall into a crouch that brought him even with Wallace. A quick glance confirmed his suspicion. The wound was bad. Mark had propped himself up into a sitting position and shoved a field dressing against his shoulder, but blood had already soaked through it. The kid's face had lost all color, and the mouth famous for charming ladies with a roguish smile and flattering tongue was pulled down into an agonized grimace that boded ill.

Wallace needed a doctor. Fast. But they were in the middle of nowhere with nothing around but ranches and a ragged handful of buildings pretending to be a town. The closest city of consequence was San Marcos, ten miles away. Chances were good Mark wouldn't survive the trip there, and waiting for someone to fetch the doc would take at least two hours, if not more.

As soon as Jonah and Preach came into view from opposite directions, herding the rustlers between them, Matt holstered his weapon and focused all his attention on Wallace.

"The kid hit, boss?" Jonah asked as he took charge of the man who seemed to be the gang's leader, tying his hands behind his back with a strip of rawhide.

"Yep. Right shoulder," Matt answered as he changed the field dressing with one of his own and wrapped a bandage as tight as he could manage around the underarm and torso. "I'll patch him up best I can, but he's gonna need a doctor. Sooner rather than later."

"I need the doc too," one of the rustlers whined. Probably the one with a bullet in his leg, not that Matt made the effort to look up and check.

"Dalton," Preach called out, "where's the closest doc?"

Matt did look up then. Terrance Dalton, owner of the Circle D, stepped into the small clearing behind the line shack. Apparently Preach wasn't the only one to circle back. The local ranchers had pooled their funds to hire Matt's crew, but Dalton owned the largest herd and therefore had the most at stake. It spoke well of him that he cared enough for the lives of the men he'd hired that he'd leave his stock to lend his gun to the fight.

"Dr. Joe can tend 'em," Dalton said. "Got an office right here in Purgatory Springs. Across from the post office. Less than a mile away."

Best news Matt had heard all day. "Great. I'll get Wallace to Purgatory. Preach, you and Jonah take that bunch to the sheriff in San Marcos."

"What about me?" the whiny rustler complained. "I'm bleedin' all over the place."

"Preach?" Matt looked to his second-in-command.

Dalton moved in closer, gun at the ready while Luke bent to examine the criminal's leg.

"Looks like a through-and-through, Cap. I'll give him a

few quick stiches and bind it up. He should make it to San Marcos."

"I don't want you stitchin' me!"

Luke straightened and shrugged. "All right. Cauterizin's easier anyhow." He unsheathed his overlarge hunting knife and held it up between them. "Just need to light a fire and get this blade red-hot. Shouldn't take too long."

"N-n-never mind. Stitchin's fine."

Matt hid a grin and turned back to Wallace. The pain etched on the kid's face killed his amusement in a blink.

"Can you stand, soldier?" Matt hunkered down and lifted Wallace's left arm over his shoulders, then wrapped an arm around his waist.

Mark nodded, grimacing as he strained with the effort of standing.

The kid might be a mere twenty-seven, ten years Matt's junior, but he was no reedy youth. He had the lean, muscular build of a cavalryman, and it took all of Matt's grit to get them both upright.

Matt whistled, and half a minute later, Phineas trotted out of the trees. Wallace's gray trailed behind.

"Come on," Matt ground out as he moved them both toward the horses. "Let's get you to Purgatory."

"If it's all the same to you . . . Captain"—Wallace groaned as Matt jostled him—"I'd prefer . . . Paradise for my . . . final rest. Better company . . . you know? Gets a little . . . hot . . . in Purgatory."

Matt scowled at the poor jest and took on more of Wallace's weight, practically dragging the young man now. "There'll be no final resting today, soldier." He lifted Wallace higher, as if making him look like he was strong enough to walk would actually cause it to be true. "That's an order."

"Do my best . . . sir."

"That's all I ask, son." Matt clenched his jaw as Preach stepped up to hold the kid while Matt mounted.

Matt glanced heavenward as he swung into the saddle, knowing God would read the plea on his heart to spare Wallace's life. *All I ask.*

Matt rode to town as fast as he dared with Wallace fading in his arms. By the time he got to Purgatory Springs, the kid slumped against him, unconscious.

"Hang on, son," he murmured, shoving the panic away and focusing on what he could control—getting Wallace to the doctor.

Purgatory Springs consisted of nothing more than a half-dozen nondescript buildings along a single main road. Matt scanned for the post office sign, spotted it, and immediately steered Phineas to the white clapboard building across the street.

"Dr. Joe!" he yelled as he halted Phineas. "Get out here! Got a man down."

He pulled his right foot from the stirrup, braced his left leg, and shifted Wallace's weight against his shoulder. Slowly, he swung his right leg over the back of the horse, concentrating on keeping Mark steady.

"Here. Let me help." A woman reached up to support Wallace and take a good portion of his weight.

Where was the doc? It didn't seem right for a woman to be doing the heavy lifting. Though, Matt had to admit, she seemed capable. Strong too. She propped up Wallace's back as Matt eased to the ground. As soon as he got his foot free of the stirrup, he relieved her of her portion of the burden and caught Wallace beneath the knees.

The sensible woman didn't stand around gaping but immediately pivoted, scurried back to the office door, and held it open. "Bring him this way."

Matt had already followed on her heels and angled Wallace through the door. The nurse—for that was what she must be, with her bibbed white apron and dark blue dress—seemed to catalog Wallace's condition with her gaze as Matt eased him past her.

"Gunshot?" she asked as she scooted around him in the hall and led the way to an oak-paneled room filled with glass cabinets and a wooden examination table.

"Yep." That was all the answer Matt could manage while lugging around 175 pounds of dead weight.

It seemed to suit the nurse, though, for she asked nothing more. Just skittered around the cabinet and stomped on a pedal of some sort. The inclined table lowered into a horizontal position.

"Lay him here."

Matt did so. She immediately pressed two fingers to Wallace's neck.

"Weak, but regular. That's a good sign."

Matt nodded, the words easing his apprehension enough to allow him to take a full breath. But then the woman started unwrapping the kid's bandages.

Matt slapped his hand over her wrist. Her head jerked up, shocked eyes wide. Shocked, remarkably *green* eyes. The kind of eyes that could make a man forget what he was about. Or would have, if he wasn't in charge of fetching competent medical attention for a man he loved like family.

"The kid's lost enough blood already. I'd just as soon wait for the doctor to get here before you go unraveling things."

Those wide eyes narrowed as she tugged her hand free of his grasp. She straightened to her full height, which placed the top of her head even with his chin. "The doctor *is* here," she said, enunciating each unbelievable word with metronomic precision. "Dr. Josephine Burkett at your service."

Dr. Joe was a *woman?*

"Now, if you and your antiquated assumptions will get out of my way," she said as she pushed past him and reached for the bandages again, "I have a patient to tend."

TWO

Josephine turned her back on the frowning stranger whose broad shoulders took up far too much space in her examination room and focused instead on the more compliant one sprawled unconscious on her table.

Whoever had applied the dressing had done a fine job. Even with all the jostling the two men must have endured on horseback, pressure on the wound had remained steady and minimized blood loss. She stole a peek at the stiff fellow who had yet to reanimate after suffering rapid-onset paralysis. A condition commonly brought on by the pronouncement of her medical expertise. Josephine shook her head. The poor male brain. So susceptible to gender-oriented shock. Unable to process female capability in areas beyond child-rearing and housekeeping. Women doctors existed only in myth. At least that was what most military men believed. And this gent had *military* written all over him.

The posture. The bearing of command. The blue vest that buttoned all the way to his collar. An officer, most likely. Ex-cavalry, if she didn't miss her guess. She'd seen enough of his kind at her father's ranch to recognize the type. Sure of themselves and their ideas. Even when they were wrong.

The end of the unraveled bandage drew her complete focus back to her patient. She gently pried the dressing away from the wound and frowned at the torn, bloodied flesh marred by a weapon that civilized people should be able to settle disputes without. Then she pressed the dressing back in place and attempted to roll the young man over far enough to check for an exit wound.

Before she could adjust and find the proper leverage to manage the task on her own, the scowling chauvinist next to her broke out of his stupor and grabbed his friend's side.

"Thank you." She offered a brief smile. Not that she *needed* the ruffian's help, of course, but she was pragmatic enough to accept it if it sped the examination process.

Josephine eyed the back of her patient's shirt. No hole. She ran her hand over his shoulder and back, feeling for a bulge to indicate the bullet had attempted an exit. She found nothing. She rolled him onto his back again and started cataloging what needed to be done. Cut away the shirt. Clean the wound. Find the bullet. Extract. Stitch. Guard against infection.

"You able to help him, Doc?"

Josephine glanced up as she retrieved a pair of scissors from the surgical tray she always kept readied. Concern was etched as deeply into her visitor's face as the squint lines at the corner of his eyes.

Yet he'd called her *Doc*. Not *Miss* or *Nurse*. She'd had to prove herself by bringing old man Johnson back from the grave with a cholecystectomy before the men around Purgatory Springs had honored her with that title. After she'd removed his gallbladder, Hiram Johnson bragged to all who would listen that his pain had disappeared virtually over-night, finally garnering her the respect she'd worked months to build. The fact that her professional title rolled off this military man's tongue on nothing but her say-so was really rather remarkable.

Maybe he wasn't quite the chauvinist she'd taken him for. Then again, he *was* still questioning her skills.

Meeting his earnest hazel eyes straight on, she gave him the calm authority she'd been trained to impart upon worried friends and family. "Yes. I've extracted bullets before." Only two, and never in an area quite so rife with major blood ves-sels, but he didn't need to know that.

Despite the name, Purgatory Springs had been a peaceful little town until the rustling started. Jeffrey Cawyer shoot-ing himself in the foot had been her only active gunshot case since medical school, though she had expertly pulled a slug from the Williams' family turkey her first Thanksgiving in town when there'd been some concern over the new cook mangling the prize-winning poultry with her heavy-handed hacking. Mrs. Williams insisted on a pristine bird for her table, and since Hiram Johnson had still possessed his stone-laden gallbladder at the time, Josephine had been willing to demonstrate her surgical skills in any way pos-sible.

Her lack of abundant experience was immaterial at the moment, however. She knew the anatomy, had been trained by the best surgeons the Women's Medical College of Penn-sylvania had to offer, and possessed the steadiest hand in her graduating class. With God guiding her, she could handle any task placed before her.

Josephine gripped the scissors with authority and angled

them along the button line near the injured cowboy's throat. First rule of dealing with antsy bystanders: reassure them. Second rule: give them something to do.

"There's a basin by the window," she said without looking up from her work. "Wash up. Once I get this shirt out of the way, I'm going to clean and examine the wound. It'll be painful, and your friend might rouse. I may need you to hold him down while I work."

Boot heels clicking sharply on her floor followed by the sound of pouring water told her he'd followed her instructions. One benefit of working with military men—they were good at obeying orders. As long as they recognized the authority of the person administering them. The fact that this one was washing dirt, blood, and grime from hands and arms without a single question or comment increased the likelihood that he'd actually be useful to her during the upcoming surgery.

Turning her scissors down the sleeve, Josephine finished cutting away the injured man's shirt. She set her scissors aside, removed the field dressing from the wound, then gently pulled the tan cotton fabric away as well. Blood seeped from the hole, already thick with coagulation.

"What can I do?" He'd returned, hat gone, vest removed, sleeves rolled to elbows, and hair damp around his face.

Josephine bit back a smile. This one didn't do things by half measures. He'd washed from stem to stern. Good. The cleaner the surgical environment, the better for her patient.

She took a clean dressing, one pretreated with carbolic acid to guard against sepsis, and pressed it to the wound. "Hold this," she instructed. "And keep pressure on it."

He did so.

She needed to do her own washing. Once her hands were

scrubbed to her satisfaction, she returned and relieved him of duty. Peeling back the dressing, she bent close to examine the wound. It looked relatively clean. Not too deep. Little to no debris. Just some fibers from where the bullet had torn through the shirt. A simple irrigation should be sufficient. She reached for a syringe.

"What is his name?" she asked.

"Wallace." Her new assistant had a rough, gravelly voice. Strong, yet worn down by life. "Mark Wallace."

She swabbed away the few fibers she'd spotted and irrigated the wound for increased visibility. Dabbing the excess liquid from the surrounding flesh, Josephine glanced up at her assistant. "And *your* name?"

He didn't meet her gaze. He was too busy staring at the hole in his friend's shoulder. "Matthew Hanger."

Josephine started. *The* Matthew Hanger? Decorated cavalry officer who'd joined General Nelson Miles in speaking out against the atrocities that had transpired at Wounded Knee?

She knew Terrance Dalton and the other ranchers had hired extra firepower to deal with the rustling problem, but she hadn't realized they'd hired Hanger's Horsemen. The famed foursome had made a name for themselves in the last couple years by taking on problems the law either couldn't or wouldn't handle.

Rumors and tall tales had spread through schoolyards and saloons, growing out of proportion. Josephine had ceased listening to the fantasy and speculation whispered in corners about the group of near-mythical heroes, her scientific mind less than impressed. Ordinary men couldn't accomplish half the feats credited to the Horsemen. The men themselves probably didn't even exist. They were no doubt the product of some newspaperman's imaginative scheme to increase subscriptions with a bit of sensational journalism.

Yet the leader of the Horsemen stood in her examination room. Matthew Hanger. His jaw clenched. His stance braced. His eyes carrying the determination of one who would do whatever it took to accomplish his objective— saving his friend's life.

Her role in that objective suddenly weighed more heavily upon her shoulders than it had a moment before.

Josephine gave herself a mental shake. It didn't matter who these men were or what heroic feats they might or might not have undertaken. They needed help, and God had led them to her.

"Well, Mr. Hanger, I'm about to start probing for the bullet, and it's bound to make Mr. Wallace cranky. The more you can calm him, the easier time I'll have of extracting the ball. Your friend is fortunate. The wound is fairly shallow. Neither the clavicle nor the scapula was impacted, so we don't have to worry about broken bones. However, there are a lot of blood vessels and nerves in this area. I don't think the bullet damaged the subclavian artery, but the brachial plexus is delicate and could affect future arm functionality, so I must take great care."

"Understood." Mr. Hanger leaned forward and locked his hands over Mr. Wallace's wrists. "Proceed."

As soon as Josephine fit her finger inside the bullet's hole, Mr. Wallace stiffened and groaned. He eyes opened, though they were glassy and unfocused. His head raised off the table, the tendons in his neck standing at attention. Mr. Hanger instantly moved his grip from Wallace's left wrist to his left shoulder and pinned him down.

"Easy, soldier." His tone carried more command than consolation, but it seemed to soothe her patient anyway.

"Captain?"

"I'm here, son. You're safe. The doc just needs to dig that bullet out of your arm, so lie still, all right?"

When her patient quieted, Josephine eased her finger deeper into the hole, carefully probing the torn tissue and noting damage done along the way. Mr. Wallace grunted softly and turned his head in her direction. His eyes widened slightly.

"Guess you . . . brought me to Paradise . . . instead of Purgatory . . . after all, Captain."

Josephine raised a brow. Was the rogue actually flirting with her?

"Doctors . . . wouldn't be this . . . pretty in Purgatory."

Guess so. She grinned and shook her head as she turned her attention back to his wound. "I assure you, Mr. Wallace, that my idea of Paradise does not include cowboys bleeding all over my fine wood floors." She probed deeper.

Mr. Wallace grunted. "My . . . apologies . . . ma'am."

"Quit wasting energy tryin' to sweet-talk the lady doctor," Mr. Hanger groused, though no real heat laced his tone. "She's got more important things to occupy her at the moment."

True. Josephine nibbled the edge of her tongue as the tip of her finger encountered a hard lump. Her stomach leaped. The bullet. It was close.

Mr. Wallace's grunts turned into extended guttural groans, but Josephine barely heard them. Her world had shrunk to include only muscle, sinew, and the foreign particle that must be removed.

It took an extra incision, her narrowest set of forceps, and more digging than she would have preferred, but the *ting* of the metal ball when it finally hit the surgical tray echoed through the examination room like the triumphant final chord of a great symphony. Satisfaction incarnate.

Somewhere along the way, Mr. Wallace had passed out again, but that was to be expected. What wasn't expected was the fluttering in her belly when Mr. Hanger shared in her symphonic moment by giving her a nod of approval.

It shouldn't have meant anything special. She'd become a doctor to help the hurting, not to impress those who watched. Yet the gesture of respect flushed her with unexpected pleasure. She doubted Matthew Hanger gave those nods out with any great frequency. He seemed a man of high standards, hardened by war and ungenerous with commendations.

Not that she actually knew him, she reminded herself sternly as she wiped the blood from her hands and took up a suturing needle. For all she knew, he could dole out approving nods like a politician did campaign promises, and with just as much meaning behind them. But when she lifted her gaze from her instrument tray and his brown-green eyes latched on to hers, the frank honesty in his face confirmed her initial impression.

"Thanks, Doc," he said. Two simple words, but the emotion behind them was palpable.

He cared for this man. Had been afraid for him. Probably even held himself responsible for putting him in harm's way. He'd taken a chance trusting her with his care—a chance that, thankfully, had paid off.

Unless . . .

"There's always a risk of infection," she informed him, returning honesty for honesty. "He'll need to stay in my infirmary for a few days until I'm sure everything's healing the way it should."

Mr. Hanger crooked a grin at her. "Then I suppose you and I will be seeing a lot of each other over the next few days."

Josephine swallowed. The prospect of having a dictatorial military type underfoot should annoy her. So why did the twisting in her belly feel less like annoyance and more like anticipation?

CHAPTER THREE

Taking advantage of the muscles hanging about in her waiting room, Josephine instructed Mr. Hanger to move his friend into her infirmary once Mr. Wallace regained consciousness. The two large men dwarfed the tiny closet of a room that served as her recovery area, but they managed to hobble inside, and Mr. Hanger soon had her patient settled on the narrow bed. Bandages covered much of Mr. Wallace's bare chest, but the captain seemed intent on pulling the sheet up to cover as much exposed flesh as possible.

Josephine bit back a grin. Whose modesty was he trying to protect? Hers, or that of his friend? The teasing rogue who'd flirted with her while she delved for the bullet in his arm didn't strike her as the bashful type, so the efforts must be for her sake. Which meant Mr. Hanger viewed her more as a woman than a doctor now that they were out of the examination room. Her feminine side appreciated the gesture even though her professional side scoffed at the needlessness of it. Anatomy was just anatomy, after all.

Mr. Wallace's eyelids drooped. "I'm good here, Captain," he murmured when Mr. Hanger started folding himself into the small chair next to the bed. "No need to keep vigil. More important things to do."

A muscle ticked at the corner of the captain's mouth, twitching the square horseshoe mustache that fed into the well-trimmed beard outlining his jaw. "Nothin's more important to me than my men. You know that."

Wallace quirked a half-grin. "Not even the horses? Phineas and Cooper have been standing out there a long time, Matt. Go see to them while I catch a little shut-eye."

A stubborn look tightened the captain's mouth, heralding a coming argument. Josephine headed it off with a touch to his arm. His attention flashed to her.

"Rest is the best thing for him now, and that'll be easier without you hovering."

Mr. Wallace chuckled weakly. "That's the truth."

"Shut up, Wallace."

The growled response elicited another unrepentant chuckle from her patient. "Go on, Captain." The laughter faded from Mr. Wallace's voice. "I'll rest better knowing Coop's been taken care of."

"Fine, but I'll be back in an hour." The last part of that statement was aimed at her.

Josephine nodded. "I'll keep an eye on him."

Matthew Hanger held her gaze for a long moment, his expression stern and unrelenting, as if trying to impose his will upon her—a will that clearly insisted he not be dismissed next time.

Josephine met his challenge, chin raised. He was afraid. She understood that. Felt compassion, even. But she'd not be cowed. This was her campaign, not his. He could join her on the field of battle if he wished, but she was the general, and she'd make the decisions about what was best for her patient.

Finally, he broke eye contact and pivoted toward the door. Josephine gave her patient a quick once-over to ensure all was as it should be, then followed the captain out.

He stopped at the bench in her waiting room to collect his things. All right, it wasn't really a *room*. More like the front entryway. The small building she rented for her practice didn't afford space for anything more substantial. She'd brought in a bench and set it against the wall in order to have a place to shoo people when they started getting underfoot or hindering the confidentiality of doctor-patient conversations. Today, it apparently doubled as a hat and coat rack.

Maybe she should bring in one of those as well. Her clientele still skewed heavily toward the feminine side of the population despite her success with Hiram Johnson, but maybe if she made her office more male-friendly, the masculine citizenry would be more likely to come in.

Then again, most of the men of her acquaintance had to be near death before they'd seek out a doctor of any gender. She eyed the man in front of her as he fit his tan hat to his head, covering the short dark hair that life had dusted with a smattering of gray strands. She doubted Matthew Hanger would seek a doctor for anything less than a bullet. Even then, he'd probably prefer to throw some whiskey on the wound, dig out the ball with his hunting knife, and sew it up himself. He'd probably even manage the feat with relative success if the wound were in a place he could reach. He had done an admirable job with Mr. Wallace's field dressing, after all, and he struck her as the warrior type. Nothing would stop him except death itself.

Or his own stubbornness.

Josephine picked up the vest with gold buttons that had been tossed on the bench's seat and handed it to its owner after he unrolled his sleeves and fastened his cuffs. "Cavalry?" she asked, nodding toward the distinctive light blue wool.

Mr. Hanger's hand paused mid-reach.

She'd surprised him. Good. She liked keeping military types on their toes. Reminded them they didn't always have all the answers.

"Retired," he ground out as he accepted the vest from her and slid his arms through the holes.

"I thought so. My father supplies horses to the army. We had cavalrymen around the ranch a lot when I was growing up."

"Burkett . . ." The captain's brows lifted a fraction, and a hint of excitement danced in his hazel eyes. "Thaddeus Burkett? Of Gringolet Farms?"

"You've heard of him?" Josephine smiled. Of course Mr. Hanger had heard of him. Her father produced some of the most sought-after horseflesh in the country.

He'd ridden for the US Cavalry during the War Between the States, and after the conflict ended, he sold the small breeding farm he'd inherited from his father in Pennsylvania, took his stock, and moved west, wanting to breed a horse more suited to the rugged territory of the expanding frontier. Mustang mares provided the perfect foil for his eastern studs. As army forts sprang up to protect settlers from bandits, Indians, and general lawlessness, the need for good horses bred for endurance and intelligence abounded. Her father met the demand with outstanding mounts that had the army coming back year after year.

"Heard of him?" Mr. Hanger's entire demeanor changed. For just a moment, the worry for his friend disappeared, and a lightness came over him. "Gringolet mounts are the most coveted horses in the regiments. I've seen officers fight over them."

"You were an officer, right? Mr. Wallace called you Captain. Did you ever have a Gringolet horse?"

Mr. Hanger shook his head. "No. By the time I received my rank, I'd already been paired with Phineas and had no desire for a different mount. We've been together nigh on ten years." He spoke with a level of fondness most people reserved for family. But then, to a cavalryman, his horse *was* family.

Josephine opened the clinic door and led the way down to the street. She walked up to the blood bay standing patiently where his owner had left him, fully tacked and unhitched. The animal was well-trained. She held her hand out to the gelding to let him become familiar with her scent, then stroked his neck, letting her fingers sift through his dark mane. "Well, when Phineas is ready for the rocking chair, I'd be happy to introduce you to my father. Should you be interested in a private purchase."

"Thanks." Mr. Hanger grinned at her, his own hand reaching up to pat his faithful companion's neck.

Something flickered in her belly. Not attraction, surely. She despised arrogant military types. But the man before her didn't look arrogant at the moment. Or even all that militaristic. He simply looked like a man who loved his horse.

Josephine snatched her hand away from Phineas and took a step toward the gray horse beside him, who suddenly seemed a much safer target for her affection. "There's a livery just past the mercantile." She pointed, as if the captain would have trouble finding it on a street that contained less than a dozen buildings. "They should have everything you need. Oh, and if you let me know where you'll be staying, I'll send word if there is any change in Mr. Wallace's condition."

Mr. Hanger sobered at the reminder, and Josephine wished she could take the words back. Well, not really. They'd needed to be said. But still . . . she hated to see the weight return to his shoulders.

"No need to send word," he said. "I'll be parked in that infirmary chair tonight." He speared her with a look that made it clear arguing would do no good.

Her pulse ratcheted up a notch. In irritation, she assured herself. "Your choice," she said as if she didn't care where he passed the night. "But don't expect me to fix the crick in your neck tomorrow morning."

With that, she left him to stew in his own stubborn juices and marched back into her office. At least Mr. Wallace didn't give her any trouble. Sleeping, injured military men were much more compliant than the healthy, alert ones.

Josephine checked the pulse at Mr. Wallace's wrist and was satisfied with the steady beat beneath her fingertips. The loss of blood had weakened him more than the gunshot itself. Once he regained his strength, he and his captain would be out of her hair. They didn't seem the type to hang around if they could sit a saddle, and one didn't need both arms in working order to accomplish that feat. She'd advise against it, of course. The body healed faster when not strained by unnecessary exertion. But she doubted Matthew Hanger would listen. Warriors didn't loll about when there was a battle to fight.

Although, if they'd managed to capture the rustlers, they might be between battles. Josephine glanced in the direction of the street where she'd left Matthew Hanger, even though she couldn't actually see him through the walls of her clinic. What did cavalrymen do when there was no battle to fight?

"That's none of your concern," she murmured under her breath as she straightened her patient's bedding.

She turned to leave and spotted the wooden ladder-back chair sitting stiffly in the corner. It was about as pliant as the man who planned to spend the night in it.

"Oh, for pity's sake." Josephine rolled her eyes, flounced out of the infirmary, and mounted the stairs on a quest for pillows.

Matt led Phineas and Cooper to the livery, paid extra for a bag of oats for each animal in addition to the hay that came with the boarding fee, then set to work relieving them of their gear and brushing them down. He tended to Wallace's horse first, ensuring Cooper had fresh water, clean hooves, and a liniment rubdown. The kid always pampered his gray. A carryover from his own pampered upbringing back east. Not that the horse didn't deserve it. A cavalry mount was as much a part of the regiment as the soldier on its back. Taking care of the horse's needs wasn't just a responsibility, it was an honor.

Matt moved to the next stall and patted Phineas's dark red coat as he eased in alongside him. A vision of the lady doc's hand brushing Phin's neck, her long, pale fingers combing through the black of the horse's mane, jabbed into his brain. He frowned.

The last thing he needed to be thinking about was a woman. Especially a bossy one who thought she could keep him away from his team. She might have managed to remove a bullet, but that didn't mean he trusted her with Wallace's life. She didn't know the kid. Didn't share a history with him. She might care about his health on a professional level, but she could never care the way Matt and the other Horsemen did. Bonds forged in the heat of battle were ironclad.

A woman couldn't understand that. Shoot, most men couldn't understand that.

Matt had seen soldiers sicken after being injured on the battlefield. Blood poisoning. Fever. Gangrene. All after *successful* surgeries. He'd keep his own watch on Wallace. The lady doc with her sassy mouth and gut-slamming green eyes would just have to accept that.

He lingered in the stable for the hour he'd promised, giving Phineas and Cooper the thorough care they deserved and giving his head a chance to clear. Seeing Mark go down had shaken him. He'd been able to concentrate on nothing past getting the kid the help he needed. But he'd accomplished that objective, at least in the immediate sense, which meant he could turn his mind to other matters. Like the rustlers and ensuring they received the punishment they deserved. Like the next job the Horsemen would take.

Francis Kendall had funneled a handful of requests to him, but none of them seemed terribly urgent. The Austin newspaperman who managed their correspondence in exchange for reporting their stories researched the letters sent to Hanger's Horsemen in care of the paper and verified the authenticity of the requests before passing them along. The thin, bespectacled reporter made an odd member of their team, but he served his purpose and saved Matt the headache of culling through the letters himself.

Maybe he'd read through the requests again. He had to pass the time somehow while he waited for Wallace to wake up.

Matt swung his saddlebags over his shoulder, then grabbed the pair that belonged to Wallace. He pulled both rifles from the saddle scabbards, then trudged back to the clinic. He wasn't about to leave their guns unattended. Preach and the others would be back later tonight. They could take charge of the weaponry then. In the meantime, Dr. Jo's infirmary was going to double as an armory.

A grin quirked Matt's mouth. She was gonna love that.

FOUR

"You can't bring all of that in here!"

Somehow Matt managed not to smile at the sputtering doctor as she sprinted from the examination room to run him down in the hall. He'd made no effort to silence his entrance, knowing the picture he made strapped shoulder to boots with guns, ammunition belts, and knives. Too bad he didn't have Preach's saber. It would've been a nice addition. He knew he was being ornery, but he couldn't resist the opportunity to get a rise out of Miss Josephine. She was as headstrong as they came. Opinionated. Obstinate. Taking her off her high horse would be just the distraction he needed.

She squeezed past him and used her body as a blockade to keep him from advancing down the hallway. Arms spread wide, her fingers brushed the top edges of the white wainscoting. Her chest heaved slightly, either from her mad dash to stop him or from the passion that set her green eyes ablaze. Either way, it looked good on her.

"This is a place of healing, not a . . . gladiatorial arena."

He raised a brow at her. "You thinking to hold me at bay

by stackin' a bunch of highfalutin words between us? Won't work."

She blinked, then tilted her head. Frown lines creased her forehead.

Yep. Throwing her off her game was a pleasure, indeed.

"I know you're an educated woman while I'm just a . . . what did you call me? A gladiator?" He could think of worse monikers. He kind of liked that one, actually. "But I ain't afraid of fancy vocabulary. Spout it all you want. I'm used to dodging real bullets. Verbal ones won't scare me."

"What are you talking about?" Her arms slowly lowered. "I'm not trying to engage you in . . . linguistical fisticuffs. That's just the way I speak."

Uh-huh. She was searching for big words now. On purpose. That slight pause was a dead giveaway. She apparently enjoyed a good sparring match as much as he did.

"Speak however you like," he said with a dismissive shrug. "Just don't expect it to deter me." He took a step forward.

Dr. Jo didn't move. Well, she crossed her arms, but that was a fortification of her stance, not a retreat. "Glower as much as *you* like," she countered. "Just don't expect it to deter *me*. Your weapons must be stored elsewhere."

"Where would you suggest? Want me to dig a hole out back and bury them? I can't just leave them out on the front stoop or in the tack room at the livery. As much as I'd like to believe that all the people in Purgatory Springs are honest folk, I'm not about to tempt fate by leaving my valuables unsupervised. The guns stay with me."

"Those guns are the reason Mr. Wallace nearly bled to death. I won't have them in my infirmary."

Matt's jaw tightened at the not-so-subtle hint that he and his lifestyle were responsible for Mark's condition. "These guns aren't responsible for Wallace's injury," Matt said, giving the rifles in his hands a lift. "These guns are responsible for saving our lives when the rustlers attacked. Rustlers who are all alive, having sustained only minor injuries, by the way. Because *these* guns were handled by men who respect human life and do all in their power to preserve it."

She frowned at his argument but didn't offer a reply. Hopefully that meant his logic had found a crack in her opinions.

"These are the tools of my trade, the key to my livelihood," he said. "You wouldn't appreciate someone demanding you leave your doctoring bag outside simply because they didn't approve of scientific advancements. You'd want to keep it close at hand because it is part of who you are. I'm asking for the same courtesy."

"Fine. But will you at least unload them? I doubt an invading army is planning to storm the clinic any time soon."

He supposed he could grant her that concession. With the rustlers rounded up and taken into custody, there was no immediate threat. It might go against his grain not to be battle-ready at all times, but if she was willing to let him keep the guns, he'd see they were unloaded.

"Deal." He set the rifles against the wall and held out his hand.

Slowly, she uncrossed her arms, then reached out and clasped his hand in a firm shake. The contact sent an unexpected frisson charging up his arm, and a wave of warmth pulsed through his chest. Her eyes widened slightly, as if she'd felt it too, but she withdrew her hand, and the sensation abated before he could examine it more closely.

Miss Josephine stepped aside and allowed him access to the small recovery room. He just couldn't think of her as Dr. Jo when she wasn't actively tending a patient, since the

Dr. Joe he'd conjured in his mind at first hearing the name was a portly fellow with white muttonchop whiskers, spectacles, and a paunchy midsection. Matt retrieved the rifles, but instead of striding through the now unobstructed doorway, he held his position and allowed his gaze to follow his opponent's retreat.

"I'll bring dinner for the two of you in a couple hours," she said, her back turned to him as she marched down the hallway.

Her hospitality surprised him. She clearly didn't want him here, yet she offered to feed him. She was a contradiction.

"Thanks."

Miss Josephine glanced over her shoulder, her eyes dancing with mischief. "Broth." A touch of triumph quirked the edge of her mouth. "Residents of the infirmary eat from the invalid's menu." She gave him a quick examination, as if inspecting his health and evaluating his ability to eat solid food. "Perhaps I'll add a little milk toast."

"Sounds hearty." Only a touch of sarcasm laced his words. In truth, it was all he could do not to laugh outright. She dueled with words the way Preach fenced with his cavalry saber. Matt would have saluted her for her combat skills if his hands hadn't been full.

A wide smile blossomed, exposing white, straight teeth and transforming her face from that of the contrary doctor he'd been sparring with to an enticing woman he suddenly wanted to get to know a whole lot better.

She's not for you, Hanger. Matt frowned as she disappeared back into her examination room. Josephine Burkett was a settling-down kind of woman, and Matt was about as unsettled as a fella could get. Too rough around the edges. Too hardened by war. Too dependent on violence for his livelihood. The exact opposite of what an educated woman who hated guns and lived to heal people would want.

"Is it true?" Elizabeth Carrington burst through the clinic's back door, slightly out of breath, her toddler son, Grant, braced on her right hip and a basket slung over her left arm. "Do you actually have two of the Horsemen here?"

Josephine turned from where she stood at the stove in front of a pot of boiling water. "Good evening to you too, Lizzie."

Her friend pulled up short at the sight of Josephine at the stove. Lizzie raised a brow and twisted Grant slightly behind her as if to shield him from an atrocity. "You're not *cooking*, are you?"

Josephine laughed. "Of course not. I want my patient to recover." Although the other occupant of her infirmary might have earned a dose of gastrointestinal distress with his gun-toting stubbornness. Then again, she'd taken an oath to do no harm. "I'm just sterilizing my surgical instruments. I know better than to infringe on your territory."

She and Lizzie had struck up a partnership soon after Josephine opened her practice in Purgatory Springs. Josephine paid her a monthly stipend to provide evening meals for herself and any patients staying at the clinic. As the wife of the local mercantile owner, Lizzie had ready access to foodstuffs and could make even the simplest dishes taste better than most of the restaurant food Josephine had eaten back in Philadelphia. Plus, she always had the latest news to impart, and since she was the only woman in town close to Josephine's age, they had quickly become fast friends.

"I brought some chicken soup for the injured one," Lizzie said as she set the basket on the cabinet closest to the stove.

She pulled out a jar filled to the brim with golden broth and chunks of chicken, carrots, and celery. "Then I have roast beef with potatoes and onions, corn bread, green beans, and a slice of cake for the other one."

Josephine left her instruments to simmer and swooped in to steal the most adorable male in her clinic from his mama. "Anything for me?" she asked as she zoomed Grant through the air before snuggling him in for a hug. "Or are the Horsemen the only ones eating tonight?"

"It would serve you right if I left you to fend for yourself."

A dire threat indeed. Josephine kept store-bought bread and jam on hand for breakfast, and since she could boil water successfully, she managed tea without much trouble. But anything that required actual chemical transformation from raw ingredient to baked/fried/roasted edibleness was best left to the experts. Lizzie knew this, of course, and wasn't above using such knowledge to her advantage.

Lizzie retrieved a pot from the cabinet and poured the soup into it. "You still haven't answered my question, you know."

"Did I need to?" Josephine grinned at Grant and took his small, fisted hand inside her own. "You obviously knew the two men were here."

"I knew two men of some sort were here. The town's been buzzing ever since the one rode in on that big red horse of his and carried the other into the clinic." Lizzie rolled her eyes. Not that Josephine could see it, since her attention was wrapped up in making faces at the towheaded boy in her arms, but she could definitely hear it in her friend's tone. "What I didn't know was if these two men are *the* two men— two of the four Horsemen that Daddy hired to help fight off the rustlers."

Lizzie's father was Terrance Dalton, the rancher who had

organized the cattlemen in the area to pool their resources and hire outside help. She probably knew more about the two men in the infirmary than Josephine did.

"I can't say for sure," Josephine said. Lizzie was the root stalk of the Purgatory Springs grapevine, and torturing her for just a little longer was too rich a temptation to resist. "They didn't proclaim themselves Horsemen when they came in. The bullet lodged in the younger one's shoulder left little room for chitchat."

"Oh, for heaven's sake. Out with it!" Lizzie brandished a wooden spoon in a manner that would have been menacing had her son not started clapping and reaching for it as if *grab-the-spoon* was a game he played with her regularly.

"All right." Josephine laughed as she pulled Grant out of reach of the spoon. "One of them did happen to mention fighting rustlers. Same one who wears a vest that closely resembles US Cavalry attire. Oh, and his name is Matthew Hanger. Does that help?"

"I knew it!" Lizzie thrust her spoon into the air in victory before retreating back to the stove. She might adore amassing information for the purpose of redistribution, but she always confirmed her facts before sharing. Unfounded gossip had no place on Elizabeth Carrington's grapevine. In truth, she was more of a journalist than a rumor mill. It was why everyone came to the mercantile for the scoop on local happenings. They knew her information could be trusted.

Grant's lower lip started to quiver as his mama left with the spoon. Diagnosing the problem and quickly devising a treatment, Josephine lifted the boy in front of her, then leaned in and blew on his neck in a loud, messy fashion. Grant dissolved into giggles, and Josephine's heart dissolved into mush.

Lizzie grinned at her son's laughter, then caught Josephine's eye. "Any news on your brother?" she asked as she stirred, her expression growing more serious. "I've been praying for him."

"Nothing good to report, I'm afraid. According to Darla, Charlie's still running with a rough crowd. I worry about him."

Charlie and her father were at odds more often than not these days. Two stubborn men set on having things their own way. The last she'd heard from their housekeeper, Father had threatened to cut off Charlie financially in order to force him into an honest day's work. It might be just what Charlie needed, but then again, it might widen the divide between them instead. If that gulf expanded any further, she feared Charlie might be lost to them forever.

"I'll keep praying for him," Lizzie said, her eyes aglow with sympathy.

"Thank you." The heartfelt words barely scratched the surface of her gratitude.

Tiny hands patted Josephine's cheeks, bringing her attention back to lighter matters. She shifted Grant to her hip, bent forward, and nuzzled his neck. "Auntie Jo's going to get your tummy!"

The little boy squealed and bent backward over her arm as she tickled his rib cage. Josephine grinned. Nothing in the world could instill more joy and hope into a person than the laughter of a child.

Grant was the first baby she'd delivered in Purgatory Springs, so she naturally felt a special attachment to him. But when the grinning fifteen-month-old's sparkling blue eyes looked at her with complete trust and acceptance, she couldn't help wishing, for just a moment, that she could be in a position to have a child of her own.

Few men considered twenty-eight-year-old, career-focused

women prime wife material, however, and the men willing to overlook her shortcomings in those areas had significant enough shortcomings of their own to keep her firmly on the unmarried path. In truth, as much as her heart panged at the thought that she might never have children, she was content with her lot. God had called her to medicine. Of that she had no doubt. He'd placed a passion within her for scientific learning and a heart that ached on behalf of the hurting. She might never have what other women did, but what she *did* have was special, and she wouldn't regret making whatever sacrifices were necessary to fulfill her vocation.

Besides, the only man to stir even a hint of romantic interest in her in recent memory was more likely to court death than a woman of medicine. He was a mercenary, for crying out loud. A man who made his living with his gun. The exact opposite of everything she believed in.

Well, maybe not *everything*. Yes, she believed the majority of bloodshed could be avoided if people would handle their disagreements in a civilized, intelligent manner, yet she realized such a view was rather utopian. The arguments Matthew Hanger had made earlier today held truth. As long as evil existed in the world, good men would be called to fight it. And afterward, doctors like her would be left to mend the brokenness.

Just because something palpable had passed between her and Mr. Hanger when her hand connected with his didn't mean new doors were opening. Attraction was simply a physiological response, an innate feminine recognition of virility in the male of the species. Nothing more. She could have the same response to any number of men.

Only she hadn't. Which meant there was something unique about Matthew Hanger that drew her to him.

Josephine set the disquieting observation aside and turned her attention to eliciting another laugh from the baby in her arms.

Matthew Hanger and his virility would be gone in a few days. She could ignore his effect on her until then.

— CHAPTER —

FIVE

Miss Josephine hadn't followed through on her threat to make him eat milk toast. She'd fed him roast beef, vegetables, and a sweetened corn bread that could have been dessert had she not thrown in a piece of vanilla cake too. She'd blamed Mrs. Carrington for the excess and insisted that had it been up to her, he would have received bread and water. Dalton's daughter had laughed at that and made some quip about that being true because it was the only meal Miss Josephine knew how to make. Apparently, the doctor wasn't much of a cook. Handled children pretty well, though.

Mrs. Carrington had delivered the meal to the infirmary herself in order to thank him and his men personally while Josephine lingered outside the door, playing with the woman's son. The lady doc had looked good with the babe on her hip. The kid seemed to soften her. The headstrong physician battling for respect faded behind the affectionate woman doting on a little boy who obviously adored her. Matt found it hard to concentrate on what Mrs. Carrington was saying, his gaze constantly wandering to the hall. Thankfully, Wallace had roused and carried the conversation for him, per usual.

Once Mrs. Carrington and her son departed, Josephine took her turn in the infirmary.

"How are you feeling?" She completely bypassed Matt and went straight to Wallace's bedside.

The kid grinned that charmer's grin of his—the one that never failed to gain an answering smile from whichever woman he aimed it at. "Like I have a hole in my shoulder."

And there it was—the answering smile. Josephine's mouth curved upward, and Matt's grip on his dinner plate tightened so much, the ceramic threatened to crack. Her reaction shouldn't bother him. All women reacted to Wallace that way. His good looks. His sense of humor. His affable personality. It shouldn't bother Matt.

But it did.

"After you eat, I'll bring you something for the pain. It'll help you sleep too." She tugged down the sheet to examine the skin around Wallace's bandage.

Matt forced himself to let go of the plate before he cracked it for real, and balanced it on his knees.

"I already slept half the day away, Doc. I could stand to be awake for a while."

She took his wrist and fit her fingers to the edge to find his pulse, then felt his head with the back of her hand. "I'll prepare a willow bark powder for you and set it on the table with a glass of water. You can stay awake as long as you like, but when the pain starts to wear on you, I want you to take the medicine and get some sleep." She helped him sit up and propped several pillows behind his back. She moved the tray that carried his soup from the floor where Mrs. Carrington had left it to the bed to bridge his lap.

After spreading a large cloth napkin over Wallace's torso, she finally turned her attention to Matt. Unfortunately, the solicitous smile bestowed on her patient stiffened into stern lines.

"You're in command, Captain." Her gaze captured his, making it clear that, in truth, he was *second* in command. "If he starts to tire, give him the powder whether he wants to take it or not. Pull rank if you have to."

"Understood." He held her gaze, and something passed between them—an undercurrent of awareness and growing respect. Maybe even cautious trust. She jerked her gaze away before he could analyze it further, but his gut didn't need his head to comprehend all the ins and outs.

Josephine Burkett intrigued him. Plain and simple. Intrigued him and appealed to him in a way no woman had in a long, long time. Crossing paths and wits with her over the next few days would be a nice change from guarding cattle and hunting rustlers. But he'd make sure nothing more came of it. He'd already lost one family. He wouldn't risk that kind of devastation a second time. The Horsemen were all the family he needed. No matter how much the lady doc appealed to him, when Wallace was well enough to travel, she'd be nothing more than a pleasant memory to keep him company on long nights in the saddle.

"I'll be back with the powder after you've had a chance to eat. I'll clear the dishes away then and will return to check on you one final time before I retire for the night." She spoke to Wallace, but Matt caught an occasional side glance darting his way. "Mrs. Carrington will send word to my night nurse, Alice Gaither, so you will probably see an older lady roaming the halls later this evening. She's more of a chaperone than an actual nurse," she explained, another glance darting Matt's way, "but she can bring you water, food, or a clean chamber pot should you need it. She can also fetch me if your pain worsens or if signs of a fever appear."

Fetch her? Matt straightened in his chair. "Where will you be?"

She turned his way, a smile—this time for him—twitching the corners of her lips. "Upstairs. I never leave the premises when I have patients in the infirmary, but the ladies of Purgatory Springs insist I have a night nurse in the clinic whenever those patients are of the male variety. To protect my reputation. Of course, any man ill enough to require an overnight stay poses no actual threat to my virtue, but perception can sometimes carry more weight than reality."

"Especially if there is a second man who is not ill in your infirmary." Matt frowned. He hadn't considered the consequences to her when he'd insisted on being allowed to stay with Wallace.

She nodded. "Precisely." She stepped away from the bed and crossed to the doorway. Then she turned back to her patient. "I'll leave the two of you to enjoy your meal. If you need assistance with the soup, just ring the bell." She pointed to the small handbell on the back corner of the bedside table. "Sometimes it's difficult to navigate everyday tasks when you're not accustomed to using your non-dominant hand. There's no shame in asking for help."

Wallace winked at her. "I'm sure I'll manage, though the thought of having a woman as lovely as yourself feeding me does tempt me to act the invalid."

Matt rolled his eyes.

"Well, I'm here if you need me."

Wallace grinned. "Thanks, Doc."

Her gaze briefly passed over Matt as she crossed to the

door, but she said nothing. Just made her exit and left Matt feeling . . . neglected. Which was ridiculous. He was perfectly healthy. In no need of medical care or nursing. Yet every time she'd touched Wallace or smiled at him or offered her help, it made Matt's hide itch as if someone had wrapped him in a flea-infested blanket.

Which was why he secretly enjoyed watching the kid struggle to keep soup in his spoon as he attempted to eat. Guilt kicked in after a moment, though, and Matt set his half-finished plate on the table and leaned forward in his chair.

"Want some help?"

Wallace shook his head. "No, thanks, Captain. I'll get it. Just need a couple practice runs."

"All right."

Matt sat back and made a show of tucking into his own food. Heaven knew he wouldn't want his men watching him make a muck of feeding himself. But if the kid didn't get the hang of things soon, Matt would have to find a way to intervene without dashing his pride. Wallace needed nourishment to regain his strength, and Matt would see he got it, one way or another.

After struggling through about half his bowl of soup, Wallace set the spoon aside and leaned back against the wall at his back. Tired or frustrated? Maybe both.

Matt cut a slice of beef from his own plate, stabbed it with his fork, and held it out to his former trumpeter. "Want something to sink your teeth into?" With the food already speared, all the kid had to do was stick it in his mouth.

Wallace's eyes brightened. "Sure." He took the fork with his left hand and herded the roast squarely between his teeth. "Mmm. That's good." He leaned forward a bit and scanned the rest of Matt's plate. "Don't suppose you could spare some of that corn bread?"

Matt handed over a chunk, putting it directly in Wallace's hand. While his friend chewed, Matt took another gander at the soup bowl. It wasn't so much the soup that was the problem. It was transferring the liquid with an unsteady spoon that created the difficulty. Maybe instead of changing the food, he should change the transport.

Matt took the coffee cup Dalton's daughter had delivered along with his plate of beef, and drained the contents in a long gulping swallow. His gullet complained at the deluge of hot joe, but he ignored the discomfort. "Here," he said as he reached for the bowl on the tray. "Let me see that soup."

"You want some?" Wallace asked, his forehead crinkling. "It's tasty, but it can't compare to that beef."

Matt didn't answer. Just took the bowl in one hand, his coffee cup in the other, and poured the soup into the handled mug. Not all of the liquid would fit, so Matt put the rim of the bowl to his mouth and drank the excess broth. "Not bad." Then he plopped the mug on the tray and angled the handle to the left. "Try it this way."

Wallace lifted the cup to his lips, then set it down with a satisfied thump after consuming a goodly portion. "This is why you're the one who strategizes all our missions, Captain." He grinned. "No problem exists that Matthew Hanger can't outthink."

Matt ducked away from the praise. There were plenty of problems he couldn't solve. Like losing his parents, avoiding a senseless massacre, or even stopping himself from being attracted to a lady doctor who was far too fine for the likes of him. "It's just soup."

"It's ingenious, is what it is."

Matt jerked his head toward the doorway where Miss Josephine stood, a paper packet in one hand, a glass of water in the other.

She stepped into the room, her gaze skittering over Matt before landing on the mug in Wallace's hand. "Such a pragmatic solution, and so obvious, now that I see it in action." She shook her head, a self-deprecating grin spreading across her face. "Mama's etiquette rules have served me well over the years, but they're so ingrained, I never once thought to serve soup with anything other than a bowl and spoon." Her attention settled over Matt and warmed him like a blanket on a cold night. "I congratulate you, Mr. Hanger. You have singlehandedly changed the course of invalid nutrition in my practice. I'll be instituting new meal-serving practices forthwith."

His gaze melded with hers, the oversized vocabulary bouncing off him like harmless pellets, not warranting his notice. He read the appreciation and respect in her eyes, and that communicated the message most important to him at the moment.

"Military men don't have much use for fancy manners when out on campaign," he said with a shrug. "But we do like to keep our bellies full and will improvise when necessary."

"A laudable skill."

If she kept looking at him like that, he'd never move from this spot. "Comes in handy."

"The captain has gotten us out of more than one tough spot over the years," Wallace said, drawing the doctor's attention back to him. "Of course, the majority of those challenges dealt with threats much more dire than slurping soup, but I'm glad to be the beneficiary of his problem-solving skills no matter the situation."

Josephine smiled and set down the water glass and medicine packet before lifting the tray from Wallace's lap. "Recovery from an injury might not *feel* as dire as facing an enemy in combat, but I assure you, it's still a battle that must be fought strategically. The more you can do to regain your strength, the better your body will heal. So don't wait too long before you take this powder. All right?"

Wallace nodded. "Yes, ma'am."

"Good."

She pivoted toward the door and held the tray out to Matt. "I'll take your dishes if you're finished with them."

Matt placed his dinner plate on the tray but held back the cake he hadn't had a chance to eat yet. "I'll bring this to the kitchen when I'm finished."

"Leave it in the dry sink. Alice or I will take care of it later. Alice usually keeps a pot of coffee on the stove. She's a bit of a night owl. Prefers to stay up reading in the parlor across the way when she's on duty. I'm sure she wouldn't mind if you helped yourself to a cup should you need to stretch your legs during the night."

Already feeling cramped in the small, hard chair, Matt appreciated the offer. "Thanks. Oh, and thanks for the pillows as well." He shifted his back against the cushion that softened the hard oak of the chair slats. Another had been propped against the wall for him to use as needed.

"You're welcome." She lowered her voice to a whisper. "I know how long the night can stretch when you're keeping vigil."

Of course she did. She'd no doubt kept watch over dozens of patients during her years of doctoring. Yet it was the fact that she'd provided for his comfort despite his overbearing demands to invade her infirmary that revealed her character.

She might be opinionated and highfalutin, but she was a nurturer at heart. A woman who thought of others before herself.

"The two of you aren't whispering secrets about me over there, are you?" Wallace teased.

Josephine glanced over her shoulder. "Just scheming about how best to get that willow bark into you should you prove more stubborn than intelligent."

"Shoot. That's easy." Matt swore he could hear the charm thickening in Wallace's voice as he stole Josephine's attention once again. "All you have to do is smile at me when you ask, Dr. Jo. I'd do anything to please a woman as beautiful as you."

"If that's true, it's amazing you've lived this long."

Matt coughed, so shocked by her reply he couldn't even manage the simple task of breathing properly.

"A man who blindly follows a woman just because she's beautiful will eventually find himself tumbling over a cliff," she said. "Better to think for yourself and make decisions based on wisdom and sensible advice." She strode to the doorway, turned, and gave her parting shot neither smiling nor asking. "Take your medicine."

Then she left, her shoes clicking a sharp staccato beat on the floorboards.

Matt cast a cautious glance at his friend to judge his reaction. Wallace wasn't used to having his charm thrown back in his face with such force. Surprisingly enough, he was grinning.

Wallace nodded at Matt. "I knew she liked you better." His face sobered a bit. "Now you know it too."

Matt's gut clenched at the thought, but he steered clear of the tempting trail Wallace's words opened up. "All I know is that she's too smart to be taken in by your bunkum. Besides, it doesn't matter which of us she prefers. As soon as your shoulder heals, we're leaving Purgatory Springs behind."

"We don't have to, Matt." Wallace met his gaze, no hint of his usual carefree nature in evidence. "As much as I love the Horsemen and the good we've been able to achieve these past few years, there's nothing wrong with hanging up the spurs and carving out a life for yourself that doesn't involve flying bullets and enemies behind every corner."

Matt stiffened. "You sayin' you want out?" What would he do without the Horsemen? He didn't even know who he was without them, without the work they did.

"Nope." Wallace shook his head, weariness etching his features as his posture slumped and he slipped a little lower on the wall. "Just saying we can't do this forever. And when the end comes, I'd much rather go home to a good woman than an empty cabin with nothing but old ghosts to haunt me."

Matt said nothing. The kid painted a nice picture, but that was all it was—a picture. One built on imagination instead of substance. No woman deserved a life with a man who carried demons in his saddlebags.

Mr. Wallace made it through the night with no incident of fever. Josephine had checked on him twice. The first time after midnight, and the second at three o'clock. Both times, Matthew Hanger had awoken the instant she stepped foot in the room.

He had set the chair out in the hallway and stretched out on the hardwood floor with nothing but one of her cushions to pillow his head. It had to be dreadfully uncomfortable, but then, he was a cavalryman, accustomed to sleeping on the ground. Finding him thus had unnerved her, though. Not because he was on the floor, but because the moment she padded on stockinged feet into the infirmary, he jerked to a sitting position with fists clenched and eyes instantly alert. The movement had been so sudden and unexpected, she'd nearly screamed. Thankfully, she contained her shock, only allowing a small gasp to escape and thereby avoiding complete humiliation.

He had jumped to his feet, apologized for frightening her, then immediately started quizzing her about Mr. Wallace's condition. She conducted a minimal examination, checking for red streaks from the site of the wound, feeling his head for fever, and checking to ensure his breathing was deep and steady. He passed each of her inspections, but she left another dose of willow bark powder on the bedside table anyway and instructed Mr. Hanger to administer it should his friend awaken in pain.

It had been a brief visit, five minutes at most, yet she left the infirmary with an odd level of reluctance. Usually she couldn't wait to return to her bed and get a few more hours of sleep, but it had been different this time.

Because of *him*. Matthew Hanger, with his sleep-mussed hair and intense concern for his friend. The way he looked at her, hungry for good news. And when she'd confirmed the absence of infection indicators, the lines around his face had disappeared, giving him a much younger appearance, one certain women might consider handsome.

All right. One *she* considered handsome.

Josephine had not lingered, however, keenly aware of the need to maintain propriety. Matthew Hanger had still been fully clothed, having only removed his hat and boots, and she'd been the same. She'd kept on the dress from the day before, her only concession to comfort the removal of her shoes and the taking down and braiding of her hair. Still, it wouldn't do to engage in personal, non-medical-related conversation, especially when Alice was almost certainly listening at the parlor door for any excuse to put in a chaperone appearance. So Josephine had returned to her room with a brief detour to the parlor to request the industrious Alice bring Mr. Hanger a stack of quilts to use as a pallet.

Her predawn visit had gone much the same, although the temptation to linger in the infirmary had intensified. Alice's snores echoed from the parlor sofa throughout the clinic, making it clear that her chaperone was off duty. Nevertheless, Josephine held to her professional standards and conducted herself as any proper physician would. She tended her patient, reassured his companion, then returned to her room, where she fell asleep praying for Mr. Wallace's continued recovery.

It was a different Horseman who slipped into her dreams, however. One with hazel eyes, an uncompromising jaw, and a protective drive that her dream self imagined extended to her.

Thankfully, the light of day brought a return of her scientific mind-set and banished imaginative tendencies to the mental closet where she locked away any thoughts that threatened to distract her from her calling. She was a doctor, not a debutante. Attraction, admiration, and any other *-tions* set on disrupting her medical routines would be kept sequestered for the duration of Mr. Wallace's internment.

Which wouldn't be much longer, judging by the healthy tissue beneath the bandage she'd just unwrapped.

"Things are progressing very well, Mr. Wallace." Josephine set aside the used dressing and replaced it with a clean one. "I see no signs of infection."

"I aim to please." He grinned at her in a way that reminded her of her brother.

Charlie was a bit of a scapegrace, but he had a knack for talking his way out of trouble that left all concerned smiling and wishing him well on his next adventure. Her father hated his glibness, preferring he take responsibility for his actions—let his *yes* be *yes* and his *no, no,* like Scripture taught. But Josephine had too many memories of times when Charlie had teased her out of a somber mood after their mother had died to hold such an unforgiving position. He'd reminded her how to laugh with his silly antics and kept her from getting lost in her grief even while being mired in his own. Charlie might not be the studious type like she was or the businessman Father wished him to be, but he had the gift of making people happy and had healed the broken places of a young girl's heart that medicine had been unable to reach.

"Can he leave the infirmary?"

Ah, there was the practical voice of which her father would approve. No superfluous repartee, just cutting straight to the chase.

Josephine glanced away from bandaging Mr. Wallace's shoulder to answer Captain Hanger's question. "I'd like him to stay a full twenty-four hours as a precaution, but if his recovery continues along this trajectory, I don't see any reason the two of you can't depart this afternoon."

The captain nodded. No other comment. Josephine turned back to her patient, absolutely *not* disappointed that he didn't try to engage her in further conversation. Matthew Hanger was a man who accomplished objectives with single-minded focus, not one who wasted time on unnecessary chatter.

Mr. Wallace smiled at her, softening the hard edges of his compatriot. "I'll be sad to leave your esteemed company, Doctor Burkett, but I can't say I'll miss being imprisoned in this bed. I fear if I don't stretch my legs soon, they might just run off without me in a fit of pique. I tend to stagnate if I don't move around on a regular basis."

"Well, we can't have algae growing on you, now, can we?" She tied off the bandage and tucked the ends under one of the folds. "You have my permission to take a lap around the parlor this morning, if Mr. Hanger accompanies you. Don't push too hard, though," she warned with a point of her finger.

"Wear yourself out, and you'll set back your recovery, which means more stagnation time in bed."

He shivered with theatrical aplomb.

She bit back a grin and imitated her most pompous medical school professor, peering down her nose at the mere mortal beneath her from her seat atop the exalted Mount of Wisdom. "Slow and steady wins the race."

Mr. Wallace chuckled. "So I'm to mimic Aesop's tortoise, am I?"

She forfeited her pretentious posture and offered a conciliatory smile. "I'm sure it will be taxing for someone of your active nature, but I promise it will pay dividends in the end."

"I'll see he doesn't overdo it." Matthew Hanger's blunt statement should have spoiled the lighthearted mood Mr. Wallace's colorful commentary had created, but it only made Josephine's smile widen.

"Thank you, Mr. Hanger." She nodded at him, then moved toward the door. "I have full confidence that you will execute your duties with the greatest diligence." She paused at the doorway. "I'll have Alice bring you both some breakfast before she leaves for the day. Eggs and hash sound all right?"

"Yes, ma'am!" Mr. Wallace's enthusiastic agreement echoed behind her, but Josephine's gaze remained on the man standing at attention near the door.

The slight dip of the captain's chin was answer enough, and oddly more satisfying than the exuberance of his friend.

Suddenly hungry herself, Josephine left the infirmary to check on Alice in the kitchen.

Matt finished his coffee, then tipped his chair back on two legs until his head banged softly against the wall. He needed to get out of here. Soon. Before that woman got any further under his skin. The kid wasn't helping any by planting crazy ideas in his head about the Horsemen retiring, and worse yet, about how Miss Josephine Burkett might actually prefer a more mature, stoic fellow to the smooth-tongued young charmer.

Not that Wallace was all flash and no depth. The kid was as loyal as they came to the people he committed himself to. He just preferred to keep most folks at a distance to avoid the pain that came from getting too close. Matt understood that. Lived that way himself. Just carried a different shield. Wallace wielded a golden shield of light and shine. Matt carried one of iron, heavy and impenetrable. Or so he thought. Until a certain lady doctor started chiseling cracks into it.

The sound of the clinic's front door opening yanked Matt back to the present. He lowered the chair's legs back to the floor, pushed to his feet, and stepped through the open infirmary door into the hall. Out of habit, his hand hovered over his hip until he recalled that his gun belt was stored under the bed with the rest of the weaponry.

"Hello?" A familiar voice echoed down the hall, bringing a smile to Matt's face. "This Dr. Joe's place?"

Matt marched toward his corporal and nearly collided with Miss Josephine when she stepped out of her examination room.

"Can I help you gentlemen?"

Preach tugged his hat from his head and smiled politely as he stepped inside. Behind him, Jonah removed his hat as well, but his face wore the same weighty expression it always did in a new place, as if he expected to encounter enemies instead of friends. Though, as much as Matt wished it otherwise, as a black man in Texas, Jonah probably had the odds figured correctly.

"They're looking for me," Matt said. "For Wallace, really." He felt a smile tug on his mouth as pride for his men expanded his chest. "Dr. Josephine Burkett, meet the rest of the Horsemen."

"Doctor?" Preach's brows rose, but he recovered quickly and tipped his head in a small bow. "Luke Davenport, ma'am. Pleased to meet you."

Josephine's lips quirked. "Luke? You're kidding, right?"

Preach shot a confused look at Matt before turning back to the doctor. "No, ma'am. That's my name."

"Matthew, Mark, Luke, and . . ." She turned an expectant look at the fourth man.

"Jonah. Jonah Brooks." The former buffalo soldier dared her to comment with his gaze.

Josephine, being Josephine, did just that. But not in the way Matt expected. "Well, that's a relief. For a minute there I thought you were going to say Thessalonians. How wonderful to have the Old Testament represented, Mr. Brooks."

Jonah blinked. Apparently not the response he'd expected either.

Matt had lost count of the number of people they'd met after forming the Horsemen who tried to tease the sharpshooter into shortening his name to Jon. They all thought themselves quite clever. Jonah, however, found them insulting. A man owned his name. His identity. To suggest he change it to suit another's whim smacked a little too much of one man trying to own another for Jonah to see the humor in it.

Brooks offered Josephine a small nod, then blurted, "How's Wallace?"

"Come back here and find out yourself," Mark called

from the infirmary, bringing a grin to Preach's face and a soft chuckle from the doctor.

"As you can hear, he's doing quite well," she said.

But the impatient patient wasn't finished. "You know, it's rude to talk about a fellow behind his back."

Matt rolled his eyes. "We're in front of you, Wallace."

Preach slapped Matt on the back and charged down the hall.

"You're welcome to visit," Josephine called after him, "but don't wear him out." She turned to Matt, but he knew his orders.

"I'll keep an eye on him."

Her smile did odd things to his chest when she looked at him like that, as if they were connected at some level, knowing what the other was thinking. Of course, he'd have to be an idiot not to know what she'd been thinking, since she'd been harping on him about watching Wallace the entire time they'd been here, but that logic didn't stop his chest from expanding beneath her approving gaze.

"The infirmary will get terribly crowded if all three of you try to squeeze in there," she said, her voice low, as if only meant for him. "If he feels up to it, this might be a good time to help Mr. Wallace stretch his legs. The four of you can make use of the parlor, but I expect my patient to be back in bed in an hour."

"Understood."

She gave him a nod, offered a smile to Jonah, then returned to her duties in the examination room, leaving him and his men to converse in private.

Matt watched her go, his gaze lingering a hair too long on the doorway she'd disappeared through, judging by Jonah's raised brow.

"What?" he snapped.

Jonah raised a hand in surrender, a hint of a smile playing at the corner of his mouth. "Nothin'. Just never seen you bowled over by a woman, is all."

"She's a doctor," Matt said, exasperated. "She gives the orders here."

Jonah patted him on the shoulder. "I ain't referrin' to the doctor, Cap. I'm talkin' 'bout the *woman*."

"Shut up, Brooks."

Jonah chuckled and strode down the hall. Matt followed, a scowl on his face. A scowl that deepened when he realized his gaze had traveled back to the examination room doorway without his permission, searching for a glimpse of a certain chestnut-haired female. He jerked his attention back to his men and lengthened his stride.

Yep. The sooner he got out of this clinic, the better.

SEVEN

"My legs still work, fellas," Wallace grumbled as Matt flanked him on the left and Preach on the right while he gingerly swung those legs around to make his exit from the bed. "You don't have to hover so close."

Preach stepped back a pace, but Matt held his position. Wallace's care was his responsibility, and he wouldn't shirk his duty, even to spare the kid's pride.

"Brought you each a set of clothes." Jonah tossed a small gunnysack through the doorway to Matt. "Figured you'd want to change."

"Thanks." Matt upended the bag onto the bed behind Wallace and collected the gear that belonged to him.

He'd cleaned up as best he could in the kitchen before dawn this morning while Josephine slept upstairs and the night nurse snored in the parlor. He'd been tired enough to force himself back to sleep after the lady doc's first visit of the night, but not after the second. Even with the pallet she'd provided to soften the hard floor.

Too many scenarios had spun through his mind. Most with

an intriguing female doctor square in the center. With pretty green eyes and a stubborn chin. A chin he imagined tipping up to meet his kiss. Which was when he knew he needed to get off the floor and squash his wayward thoughts with practical action. So he'd ventured into the kitchen, found some bread to snack on, then heated a kettle of water and scrubbed himself clean from head to waist. Then he pumped some cold water into the empty dishpan, washed Wallace's blood out of his vest, and hung the garment over the back of a chair to dry. Then he'd washed the handful of dishes sitting on the counter. Then he'd washed the counter.

Once he was out of things to wash, he'd made fresh coffee, brewed the way he liked it. Thick, black, and potent. Guaranteed to paste a man's eyelids open and clear his mind of distractions.

He found a pair of scissors in a drawer and trimmed up his beard, sorely wishing he'd had a razor to clean away the scraggle growing on his neck, but that would keep until he was back at Dalton's ranch. He'd filled the rest of the time sitting in the hall with a lamp pilfered from the parlor, going over options for their next job. Completely expelling Dr. Josephine Burkett and her green eyes from his mind.

Until he heard her stirring above him.

Thankfully, Wallace awoke around the same time and provided Matt a more appropriate target for his attention.

Now he had *all* his men with him, and he was finally starting to feel like his old self. Focused. Taking care of business.

"Preach, help Wallace with his shirt. Can't have him sitting in Miss Josephine's parlor half-naked. Take care with his arm, though. Just leave the right sleeve hangin'." Man, but it felt good to be giving orders again.

Matt untucked yesterday's shirt from his trousers, unbuttoned the top buttons, and pulled it over his head. He tossed it onto the empty chair, then reached for the clean shirt on the bed.

"Excuse me, Mr. Brooks. I have a sling for Mr. Wallace's arm . . . oh." Josephine pushed into the infirmary and stopped, her gaze stuck on Matt's chest. "I . . . um . . ."

Embarrassed, Matt grabbed for his shirt and held it up in front of him, not that the wadded-up fabric covered much. Most of his battle scars, ugly puckers and reddened slashes that no lady would want to see, were no doubt still on display.

Yet Josephine showed no disgust or pity or even medical interest. She just stared, her jaw slightly slack, her eyes . . . warm?

"Thanks, ma'am," Preach said, breaking the spell as he reached for the triangle of white muslin she held.

Josephine blinked a couple times, then tore her gaze away to focus on her patient. She shook her head slightly. "I'll just . . ."

"I got it." Preach took the fabric from her. "I got experience fittin' slings."

A spark entered her eyes. "That may be, Mr. Davenport, but I'm the doctor here." She cleared her throat, snatched the sling back from him, and waved him aside.

Matt grinned. That was the Josephine he knew.

With the doc's attention aimed at Wallace, Matt got his shirt on and tucked into his trousers. A tricky task when a fellow had to dodge knowing grins shooting at him from every other man in the room.

"Keep your arm angled upward across your chest," Josephine instructed as she curved the fabric around Wallace's elbow and behind his back.

The sling-fitting procedure brought her curves far too close to the grinning trumpeter's face. Matt frowned. Which, of course, only made Wallace grin wider. Once she had the ends tied off, she stepped back, and the jealousy twisting Matt's gut dissipated.

"All right, then," she said, carefully keeping her gaze averted from Matt's position. "I'll leave you to your visit."

Preach nodded to her. "Thanks, Doc."

No one said another word until the sound of her footsteps faded down the hall.

"Only Wallace would get shot in a town with a female doctor on duty." Preach grabbed the kid's shirt and held out the left sleeve for him to slip his good arm into. "You just can't help yourself, can you? Always got to make an impression on the ladies."

Wallace winced as Luke brought the shirt around his back and gently pulled it closed around his bandaged shoulder. "You'd think bleeding like a stuck pig would do the trick, wouldn't you? Unfortunately, despite my best efforts and this particular lady's affinity for wounds and bandages, I seem to have come in second in the favorable impression contest. And that was even before the captain decided to hedge his bets by allowing her to *accidentally* catch him with his shirt off." He shot a wink at Matt. "Good timing on that one, Captain. I'll have to remember that strategy."

Heat flared along Matt's neck as Preach and Brooks made pitiful efforts to muffle their snickers. "Maybe we should tie another sling around your mouth," Matt groused. "Stop all that nonsense rattling around inside your noggin from leaking out."

Wallace laughed.

"Good luck with that," Preach said after fastening the second-to-top button of Mark's shirt and taking a step back from the bed. "Wallace, here, has twice as much nonsense inside him as the average fella. I don't think a sling would contain it."

"Thanks a lot, Preach." Wallace shoved him with his good arm. Luke made a show of staggering backward even though Wallace was still too weak to put much *oomph* behind the gesture.

Luke clapped a hand to his chest and schooled his features into a semblance of piety. "'Even a fool, when he holdeth his peace, is counted wise: and he that shutteth his lips is esteemed a man of understanding.' Proverbs 17:28. In case you want to skip the extra sling option."

Wallace rolled his eyes. "I'm pretty sure you're breaking some kind of infirmary etiquette by picking on the patient."

"Then I guess we better get you out of the infirmary." Matt enjoyed the comradery shared by his men, but he knew their patterns all too well. The teasing was fixing to cycle back around, and he could do without talk of him and the lady doc bouncing off the walls and carrying down to the examination room. He could handle the ribbing, but he didn't want Josephine embarrassed or made to feel uncomfortable.

He gripped Wallace's left elbow and helped him to his feet. A bit of color drained from the kid's face, but he managed to stand. His battle-hardened tenacity kicked in as he conquered the wobble in his legs and walked to the door. Matt released his elbow, letting him make his own way, but he and Preach flanked him on either side, ready to step in if needed, as Jonah cleared a path to the parlor.

The kid made it to the next room under his own power and even managed to lower himself onto the upholstered settee by bracing his weight on the sofa arm as he eased down. Matt wasn't thrilled at the sweat beading Wallace's brow, but the kid didn't seem to be breathing too hard, so he let it go without comment and turned his attention to the other two Horsemen.

"How'd the delivery go in San Marcos?" he asked.

Preach's gaze lingered on Wallace, concern evident in the lines of his face, but he followed Matt's cue and took a seat in one of two matching armchairs across from the settee. Jonah slid into the other, leaving Matt to share the sofa with Wallace.

"There was much weeping and gnashing of teeth during the wound stitching." The disgust on Luke's face made it clear what he thought of the mettle of the injured rustler. "But we got 'em all delivered in one piece to the marshal. Ringleader had a price on his head, so we earned a nice little bonus to go along with our fee."

Matt nodded. He'd had no doubts his men could handle the rustlers. But the news of the reward was a welcome surprise. The Horsemen donated all reward money to the army's widow-and-orphan fund, earmarking their donations specifically for families of fellow cavalrymen.

"Dalton said we can stay at the ranch as long as we like," Jonah added with a tip of his head toward Mark. "So you got plenty o' time to heal up afore we move on, Wallace."

"The doctor expects my arm to be out of commission for a couple weeks, but I should be good to sit a horse in a few days."

Matt cut him off. "We'll stay a week."

The kid didn't want to be seen as a hindrance. Matt understood that. The army taught a man to be ready to go when the bugle blew no matter what aches and pains he suffered. But a hole in the shoulder was more significant than a bruised rib or strained back. He needed more than healthy pride to make a full recovery.

"I can be ready sooner, Captain. I—"

Matt raised a brow and toughened his tone. "A week, Wallace." He'd not budge on this point. "Longer, if the doc thinks you need it."

Wallace slumped a tad at the pronouncement but acquiesced with a nod.

"Now," Matt said, reaching into his pocket for the scrap of paper he'd written his notes on during the wee hours of the morning, "I got a few job possibilities for us to vote on. We'll be down one gun for a bit, but there's one item in particular that seems geared to Wallace's other talents."

"You mean women." Preach smirked.

Matt grinned. "Among other things."

"What you got, boss?" Jonah leaned forward in his seat, neatly getting them back on topic and sparing Wallace from further ribbing.

Matt examined the three items on his list. "Kendall forwarded me a letter from a widow who can't seem to hire any men to work her ranch. Ain't a lot of cowpokes willing to take orders from a woman to start with, but after one of her men was threatened and bloodied by a group of masked thugs, no one's even applied. She's pretty sure the thugs work for her late husband's rival, but with no proof, local law enforcement refuses to step in."

Jonah let out a soft whistle. "None of her hired men stayed on after her man kicked the bucket? Don't sound like there's much respect for the widow, if'n that's the case."

Matt thought back to the letter he'd read that morning. "I think she's still got her husband's foreman sticking around, but the rest have scattered."

"Hmm." Preach leaned back in his chair and rubbed his jaw. "This foreman single?"

Matt shrugged. "Don't know. Why?"

Instead of answering, Preach asked another question. "You know how the husband died, or how long ago?"

"Fella's been gone three months, but her letter said nothing about how he died. What're you thinking?"

"Just seems odd for men to abandon the brand they'd been riding for so easily. Jonah's right. Something's wrong there."

Wallace sat up straighter, interest flaring in his eyes. "You don't think the threat of violence explains the defection?"

"Maybe." Luke crossed his ankle over his knee. "But most cowmen I know are tough. If one of their own got singled out for a beating, they'd retaliate in a group themselves, not pick up and leave. But if they didn't respect the man or woman giving the orders . . ."

"But they'd been working for this foreman already," Wallace insisted. "Wouldn't that indicate trust and respect?"

Jonah tapped his thumb against the chair arm. "He coulda done something to break their trust."

Wallace frowned. "Like what?"

Luke scratched at a spot behind his right ear. "Like murder their boss."

"Whoa." Matt shook his head. "That's a big leap, Preach."

Luke held out a hand. "Hear me out. What if this foreman's been sweet on the cattleman's wife and decided to rid himself of the competition? He takes out the owner, the wife inherits, he gets to run the ranch however he sees fit, and if he convinces her to marry him, he gets everything. Any hands who don't like it can leave. Men loyal to the original owner and not the foreman would leave."

Matt shook his head. "But why scare off new hands? And why ask for help from the Horsemen?" Preach's story might be plausible, but it was too convoluted to be probable. Yet this was exactly why they discussed the jobs they took. Four different men with varied life experiences saw things from four different angles. Kept them out of trouble more often than not.

"What if scaring off the new hands was an accident?" Preach insisted, warming to his tale even more. It wouldn't surprise Matt if his corporal took up writing dime novels someday. "Maybe one of the old hands threatened to take his suspicions to the sheriff. Foreman gets wind of it and hires a gang of masked bullies to rough him up and feed him a story about how anyone choosing to work for the widow would pay the price. It works too well. Word spreads, and no one wants to ride for the brand. As for her asking for our help, maybe the widow doesn't see the foreman for the fiend he is. She's seeking help because she believes the lies he's been feeding her."

"Well, if that's the case," Wallace said, "she needs our help more than ever! If this cad killed her husband, there's no telling *what* he'll do to her if she spurns his advances after all the trouble he went through to get her all to himself. I say we take the job."

Matt grinned. Always the gallant gentleman riding in on the white horse to save the damsel. Though the kid did have a point. *If* Preach's story held water. Matt wasn't convinced it did.

"Or this could be exactly the situation she describes." Matt injected some common sense into the conversation. "A cattleman is taking advantage of the widow of his rival and trying to run her into the ground financially so he can corner the local market."

Jonah's thumb ceased tapping. "I think we should scout it out before deciding one way or the other. Too many variables in play."

Preach uncrossed his leg, his boot heel thumping against the floor. "Agreed."

"Might need to use assumed names." Wallace's eyes glowed with excitement. Apparently he wasn't ready to let this one go just yet. "One of us could hire on undercover. Check things out from the inside. Once we get the lay of the land, Matt can meet with the widow to secure payment for our services, but we'd have to swear her to secrecy. Ensure she doesn't tell the foreman who we are. It'd be the only way to learn the truth. I could get her to open up to me—"

Matt scowled. "*You've* got a hole in your shoulder. No one's going to hire a cowhand with only one working arm."

"Then I could coach Preach on how to earn her trust."

"As if I need help sweet-talkin' a woman." The largest Horseman leaned forward in his chair and scowled with enough heat to send a lesser man running for cover.

Wallace only scoffed. "Preach, you couldn't sweet-talk a woman with a bucket full of peppermint sticks in hand."

"Enough!" Matt clapped his hands against his thighs, too tired to put up with this nonsense after the restless night he'd had. "No one's sweet-talking anyone, all right?"

"Well, that's unfortunate."

Four sets of eyes swiveled to the doorway, where Josephine stood with a tea tray in hand.

"I'd hoped to sweet-talk my way into the room with tea and cookies."

EIGHT

Josephine smiled at the men before her, all of whom were rising to their feet. Even Mr. Wallace made the effort until the captain signaled with a sharp hand motion for him to remain seated.

She'd obviously gotten here just in time. The last thing her patient needed was to get worked up emotionally. The increased vocal volume coming from the parlor as she approached proved that she'd been right not to leave the men completely unsupervised.

"Don't worry," she said with a slightly sheepish glance at Mr. Hanger, "I didn't make the cookies. Mrs. Carrington brought over a batch this morning. I did make the tea, but I've been told by reliable sources that my brewing skills are semi-competent."

"I'm sure the tea is excellent," Mr. Wallace said from the sofa, his charm apparently unimpaired by his exertion. She'd take that as a good sign. Had his charisma been absent, she would have ordered him to bed immediately.

Mr. Hanger suddenly appeared before her, having crossed

the room while she visually examined her patient. He relieved her of the tray and turned to set it on the low table in front of the settee.

"Thank you." Her mouth dried slightly as she watched him handle the heavy tray with ease, the play of his muscles visible to the discerning eye through the cloth of his shirt. And her eye was definitely discerning. Disconcertingly discerning.

Josephine bustled forward, poured tea, set cookies on plates, and absolutely did *not* think about Mr. Hanger's muscles.

She'd seen countless men shirtless over the years. Her brother and his friends at the swimming hole. Cadavers in medical school. And, of course, patients with injuries to the torso or upper extremities. Goodness, she'd seen Mr. Wallace's chest, and he was just as virile a specimen as Mr. Hanger. Well, perhaps not *quite* as virile, but certainly robust enough to create an impressive muscular display. Yet nothing about the younger man's form drew her eye for any purpose other than professional inspection. The captain, on the other hand . . . well, the current fluttering in her abdominal region symptomized a disorder of decidedly non-professional origins.

Which meant it had no place in her clinic. And *she* had no place in this room. At least not until she had her unprofessional fluttering under control.

"Physician, heal thyself," she muttered under her breath.

"What was that?" Captain Hanger looked at her oddly.

Rats. Apparently her comment had not been far *enough* under her breath.

Josephine covered her discomfort with a grin and straightened from bending over the tea table. "I know I interrupted your conversation, and I apologize. I'll leave you gentlemen to your business."

She kept her gaze averted from the captain, finding Mr. Wallace's easy smile far less disruptive to her pulse.

"Your interruption is always welcome, Doctor Burkett." Mr. Wallace winked at her. Almost as if he were privy to her wayward thoughts.

"Yes, well, *you*," she instructed the hopefully not-as-insightful-as-he-seemed fellow with a point of her finger, "should take it easy on the flirtation. In my experience, men trying to impress those around them tend to push themselves harder than they should and end up impeding their recovery."

He schooled his features. "Yes, ma'am."

Of course, both of them knew it wasn't *her* he was trying to impress.

Leaving the men to enjoy their refreshments, and putting some much-needed distance between her abdomen and Mr. Hanger's muscles, Josephine headed for the door.

Unfortunately, Mr. Hanger and his muscles decided to follow, and as soon as she stepped into the hall, he opened his mouth and made it impossible for her to continue pretending he wasn't there. Etiquette dictated that one look at a person when being spoken to, after all.

"Thank you for the tea." The captain's weight shifted from one foot to the other, his usual aura of confidence strangely absent. "I, uh, want to apologize . . . for earlier."

"Earlier?" Were the tips of his ears turning red?

"In the . . . infirmary." The ruddiness spread to his neck and made a steady climb toward his jaw. "I never should have . . . disrobed with the door standing open."

Oh, good heavens. He was apologizing for *that*? The image

she'd fought so hard to banish jumped right back into her cerebrum and posed for her appreciation. Josephine ducked her head. She'd been doing so well focusing on *his* discomfort that she'd successfully forgotten her own. Now her cheeks rivaled his neck.

"Too many years surrounded by military men, I suppose." He grabbed his nape, his gaze skittering away from hers. "I didn't even consider a woman . . . walking in."

"I took no offense." What she *had* taken was a nice long look, one that lasted far longer than it should have. "I'm a physician," she said with a wave of her hand, as if the vision of him half-dressed hadn't seared itself on her brain. "I'm accustomed to viewing human anatomy." Which was true. It was also why the lingering effect was so disturbing. She should have gotten over it by now.

His eyes finally met hers, and her stomach flared. She pressed her palm against the out-of-line organ, warning it to behave. Not that it listened.

"Still," he said. "I'm sor—"

The clinic door flew open. "Dr. Jo!"

Douglas Flanders burst into the front hall, and Josephine nearly jumped out of her skin.

The captain had her shoved halfway behind him before he realized the threat was only a twelve-year-old boy.

"Oh, there you are." Doug peered around Mr. Hanger as if a cavalryman standing guard over the local doctor was business as usual. "Good."

Josephine stepped around the captain, her healer instincts on full alert. "What's wrong?"

"Ma's got one of those spots on her back again. Says it's really sore. Wants you to come take a look."

Josephine nodded. "I'll get my bag."

She strode off to her examination room without a glance at Matthew Hanger. Hoping he'd be back in the parlor by the time she returned, she took an extra minute gathering her supplies. The delay didn't help. He stood in the hall, patiently answering Doug's multitude of questions.

Mrs. Flanders was prone to carbuncles, but she hadn't mentioned anything to Josephine two days ago when they ran into each other at the mercantile. Most likely she had decided she needed a doctor today after rumors of the Horsemen spread. Which explained why Douglas came to fetch her instead of his older sister, Dorothea.

"I won't be gone long," she informed the captain while trying not to look at him. She caught his nod from the corner of her eye, then turned her full attention on Douglas. "Let's be off, shall we?"

Douglas was as reluctant to leave as she was eager. Taking the boy's arm, she steered him down the clinic's front steps and closed the door behind them.

Never had she actually looked forward to the unpleasant business of lancing and draining a boil, but given the choice of Mrs. Flanders's carbuncle and continued awkward conversation with Captain Hanger about his state of undress, she was opting for the carbuncle.

By the time Josephine returned to the clinic, three of the four Horsemen had disappeared. Mr. Wallace napped quietly in the infirmary, and a note lying atop her vacant examination table explained that the captain had gone to the livery to see to the horses.

Telling herself that the slight deflation in her midsection was a symptom of relief, *not* disappointment, she set about cleaning the instruments she'd used with Mrs. Flanders and replenished the medicinal supplies in her doctor's bag.

Twenty minutes later, the bell on her door jangled. Josephine looked up from the medical journal she'd been reading at her desk and spied Captain Hanger's distinctive hat. Stashing the cookie she'd been nibbling under the magazine's pages as if it were illegal contraband, she pushed to her feet and brushed a hand over her skirt to ensure a crumb-free ensemble, then hurried to the doorway.

"Mr. Wallace is still resting," she called softly after the man walking down her hall.

The captain turned and tugged the hat from his head. "I thought I'd sit with him a bit. The others are fetching a wagon from Terrance Dalton, so we should be out of your hair by early afternoon."

Josephine nodded. "I'll ride out to the ranch a couple times this week to check on him, but if he starts running a fever or if you notice unusual swelling or redness around the wound, come get me right away. Day or night."

"I will, Doc. Thanks."

Then he strode down the hall to the infirmary and disappeared from sight.

Well, good. Now that he was tending to Mr. Wallace, she was free to return to her medical journal and the utterly fascinating article on tuberculous peritonitis she'd been reading. Yet not even laparotomy discussions kept her mind from wandering to the cavalryman keeping vigil in her infirmary.

Thankfully, Mr. Albertson arrived with an ingrown toenail that proved an adequate distraction. By the time she had his toe cleaned, treated, and bundled back up into a loosened shoe, the remaining two Horsemen had arrived with the wagon.

Demonstrating admirable military efficiency, the three healthy Horsemen had the horses retrieved from the livery, Mr. Wallace bundled into the back of the wagon, and all of that awful weaponry cleared out of her infirmary in mere minutes.

Having seen Mr. Albertson on his way, Josephine strolled down to the street and leaned over the edge of the wagon bed to bid her patient good-bye. "Don't go undoing all my fine needlework on that arm of yours, Mr. Wallace. Wear the sling whenever you're up and about and get plenty of rest."

He gave her a two-fingered salute. "Yes, ma'am. I'll follow your instructions to the letter."

"See that you do." She wagged a finger at him in mock sternness. "I'll be out to check on you, so I'll know if you misbehave."

"That rogue always misbehaves," Mr. Davenport said as he finished tying Wallace's gray horse to the back of the wagon. He left Phineas tied to the hitching post, then moved past her to climb into the front of the wagon. "The captain will settle up our account, Doc," he said with a tip of his hat.

She stepped back from the wagon, then lifted a hand to wave as Mr. Brooks set the team in motion. "Keep the pace slow," she called as they pulled away.

"They will." The captain's voice rumbled close behind her.

She pivoted sharply and came face-to-back with the man she'd been trying so valiantly to eradicate from her mind. His gun belt had returned to his hips, and as she watched, he slid a rifle into the scabbard on his saddle. Apparently not all of the weaponry was in the wagon. A good deal of it was on the captain.

Josephine frowned. How had she forgotten the reality of who he was? He might be fiercely loyal to his men, patient and kind to young boys, and respectful to her, but he was still a man of war. Once again draped in the tools of his trade. Wasn't that what he'd called them? These horrible contraptions of metal and gunpowder that were designed to maim and kill? Yes, they could also be used to defend the innocent and feed the hungry, as he'd claimed, but looking at them now, she couldn't ignore the truth. He was a man of violence. A warrior who had undoubtedly taken lives on the battlefield. Perhaps he fought now to protect the weak and preserve justice, but the fact was, he still chose a path of violence, not one of peace. The very opposite of the oath she'd taken to first do no harm.

Maybe it was a good thing he was leaving.

"This should be enough to cover your fee," Captain Hanger said as he slowly turned to face her, a couple folded banknotes in his hand.

"Thank you." She slipped the money into the pocket of her apron without looking at it. Without really looking at him either.

He stood there for a moment, and she thought he might say something. But he didn't. He just turned back to Phineas, swung up into the saddle, then tipped his hat to her.

"See ya around, Doc."

"Good-bye, Captain."

Then, without a backward glance, Matthew Hanger rode out of her town and out of her life.

"It's for the best," she mumbled as she watched him ride away. He belonged with his men. Just as she belonged in her clinic. Where things would finally revert back to normal now that Captain Hanger, with his intense hazel eyes, fierce loyalty, and impressive musculature, had removed himself.

A week later, she was still waiting for the reversion to occur. Stubborn reminders lingered, like campfire smoke infused into clothing. It was as if someone had taken her perfectly ordinary rooms and nailed brass nameplates above each doorway to assign them new identities.

The Parlor of the Carried Tea Tray. The Hall of Awkward Apologies. The Infirmary of Dedicated Vigils. The Examination Room of Averted Crisis. She even had a Kitchen of the Drying Vest, since she'd discovered his damp cavalry vest hanging on the back of one of her chairs the morning after he'd slept in her infirmary. Or not slept, if the cleanliness of her kitchen and his clothing was any indication.

It had been eight days since the Horsemen left. Eight days. And *still* her gaze darted to the chair in question when she crossed the kitchen to fetch the kettle for some late-morning refreshment, hoping to see a familiar flash of blue.

For pity's sake. She couldn't even fix herself a cup of tea without Matthew Hanger intruding. Josephine abandoned the kettle and marched out of the kitchen. Forget the tea, she needed some fresh air.

Josephine left the clinic and strode down the street. In the *opposite* direction from the one the Horsemen had driven when returning to Dalton's ranch. The sun shone in the sky. A gentle breeze cooled her nape. There were probably even wildflowers blooming down along the creek. Perfect conditions for a country stroll. And the perfect prescription for an ailing mind: Take in a healthy dose of God's creation. Allow his spirit to soothe hers. Let go of *what-if* and focus on *what was*.

"Josephine! Wait!" Lizzie bolted out of the post office, waving a piece of mail above her head. "There's a letter for you."

Biting back a sigh, Josephine turned and pasted a grateful smile on her face. Hopefully the grin hid her irritation. After all, it wasn't Lizzie's fault that she suffered from a frustrating case of man-brain. The infection would clear eventually. In the meantime, she'd just have to think sterile thoughts when her friend brought up the Horsemen. Because she would. Lizzie had spoken of little else over the past week. Recounting their heroics in taking down the rustlers. Going on about how much her father respected them not only as hired guns, but as men. She even felt it necessary to relate the various singing styles of the four men, since they'd joined her father on the Dalton family pew in church on Sunday. Apparently Mr. Wallace sang a lilting tenor that had actually caused Mabel Yarbrough to swoon. Mr. Brooks rumbled a low bass almost too quiet to hear. Preach Davenport couldn't carry a tune in a bucket. And the captain? Well, his voice was as no-nonsense as the rest of him. He hit the notes he aimed for and left it at that.

"You didn't have to chase me down," Josephine teased as she retraced her steps to meet her friend. "You could have just brought it when you delivered supper, like you usually do."

Lizzie, slightly out of breath, held an ivory envelope out to her. "I thought it might be important. It's from Gringo-let."

Her father?

Josephine took the envelope. The penmanship didn't match the slashing, powerful strokes she'd expected to see. The address had been scribed in a softer, more feminine hand. Darla? Why would Father's housekeeper write to her? Josephine's heart flip-flopped. Had something happened to him?

Josephine tore open the letter and consumed the words as fast as her eyes would allow. Father was in good health, thank the Lord, but Charlie . . .

She clasped Lizzie's arm. "Have the Horsemen left yet?"

Josephine had paid a call to the Dalton ranch yesterday, removed Mr. Wallace's stitches, and given him permission to engage in mounted travel as long as he wore the sling for at least another week. Now she wished she hadn't been so eager to rid herself of them.

"They left early this morning," Lizzie said, confirming Josephine's fears. "They stopped by the mercantile to purchase supplies."

"Did they say where they were going?" She had to know. *Please, Lord. I need a direction.*

Lizzie scrunched her nose like she did when totaling a grocery bill. "North, I think. Paul put their order together. I was in the storeroom with Grant."

Listening at the door, thank heavens. Never had Josephine been more grateful for her friend's penchant for information gathering.

"I think they said something about a ranch." Lizzie's eyes brightened. "Burnet! A ranch outside of Burnet."

"Thank you." Josephine gave her friend's arm a squeeze, then dashed for the clinic.

She was already two or three hours behind them. She'd have to rent a horse, and nothing at the local livery would compare to the cavalry mounts the Horsemen rode. Her only hope was that Captain Hanger would enforce a slow pace in deference to Mr. Wallace's injury.

In truth, their pace didn't matter. She'd ride through the night if necessary. Her brother's life depended on it. Matthew Hanger might be a bur in her brain that wouldn't shake free, but right now he was her best hope to save Charlie.

CHAPTER
NINE

Josephine pounded up the clinic steps to her bedroom and stripped out of her skirt and petticoats. Rolling them into a ball, she shoved them into a carpetbag and dug through her bureau drawer for the trousers she kept for emergencies. One couldn't grow up at Gringolet with a former cavalry officer as a father and not know how to ride. Not only ride, but ride like a soldier. Astride. And ready for anything.

Which meant donning the black pantaloons she hadn't worn since graduating from medical school. But if Dr. Mary Edwards Walker, renowned war surgeon and recipient of the Medal of Honor, could don men's clothing for ease of work, Dr. Josephine Burkett could don trousers to save her brother.

After pulling on the trousers, she grabbed the longer of her two jackets, the one that fell past her hips, and shoved her arms inside. She tossed a hairbrush, pins, a clean shirt-waist, and clean stockings into her bag, then ran downstairs to grab foodstuffs. Not knowing how long she would be on horseback, and not wanting to be a burden to Captain Hanger and his men when she caught up to them, she scraped all the tins from her kitchen shelves into the top of her carpetbag, remembering at the last minute to pull a can opener out of the drawer and add it to her supplies. Crackers, tinned salmon, kidney beans, peaches, condensed milk. If it was edible, she grabbed it. For once in her life, her inability to cook was an asset instead of a liability.

With her carpetbag stuffed and heavy enough to make her waddle, Josephine headed to the examination room and collected her doctor's bag. She never traveled without it. And while she prayed she could reach Charlie before he needed her professional skills, she planned to be prepared for whatever she might encounter once she found him.

Mr. Radisson at the livery gave her an odd look when she showed up in trousers. His eyebrows climbed clear into his hairline when she propositioned to purchase his hat.

"My hat?" He pulled the black slouch hat from his head and looked at it as if he'd never seen it before. "I just bought it a couple days ago. Ain't even got it properly broke in yet."

"Then you won't mind breaking in another one, will you?" Josephine smiled and handed him five dollars, which was likely twice what he'd paid. "I'd buy one myself, but I'm in a terrible hurry. I need your fastest horse with saddle and tack. And your hat."

The wider brims of men's hats offered much better protection against sun and rain than the stylish bonnets she owned, and right now fashion held no place on her list of priorities. The only things she cared about were items that would help her get to the Horsemen and then to Charlie. In fact, she hadn't given headgear a second thought until Mr. Radisson sauntered out of his office to assist her and the newness of his chapeau caught her attention.

His gaze zeroed in on the money she offered, and he slowly

handed over the hat. "Well, if it means that much to ya, I 'spose I can let ya have it."

"Wonderful." Josephine snatched it from his slow-moving hand and flopped it onto her head, trying to emphasize her need for haste. "Now, if you'd fetch your best horse, please? I really must be on my way."

"I got a nice, gentle mare that'd be a good mount for a lady such as yourself," he said as he turned.

"You're not speaking of that swayback nag with the spotted flanks, are you?" Good heavens. That horse had to be at least twenty years old and probably wouldn't even survive the trip.

Radisson stopped. "Myrtle is a sweet little lady with an easy gait. She'll suit you just fine, Dr. Jo."

"I'm not paying a social call, Mr. Radisson. I'm riding cross-country and need a mount with speed and stamina. A sturdy quarter horse with a deep chest or a mount with some mustang blood in him. Do you still have that palomino I saw in your corral last week? That one would suit my needs."

The livery owner stared at her as if she'd just spoken in a foreign tongue. "Sandy's a cow pony, ma'am. He won't take to a sidesaddle."

"Well, I don't take to them much, myself. I'll be riding astride, hence my unconventional clothing, in case you were wondering."

He kicked at the dirt. "Well, I didn't want to say nothin' . . ."

Josephine shoved twenty dollars at him, enough to cover a multiday rental plus a generous bonus to help him find a sense of urgency. "Just have Sandy saddled and ready to go in five minutes. I need to leave immediately."

Radisson's eyes lit up. He took the money and stuffed it in the pocket on the bib of his overalls. "Yes, ma'am. I'll have him ready."

Josephine nodded, then rushed over to the mercantile. Lizzie was assisting a customer with a length of fabric, but as soon as she spotted Josephine, she excused herself and hurried over to her friend.

Lizzie's gaze skittered to a halt on Josephine's legs, but she recovered quickly and made no mention of the trousers. "You're going after them, aren't you?"

Josephine nodded. "I have to. My brother's in trouble, and my father refuses to help. The Horsemen are my only option."

Lizzie gave her a serious look. "They don't work for free, Jo. Daddy had to pool money with the other ranchers in the area to afford them. They might help out in gratitude for what you did for Mr. Wallace, but this is their livelihood, so . . ."

It didn't matter that she left the sentence hanging. Josephine heard the unspoken words anyway. *Don't get your hopes up.* Unfortunately, she didn't have a choice. Captain Hanger and his men were all the hope she had at the moment.

"I'll think of something." She had several hours on horseback to come up with a plan to pay them. "If you could help spread the word that I'll be gone for a few days, I would appreciate it."

Lizzie grinned. "Spreading words is my specialty."

"I know." Jo smiled, her first moment of lightness since Darla's letter arrived. "If there are any medical emergencies, you can send for Dr. Carlton in San Marcos." She hated leaving her community without medical support. What if something happened to little Grant or old Mrs. Peabody while she was gone?

Lizzie touched her arm. "We survived without a doctor in Purgatory Springs for years before you came, Jo. We'll make do until you get back." She wrapped Josephine in a quick embrace. "Go after your brother. He needs you more than we do at the moment."

Josephine hugged her friend, then stepped back. "I'll return as soon as I can."

"Godspeed."

Yes, Lord, Josephine prayed as she hurried back to the livery. *I'm going to need all the speed you can give me.*

Matt's eyes scanned the landscape in front of him out of habit, but his mind only half processed what he saw.

He should have stopped by the clinic before he left. After she'd done her best to avoid him at Dalton's ranch yesterday when she checked on Wallace a final time, he'd decided that avoiding her in return would make things easier for them both. But now he feared that choice had only made him appear rude. Ungrateful. She'd likely saved Wallace's life, after all, and he couldn't be bothered to bid her a decent farewell.

He probably should've warned her about Kendall too. Preach had wired the reporter while he and Jonah were in San Marcos, letting him know they'd finished the job and giving him the names of key people he'd want to interview. Dr. Jo was sure to have made that list.

That was one of the things Matt liked best about their arrangement with Francis Kendall. He never insisted on interviewing them directly. He was content to interview those who hired the Horsemen and any other locals who witnessed their efforts. Of course, that led to some inflating of the truth from time to time, but Kendall made sure not to let the facts get lost in the storytelling.

Josephine would be one to stick to the facts. If anything, she'd downplay her role. Probably shrug Kendall off with some statement about just doing what she'd been trained to do. Maybe he should wire Kendall himself, make sure he knew exactly how vital she'd been to Wallace's recovery. Emphasize her skill and compassion. Matt frowned as he squinted into the western sun. Nah. She struck him as being as unappreciative of the limelight as he was. She deserved respect, but she wouldn't want it handed out for free through a newspaper article. She'd want to earn it face to face. The way she'd earned his.

The sound of hooves approaching from the rear of their small party drew Matt from his musings and sharpened his focus. He brought Phineas's head around and kicked him into a trot to meet Jonah, who'd been scouting their back trail while Matt attended to what lay ahead. Preach and Wallace reined in their mounts as Matt rode by. They'd watch for any encroachers from the north. Not that this was particularly hostile country, but if trouble was coming, it was better to have time to prepare before meeting it.

Jonah slowed his cantering horse to a walk as he met up with Matt.

"Something to report, Sergeant?" Matt scanned the area behind them, the dip of the terrain preventing him from seeing much of what fell to the south. "You rode in at a faster clip than usual."

"Rider on our back trail. Gained on us over the last hour."

Matt frowned. "Single rider?"

Jonah nodded. "Yep. On the small side too. Could be a boy."

Matt groaned. It wouldn't be the first time a kid had ridden out after them with some crazy notion about joining the Horsemen. The boy he'd met in the clinic, what was his name? Donald? Dennis? Douglas! That was it. He'd had a hundred and one questions about the Horsemen. Could be he'd followed them. He seemed a mite young, but stranger things had happened.

"I'll check it out. Stay with the others." If it *was* a kid, Matt would have to see him home. He couldn't let a young'un wander around on his lonesome. If it wasn't a kid . . . well, Matt would have a friendly chat with the fellow. Determine his business and see if he posed a threat. "Wallace can probably do with a rest about now, anyway. Have the others hold up until I return."

Jonah tapped the brim of his hat. "Will do, Captain."

Nudging Phineas into a canter, Matt set off in the opposite direction from his men. He should probably thank the mysterious rider for giving him an excuse to force Wallace to rest without sounding like a nagging old woman for once. The kid's pride was already rubbing raw with the slower pace Matt had forced on the group for his benefit. Having a reason to stop that didn't center on his injury would be a blessing.

Matt crested the hill that had obscured his view of the back trail and reined Phineas in. He scanned the road that stretched out to the south. There. About a mile back. A rider with a black hat on a pale horse. Rode well for a youngster. Too well. The rider had the seat of an experienced horseman, one with years of training. Matt shaded his eyes with his hand and squinted. Fellow might be small, but not likely a boy.

Unsnapping the guard on his holster so his revolver would be ready for a quick draw if needed, Matt touched his heels to Phineas's flanks and set an intercept course. Could be nothing, or could be trouble. Time to figure out which.

With both horses cantering, the distance between them shrank quickly. As they drew near each other, the rider in the black hat straightened in the saddle, then waved an arm above his head as if signaling him. Matt leaned forward over his mount's neck and strained to make out distinguishing features. Was one of Dalton's ranch hands chasing him down for some reason? Had they left something undone with the rustling job?

The color of the mount was wrong, though. He didn't recall any palominos in Dalton's corral. Of course, he likely hadn't seen all the horses in the rancher's remuda.

The rider waved again. The skin on Matt's nape tingled. Who was this? And what did he want?

As the distance between them closed, something about the horse struck Matt as familiar. The palomino. When he'd boarded Phineas and Cooper at the livery in Purgatory Springs, there'd been a palomino there. American quarter horse. Good lines. Strong chest. But the rider?

"Captain Hanger!"

He barely made out his name over the sound of pounding hooves, but it was the frequency of the voice that brought him up in his saddle. High pitched. Like a boy or a—

"Matthew!"

Female. And one who made his heart skitter sideways by calling him by his given name.

Josephine.

Twice now he'd mistaken her for a man. An unbelievable happenstance, given how much he was drawn to her as a woman.

The weight of the situation suddenly hit him. She wouldn't have chased him down just to wheedle a proper good-bye out of him. Something was wrong. Something serious.

As they came together and reined in their mounts, Matt urged Phineas alongside the palomino.

"What is it, Josie? What's wrong?"

The desperation in her face made his gut churn. "My brother. Please. I don't know who else to turn to."

Her lack of ten-dollar words or even complete sentences told him more than anything else how frightened she was.

He leaned forward in his saddle. "Tell me."

Josephine turned away from Captain Hanger's intense hazel eyes, needing a moment to collect herself. She'd been so driven to reach him. Now that she finally had, it was all she could do not to disintegrate into a weepy mess of gratitude. But she wouldn't do that. She wouldn't be the type of woman who used tears to sway a man into solving her problems for her. She needed his help, but she fully intended to be a partner in this rescue mission, and if she fell apart now, he'd never deem her strong enough to ride alongside them.

Inhaling a deep breath, she ordered her trembling insides to still. His nearness proved an apt distraction from her distress, but it did little to focus her mind on her well-thought-out speech. She'd rehearsed for miles what she would say to him, but she needed her wits intact to competently plead her case.

Sliding her right foot out of the stirrup, she shifted her weight to her left side. Matthew took the hint and urged his mount back a step, thereby allowing her to dismount without hindrance. After a moment, she and the captain walked side by side up the road, their horses trailing behind them.

"I received a letter from home this morning. My brother, Charlie, is being held hostage. A ransom demand was sent to my father, but he refuses to pay."

Matthew twisted to face her. "Seems harsh."

Her shoulders drooped. How to explain the complicated nature of her father and brother's relationship?

"Charlie's a bit of a rascal. Always getting into one scrape or another." She pressed her lips closed over the well-worn excuse. Sugarcoating the truth wouldn't serve any purpose. "He'd rather live off my father's money than apply himself to establishing his own career. He wants nothing to do with running Gringolet, much to my father's consternation, and prefers gambling and racing. A few months back, Charlie 'borrowed' several Gringolet horses on a dare, and he and his drunk friends raced them cross-country. One of the animals came up lame. It was the last straw. Father was so furious, he cut Charlie off financially and kicked him out of the house. According to Darla, our housekeeper, Father has refused even to speak Charlie's name since that day.

"It sounds harsh," she said, drawing to a halt in the middle of the road, "but I believe Father still loves Charlie. He's trying to save him from a path of destructive behavior. Hoping he'll sever ties with the bad company he's been keeping and recognize the importance of integrity and the value of hard work." Josephine shook her head, tears welling despite her determination to stay strong. She blinked them back. "I never thought he would go so far as refusing to pay a ransom, though."

The captain made no comment, and his face was impossible to read.

"According to Darla, Charlie was seen in the company of these outlaws before the ransom demand was issued, so Father doubts the veracity of their threats. He doesn't think they will actually hurt him. He believes they're just trying to leverage the family for money Charlie can no longer provide. Most likely to cover gambling debts."

Worried that Matthew would take the same stance as her father, Josephine grabbed his hand and squeezed it tight. "Even if this trouble is of Charlie's own making, I can't leave him in the hands of violent men with nothing more substantial than a . . . a *theory* that they won't harm him. He's my baby brother. If there's even a chance that his life is in danger, or that he might suffer bodily injury, I have to help him."

Captain Hanger turned to gaze at something off in the distance, making him even more difficult to read. "You plannin' to pay the ransom?"

She bit her lip. "No. They're asking for three thousand dollars. By Friday. I can't afford half of that." Here it came. The moment of truth. Straightening her backbone and lifting her chin, Josephine gathered her courage and made her outrageous request. "I want to hire the Horsemen to rescue my brother."

A tiny muscle ticked in Matthew's jaw beneath his ear. Was he angry?

"I'll pay you, of course," she hurried to assure him, in case he thought she was trying to take advantage of their acquaintance. "I remember your enthusiasm for Gringolet horses. When I graduated from medical school, my father promised me my pick from any of the mounts in his stable. I've been saving that pick, knowing it would take several years to build my practice. I hoped that when I was more established, I would be able to stable a horse and ride regularly.

But I'll give my pick to you." It was the only thing of value she owned. "Agree to rescue Charlie, and you can have any horse Gringolet has to offer."

He said nothing. Just slowly turned back to face her. His face a mask.

Her heart rate tripled. Her breath shallowed.

Please say yes. Please say yes.

"Hard to split a horse between four men," he finally said, his voice flat. "You aren't just hiring me, Josie. You're hiring *all* the Horsemen."

She swallowed. She'd been so focused on convincing Matthew, she hadn't given the others more than a cursory thought. Her mind spun, desperate to find a solution.

"Perhaps you can sell the horse and split the profits," she blurted. "Gringolet stock brings top dollar at auction." The idea was paper-thin, but it was all she had to offer. "Please, Captain Hanger."

Something hardened in his eyes. "I liked it better when you called me Matthew."

Josephine blinked. Then hope speared upward through her core like water from a geyser. He hadn't said no. In fact, he'd just invited a greater level of intimacy. And—wait a minute. Had he called her Josie? He had. Twice. She'd been too consumed with spitting out her proposal that she hadn't fully registered the pet name.

Josie.

Her mother had always insisted on using her full name, while her father and Charlie had shortened the moniker to Jo. As a youngster who idolized her father, she'd enjoyed being *one of the boys* with a more male-sounding name. But once she took to wearing long skirts and pinned-up hair, the desire to be *one of the boys* proved less enthralling. She'd leveraged the name with her medical practice, thinking people might be more accepting of her as a physician if there were something about her that reminded them of a man.

But *Josie?* It felt feminine. Maybe even affectionate. It opened a door between them that had previously been closed and invited her closer.

Her head warned against the lure. He was a man who lived by his gun, who profited from violence. Yet her heart argued that he fought for justice and was no different than her father—a man trained for war who had turned that training into a livelihood that not only provided for him and his men but contributed to the good of society. And, most telling of all, Matthew Hanger was the man she had instinctively run to for help. How hypocritical would it be to condemn him for his warrior skills even as she pled for him to use them on her brother's behalf?

"Matthew." As she said his name, acceptance of who he was resonated in her chest. She shifted nearer to him. Touched his arm. "Please. I need your help."

Matt fell into those pleading sea-green eyes and knew at once he was lost. Who was he kidding? He'd been lost the minute she flagged him down. Now she was touching him. Calling him by his given name. Looking at him as if he were some kind of hero.

He would help her, but then, he'd decided that from the beginning. Didn't even need her horse, though a Gringolet mount *would* be a mighty fine prize. Phineas had served him well, but the old boy deserved greener pastures and an easy retirement in the next year or two.

The others would give him a hard time for even bringing

up the idea of taking a job for free. If word got out, they'd be swamped by charity cases. They'd have to leave Kendall in the dark. Of course, the others might think him a sentimental fool and turn down the job. They always put jobs to a vote. Three against one wouldn't cut it, and even though he could probably convince Wallace to take his side, since the doc saved the kid's life, two votes still weren't enough. It took a majority to contract a job. And despite what he'd said about the Horsemen being a package deal, if they decided that risking their lives for a man they'd never met and a woman they barely knew wasn't a job they were willing to take, he'd strike out on his own for a week and do it himself.

Because he couldn't tell her no.

He didn't *want* to tell her no. And that right there should send him riding in the opposite direction as fast as Phineas could carry him.

He knew better than to fall for a pretty pair of eyes and a feisty temperament. Female entanglements left a man vulnerable. He'd already lost one family. If he let himself care for Josie, he'd run the risk of suffering that agony all over again. He couldn't do that. *Wouldn't* do that.

Yet he also couldn't leave her stranded. She needed him.

No, he corrected himself, she needed the *Horsemen*. That was all this was. A job. Nothing personal.

Needing a clear head, he moved away from her touch. "Mount up. We gotta run this by the others before I can give you an answer."

He might have already decided to help her, but she didn't need to know that yet. He wanted to discuss it with his men first. Get their opinion. An objective opinion.

To her credit, she didn't balk at the delay. Just said, "Of course," and moved straight to her horse. Not a whiff of chicanery. Just an eagerness to do whatever needed to be done to achieve her goal.

In two quick strides, Matt arrived at her side and offered a leg up. She smiled her thanks and fitted her foot into his laced fingers. He made a point not to stare at the snug way her trousers outlined her legs when she mounted. He *looked*—how could he not—but he didn't stare. He didn't have to. His memory and imagination captured the images for him. As he turned away to mount his own horse, the feel of her calf brushing against his arm lingered to taunt him. He did his best to banish the sensation, but it proved stubborn.

He couldn't recall ever seeing a lady in trousers, and now he understood why. It put thoughts in a man's head. Thoughts about limbs. Shapely limbs, in Josie's case. With the way she rode, her trousers had to encase well-defined legs. She couldn't have endured several hours of hard riding otherwise.

Get your mind back where it belongs, Hanger. She chased you down so you could save her brother, not so you could obsess over her legs.

Matt blew out a sigh and urged Phineas to an easy canter. Josie stayed right with him, as he knew she would. A capable horsewoman. One who'd been smart to wear trousers. They were a practical garment for long rides. It spoke well of her common sense. It wasn't her fault his mind kept wandering where it had no business going.

Her brother. That was what he should be thinking about. Matt knew the type. Privileged. Spoiled. Eager to earn the respect of their peers with money and stupid stunts, not realizing that the very friends they worked so hard to impress cared nothing for them. Would desert them the instant things grew dull or difficult. He'd trained more than a few recruits with similar backgrounds. He'd tried to instill a sense of purpose in them. Teach them to fight for something bigger than themselves. To find honor in serving their country, protecting others, and defending the men at their sides. Men who wouldn't abandon them in battle, who cared more about mettle than money. Some couldn't handle the strict military lifestyle, having every moment dictated by bugle calls or orders from others. Some couldn't handle the grueling training and loneliness of long patrols. But some . . . some found the inner strength to apply themselves, to become men of character, men worthy of genuine respect.

Men like Mark Wallace. Wallace had come to him as a flamboyant kid with a talent for horsemanship and a reckless craving for adventure that endangered all around him. Now he was a man others depended upon, one who'd taken a bullet for his captain. His friend.

Perhaps he could do the same for Charlie. Matt had heard the sorrow, the embarrassment in Josie's voice as she explained the situation. She loved her brother, wanted him to be a man of character, a man who would bring the family honor instead of disgrace. Maybe Matt could put in a good word for the kid with the commanders of the 7th. Get him some military discipline and pride. Maybe . . .

"I think I see Mr. Brooks." Josie raised her voice to be heard above the hoofbeats.

Matt jerked himself out of his own thoughts, swiveled his head to the side to look at her, then peered in the direction she pointed.

Sure enough, Jonah sat atop his horse at the edge of the rise, rifle draped across his lap in readiness, waiting for them to crest the hill.

"Yep," he snapped, angry at himself for dropping his guard. If Jonah had been foe instead of friend, Matt could have led them straight into an ambush. "Let's go." His voice was sharp, even to his own ears, but he made no apology.

The time for tenderness had passed. If he was going to lead the Horsemen into battle, he couldn't allow distractions. And there was no bigger distraction than the woman riding at his side.

ELEVEN

Matt reined Phineas in as he topped the rise where Jonah waited. The sharpshooter didn't seem shocked in the least by Josephine's appearance. Although he'd probably deduced her identity halfway up the hill with those keen eyes of his.

"Ma'am." Jonah tugged on his hat brim as if he'd just met her crossing the street in town instead of out in the middle of nowhere, dressed in a hodgepodge of men's and women's clothing.

Josephine nodded to him as she leaned forward in her saddle and patted the palomino's neck. "Mr. Brooks. Fine day for a ride, don't you think?"

"Beats walkin'."

She smiled as she straightened. "That it does."

"The others are just up the road a piece." He gave a little nod to indicate the direction, then turned to meet Matt's gaze, a teasing gleam in his eyes. "I'll bring up the rear. Keep an eye out for any more trouble."

"*More* trouble?" Josie scanned the surrounding countryside

as if an attack were suddenly imminent. "Just how much trouble have you faced so far on your journey?"

"Not a lick 'til you showed up." The former buffalo soldier chuckled, his grin wide as he circled his mount behind them.

A tinge of pink colored Josephine's cheeks.

Matt scowled a reprimand at Brooks as he passed. Jonah swallowed the sound of his laughter, but his shoulders kept right on shaking, making his opinion on women in the ranks abundantly clear.

Not that Matt could argue the point. Josephine had already proven a distraction. The sooner the other Horsemen heard her out and made a decision, the better. Once she was back in Purgatory Springs, he'd regain full use of his wits and could take care of business. He'd deliver the kid to his sister, then be on his way. Free of entanglements. He might have a few new regrets to add to the sack he carried, but better to take 'em on when they were small than to let them grow to a size that could break him later.

"Ignore him," Matt groused as he moved Phineas to block her view of Sergeant Brooks and his shaking shoulders. "The others are waiting."

She didn't quite meet his gaze, but she nodded and nudged her mount into a trot.

Ten minutes later, Preach was waving them over to a small stream a hundred yards or so from the road. He meandered out to meet them, squinting and craning his neck as he tried to discern the identity of their guest. "Is that . . . Dr. Jo?"

Josephine drew her mount to a halt and pushed the too-large hat higher on her head. "Mr. Davenport," she said in acknowledgment.

Luke raised a brow. "You come all the way out here to check on Wallace?" He glanced over his shoulder to where

Mark had pushed to his feet from sitting with his back against a tree. "The kid's a little cranky, but I checked his arm when we stopped, and it seems to be holdin' up just fine."

"I'm glad to hear it," Josephine said, "but I'm not here as a doctor today. I'm here as a client." Her gaze swept over each man in turn. "I want to hire the Horsemen."

Matt tried to gauge Luke's reaction, but the big man gave little away beyond a small start of surprise.

"Well, then. I guess we better get you down from there so we can have ourselves a powwow." Preach strode forward and reached for her, but she waved off his assistance.

"Thank you, but I can manage." And she did, her feet coming to rest on the ground in a smooth, controlled motion even with the stirrups shortened to accommodate her smaller stature.

Matt grinned in appreciation. Not only because she knew her way around a horse, but because Preach's hands weren't locked on her waist right now. He trusted the corporal with his life, but that didn't mean he wanted his friend's hands on his woman.

His woman?

Matt's abdomen clenched. Where had *that* thought come from? Hadn't he just resolved to conclude their business and get her firmly out of his life as soon as possible?

Good grief, Hanger. Get your head on straight.

"Dr. Burkett, what a delightful surprise!" Wallace swooped in, good arm extended to take her hand. "Here, let me see you to the stream. I'm sure you'd like a moment to refresh yourself after such a long journey."

"I *am* rather thirsty." She didn't take his offered hand, just glanced down at herself and swiped at the edge of her jacket. "And dusty. But I fear the situation that sent me riding after you is urgent. I'd prefer to explain my proposal first, then seek refreshment while you and the others debate its merits." She darted a glance toward Matt. He caught and held her gaze, shoving down the pleasure that tried to rise when she sought him out above the others. "I'm sure you'll want privacy for such a discussion."

Preach crossed his arms and neatly inserted himself between Matt and Josephine. He scowled briefly at Matt before turning to face their guest. "I reckon your proposal has at least some merit, or the captain wouldn't have brought you here, so go ahead and spill it."

She stepped sideways to peer around Davenport's sizeable shoulders, her brows raised in silent question. Matt nodded, taking charge of Jonah's horse as the last Horseman joined the group. Josephine began her explanation, and Matt distanced himself slightly from the others, not wanting to influence the way they heard the tale. He listened for any new information that might arise in the second telling as he loosened the cinches on the three horses in his care, then led the animals to the stream. By the time he returned, she'd covered the basics and even produced the letter from her father's housekeeper and handed it to Wallace, since he stood closest to her. The kid scanned the missive as she made her plea, then passed it to Jonah.

"I realize that the price a single horse can fetch, even a Gringolet horse, fails to meet the standard rate for hiring your services," she said. "It's not fair of me to take you away from whatever better-paying job awaits you in Burnet. Nor is it fair of me to ask you to risk your lives when I can't pay your price, but I'm asking anyway. I have no choice. My brother's welfare hangs in the balance." Her lower lip quivered slightly, but she fisted her hands around the hem of her blue jacket and lifted her chin. "I'll pay as much as you need. A little each month to cover whatever debt remains. I'll sign a contract to that effect, if it will help. Whatever you want."

It killed him to see the proud Josephine Burkett groveling, but his men needed to see her desperation. Her love for her brother. Money had never been the Horsemen's primary motivation. Yes, it was how they made their living, and yes, a man who risked his life for trouble that wasn't his own deserved to be compensated handsomely, but the jobs they took were about more than that. They were about protecting the innocent and righting wrongs. Fighting the battles ordinary people couldn't fight for themselves.

After the horrors of Wounded Knee, they'd all sworn an oath to do everything in their power to preserve life and justice. That was their penance. Their calling. The money kept them in ammunition, fed their horses, and allowed them to put a little away for the day they'd be too old to play the mercenary game, but it wasn't what drove them. Guilt and a craving for redemption drove them.

At least, that was what drove Matt.

"We don't work on a contract basis, ma'am," Jonah said, his words firm but polite. "We either agree to take on the job for the price you're offerin' up front, or we walk away."

"I understand." Her posture drooped a bit, then bounced back as a new light entered her eyes. "Free medical treatment." She nodded toward Wallace, then eyed each man in turn, renewed energy zinging through her. "You men are in a dangerous line of work. If you agree to rescue my brother, I'll agree to come to you, *any* of you, anywhere in Texas, whenever you need my services. Injury. Sickness. I'll treat you for free. For life. Should you marry, I'll even deliver your babies. You'll have your own personal physician on call."

Preach scratched his jaw. "Could come in handy."

Josephine beamed, her hope-filled eyes meeting Matt's with an impact that sent vibrations coursing over his skin. Man, but he wanted to make this woman happy. To give her the answer she wanted to hear. But it wasn't up to him. It was up to the Horsemen. As a group. He killed the smile twitching at the corners of his mouth before it could break free, not wanting her to think her latest offer would sway the Horsemen in her favor. It might, but it might not. Better to temper her expectations.

Her smile dimmed a bit, but her chin remained high. "I'll let you talk things over," she said, casting a final glance his way before she retreated to where the horses drank from the stream. She patted her palomino's hindquarters, then unstrapped a canteen from the back of the saddle before heading upstream, where a clump of scraggly brush provided a bit of privacy.

"Well, boss," Jonah ventured once Josephine was out of earshot, "what do you think?"

Preach scoffed. "You *know* what he thinks. He's got it so bad for the lady doc, he's ready to ride to her rescue all on his lonesome."

"Preach . . ." Wallace's tone asked for a level of tact the big man rarely showed.

"What?" Preach shot a glower at Wallace. "You gonna tell me I'm wrong?"

Matt stuck his hand between them. "Whether or not I have a personal interest in the lady is not the issue under discussion."

"Which means he definitely has a *personal interest*," Preach stage-whispered to Wallace out of the side of his mouth. Wallace tried to fight off a grin but failed miserably.

"We're discussing the job."

"I'm not likin' the location of the drop." Jonah, thankfully, could be counted on to keep to the business at hand. Always serious, always focused. He'd pull no punches when it came to giving his honest opinion. "Uvalde's a rough town. Outlaws and banditos crossin' in and out of Mexico on a regular basis. Hard men who won't take kindly to someone interferin' with their business."

"Uvalde?" Preach snatched Josephine's letter out of Jonah's hand. "Let me see that."

Matt clenched his jaw. He hadn't known where her brother was being held, since he hadn't yet seen the letter. Uvalde had a reputation for lawlessness. The few decent folk who lived there gave the outlaws free rein in the interest of self-preservation. Made things a mite more complicated. He'd still go, but not alone. He'd have to hire men to ride with him if the Horsemen voted him down. The prospect didn't sit well. New men wouldn't know how he worked. Couldn't anticipate his moves. And couldn't be counted on to have his back if things went south.

I need the Horsemen, Lord. Matt looked at each of his men in turn. Each of his friends. *Not sure I can do this without them.*

"I don't like it, Matt." Preach handed him the letter. "Uvalde's a solid two-day trip. That's *if* we cut across to Austin and catch the train down through San Antone. We'd have to leave the train at least one stop early so we could keep our arrival a secret. That'd only leave a few hours Friday morning to scout and plan before the ransom is due at noon. That's a pretty tight window."

"Won't know how many men we're up against until we're there either," Jonah added. He thumbed his hat up higher on his head. "Plenty of men with stunted morality to recruit hanging around the saloons and brothels down there. Some might even jump into the fight just for the sport of it."

"The deck certainly isn't stacked in our favor on this one," Matt acknowledged, "but I'm still gonna vote yes. Josephine Burkett's a good woman who needs help. I want to help her."

"She did save the kid's life," Preach conceded. "And I ain't gonna lie, I like the idea of having my own private doc on call if I end up on the wrong side of a bullet."

Matt's hope spiked. If Preach voted in favor of the job, that would give them three votes. Which would be enough.

"What about the widow in Burnet?" The question thudded to the ground at the men's feet. From Wallace of all people. The one Horseman Matt had expected to be on Josephine's side. "She might be in real danger if our theory about her foreman is correct. Don't get me wrong, I owe Dr. Burkett my life, and if she was the one in danger, I would be the first to suggest we drop everything to help her. But she's not. Her brother is. A man who, by the lady's own admission, is in a predicament of his own making. Outrageous wagers. Irresponsible, nearly criminal behavior." Wallace met Matt's gaze. "We made a pact to protect the innocent, not fools who snare themselves in their own webs."

Preach folded his arms. "Kid's got a point."

Matt clenched his jaw, unable to deny it. But he couldn't let it lie either. "Look. I'll respect whatever the group decides. You know that. If you agree that it's better for the Horsemen to head to Burnet to help the widow, I won't stop you. But I won't join you either." Disturbed murmurs and raised eyebrows had Matt bringing his hand up in reassurance. "I'd join you as soon as I could, but you wouldn't need me for the reconnaissance portion. Preach can hire on like we talked about, learn all he can about the widow and her foreman, and by the time I get there, you'll have gathered enough information for us to make a decision about taking the job. In the meantime, I'll hire a few extra guns and make the trip down to Uvalde.

"I know you think I'm soft in the head over this woman, and you might be right, but my conscience won't let me turn her down. My gut tells me she's stubborn enough to go down there herself and try to bargain with the crew holding her brother hostage. Probably try to trade her horse for her brother or something equally wrong-headed. They'd be more likely to take what Charlie owes out of his sister's hide than wait for a horse the old man might or might not hand over." The more Matt thought about all the things that could happen to Josephine if she tried to save her brother on her own, the harder his blood pumped. "I can't take that chance."

Silence fell over the group for a long moment. Matt said no more. He'd made his plea. It was up to the others to decide what they felt called to do.

It's in your hands now, Matt prayed. *I trust you to know what's best.* But he couldn't help hoping that God's idea of what was best matched up with his own.

Jonah was the first to break the silence. "The Horsemen stand together." He looked Matt square in the eye. "If your gut is tellin' you to help the lady doc, that's good enough for me." He turned his gaze to the others. "I ride with the captain."

Preach unfolded his arms. "Can't say I care much about this Charlie fella, but I'd sure hate for something bad to happen to Dr. Jo. Count me in."

Matt turned to Wallace. The kid had saved his life by taking that bullet. The last thing he wanted was for a woman to come between them.

Wallace sighed. "I suppose the widow in Burnet can wait a few days."

Matt nodded solemnly, even though he wanted to grin like a maniac. "Thanks. I promise we'll head up there the minute this job with Josie is finished."

In his relief, the nickname slipped out before he could catch himself. Wallace's gaze sharpened knowingly, and Matt had to fight the urge to justify himself.

"I get that you care for Miss Josephine, Matt, and I respect that," the kid said. "But I can't shake the feeling that something is off about this job."

Matt laid a hand on Wallace's good shoulder, a tickle of foreboding itching against his nape. "Then I'm glad you'll be there to watch my back."

TWELVE

Josephine ran her dampened handkerchief over the back of her neck for what must have been the tenth time. The cool cloth felt good against her heated skin after the long ride, but the action had nothing to do with cleaning away perspiration. Her mind simply couldn't handle a more complicated task. Not when all of her energy was focused on the men standing less than fifteen yards away, their discussion varying enough in volume that she managed to catch a word every once in a while. A happenstance that only added to her mental strain as dozens of conversational scenarios zipped through her head, torturing her with phantom wisps of what they *might* be saying.

So when footsteps finally crunched the dirt and leaves along the creek bed, Josephine stuffed her handkerchief in her jacket pocket and nearly pounced on the man who'd come to fetch her.

"What did they say?" She searched Matthew's face for the answer she sought. He smiled slightly, and her heart pounded.

"Preach really likes the idea of having a personal physician at his beck and call. You might end up regretting that offer."

"Not if I have my brother returned to me alive and well." Her stomach danced in giddy little circles as she peered into Matthew's hazel eyes, seeking the confirmation she so desperately needed. "Does that mean the Horsemen are taking the job?"

"Yep."

"Oh, Matthew." Joy and relief swept over her in such a wave that it picked her straight off her feet and splashed her into his arms. She hugged his neck. "Thank you!"

There was not a doubt in her mind that he was the reason they'd agreed to help her. If he hadn't given her his support, they never would have taken the job. Not for the pitiful fee she offered and the trouble they would incur.

It wasn't until she felt the warm pressure of his hand against the small of her back that she realized she'd thrown herself at him.

"Sorry. I . . . ." She ducked her head and stepped back. "I got a little carried away."

"I didn't mind."

She jerked her chin up. There was no charmer's smile on his face. Neither was there an abundance of politeness in evidence, as would be the case if someone meant to smooth over a social gaffe. There was only Matthew. The rugged, straightforward captain, with his square jaw and horseshoe mustache, looking at her with an intensity that made her believe cardiac somersaults were anatomically possible.

"Your horse is too spent for us to travel much farther. Cypress Mill is close. We can stay there tonight. I don't think they have a hotel, but there's probably someone who'd take in a female boarder. The men and I can bed down at the livery."

She nodded. Traveling with a group of men wouldn't do her reputation any favors, but having a chaperoned place to pass the night would ease things. She appreciated his thoughtfulness in taking that into account.

"Tomorrow we can cut across to Austin and catch the train. You can ride with us as far as San Marcos, then take your mount back to Purgatory Springs. I'd prefer to escort you home, but our timetable is too tight for me to take a side trip."

Josephine frowned. "I'm not going back to Purgatory Springs. I'm going with *you*."

Matthew's face hardened. All chivalry disappeared beneath the absolute authority of a US Cavalry commanding officer. "No. You're not."

Had she really just been appreciating his thoughtfulness? Ha! He was a dictator. She straightened her spine and glared at him. "You might order your men about, Captain Hanger, but I am not one of your soldiers. I choose where I go and what I do. My *brother* is being held hostage. I'm going."

Matthew grabbed her arm and dragged her close, his voice deadly quiet. "Uvalde is a den of outlaws, Josie. No place for a woman. I couldn't keep you safe."

She tossed her head, modulating her tone to match his volume. Neither of them wanted their disagreement overheard. "I'm not hiring you to keep me safe, *Captain*. I'm hiring you to rescue my brother."

He made a growling sound in his throat, then released her arm. "Quit calling me Captain."

She blinked. "What?"

He blew out an exasperated breath. "My military rank obviously holds no sway over you, and even in trousers there's no way I could ever confuse you for one of my men, so let's just keep formal titles out of this. Unless you want me to start calling you Doctor at every turn."

No. The forced formality would itch under her skin. Much like she supposed her sarcastic use of his rank was doing to him now.

"I encouraged the men to take this job because I wanted to help you," he said. "*You*, Josie. Not your brother. If you came to Uvalde with us, I'd be little use to my men or to your brother, because I'd constantly be worried about your well-being. If it came down to keeping you safe or rescuing your brother, I'd abandon your brother and my men in a heartbeat."

He'd abandon his men? For *her*? Josephine's pulse accelerated so quickly, she became a little light-headed. His men meant everything to him. She'd seen that truth in how he cared for Mr. Wallace. It reflected in the way they all trusted him, looked up to him. Was it just because she was a woman that he made such a claim? Some chivalrous impulse to save women and children first? Gazing at his earnest face, it felt like more. It felt . . . personal.

"I need to be there, Matthew," she pleaded. "I want Charlie to know that despite Father's rejection, his family still supports him. Still cares." He started to shake his head, and she jumped in with a compromise. "What if I didn't come to the rescue itself, but simply stayed nearby? Somewhere close enough that I could meet up with you as soon as you get Charlie away?"

His gaze sharpened. "It would have to be outside Uvalde. That place is a viper's nest."

She nodded quickly, not wanting to give him the chance to second-guess the offer.

"We plan to disembark at Chatfield in order to do some

reconnaissance on the outskirts of Uvalde without anyone being aware of our presence. You can stay there." He was dictating again, but she didn't care this time. He was giving her what she wanted. Or close enough to satisfy.

"I'll wait for you in Chatfield," she vowed. "Out of harm's way. You have my word."

He held her gaze for a long moment. At first he seemed to be ascertaining the reliability of her promise, but then something changed. Softened. Heated. Her heart responded with a thrumming vibration, but he turned away and glanced toward his men. He caught Mr. Davenport's eye and gave a little sideways jerk of his head. Some kind of signal, apparently. Then he turned back to her, the heat she'd seen in his eyes banked to something far more polite and far less interesting.

"Walk with me?" He extended his arm.

What was he about? Was he trying to distract her? Or did he want to spend time with her away from his men while their horses rested?

Hoping he was motivated more by the latter than the former, she slid her hand into the crook of his elbow. "All right."

Some of the tension radiating from him eased at her acceptance, and she hid a smile. Could it be that the mighty Matthew Hanger was nervous around women? It was such a departure from the always-in-control cavalry officer that she found the discovery quite delightful. Especially if his reaction had more to do with her specifically than women in general.

That would be a helpful piece of knowledge to obtain. Of course, testing the theory would require surrounding him with other unmarried women to observe his reaction. Her smile dimmed. A passel of beautiful variables flirting with her subject failed to thrill her research-loving soul. Perhaps scientific inquiry was not the proper course of action in this situation. Besides, her method was bound to be flawed. As invested in the outcome as she was, she wouldn't be an objective observer. She *wanted* to prove that he had a special interest in her, because she had a special interest in him. One that seemed to grow stronger the more time she spent in his company.

Once they were a fair distance away from the others, Matthew broke the silence. "Tell me about your brother." He glanced her way, any evidence of nervousness swallowed by pragmatism. "Physical description, personality, how he's likely to react when we arrive."

Ordering herself not to be disappointed in his chosen topic of discourse, Josephine turned her mind to Charlie. She was here to secure his rescue, after all, not to secure herself a beau.

"He's slender in build," she said, "taller than me, but an inch or two shorter than you, I would say." She eyed Matthew's height, only getting a little distracted when her gaze tangled with his on the way back to the ground. Thankful for the trousers and boots that made tromping through tall prairie grass an uncomplicated matter, she lengthened her stride, enjoying the stretch of muscles long confined while riding. "His hair is dark brown and curls a bit around his collar. His face is clean-shaven." She tried to think of anything that would make him easy to identity, besides the fact that he would most likely be in restraints. "He wears a black hat with a band made of silver conchos. Never goes anywhere without it." Her pace slowed as a disheartening idea occurred to her. "I suppose they could have stolen it. The silver's not worth much, but these men seem desperate to wring every last coin from him that they can." She stopped altogether.

"Do you think—" Her voice cracked. "Do you think they've beaten him?"

She hadn't allowed her mind to consider what kind of torture Charlie might be enduring, choosing to focus instead on what she could do to help him. But now that she had handed her burden to the Horsemen, the floodgates opened. Visions of his face swollen and bloodied. His posture bent sideways as he cradled broken ribs. His body riddled with bruises and welts. Josephine trembled at the horrible pictures her imagination painted, her own body aching in sympathy.

Matthew moved to stand in front of her and cupped his hands around her upper arms. His touch was gentle. Comforting. And as she raised her chin to meet his gaze, she felt his strength seep into her, helping her banish her fears with logic and hope.

"They won't hurt him," Matthew said, his voice firm, confident—as if he had no doubt that what he said was true. "Not yet, anyway." That was slightly less inspiring, but the fact that he wasn't glossing over things for her sake made it easier to believe him. "If they want to collect a ransom, they won't damage the merchandise. It's not in their best interest."

She gave a jerky nod. It was all she could manage as she struggled to control her emotions.

He seemed to sense her turmoil, for his grip tightened slightly on her arms and he leaned closer, his face mere inches from hers. His hazel eyes glowed with promise, a promise she fought to believe.

"I'll get him back for you, Josie. I swear it."

"I know." Her lips curved of their own volition, so moved was she by his vow. They'd known each other for such a short time, yet in that moment she had no doubt that he would sacrifice his life to accomplish his mission. It was just the kind of man he was. Honorable. Capable. Selfless. The kind of man this world needed.

But the idea of him giving his life for her brother stirred fear instead of bringing comfort.

She raised her hands and grasped his arms above the elbows, closing the chain that held him to her and her to him. "As much as I want my brother back, I want *you* to come back too, Matthew. Promise me you will."

His throat worked, but he said nothing.

Josephine bit her lip, her gaze falling to somewhere around his collarbone. "The only thing worse than losing my brother would be carrying the knowledge that I was the cause of a great man's death." She forced her gaze back up to his face, a face lined with experience, hardened by war. Yet in his eyes she saw his noble soul and champion's spirit. "I might not know you well, Matthew Hanger, but I've seen your heart. The world would be a darker place without you in it."

THIRTEEN

Matt stared at the top of Josie's head, her admiration crawling over him like a colony of fire ants, nipping at his conscience, at his honor. She was saying those words to the man she thought he was, not to him.

"I'm not a great man," he ground out, his voice like gravel. "You don't know the things I've done." He released her arms and stepped back.

Her hands fell to her sides, but they soon found their way onto her hips. The confusion he expected to see on her face was nowhere in evidence. Instead, she looked downright miffed.

"Must you be so contrary? Contradicting me at every turn? It's really quite tiresome."

"I'm trying to be honest." And heaven help him if her combative stance didn't get his blood firing. The self-pity that had slumped his posture a moment ago ceded to the warrior inside who insisted on winning whatever battle he faced.

"Good," she said. "I like honesty. What I don't like is a man assuming he knows better than me and running roughshod over my opinions." She lifted her right hand from her hip and jabbed her index finger into the dip of his shoulder. "I've seen your dedication to your men. I've seen your patience with young boys barraging you with questions. I've heard accounts of you risking your life to fight for those beset by wicked men. I've seen you worship with a Bible in your lap and a song on your lips. I didn't make up my opinion on a whim, Mr. Hanger. I have empirical evidence to back my claims."

Matthew crossed his arms. "Your *evidence* don't show the whole picture. You haven't seen me kill."

She flinched but didn't back away. "My father was a soldier," she said. "He killed men in battle. Yet I respect him more than any man I've ever known. I might despise humanity's need to solve disputes with guns instead of words, but I understand the nature of war and don't lay blame on those who wage it."

He should just surrender now, accept her terms, and allow her to keep her heroic opinion of him. But he couldn't. Some perverse need drove him to expose the dark places of his soul, to prove that he wasn't the man she thought him to be.

"I'm a harsh taskmaster." He jutted his chin, daring her to see the real man beneath the façade. "I'd drill new recruits until they broke—insulting them, torturing them for hours in the hot sun or the freezing snow. More than one have called me a monster."

She raised a brow. "Yet your men would follow you into Hades if you asked it of them. That tells me that even at your worst, you are thinking about what is best for them, and they know it. You're training them to survive."

He frowned. Stubborn woman, insisting on believing the best of him when she didn't know the worst. Time to bring out the big guns. His heart pounded in his chest, and his throat tightened around the words marching up his craw.

"You haven't seen me fail to save women and children from a slaughter my own troops rained down on them."

Her eyes softened, but the line of her mouth remained as firm as ever. "And you haven't seen me fail to save patients who died under my scalpel."

The statement brought him up short. He'd never considered that someone outside the military could understand the deep-seated regret and self-blame inherent in watching a person die, one he'd sworn to protect. Matt looked at Josie with new eyes—eyes that didn't just see a beautiful woman and a skilled doctor, but someone familiar with the path that led through the valley of the shadow of death.

"I still see their faces." He clamped his jaw closed. He hadn't meant to divulge that. Commanders didn't admit weakness in front of their men. But then, she wasn't one of his men, was she?

The horrors of Wounded Knee flashed through his mind. The sharp scent of gunpowder wafted into his nostrils. The boom of the Hotchkiss guns echoed in his ears. As he looked out over the Texas prairie, he didn't see grass. He saw blood-stained snow. Scores of dead Lakota. The old woman he'd tried to save. The children. The boy with Matt's bullet in his shoulder. All gone. Slaughtered. And he'd been part of the massacre.

A gentle touch on his upper arm cleared the choking haze of memory. He blinked the smoke of past battles from his eyes and focused on lovely green eyes shining not with pity or disgust, but with understanding.

"I see them too," she said. "The old man whose heart was too weak to endure the stress of removing the cancer that was killing him. The woman crushed by a wagon who'd lost too much blood by the time I got to her. The stillborn babe who never took a first breath." Her lashes dipped, brushing across the freckles lining the tops of her cheeks. "I tell myself I did everything I could. That their deaths were outside my control, but I still feel regret." She raised her lashes and peered into his eyes with a vulnerability he'd never thought to see on her face. "And when I'm particularly tired or discouraged, I torture myself with questions of what I could have done differently."

"How you could have saved them." He did the same. Not only with how he could have saved the old woman and those kids, but how he could have stopped the entire fiasco from happening in the first place. If he had forced the Lakota to surrender their weapons when they'd first tracked them down. If he had restrained the medicine man who'd incited the rebellion. If he had—

"But torture isn't healthy," Josie said, cutting off his spiraling thoughts. "It tears apart the soul." She smiled at him, a knowing smile that made him suspect she knew exactly where his brain had traveled. "One of my medical professors liked to say, 'You won't find success with patients in the present if you dwell on the failures of your past.' I think he was right. So when a loss comes, I examine what went wrong, learn what I can to inform future decisions, then leave it behind. I have to if I want to serve my patients to the best of my ability."

"'But this one thing I do,'" Matt murmured softly, "'forgetting those things which are behind, and reaching forth unto those things which are before.'"

138

Her smile stretched wide. "Exactly! I love that verse from Philippians. It's seen me through many a late-night mental battle."

He had a hard time imagining this strong-willed woman losing ground in any battle she waged, but he knew better than most how different things were in the dead of night, how nightmares could distort reality, and how shadows of doubt and recrimination loomed large.

"Preach quoted it the day we decided to leave the army and start the Horsemen," he said. "It kind of became our creed."

"A fitting motto."

They fell into an easy silence after that and began walking again. Their arms hung loose at their sides, his knuckles brushing the back of her hand on occasion. Whenever the unintentional touch occurred, awareness zinged up his arm and shot into his chest, causing his lungs to constrict and his breathing to become slightly erratic. He could feel the pull of her. So close. Mere inches of no-man's-land separated them. Territory yet unconquered. He steered his step minutely closer to hers, the warrior inside urging him to lay claim even as the gentleman insisted he hold the line.

The back of her hand brushed against his. At her instigation, not his. By accident or design? He slanted a look at her, but the hat she wore hid her eyes from him.

He chomped at the bit holding him in place. Her hand swung past his in a near miss just as a bird called from the south. The sound blasted through his ears like the bugle call to advance. The soldier surged forward. Crossed no-man's-land. And claimed the fair maiden's hand.

When she offered no resistance, his galloping heart

slowed to a canter, the triumph rising in his chest tempered by the sheer wonder of the feel of her fingers resting against his.

"How long did you serve in cavalry?" she asked, finally breaking the silence that stretched between them.

"Thirteen years. Joined up after Custer's defeat at Little Bighorn." Matt thought back to the naïve kid he'd been, so eager to make a difference, not realizing the price he'd be asked to pay.

She tilted her face to peer up at him. "You must have been very young."

He grinned. "I didn't think so at the time. Twenty-two was a man grown. But looking back, the man I am today feels ancient in comparison."

"Not ancient," she said, humor sparking in her eyes, "just well-seasoned. At least, that's what I tell myself when I overhear the old-maid whispers."

"Old maid?" Matt's feet planted in the ground as the need to defend her against such outlandish accusations fired his blood. "You are nothing of the sort. Old maids are spinsters who are either too timid to face the world or such grouches that they find nothing but fault in it. You are far too vibrant, intelligent, and kind to fall into either category. Not to mention the fact that the idea of you being old is ludicrous. Me? I'm practically in my dotage. But you?" His voice softened as he reached between them and ran the back of his finger across her cheek. "You are a rose in full bloom."

A touch of pink colored her skin, and her lashes lowered to hide her eyes. He clenched his jaw. He'd said too much. Gotten too personal. But the idea of some snoopy busybodies calling Josie an old maid just because she wasn't married riled him so much that words had just tumbled out of him before he could think better of it.

"Sorry. I know it ain't exactly polite to comment on a woman's age."

Her head came up, and she pinned him with her gaze. "Don't you dare apologize, Matthew Hanger."

There she went again, throwing around his full name as if it were the exclamation mark on her sentence. A man really shouldn't enjoy being harangued, but Josie's rants were more like teasing in disguise, having more to do with lifting him up than tearing him down. And while her highfalutin vocabulary might intimidate him just a tad, it was hard not to appreciate her wielding it on his behalf.

She jabbed him with her finger again. "You will not retract that compliment. Do you hear me?"

"Yes, ma'am." He gave a sober nod. It really was hard not to grin, but she was making such an effort to look fierce, he didn't want to ruin the game.

"Good, because I plan on holding on to those fine words for a good long while. And another thing." She jabbed him again, though this time it was more of a full-handed pat than a jab, one that lingered against his chest, giving him the oddest urge to flex his muscles. "You are far from being in your dotage. I've seen your physique, if you'll recall, and as a doctor, I can assure you that among male *Homo sapiens*, you fall far above the average."

The fact that he had never heard the term *Homo sapiens* did nothing to impair his understanding of her meaning. She didn't see an old man nearing his fourth decade with graying hair and aching bones when she looked at him. She saw a man in his prime. He did flex his muscles then, and that grin he'd been fighting found its way onto his face. Only it wasn't humor inspiring its appearance this time. Nope. It was full-on swagger.

"And what if I'm more interested in your opinion as a woman than a physician?" he asked as he set a hand to her waist and tugged her closer.

"A physician is trained to catalog the strengths and weaknesses of the human anatomy," she said as her palm flattened against the wall of his chest, "and report accurate findings. But a woman?" Her gaze lifted from his chest to his face. "A woman keeps her secrets."

As close as they were, she had to tip her chin to meet his gaze. Her lips beckoned, and the urge to kiss her was so strong it required physical effort to hold himself back.

"I promise not to tell anyone," he whispered.

Her attention slid to his mouth, and the kissing side of the tug-of-war inside him gained momentum. He lowered his head an inch.

"Hey, Captain!" Preach's voice boomed from somewhere behind them.

Matt jerked his head up even as Josie stepped away and started brushing at the edge of her jacket. A growl built in his throat. His corporal was going to get an earful later tonight.

"What?" he shouted at the man who stood a fair distance away, carefully turning his attention to the east so as not to look directly at the couple whose position had been rather cozier than dictated by the client-Horseman relationship.

"Gettin' late. If we're gonna make Cypress Mill before nightfall, we gotta get a move on. Horses are rested, and provisions are packed."

Matt let out a sigh. He couldn't blame Preach for being practical. "Very well, Corporal. We'll be right there."

But when he turned to offer Josie his arm, she skittered past him and hurried back toward the other Horsemen without a single backward glance.

He guessed she'd be hangin' on to those secrets of hers a while longer.

FOURTEEN

The *clickety-clack* of the train rocking along the rails should have lulled Josephine into a doze, but she was too busy trying to eavesdrop on the conversation happening behind her to allow her weariness to have its way. Matthew had been sitting in the backward-facing seat in front of her, but he'd abandoned her company an hour ago to talk in hushed tones with his men.

She hated not being privy to their discussion. She wanted to know their plans, their strategy for extricating Charlie. Yet they probably wouldn't speak freely in front of her. Her father never had.

As a girl, whenever she happened to enter the stables while he was discussing business with one of his army buyers, he'd interrupt himself mid-sentence in order to avoid tainting her delicate female ears with talk of breeding or financial concerns. He always greeted her warmly and made time for whatever questions she had, but then he'd send her on her way, taking care not to resume his business dealings until she was out of earshot.

Which was probably why, on such occasions, she made a beeline for his study. If her father didn't think it proper to teach a girl about horse breeding and economics, she'd simply teach herself. Books didn't care if she wore skirts instead of trousers. Their knowledge belonged to anyone with the courage to open their covers. And she had courage in spades. The size of the tome and the length of the words didn't dissuade her. She pursued them all, though the treatises on commerce quickly grew tedious. The books on animal husbandry, however, fascinated her and beckoned her back again and again.

God's creation was a marvelous machine, each cog and gear accomplishing a unique purpose within its own sphere that then affected the health and function of the overall animal. Those early forays into her father's study had lit a fire within her to understand the workings not only of four-legged creatures, but two-legged ones as well.

She had been fighting against male notions of what the female brain could handle ever since.

To be fair to Matthew and the other Horsemen, her exclusion from their conversation was most likely not based on gender. Matthew was too practical not to take the shortest distance between two conversational points. And he seemed to appreciate her general intelligence. No, her lack of military training was her disqualification. A fair omission, since she'd never engaged in a rescue mission. They had no reason to include her. Just as she would have no reason to include any of them in a discussion on the proper course of medical treatment for an incapacitated patient.

Still . . . being left out rubbed with all the discomfort of a cat being petted against the grain.

But enough of this moping. She'd hired Matthew and his men because she believed them capable. Time to trust them to do their jobs and quit trying to listen in on their plans. Craving knowledge might be her greatest strength as a doctor, but it was her greatest weakness when it came to matters of faith. Faith in people *and* faith in God. Knowledge inspired confidence. A lack of knowledge left her feeling powerless and afraid. And weak. As someone who thrived on being in control, weakness was hard to stomach. As was relying on someone else to solve her problems. Yet she had no choice in this case. She didn't have the expertise or skill to rescue Charlie on her own, so she had to rely on those who did. And not just the Horsemen.

Her eyes slid closed. *Grant them success, Lord. Shape their plans with your potter's hands. You know all. See all. Therefore, your power is infinite. Cover Matthew and his men with your protection. Guide their steps. And please . . . take care of Charlie. He's made myriad mistakes, but you are a God of mercy as well as justice. Let mercy reign.*

A yawn overtook her as she prayed. She opened her eyes and gave her head a little shake. Two full days in the saddle were taking their toll. She might still possess the skill to ride like a cavalryman, but that didn't mean her muscles were accustomed to such lengthy outings. Her thighs, back, and abdominal muscles were protesting—loudly—about their gross overuse. She hadn't just pushed her rented horse to the limit, traveling nearly eighty miles in two days. She'd pushed herself to the limit too. She was exhausted, worried, and as sore as she ever remembered being. The worry made it impossible to treat her exhaustion, but perhaps she could address her aching muscles.

Josephine pushed to her feet and stepped into the aisle, reaching overhead to grip the luggage rack for balance as the railcar swayed. A dull throb permeated her legs when she straightened, causing her to bite back a moan. The best prescription for sore muscles was stretching and gentle exercise. A walk down the aisle should ease the stiffness, if not the ache.

And if it happened to take her past the Horsemen, well, that was just a bonus.

The dapper older gentleman seated across the aisle dipped his head politely as she turned down the walkway, though his gaze raked over her with unconcealed disapproval. Probably her mismatched outfit and lack of a proper bonnet. At least she'd remembered to pack a skirt so she wasn't traipsing through the railcar in her trousers. That would have really raised his brows. A smile tugged at her mouth at the thought. Her dark green skirt might be wrinkled and the color completely unsuitable for the blue jacket that still smelled of horse, but her white shirtwaist was clean. Acting as if she wore the latest Paris fashion, she held her head high and nodded to him in return as she strolled by.

Putting the stodgy fellow out of her mind, Josephine turned her attention to the left, where the low voices of the Horsemen rumbled. They sat two to a seat, facing each other, their heads close together as they plotted and schemed. Mr. Wallace caught sight of her first. He straightened and smiled, and immediately the rumbling ceased as the other three sat up and nodded to her. Matthew twisted in his seat, his gaze finding hers.

"Everything all right?" he asked.

"Yes. I'm just stretching my legs."

His gaze traveled over her, not a hint of disapproval evident on his rugged face, just concern and sympathy. This was a man who had trained new recruits. Any efforts to hide her fatigue and soreness were pointless, but her pride insisted she try.

He rose to his feet, his voice softening to a timbre that would travel only to her ears. "I'm sorry we had to push you so hard yesterday."

She touched his arm. "Don't be. It was necessary. My brother's well-being is more important than my comfort."

"You should try to sleep. We still have at least two hours before we arrive in Chatfield."

"Maybe," she said. She doubted she'd be able to drift off with the hard wooden benches, the rattle of the rail wheels, and the frequent stops to take on mail and passengers, but it might not hurt to try. Right now, though, she had legs to stretch, and he had plans to finish.

She took a step down the aisle, letting her fingers fall away from his elbow. "I'm fine, Matthew. Truly." Her gaze swept over the other three men. "I'll let you get back to your discussion, gentlemen."

They nodded politely to her, each giving his own interpretation of the action. Mr. Davenport, seated to Matthew's left, smirked a bit, as if amused by seeing his commander so concerned for a woman's comfort. Mr. Brooks, across from him next to the window, offered a brisk nod that seemed more impatient than polite, as if he considered her a distraction they would've done better to leave behind. Mr. Wallace touched the brim of his hat with the hand of his uninjured arm, his smile pure charm as she moved past. Not for the first time, it struck her how different they were from each other, yet the tie that bound them could not be denied. These men would fight for each other. Die for each other.

A swirl of foreboding eddied in her stomach, leaving her slightly ill. She hardened herself against the unwelcome angst and made her way toward the rear of the railcar. She wasn't leading them to their death with this mission to save Charlie.

These were seasoned soldiers. Experts at defeating outlaws and criminals. They'd rescue Charlie and return unscathed.

She had to believe that God would grant them victory over the villains holding Charlie. It was all she had to hold on to in a situation residing completely outside her control. So she clung to the belief with all her strength. Every time she had rolled over the last two nights, she had prayed for Charlie's safety. But not only his. She'd prayed for the Horsemen too. For Matthew especially. He was doing this for *her*. He'd said as much. Which meant if something happened to him or to one of his men, it would be her fault.

Think on what is lovely, Jo. Not all this darkness. Think on what is virtuous and praiseworthy.

Unfortunately, the most virtuous and praiseworthy thing that popped into her mind was the man sitting behind her, which circled her back to where she'd started. She'd never get her mind off her troubles at this rate.

"Tommy?" The alarmed cry sharpened Josephine's focus like nothing else could. She knew that tone: a mother afraid for her child. "Tommy! What's happening?"

There. Four benches down the aisle. Right side. A boy, aged seven or eight. Slumped against his mother's side. Convulsions wracking his body. His arms stiff and unnatural. The mother clutching her son, trying to control the uncontrollable.

Josephine ran down the aisle. "Don't fight him. We need to lay him on the floor where he won't hit anything. Here. In the aisle."

The mother looked at her, tears in her eyes. "I have to help him."

But she wasn't. The boy's shins were banging against the seat in front of him over and over.

"I'm a doctor. The convulsions will pass on their own in a moment. In the meantime, we need to keep him from injuring himself. The best way to do that is to lay him flat in a place where he can't hit anything. The aisle gives us the most room."

People in nearby seats were gasping and shrinking away, as if afraid the boy's condition was contagious.

"It's the falling sickness," one man declared.

A woman with a high-pitched voice shrieked. "It's a demon!"

"It's not a demon," Josephine snapped. She turned to the mother, softening her voice. "Slide off the seat and onto the floor of the aisle. He'll come with you."

The woman nodded and moved to the edge of her seat. Josephine circled behind her, then gripped under her arms to help her descend. It wasn't graceful, but it worked. Josephine helped her scoot around until her back faced the opening of the seats across the aisle and her legs sprawled perpendicular across the walkway. The boy had slipped from her lap, but he lay straighter, his legs no longer beating themselves against the seat. His arms flailed, though, elbows locked, wrists bent, hands balled.

One of the fists caught his mother across the cheek. A small, surprised cry escaped her, but she didn't pull away from her son. "It's all right, Tommy. Mommy's here." She touched his shoulder. "Mommy's here."

"So am I," a deep voice pronounced. Josephine looked up to find Matthew hunkered in the aisle in front of them, her doctor's bag in his hand. "What can I do?"

The rest of the Horsemen filled the aisle behind their leader. All expressions fierce. Ready to do battle. Whatever that might entail.

"Your coats. Take them off and use them to create padding between his legs and the legs of the benches. I'm going to roll him onto his side to keep his arms more controlled and to ease the pressure on his chest. I don't like his color."

The boy's face had a grayish hue. The muscle spasms were forcing the air from his lungs.

"Move!" a harsh voice growled. Mr. Davenport's, she believed, not that she took the time to verify. All she knew was that a flurry of footsteps commenced, followed by four coats being rolled up and positioned around the boy's legs and torso with the precision of soldiers setting up a military perimeter.

"Is he dying?" The mother turned her tearstained face to Josephine.

Jo shook her head. "No. It's nearly over. Look. He's starting to relax."

The convulsions had indeed slowed. The boy let out what sounded like a sigh, and Josephine thanked God when she saw him draw a full breath.

"Tommy?" His mother ran a hand over his hair.

"It might take a couple minutes for him to wake," Josephine warned, not wanting the woman to be any more frightened than she was already. "Has this happened before?"

The boy's mother shook her head. "Never." Her eyes sought Josephine's for answers. "Is he sick?"

"Convulsions can have many causes." She placed the back of her hand against the boy's forehead. "He doesn't seem to have a fever. Sometimes high fever spikes can cause them." Or an infection of the brain. "Has he been ill lately?"

The mother shook her head. "No. He's been perfectly fine. He was running and playing at the station in San Antonio with some other children before we boarded. Well, until he fell off the railing."

Josephine immediately moved her hands to the back of the boy's head, her fingers searching for a lump beneath his hair. "Did he hit his head?"

"Maybe. He wouldn't tell me, just brushed me off when I ran over to check on him. You know how boys are."

That she did. Charlie always hated it when she tried to soothe his hurts in front of his peers.

There. Her fingers probed a large protrusion on the side of his head. "There's a knot here. Feel it?" She moved the hair aside and invited the boy's mother to find the swelling.

The woman nodded as her eyes widened. "Did he crack his skull?"

Josephine smiled reassuringly. "No. There's no blood." Though there might be swelling inside the skull as well as outside. "It could be the reason for the convulsions. You should take him to a doctor as soon as you get to your destination. Have him examined. Tell the physician about the convulsions."

The boy stirred. His eyes fluttered open. "Mama?"

"Tommy!" She bent over and kissed her son's forehead. "Oh, thank the Lord."

A lingering tightness in Josephine's chest relaxed as the boy looked around, his eyes losing their glassiness, his color improving.

"Why are we sitting on the floor?" he asked.

His mother laughed, a sound of abject relief as she recognized that the danger had passed.

"Here, ma'am." Matthew extended a hand. "Let me help you up."

Josephine had forgotten he was there. She blinked as she looked away from Tommy for the first time. Somehow the Horsemen had surrounded her. One in front, one in back in the aisle, and one on each side in the seating areas. Unconcerned with causing a scene or displacing passengers, they'd positioned themselves as her protectors.

Warmth radiated through her midsection.

"I got the boy," Mr. Davenport said as he bent down and scooped Tommy up with more gentleness than she would have thought the big man capable of exerting.

With the crisis passed, chatter inflated through the car as the other passengers tried to process what they had witnessed.

Josephine reached for her doctor's bag and stood, accepting Mr. Wallace's assistance as he cupped his good hand around her elbow. She smiled her thanks, then propped the medical bag on the seat facing Tommy's mother.

"Where are you traveling to?" she asked, smiling as if she were just making small talk. In truth, the answer mattered. Tommy needed quality medical care, and he'd be more likely to receive it back in San Antonio than in any of the small towns this train was headed to.

"We were going to Hondo to see my sister, but I think I'm going to turn around at the next stop and head home. We have a doctor there I trust."

"I think that's wise." Josephine nodded, then reached into her bag and pulled out a small packet of white powder. "This is potassium bromide. Mix a small pinch of it in some water and give it to him to drink once you are on your way back. It's a sedative that is helpful in preventing convulsions. It will make him sleepy, but it should ensure that he doesn't have another episode during your journey home."

The mother took the packet. "Thank you, Doctor . . . ?"

"Burkett." Josephine smiled. "Of Purgatory Springs."

"God's blessings be upon you, Dr. Burkett."

Josephine reached over and straightened a hank of hair that had fallen over Tommy's forehead. Such a young lad to suffer such a frightening attack. She prayed the seizure was a single incident and that the damage from his fall had not created a permanent disability. Being epileptic was a hard road to walk for anyone, let alone one so young. "God's blessings on you and your son as well."

Josephine retrieved her doctor's bag and made her way back to her seat, surprised when the Horsemen continued flanking her. Their coats tucked under Mr. Davenport's left arm, they marched two in front of her and two behind. When they reached their seats, Mr. Brooks and Mr. Wallace slid onto the two benches behind her while Mr. Davenport opted for the rear-facing seat in front of hers, tossing the coats onto the seat between him and the window. Confusion knit her brow, and it only grew when Matthew relieved her of her medical bag and stowed it overhead. Then he clasped her hand and slid onto her bench, his hold on her bringing her down beside him. He slid over to the window, propped his boot on the edge of the seat in front of him by the coats, then tugged her into his side.

"Preach and the others will keep an eye out for trouble," he murmured softly. "It's time for you to rest."

She glanced around the railcar. Passengers were staring at her strangely, as if they'd never seen a doctor treat a patient before. Then she caught a whisper. Something about the impropriety of ladies sprawling upon the floor of a public conveyance. Another about outlandish women claiming to be doctors. Another, more disturbing one about witches and exorcisms.

For pity's sake. Did small minds have nothing better to do?

Then she felt the warmth of Matthew's hand cupping

her jaw. She turned away from the disturbing whispers and focused her attention on the man at her side.

"Lay on my shoulder, Josie. Rest."

"What about your plans?"

He smiled, lines crinkling around his hazel eyes. "We've got the big things hammered out. The rest will keep. Come on." He urged her closer. "Try and grab a few winks."

I'll watch over you. He didn't say it aloud, but everything emanating from him breathed the promise into her.

He offered escape from her exhaustion, her worry and frustration, and suddenly the desire to carry her own load no longer appealed. With one more long look into his eyes, she handed over the last threads of trust she'd been clinging to and leaned into him.

Her head found his shoulder. Her eyes slid closed. And in less time than she would have thought possible, she slid into sleep.

Matt had a crick in his neck and an ache in his lower back, but he'd never felt better in his life. Josie's head lay nestled against his chest, having slipped from his shoulder somewhere between Seco and Sabinal. His arm curled around her shoulders to hold her securely against him, and his thumb idly stroked her sleeve.

Preach had rejoined the other Horsemen after the majority of the passengers debarked in Hondo, leaving Matt to enjoy Josie's company alone. Free of knowing looks and teasing eyebrow waggles from his second-in-command.

Holding Josie was about the sweetest torture he'd ever known. Having her so close, so unguarded, so soft against him had quickly become addicting. He'd studied her. Every nuance. Every detail. The moment her breathing deepened and her muscles fully relaxed into sleep. The way her fingers twitched when she dreamed. The softness of her hair against his neck. The slightly floral scent of the hotel soap on her skin. The way she felt snuggled up against his side.

For a man used to the company of other men, holding a

woman was a new experience. One he liked. A lot. But only because the woman was Josie. She did things to him. Fired his blood. Softened his demeanor. Made him want to be a better man. She called to a place buried deep inside him that felt like family—felt like love. Not that he knew much about the subject, being raised by his uncle after the Comanche killed his parents. Elijah Hanger had been a gruff man, not given to sentiment. He knew his way around a horse, though. Taught his nephew everything from grooming to riding to tending injuries and focused a young boy's grief into a serviceable skill and a soul-deep passion.

Matthew twisted his head to take one final, leisurely look at Josie before waking her. The Chatfield stop was coming up, and he was pretty sure she'd want to clear the sleep from her brain before the train pulled into the station. Even so, he hesitated. She looked so peaceful. No worry for her brother creasing her brow. No shadows of exhaustion dimming her eyes. Just smooth skin, dark brown lashes fanning upon her cheeks, freckles peeking through and dancing over the bridge of her nose. Beautiful. The kind of beautiful that put thoughts in his head that had no business being there. Thoughts about holding her like this for the rest of his days.

Well, maybe not like *this*, he admitted as the train rounded a curve and a new twinge shot up his back. A house would be better. Their house. No strangers looking on. No interfering friends on hand. No rescue mission to distract from the simple pleasure of holding her. Just the two of them. Together. Vows spoken. Bed waiting. An entire night of—

"Chatfield Station!" The conductor's voice boomed through the railcar as he made his rounds and readied passengers for the next stop.

Josie didn't even flinch. He'd known she was tired, but this was exhaustion.

"Sorry, Josie," he whispered as he gently lifted her into a more upright position. He caressed the side of her face and murmured her name close to her ear. "Josie? Time to wake up, sweetheart. We're coming into Chatfield."

Her lashes lifted slowly. She blinked. Looked around. Focused on him. "Matthew?"

Man, but he could get used to hearing his name in her sleep-roughened voice. Waking up to that every morning would be heaven. His gaze traveled over her face, settling on her mouth. The urge to steal a taste was strong. But his honor was stronger.

Dragging his focus back to her eyes, he said, "We're almost to Chatfield Station."

"Oh." The word exited on a sigh as soft as her eyes, which were still glazed with the residue of sleep.

Or was something else making her expression dreamy? His pulse kicked a little harder in his veins.

"Oh!" She stiffened and pulled away from him, as if the memory of why she was here and what she was doing had flooded her brain all at once. A touch of pink colored her cheeks as she glanced at the arm he'd casually draped over the back of the seat after her jerk forward had sent it plunging off her shoulders. "Sorry. I, ah, don't usually nap in the afternoon. Leaves me terribly groggy."

Matt grinned. Seeing her rattled was rather enjoyable. It gave a man the idea that he didn't have to be perfect to walk by her side. A mighty fine thought for a man all too aware of his imperfections.

She set about smoothing her skirt and checking her hair, as if worried she'd come undone during her slumber.

"You look fine," he assured her, deciding it best not to tell her that she had a faint line across her cheek from where it had pressed against a wrinkle in his shirt. It made him smile, though.

She caught his smile and started to return it before something out the window behind him snagged her attention. Probably the outskirts of town, judging by the way the train was slowing. Whatever she saw drained the last of the softness from her features and brought forth the determination he'd grown accustomed to seeing her exhibit whenever she had a job in front of her.

"Will you and the others stay the night in Chatfield," she asked, her tone brisk, "or will you head to Uvalde right away?"

His arm dropped from the seat back to his lap. Time to focus on the mission, not the woman. "We'll get you settled, then use what daylight we have left to start toward Uvalde. It's only about ten miles, so we should cover most of that distance before nightfall. We'll make camp away from the road, then start our reconnaissance at first light. We'll finalize our plans and make our move. Should have your brother back to you by midafternoon."

She nodded, but tension lingered in the lines around her mouth, and worry glimmered in her eyes.

He squeezed her hand. "We'll get him out, Josie. I swear it."

Her gaze met his, and his heart kicked in his chest. "I know you will." No hesitation, no uncertainty. She believed in the Horsemen. In him. "Just make sure you get yourself out too."

"That's the plan." Matt grinned. How could he not, when she'd all but announced that she cared about him?

The screech of braking wheels vibrated through the car, followed by the hollow sound of the train whistle. Matt glanced out the window and spotted the platform. His grin tightened into a firm line. Time to get to work.

Military precision wasn't all it was cracked up to be. Josephine frowned as she hustled across the road in front of her boardinghouse to join the men gathered in front of the livery. She'd barely had time to get settled in her room and unpack a few things before she'd spied the Horsemen through her upstairs window, inspecting their tack and saddlery in the same manner they did every time they'd been ready to mount up and ride out. She knew what that signaled. They were fixing to leave. Without saying good-bye.

Mr. Brooks noticed her first. He signaled his captain with a subtle tip of his head. Matthew turned. Took a step in her direction. But she didn't wait for him to come to her. She intended to share a piece of her mind with *all* the Horsemen.

"Forget something, gentlemen?"

Matthew's arched brows only fueled her irritation. "I don't think so. We're still good on supplies. Ammunition. Weapons." He glanced at his men. They nodded at his assessment.

She crossed her arms. "You didn't think to check in with your employer before heading out?"

Her question only seemed to deepen Matthew's confusion. "I explained our plan before we left the train. I thought you understood we needed to leave as quickly as possible to take advantage of what daylight we have left for travel."

Mr. Wallace cleared his throat. "I think she was expecting a more personal good-bye, Captain."

She had been, but that wasn't the only thing tweaking her temper, nor the most important. "Where's my palomino?"

The lines disappeared from Matthew's forehead, as if he

was thankful to have a question he could answer. He gestured toward the livery. "He's inside. All settled."

"Why is Sandy inside instead of saddled and ready to travel with you?"

"Because . . . he's *your* horse." Matt looked at her as if she'd lost her mind. She might yet, if these thickheaded men didn't pull the cotton wool out of their brains and start thinking clearly.

"A horse I have no need of while I'm waiting in Chatfield for your return. A horse that could serve as my brother's mount once you extricate him from his captors. A horse that could keep your own from fatiguing due to the weight of an extra man should a pursuit ensue. *A horse*," she emphasized, "I would have offered for your use had you done me the courtesy of briefly checking in before running off into the wilds of outlaw territory."

"I'll go fetch the palomino," Mr. Davenport grumbled as he ducked into the livery with all the haste of a soldier seeking cover from cannon fire.

Mr. Wallace wasn't much better, doing a quick about-face. "I'll see about getting a refund for that packhorse we rented."

Mr. Brooks apparently didn't feel compelled to offer an excuse. He just turned and rounded the corner of the livery, leaving her alone with Matthew.

"I didn't realize the horse mattered so much to you." He held his arms away from his body, palms facing forward in a non-threatening position, as if she were an unstable gunman with a loaded revolver and a hair trigger.

Josephine sighed. "It doesn't. Not really. It's just . . . I know I'm not a soldier, Matthew. My knowledge of military tactics wouldn't fill a thimble, and I have no notion of how to go about planning a rescue. But that doesn't mean I have nothing to offer. I might not be going with you, but this is still as much my mission as it is yours. I want to understand what is going on, and I want the chance to help in any small way I can." Her shoulders slumped. "If nothing else, I had hoped to offer a prayer for the safety of you and your men before you left."

Matthew ran his forefinger and thumb over his mustache, his gaze falling to the ground. "Of course you have something to offer . . ." The words died away. He cleared his throat and tried again. "It didn't occur to me . . ." He blew out a breath, then yanked the hat from his head, slapped it against his leg, and let it dangle from his fingertips. Finally, he raised his eyes to hers. "I ain't used to dealin' with women and their feelings, Josie. I'm used to the military, where you take orders and give orders without chitchat or explanation. I see something that needs doin', and I go do it. That's how I was trained."

Women and their feelings? Josephine pressed her lips together to keep from spouting her *feelings* all over his imbecilic head.

"You're gonna have to be patient with me," he said, his gaze apologetic.

Her ire softened a little.

"Give me time to adjust. I might be an old dog, but I can still learn new tricks."

She uncrossed her arms and blew out a breath, letting the last of her affront escape on the wind. "Quit calling yourself old."

He didn't smile, just held her gaze with serious intent. "You're right. I was so focused on the task in front of me, I didn't give a thought to what others might need. What *you* might need. Forgive me."

His eyes glowed with such fervor, such sincerity, she barely managed a whispered, "You're forgiven."

Finally, a smile touched his lips. A crooked half-grin that had her stomach attempting acrobatics. "Thank you for the use of your horse. It'll save us some money and perhaps some time."

Josephine bit back a smile at his attempt to soften his honesty. She was costing them time. They'd had a packhorse hired and ready to go, and they would have been on the road by now if she hadn't stormed across the street to confront them. But she didn't regret it. Time wasn't the only valuable commodity to be considered. Trust. Openness. Communication. They were important too. And had she not come, Matthew would have left never knowing how she felt, and she would have stewed over his callous disregard for her feelings. But now . . . now he stood before her, promising to take her needs into consideration and proving once again that his honor ran as deep as his loyalty. A woman could build a life with this man. Even an opinionated physician who'd thought herself destined for the shelf of spinsterhood.

Of course, he had to be agreeable to such an arrangement. Oh, and survive his mission—the mission she'd assigned him.

One by one, the Horsemen reappeared, apparently having decided they'd given their commander sufficient time to smooth the lady's ruffled feathers.

Yet Matthew never looked at them. He looked only at her. "Do you have any other questions or concerns?"

She had a lot of concerns, mostly centered around everyone making it out of Uvalde in one piece. But she shook her head. "I'd still like to say that prayer, though. If your men wouldn't mind."

Matthew raised his arm and made a sharp motion with

his hand that his men responded to without question. In the next moment, she was surrounded on all sides, the shadows from their bodies blocking out the sun.

"Hats off, boys," Matthew ordered. "Josie's gonna pray for us."

All three removed their hats and bowed their heads as if prayer was a familiar posture.

Josephine dipped her own head and folded her hands at her waist. "Dear Lord, watch over these brave men. Keep them safe from harm, and grant them success in rescuing Charlie. May they be like David's mighty men, striking fear in the hearts of the wicked and winning victory for the cause of the righteous. We ask these things in the name of Jesus. Amen."

A quiet chorus of *amens* echoed around her as faces lifted and hats found their way back to heads.

"A fine prayer, ma'am."

Josephine blinked. The compliment came from Mr. Brooks. She nodded, feeling acceptance from him for the first time.

The Horsemen moved to their respective horses and started to mount. Josephine followed Matthew, not quite ready to separate from him.

Matthew looked over the back of his horse toward Mr. Davenport. "Got a verse for us, Preach?"

The big man swung up into the saddle, peered off into the distance for a moment, then turned back toward her and winked. "Romans 8:31. 'If God be for us, who can be against us?'"

He gave a waggle of his brows, then set off. Wallace and Brooks followed. But as Matthew started to mount, Josephine took hold of his arm.

"Wait."

He pulled his foot out of the stirrup and pivoted to face her.

Without taking time to think the instinct through, Josephine pushed up to her tiptoes, grabbed his face, and planted a kiss on his mouth. "Be careful," she ordered before she turned her back and marched across the street to her boardinghouse.

Several dozen thudding heartbeats pounded in her chest before she finally heard the sound of Phineas's hooves cantering out of town. Only then did she turn to watch Matthew ride away.

He made a glorious picture. Tall in the saddle. Valiant. Unafraid of the dangers that lurked ahead. A hero on a noble quest.

A rather romantic notion for a woman who'd packed away dreams of handsome knights long ago in favor of the reality of a career in medicine. It seemed she hadn't done quite as good a packing job as she'd thought, however, for all the quantifiable scientific evidence coursing through her at the moment pointed to one undeniable conclusion. She was falling in love with Matthew Hanger.

CHAPTER SIXTEEN

Matt hunkered behind a rock at the rim of a canyon wall and lifted a pair of field glasses to his eyes. He counted twelve men in the outlaw camp below. Fifteen horses in the remuda, meaning there could be other men in the area not in his line of sight. The surplus mounts might be pack animals, but Matt preferred to plan for the worst possible odds instead of blindly hoping for the best.

It had taken nearly two hours of scouting this morning to locate the camp. The ransom exchange was supposed to take place at noon by a large dead oak known as the Hanging Tree two miles west of Uvalde. A rather grim landmark, but one the locals knew well.

Wallace had uncovered the location of the infamous tree with nothing more than a roguish smile and a listening ear. After dark fell the night before, he'd snuck into town, infiltrated the largest of the five saloons on the main thoroughfare, and worked his charm on one of the ladies employed there. Not only did he discover the location of the tree, but he gathered intelligence on a new gang holed up somewhere outside of town. A gang whose members drank hard and treated their paid companions with a rough hand. Wallace offered a sympathetic ear to one such companion and learned that her Friday night customer had bragged during their last encounter about coming into some money soon. He'd be able to afford a high-class strumpet for his next pleasuring and would no longer have to put up with her inferior attentions. Still carrying a grudge over that indignity, the woman had told Wallace everything she could about the man—mean eyes, pockmarked face, and a bright blue neckerchief riddled with tobacco stains tied about his neck.

Rather like the fellow prowling through the center of camp, talking to a man who carried himself with the bearing of one in command.

Matt adjusted the focus on his binoculars. It was hard to make out features from this distance, but the man in the blue kerchief had skin that looked different from the man at his side. Less smooth. Textured, almost. Pockmarks could explain the effect. Matt wished Jonah was here. He'd hand off the field glasses and get a second opinion. His sharpshooter had the vision of a hawk. Unlike Matt, whose eyesight had dulled in recent years, losing the sharpness of objects viewed at a distance. But the Horsemen had split up to cover more ground, each heading out from the Hanging Tree in a different direction in an effort to locate the outlaw camp more quickly. Matt took his eyes from the field glasses to pull his watch from inside his jacket and check the time. Ten minutes 'til rendezvous. He needed to gather what information he could, then meet up with his men.

Stuffing the watch back into his pocket with his right hand, he lifted the binoculars with his left and combed through the camp in search of a prisoner. He didn't find one.

Matt frowned. It was hard to know who to rescue if no one was tied up.

He spotted a man in a hat that matched the description Josephine had given him—black with a band of silver conchos. Could be Charlie. Or it could be a gang member who'd swiped the headgear. The man in the hat sported a scruffy brown beard. Not clean-shaven like Josie had described. But then, a hostage wouldn't be given access to a razor. It could too easily be turned into a weapon to be used against his captors. Yet this man didn't look like a hostage. He roamed the camp freely. No restraints. No evidence of torture. He even laughed at something his companion said.

The back of Matt's neck prickled. Something was off. Maybe Josie's father had been right about Charlie not being in any real danger. On the other hand, every man in the camp looked like the type who could shoot a friend in the back if given the right provocation. Especially the leader.

Matt moved his field glasses until the leader came into focus again. Dressed in unrelieved black with a bearing to match, he snapped at a man by a small wagon. The camp cook, most likely. The gray-haired fellow scurried forward and extended a tin cup. The man in black took it, guzzled a big swallow, then turned and spewed it from his mouth. He lashed out, slapping the cup across the older man's face with enough force to send the cook reeling backward, cradling his bloodied nose.

Words were shouted, though Matt couldn't hear them. He saw the tendons lifting in the leader's neck, though, and the blood rushing to his face as his mouth moved in exaggerated motions. The old man backed away, his posture bent in on itself. The leader let him escape but pitched the cup at his head, bouncing it off the old man's skull.

No one interfered. No one stepped up to help the man who'd been foolish enough not to keep their leader's coffee warm. Everyone kept their heads down, not wanting to attract any hostile attention upon themselves.

A sick sensation swirled through Matt's stomach. Josie had been right to be concerned. These men were violent and didn't deal well with disappointment. Charlie's life could easily be forfeit if the ransom went unpaid.

Matt swung his gaze back to the man in the concho-decorated hat. Charlie? He needed to be sure. He couldn't risk the Horsemen's lives for an unverified target. These outlaws were armed to the teeth. Guns. Knives . . .

Wait.

Matt's gaze zeroed in on Charlie's hip. He wore a gun belt, but the holster was empty. No weapon. The only unarmed man in the entire camp. Matt shoved the field glasses into the leather case hanging from his neck as he backed away from the edge of the canyon wall.

It wasn't the best verification he'd ever taken action on, but it would have to do.

He raced Phineas down the back side of the canyon and around to the abandoned line shack that sat half a mile north of the Hanging Tree. The rest of the Horsemen were already there.

"Hope you found something, Cap," Preach said as he came out to meet him. "Jonah found a small group holed up in a ramshackle old barn east of here, but Wallace and I came up empty."

Jonah didn't move from where he leaned against the shack wall, just glanced up and met Matt's eye. "The gang I found looked more like squatters than outlaws. Five men, two little more than boys. Scrawny. Didn't look like none of 'em had

had a decent meal in weeks. Not much in the way of weapons neither. A couple of old rifles. One revolver. They might be desperate enough to try ransom, but they looked too haggard to carry it off."

Matt dismounted and patted Phineas on the rump to let him know he could join the other mounts at the trough by the water pump.

"I found a dozen men holed up in a shallow box canyon two miles northwest. Pretty sure one of them was the pockmarked fellow Wallace's lady friend told him about."

"Did ya spot Dr. Jo's brother?" Preach asked.

"I think so. Found a fellow wearing the hat Josephine described. Right height and build. Same coloring as the doc. But he wasn't restrained." Matt nodded at the raised eyebrows around him. "He walked freely about the camp. The only difference between him and the other men was that he wore no weapon. The rest of the crew was armed for Armageddon."

"So what's the plan, Captain?" Not an ounce of doubt shadowed Wallace's face. "I'd guess we have about an hour before they head to the ransom site. Do we wait for them to make their move and snatch Dr. Burkett's brother when they leave the canyon, or are you thinking of utilizing a more stealthy technique?"

Matt blew out a heavy breath, praying he was making the right call. "If these were a bunch of rowdy kids trying to gouge their friend's father for money, I wouldn't hesitate to confront them. But from what I've seen of this crew, they aren't the kind to fold in the face of a well-coordinated attack. They'll rage with a wild and vicious counterattack, not caring how many of their own go down in the skirmish."

Preach let out a low whistle. "That kid got himself in way over his head."

"Yes, he did." And for the first time, Matt worried that he might not be able to keep his promise to the kid's sister.

"Goin' in from the back, then?" Jonah asked.

Matt nodded. "Best option for avoiding a shootout. Though it might still come to that." He hunkered down and used his finger to draw a crude representation of the canyon in the sand. "I spotted two sentries. Here and here." He pointed to either side of the canyon's entrance. "The horses are in a remuda here." He made a circle at the rear left side of the drawing. "Preach and I will scale the back wall." He glanced at his corporal. "It's only about twenty feet."

Preach scoffed. "Child's play."

Matt grinned, then returned to his plan. "Brooks and Wallace will be positioned up top to keep watch and lay down cover fire if needed. I'll locate the target. Preach will provide the distraction." Again, he glanced at his second-in-command. "I was thinking a nice, old-fashioned stampede should do the trick."

Preach's eyes danced. "I do love creating chaos."

"Once the horses are on the run, Preach will head to the ropes and make the climb. I'll secure the target and follow. Can't guarantee Charlie's climbing skills, so Preach will position himself at the top of the rope and reel the kid in for a quicker ascent. I'll remain below until the target is secured, then make the climb."

Wallace raised a brow. "You really think all three of you can make that climb without being discovered?"

"Nope." It would be a nice surprise to prove himself wrong, but Matt harbored no rose-colored illusions. What he *did* harbor was full confidence in his men. "You and Brooks will lay down cover fire when it becomes necessary and continue until we're all clear of the canyon. Then we mount up and ride for Chatfield." He looked at each of his men in turn. "Any questions or concerns? Improvements to offer?"

"I won't be able to handle my rifle one-handed, Captain. Not sure how much help I'll be laying cover fire." The admission left Wallace looking physically ill. He glared down at his sling. "I've never been much of a marksman with my left hand."

Matt grabbed Wallace's good shoulder and squeezed. "I ain't askin' you to shoot bull's-eyes. I just need you to keep those outlaws ducking for cover. A little wildness in your shots will keep them off guard, never knowing where the next bullet will fly. If you barrage them with frequency, Brooks will take care of the accuracy."

Jonah tipped his chin to Wallace in a nod that let them all know he'd be watching their backs.

Preach spoke up next. "You got an alternative plan if the fella you spotted turns out not to be the doc's brother?"

It was a good question. One lacking a satisfactory answer. Matt had to shake his head. "Nope. Just a quicker need for an exit."

"I suppose we could always stake out the Hangin' Tree to see who shows up," Preach said with a shrug. "Try to take them by surprise."

"And face three-to-one odds?" Jonah shook his head. "If I had a good sniping position, maybe, but the area around the Hanging Tree is flat with little vegetation. No place to set up a perch and even the odds."

"Jonah's right," Matt said. "Attacking head-on would be suicide. Stealing their prisoner from behind their backs is the only option with an acceptable level of risk. As much as I want to return Josie's brother to her, I'm not willing to throw your lives away doin' it."

He'd walk that road alone if it came to that. Matt had sworn to bring her brother back, and he refused to return empty-handed.

Of course, that meant he might not return at all. But he'd deal with that eventuality when it looked him in the face. Not before.

— CHAPTER —
SEVENTEEN

They moved silently, each man focused on his task. The horses, including Josie's extra mount, waited behind a small stand of post oak a hundred yards away. Close enough to reach quickly. Distant enough not to be spotted or heard by those in the box canyon below.

Matt shrugged the coil of rope he carried off his shoulder and looped it around the base of the boulder he'd hidden behind earlier. After securing it with a bowline knot, he gave it a hard yank to test its sturdiness, then tossed the end of the rope over the rim and quietly fed the length of it over the side. Preach did the same, using a live oak a few feet farther from the rim as his anchor.

Slipping up to the canyon's edge on his belly, Matt surveyed the action below through his field glasses. A group of men crouched in a circle near the mouth of the canyon, playing cards. Two others busied themselves checking their weapons. The abused cook banged pots and pans as he packed the chuck wagon. The pockmarked fellow with the blue kerchief had taken over guard duty for one of the sentries. And the lead outlaw stood in the heart of it all, shooting the breeze with none other than Charlie Burkett.

Crud. This plan would only work if he could cull Charlie from the herd without anyone noticing. Stampeding horses wouldn't suffice as cover if the lead outlaw stood right beside his prisoner when the ruckus started.

Matt waved Preach over. "We're gonna have to wait a bit." He handed the field glasses to his corporal and pointed toward the heart of the camp. "Charlie needs to be on the fringe before we can make a move. He's too entrenched with the others right now to risk setting the horses off."

Preach propped himself on one elbow and peered through the binoculars. "It ain't ideal," he observed as he handed the binoculars back to Matt, "but if we postpone too long, our window's gonna close. Might be a good idea to position ourselves inside the canyon, keep an eye on things, then strike as soon as an opportunity presents itself."

"Agreed." Matt placed the field glasses back in their case, then slithered away from the canyon's rim. He rose to his feet and waved Preach to the left while he edged right. "Update Brooks, then make your climb. I'll do the same with Wallace."

Preach offered a two-fingered salute and moved out, keeping his tall frame hunched over to be less visible to anyone below who might glance their way. Matt did the same, winding his way to Wallace's position a dozen yards away.

The trumpeter had found a sapling with a *v*-shaped trunk and propped his rifle barrel in the natural notch, making the weapon more manageable for a one-armed man.

"Preach and I are headed down, but we're gonna have to play the timing by ear." Matt lowered the field glasses case to the ground beside Wallace. "Charlie's too close to the outlaw leader. We'll have to wait until he separates himself."

"And if he doesn't?"

Matt shrugged. "I'll think of something."

Wallace grinned. "Don't you always?"

Only when the Lord allows. Matt shook his head as he thumped Wallace on his good shoulder and headed back to where his rope waited.

Matt wanted his men to have full confidence in his ability to lead them, but he wasn't so foolish as to believe his past successes were due to his own cleverness. His experience in battle had certainly provided wisdom and helped him anticipate an enemy's actions, but God was the master general. Matt would have no success without the Lord's leading. Some might call it gut instinct, but the feelings in his core that urged one action over another went deeper than his gut. And he never failed to listen.

Guide me, O thou great Jehovah. One of his favorite hymns and the prayer on his heart as he hurried back to his post. The mission before him required guidance. Lots of guidance.

He reached his rope, gave it another test yank, then pulled his old cavalry gloves from his belt and shoved his hands inside. The pale yellow leather snugged against his fingers like an old friend, lending reassurance. They'd seen many a battle, these gloves. Matt tugged them over each wrist and wiggled his fingers to ensure maximum movement.

Preach came up alongside him. "Jonah said he'd keep a bead on the man in all black until cover fire becomes a necessity. He can put him down if it comes to that, but he'll hold off unless one of us is under immediate threat."

Matt nodded, hearing the words left unsaid. Their vow not to take a life was sacred to the Horsemen. Only in defense of one of their own would they violate it, and even so, Matt knew Jonah would aim to wound, not to kill. But at this distance, with all the chaos soon to ensue, nothing could be guaranteed. Death was a real possibility.

"Got a verse for me?" The routine of the question calmed him almost as much as the scripture that came back in answer.

Preach peered into the canyon below, then turned and straddled the rope hanging a few feet to the left of Matt's. He grabbed hold and turned his face toward heaven. "'When thou goest out to battle against thine enemies, and seest horses, and chariots, and a people more than thou, be not afraid of them: for the Lord thy God is with thee.' Deuteronomy 20:1."

Matt closed his eyes for a fraction of a moment and let the words flow over him. He couldn't imagine a better-fitting verse. Everything except the chariots applied to their situation. And even then, he figured the chuck wagon could substitute. In either case, they were outnumbered and outgunned. Yet they need not be afraid, for God was with them. A man couldn't find a better anchor for his courage than the Almighty.

"See ya at the bottom, Cap."

Matt's eyes popped open, and he lifted a hand to salute Preach as his corporal dropped over the side of the canyon. Matt followed suit, gripping the rope in both hands and walking his legs over the side. Hand under hand, he lowered himself. Controlled. Steady. Silent.

Regular glances over his shoulder confirmed he hadn't been spotted. By the time his feet met the earth, Matt's arms burned, but in an invigorating, well-used sort of way. He gave them a little shake, then stepped away from the rope, letting his method of escape camouflage itself against the brown of the canyon wall.

Preach headed to the remuda without a word while Matt searched for cover to use while he waited for an opportunity to approach Josie's brother. There wasn't much to choose from. A couple scraggly juniper bushes jutted up from the barren ground fifteen feet into the canyon. They would have to do.

Matt strode forward casually, figuring if anyone happened to glance his way, he'd draw less notice if he looked like one of the gang moseying through camp instead of a hunched-over interloper trying to avoid detection. Once he reached the nearest of the bushes, however, he crouched behind it and shielded himself from sight.

From between the branches, he could make out Charlie's face but not the content of his conversation with the leader. The man in black grew agitated, apparently not liking something Charlie had said. Charlie smiled and gestured grandly with his hands, obviously trying to reassure his captor that everything would be fine. Probably regarding the ransom. The leader didn't like what his prisoner was selling, however, for he snatched his cigarette from his mouth and flicked it at Charlie's head. Charlie dodged. At the same time, the man in black surged forward, snatched Charlie by his jacket lapels, and hauled his face to within inches of his own.

"Better hope your old man pays, Burkett." The leader's raised voice carried through the suddenly still camp.

"He'll pay," Charlie assured him. "One way or the other. I swear it."

"He better." The outlaw released his hold on Charlie, then made a show of straightening his crumpled lapels. "I ain't in this just for kicks. I expect to get paid. And well."

"You will be."

The outlaw patted Charlie's shoulder with enough force

to send the smaller man stumbling sideways a couple paces. The leader smiled, sending a shiver running over Matt's nape. "Then you got nothin' to worry about, do you?" He started to turn away, then stopped and pivoted back to face Charlie. "Just remember what happens to folks who disappoint me."

Charlie held his ground, doing an impressive job of not looking intimidated. Matt had to give the kid credit. He might be a self-centered fool for getting himself into this mess, but he wasn't a coward.

The outlaw leader left Charlie and strode toward the men playing cards. "Dawson! Fetch the leather straps. Time to tie up our guest."

A big fellow with a shockingly red beard tossed down his cards and pushed slowly to his feet. "Sure thing, boss."

Matt's gut knotted. If he didn't make his move now, he might not get another chance. But how?

He glanced right. Nothing. He glanced left. Nothing but a fellow relieving himself behind the second juniper bush.

An idea sparked. It was brash. Risky. But it was all he had.

Matt stalked forward, angling his approach to come at the man from behind. A quick glance around told him no one had noticed the action taking place in the camp latrine. Thanking God for bushy juniper and distracted minds, Matt closed on his target. Then lunged. His right arm snaked around the man's neck and squeezed off his airflow before he could voice a protest. The outlaw grabbed at Matt's arm, trying to peel it away, but Matt held tight, locking his right hand onto his left arm to increase the pressure on the man's airway. Just a few . . . more . . . seconds. . .

The outlaw went slack in Matt's arms. Matt lowered him to the ground, then pulled the coat from the unconscious body and snatched the outlaw's hat from where it had fallen in the dirt. Taking off his own coat and hat, Matt replaced his gear with what he'd pilfered. Pushing the grimy hat brim low on his face, Matt stepped out from behind the bush and strode toward the center of camp as if he belonged there, praying the others would simply see what they expected to see and nothing more.

Keeping to the periphery, he meandered to a spot a few feet behind Charlie where someone had stacked extra branches and other kindling for the fire pit. The campfire wasn't much more than coals now, since they were fixing to leave, but it was the only excuse handy, so Matt grabbed the end of the largest branch in the pile.

"Hey, Burkett. Give me a hand with this, will ya?" Matt lowered his natural voice and roughened the tone.

Charlie turned, confusion on his face. "Dawson's fetch-ing—"

Matt, head down, waved a hand dismissively. "Yeah. Yeah. This'll only take a minute."

Another man turned. "I got ya, Granger." He gave Charlie a shove in Matt's direction. "Make yourself useful, rich boy. Oh, that's right. Ya ain't rich no more, now that Daddy cut you off. Gotta dirty your hands and work for a livin' like the rest of us."

Charlie's face tightened in anger, but he kept his mouth shut as he stumbled toward Matt.

Without looking up, Matt gestured toward the opposite end of the long branch. Charlie moved into position, bent, and lifted. Matt took the lead, carrying his end toward the juniper bush he'd hidden behind moments ago.

It only took a few steps for Charlie to start grumbling. "Where are we taking this?"

"Shut up and move," Matt ordered.

Just a little farther. Then Preach could scatter the horses. Matt adjusted his hold on the branch, sliding closer to Charlie.

"This is stupid, Granger. There's no point—"

Matt lifted his head and looked Charlie full in the face. The kid's brows shot up in shock. Then alarm lit his eyes. His gaze immediately darted back toward the camp.

Matt didn't hesitate. He dropped the wood, drew his gun with his left hand, and wrapped his right arm around Charlie in a move that would look like a friendly embrace to anyone who happened to glance their way. What they wouldn't be able to see was the pistol pointed at the underside of Charlie's chin.

"Settle down. I'm a friend. Your sister hired me to rescue you."

Charlie's face cleared. "Jo's here?" His attention darted around the canyon as if his sister might be waiting behind the juniper bushes. "Where?"

"I'll take you to her. But we have to move now."

He expected the kid to become compliant at that point, but Charlie had the gall to shake his head.

"I can't. I have to be there for the ransom exchange. If I'm not, my father will never hand over the money, and Taggart will kill him in order to take it."

"Your father's not coming."

"What?" Shock and hurt flickered in the kid's eyes before something harder took over. "Guess that tells me where I rank in his esteem."

Matt's impatience climbed. "You can be mad at your father later. Right now, we've got to get you out of here."

Before Charlie could make up his mind, the screaming

neighs of frightened horses pierced the air. Horses reared and charged. Their hooves pounded the ground as they ran for freedom. Men shouted and sprinted toward them, adding to the commotion.

"We have to go. Now!" Matt dragged Charlie toward the back of the canyon where the rope waited.

Preach was already halfway up the wall.

Charlie finally quit dragging his feet and started running in earnest. Matt drew a second weapon and watched their backs as they raced to make their escape. A spooked horse nearly took him down from behind, but Matt kept his feet and his grip on his weapons.

"Burkett's escaping!"

The cry went up right as Charlie reached for the rope. He stopped. Looked behind him.

"Get going!" Matt ordered. "I'll cover you from behind. I've got men at the top who will protect you."

Still Charlie hesitated.

Matt shoved him with his shoulder. "Go!"

The kid grabbed the rope and started to climb. Matt stood his ground at the base of the cliff and faced the outlaws charging his way.

EIGHTEEN

The first shot from above brought the outlaw leading the charge to his knees as he grabbed for his thigh and buckled. The second shot took out the pockmarked man in the blue kerchief, who dodged a horse only to fall backward when a bullet hit his right shoulder. By the time Wallace added his ammunition to the mix, the outlaws were actively retreating and seeking cover.

Unfortunately, they found it.

The red-bearded Dawson and a fellow in a brown vest dove behind the large branch that Matt and Charlie had moved. The outlaws had to lie on their bellies to protect themselves, but they didn't seem to care about aiming. They just braced their gun hands atop the thick branch and shot in Matt's general direction while keeping their heads down. Matt pivoted sideways to make himself as thin a target as possible, but bullets still zinged by him far too close for comfort.

Willfully ignoring the gunfire around him, Matt steadied his arm and shot a notch off the branch an inch from

Dawson's hat. The outlaw flinched and brought his gun hand down to cover his head. Matt didn't expect the deterrent to last, but at least it slowed the current barrage.

A movement to his left drew Matt's attention. Three men were pushing the chuck wagon, rolling it past the fire pit. Once they maneuvered it into position, half a dozen men or more would be able to take shelter behind it, leaving Matt's position vulnerable no matter how much cover fire Jonah and Wallace laid down.

He glanced up the wall to judge Charlie's progress. Halfway. Preach was dragging him from the top now, and the kid just hung on. Eyes squeezed closed. Mouth pinched tight. Hands white-knuckled as he clung to the slow-moving rope.

Matt frowned. He should've given the kid his gloves. Too late now.

Turning back to the fight before him, Matt caught a glimpse of a horse walking against the grain of the other animals. Small, controlled steps. Matt pivoted that direction to get a better view. A pair of black trousers distinguished themselves between the mount's brown legs. Someone had caught a horse and was using it as a shield.

Coward. A cavalryman might use a fallen horse as a shield in the midst of war as a last resort, but to use a live horse as protection in an offensive maneuver when other defensive options existed made his hide itch.

Another movement returned Matt's attention to the men behind the branch. Brown Vest was peeking around the end and taking aim. High aim. At Charlie. Matt fired with his left hand, then followed with his right, showering the outlaw with enough bark shards to force his eyes closed and hopefully keep him out of commission for several seconds.

The shield horse reached the chuck wagon, then shied as

the wagon jerked forward. The animal tossed his head and revealed the ingrate hiding behind him.

The leader. Taggart.

Of course.

Taggart jerked the reins down with enough force to injure the bay's mouth and tied the animal's head with no give to the side of the chuck wagon to maintain protection on his flank.

"Burkett! You worm!" Taggart yelled. "I'm gonna kill you!"

Taking care not to shoot the horse, Matt let a shot fly directly over Taggart's head, taking enormous satisfaction when he ducked behind the wagon.

His satisfaction didn't last long, however, for now that more substantial shelter was in place, the outlaws grew bolder.

Jonah and Wallace had the high ground advantage, but two couldn't hold off a dozen men forever. Bullets whizzed past Matt with greater frequency. A couple even creased his skin. He tried not to flinch when fire burned across his forearm, but when he lost a chunk of hide from his left thigh, his step faltered.

He dropped to the ground, partially to cover his injury and partially to make himself harder to hit. Yet as soon as the dust hit his face, an advantage became clear. Bringing his right hand around in front of him, he took four shots beneath the wagon. He hit three different trouser legs and a wagon wheel. Taggart's black trousers unfortunately remained intact, thanks to an inconvenient spoke. But the bullets pelting the canyon wall around him slackened as the other three outlaws behind the wagon howled in pain.

"We got him, Captain," Preach called from above. "Get to your rope!"

Holstering the empty gun in his right hand, Matt took a

few last potshots at Taggart with his left, then rolled the few feet to his rope. He scanned the area, spent his last bullet on Dawson, whose head was poking up from behind the log again, then shoved the spent revolver into its holster and leapt onto the rope. Praying for strong arms and trusting his men to cover him with all they had, Matt gritted his teeth and scaled the wall.

Jonah and Wallace picked up the shooting pace, their repeating rifles spitting in rapid-fire fashion. Preach and Charlie would be fetching the horses. The pieces of the plan clicked through Matt's brain, keeping him focused.

A bullet hit his boot heel, spinning him sideways with the force. Matt tightened his grip on the rope as his body bounced against the canyon wall. All his momentum disintegrated. He clenched his jaw and glanced up to judge the remaining distance. Ten feet. He could climb ten feet. Even with a throbbing thigh and a bleeding forearm. He was a cavalryman. Built for war. He could do this.

Ten feet.

A groan tore from his throat as he flexed his biceps and pulled his body upward. He released one hand and grabbed for a higher position. Then another.

Nine feet.

Hand over hand he climbed. But fatigue drained his strength. Despite his mental fortitude, his arms unfolded. He dangled, five feet from the top.

Gunfire continued all around him, friendly and nonfriendly alike.

C'mon, Hanger. This isn't how you want to go out. Get moving, soldier!

He pulled, then stopped when he felt his grip slipping. Heart thumping, he darted his gaze along the cliff wall, desperate to find some kind of support. He wasn't going to make it without help.

There. To the left. A root protruding from the wall.

Matt stretched his boot toward it, raising his knee at an awkward angle. There wasn't much there, but if he could plant his toe and the root held, he might be able to take enough weight off his arms to keep from losing his grip.

He jabbed the pointed toe of his boot into the wall, catching the ball of his foot on the root. He straightened his knee, letting the foothold take his weight. It held. Thank God, it held. Warm relief rushed into his fatigued muscles.

Then a deep voice rumbled from above. "I got you, Cap. Hang on."

The rope tugged, and Matt's grip instantly tightened. God bless Preach.

Matt focused all his energy on maintaining his hold on the rope as his corporal dragged him toward the rim. Three feet from the top, however, a spinning object in his periphery yanked his focus away from the rock.

A black hat decorated with silver conchos flew out over the canyon. Bullets knocked it hither and yon until it finally fell to the ground in front of the chuck wagon. The shooting slowed.

Matt grimaced as his shoulder scraped along the rim's edge and his body folded over the side. He scrambled to his feet, thumped Preach's arm in thanks, then frowned up at Charlie sitting astride Josie's horse. Without his hat.

The shooting ceased altogether as Jonah and Wallace retreated from their positions and raced to their mounts.

Questions and suspicions flooded Matt's mind, but they would have to wait. Taggart and his crew would pursue. Creating distance was paramount.

Matt jumped to his feet and slid his hunting knife from its sheath. Grabbing the rope he'd knotted to the rock, he sliced through it in two quick slashes and let it plummet to the canyon floor as he swung up onto Phineas's back. He couldn't leave the outlaws an avenue to attack from behind, and reeling the rope in would have forfeited too many precious seconds.

"Ride!" Matt's command set the Horsemen in motion.

The horses lunged forward, and in seconds, the group of five galloped as a unit away from the canyon. By tacit consent, the Horsemen surrounded Charlie in tight formation. For his protection, yes. But also because they didn't trust him. No one knew for sure where his loyalties lay.

Jonah led the way, guiding them to the main road, where their hoofprints would disappear among the myriad others cluttering the path. Not that Taggart wouldn't guess they were headed northeast. Only an outlaw would travel southwest into Mexico.

Yet the longer they rode without any sign of Taggart's men on their trail, the more uneasy Matt became. When the road crested a small rise, he called for a halt.

"Why are we stopping?" Charlie asked, glancing over his shoulder to scan the road behind him. "We need to put more distance between us and Taggart."

"Wallace, toss Brooks the field glasses." Matt glanced straight through Charlie as if he hadn't spoken and made eye contact with his trumpeter.

Mark didn't hesitate. Holding his gray steady with his knees, he unhooked the strap of the binocular case from his saddle and tossed the equipment to Jonah. The sharpshooter snagged it out of the air and brought his horse around to face the rear. He pulled the field glasses from their case and held them to his eyes.

"No sign of 'em."

Even with the delay of gathering their horses, a group of outlaws should have been visible on their back trail if they were giving pursuit.

Matt drew Phineas even with Charlie's mount and glared. "What did you signal?"

Charlie flinched and jerked backward in his saddle. "Signal? What are you talking about? I was just trying to get away. Same as you."

Matt didn't have time to play games. "Your hat," he growled. "You tossed it into the canyon. You had no reason to do that. Not unless it was some kind of prearranged signal."

Charlie's face darkened. He leaned forward, eyes narrowed and tone sharp. "In case you didn't notice, *I* was the one being held against my will. The one whose life Taggart threatened. If you think I'm working in collusion with that kidnapping scum, you better get my sister to examine your head next time you see her, because it's obviously malfunctioning." He glanced briefly at the other Horsemen, noted their frowns, then shifted in the saddle and refocused his attention on Matt. "The wind caught it, all right? I pulled it off my head to bang the dust off, and a gust of wind carried it away. Guess my hands were too shaky from that climb to hang on." When Matt failed to relent on his stare, the kid moved from angry to defensive. "You think I *wanted* my favorite hat riddled with bullets? I loved that hat."

Matt wasn't buying it. Neither were his men, judging by their closed expressions. Charlie had signaled *something* to the outlaws. The question was . . . what?

← CHAPTER →
NINETEEN

A bird twittered, and Josephine's chin jerked up. From her bench in front of the boardinghouse, her gaze scanned the road over the pages of the dime novel she'd purchased in the mercantile that morning. Nothing. Well, not *nothing*. The drugstore clerk was still sweeping the walk in front of his store, a pair of ladies chatted in front of the café a couple doors down while their children banged sticks together in a mock sword fight, and a man loaded sacks of feed into the back of a wagon across the street. They'd all been there the last time she'd looked up too. Probably because her last glance had been less than a minute ago when a horse in the livery corral had nickered.

She forced her lungs to inhale at a slow, steady rate, then exhaled on a prayer.

Please let them be safe.

Her hands crinkled the pages of her paperbound book. Not that she had read more than a handful of its words. She turned pages every so often to keep up appearances, but in truth, the only purpose the book served was to give her hands something to hold so the townsfolk wouldn't think her deranged for sitting on a bench for hours and staring anxiously down the road.

She'd been here since noon, her bag packed and waiting at her feet. She had six train tickets purchased for both the 4:18 departure and the 6:47. Josephine checked the time on the pendant watch that she'd purchased along with her reading material. Three-forty. Still time to make the earlier train if Matthew and the others returned soon.

Please let them return soon. The longer the day grew without sight of them, the harder it became to fight off the worry that had prodded her since breakfast.

A particularly loud *clack* followed by a triumphant shout drew her attention to the children. Little warriors defeating pretend foes. If only real foes were as easily vanquished.

A soft rumble caught her ear, barely audible over the activity of the town. If she hadn't been straining to hear exactly that sound for the last couple hours, she would've missed it.

The book fell to her lap as she straightened away from the back of the bench.

The rumble intensified.

She scooted to the edge of her seat.

Hoofbeats. Those were definitely hoofbeats.

Josephine stood, her gaze locked on the road leading into town, her fist mangling the dime novel's cover.

Please let it be them.

A dark spot appeared on the horizon and grew. Then separated into individual forms of horsemen. *Five* horsemen.

"Thank you, Lord." The words fell from her lips in a whisper, but they shouted in her soul.

Fighting the urge to run out to greet them, since placing

oneself in the path of running horses was not the wisest option available, she chose instead to drop her crushed novel onto the bench and collect her medical bag from where it sat on the boardwalk next to her carpetbag. She only glanced away from the approaching riders long enough to latch onto the handle of her bag, but even then her other senses remained fixed on the men. The sound of thudding hooves and the vibration of the boardwalk took precedence while her eyes were briefly engaged elsewhere.

Bag in hand, she stepped down to street level. They were closer now. Close enough for her to recognize hats. Her stomach clenched. She didn't see Matthew's tan hat. Nor Charlie's black one with its flat top and silver concho band. She looked again. Only four hats. And she didn't recognize the one in the back.

Heart thumping erratically in her chest, she adjusted her grip on the medical bag and strained to identify faces. Mr. Brooks must be in front, his darker skin distinguishing him from the others. And Mr. Davenport's bulkier build fit the large man on the right. Mr. Wallace's gray horse stood out from the rest. And there! The space between riders widened a bit and allowed her to make out Sandy's distinctive palomino coat.

Charlie! The man in the center without a hat must be her brother. And he was healthy enough to ride unassisted, thank the Lord.

That left Matthew to bring up the rear. But why would he be wearing a strange hat? The shape and dark brown color were all wrong. It *was* Matthew, wasn't it? Josephine gave herself a mental shake. Of course it was Matthew. The Horsemen would never leave him behind.

As the men closed the final fifty yards and reined in,

Josephine's gaze sought Charlie's, her doctor's eyes examining him for injury. He looked remarkably well. No visible bruising on his face. No blood staining his clothes. He looked a bit ragged around the edges, as if he hadn't been sleeping well, but that was to be expected, having been held hostage for several days.

"Charlie?" She moved forward before the horses came to a full stop. Mr. Brooks and Mr. Davenport parted their horses like the Red Sea to allow her access to her brother.

"Hey, sis." He looked appropriately abashed, his head hanging low as he walked Sandy up to her.

Charlie had mastered that repentant mien years ago when they were children. Whenever he'd gotten caught doing something naughty, he'd shrug his shoulders, soften his eyes, and give one of those half-grins that made every woman within sighing distance melt. It never worked on their father, but it had disarmed Mama every time. Charlie would say how sorry he was, and she'd wrap him in a hug and forgive him his indiscretion. After she died, Josephine stepped into her shoes and fell prey to the same tactics. A sister's place wasn't to discipline, after all. It was to protect. So she sheltered him. More than she should have. Their housekeeper, Darla, had a soft spot for him too. Which explained why she had gone behind her employer's back and written to Josephine when Charlie was abducted.

"Are you hurt?" She placed a hand on his ankle above the stirrup, her eyes doing a second, more intensive scan now that he was closer.

"Nah. Little rope burn on my hands, but nothing serious." The scruff of a half-grown beard darkened Charlie's jaw, and for the first time, Josephine saw him not as her baby brother, but as his own man. A man she didn't really know. Between medical school and starting her practice, she hadn't spent any significant time with him for close to a decade.

"Let me see." Doctoring was easier than sistering. It gave her something productive to think about instead of questioning how she might have contributed to her brother's shortcomings.

He held out his palms for her inspection. The skin was red, and there was a small tear at the base of his right index finger, but nothing a little salve wouldn't cure.

She stepped away from him and glanced at the rest of the men in turn. "Any injuries need tending? We have a little time before the train arrives." Her gaze skittered from one to another, oddly reluctant to focus on the man at the rear of the party. The man she most wanted to tend. "Better to see to them now than wait for infection to set in."

And better for her to stop acting like a suddenly shy miss, embarrassed to talk to a man she favored in front of her brother.

Josephine steeled herself and turned. Matthew was dismounting, not even looking at her. *Humph.* Nothing like a dose of humility to still one's fluttering pulse. He shrugged out of the dingy coat she didn't recognize and tossed it over Phineas's back. Then he plucked the dirt-encrusted hat from his head and hooked it over the saddle horn.

"Lose your hat?" she asked. It wasn't the most intelligent or pertinent question, but it was the first one that came to mind, and really, she was growing just a tad exasperated that he wouldn't face her.

"Decided to trade it in." He still made no effort to turn.

"For *that*?" She grimaced at the filthy hat before focusing on the man she was starting to suspect was actively avoiding her attention. "I should probably check your head for lice." She took a step closer.

"No need." He waved her off, but she ignored the gesture. So help her, if he was hiding an injury . . .

"Preach, tend the horses." Matthew retreated from her, tossing his saddlebags over his shoulder and calling out orders to his men like some kind of defensive maneuver to block her advance. "Jonah, inventory the supplies. Wallace, keep an eye on our . . . guest."

Why would someone need to keep an eye on Charlie? Josephine's mouth tightened. Matthew's tone gave the impression that the order stemmed from a lack of trust rather than a desire to protect. The implication abraded her family loyalty and left her voice a tad sharper than it should have been.

"Any orders for me, *Captain?*"

Still, he didn't turn. He simply waved her off. "Just see to your brother."

Josephine marched after him. "I will not be ignored, Matthew." She grabbed his arm from behind, then flinched when he yanked it away.

He immediately stopped and twisted his neck to look at her, his eyes apologetic. "Sorry, Josie. I didn't mean to pull away from you like that. I just—"

"*Josie?*" Charlie's voice challenged from behind her. "Who gave you the right to address my sister so informally?"

"I did," she snapped. For pity's sake. If men weren't being stubborn, they were being ridiculously overprotective. She turned back to Matthew. "Apology accepted. Now quit dissembling and face me."

Matthew quirked a half grin. "Still slinging those ten-dollar words, I see."

The grin distracted her, but only for a moment, because out of the corner of her eye she spied the large stain on the left leg of his trousers. Her gaze flew back to the arm she'd grabbed a moment ago. A smaller stain soiled his sleeve, as well. No wonder he'd jerked away from her.

"You're injured!" It emerged more as an accusation than the expression of concern most women would make over a man they cared about. But most women weren't doctors. Doctors their men should trust with their wounds because they believed them competent. "Why would you hide that from me?"

"They're just scratches, Josie. I swear. I'll rent a quick bath at the barbershop, clean 'em up, and be good to ride. Nothing to concern yourself over."

"Nothing to *concern* myself over?"

"Oh, now you've stepped in it." Charlie chuckled.

Josephine swung around and jabbed a finger in her brother's direction. "You be quiet. He wouldn't be injured in the first place if it weren't for you."

"Hey!" All jocularity fell from Charlie's face. "I didn't ask him to take on Taggart's gang for my benefit."

"No. I did." She spun away from her brother. His lack of remorse and failure to accept any level of responsibility made her chest ache. "And I paid for his services with the promise of medical treatment. Anytime. Anywhere. And I plan to hold up my end of the bargain." She met Matthew's eyes, her heart doing a little flip. "I need to make sure you're all right. Even the smallest wound, if not properly treated, can turn septic. Please, Matthew."

He blew out a breath, his face reddening slightly. "Fine. But this can't take more than fifteen minutes. Taggart and his gang didn't follow us, but I don't think we've seen the last of them. I'll feel better when we have more distance separating us." He speared her with his gaze, making it clear *she* was the part of *us* he was most concerned about.

Feeling mollified and even slightly cherished, Josephine gave a crisp nod. "Very well. I'll follow you to the barbershop. Once you're out of your bath, I can examine your wounds."

Charlie, having dismounted, pushed his way into the conversation. "Not without a chaperone, you won't. I'm coming with you."

"Guess it'll be a party," Mr. Wallace said with a smile. "I won't mind having the chance to clean up a bit." His easy manner helped diffuse the tension flaring between her brother and Matthew. They didn't seem to like each other very much. Odd, since Matthew had just saved Charlie's life.

"Let's get a move on, then." Matthew glared at Charlie, then marched off toward the building with a striped pole out front, two doors down from the mercantile.

Josephine hurried to catch up, but Charlie slowed her with a hand to her arm as the two of them followed a short distance behind.

"Is this fellow courting you, Jo?" he asked in a hushed voice, the frown on his face indicating his lack of enthusiasm over the prospect.

"There's no official understanding between us, but there's . . . potential. Not that it's any of your business."

"None of my business? I'm your brother."

"And I'm a twenty-eight-year-old professional woman who happens to be fully capable of making decisions pertaining to her personal life without the opinion of a male family member."

Charlie shook his head. "Still bossy as ever, I see." They reached the boardwalk, and he tugged her to a stop.

Matthew continued on to the barbershop, and Mr. Wallace hung back a few steps to give the siblings some privacy.

"I'm not putting myself in your business because I think

you need me," Charlie said. "Heaven knows you have too much stubborn pride to need anyone." The trace of bitterness in his voice made Josephine frown. "It's just that I care about you, and I don't want to see you hurt." He glanced at Mr. Wallace, then modulated his tone to a softer decibel. "This man's not good for you, Jo. I know men of his kind. Men who make their living with their guns. He's violent and cold. You didn't see how he fought back there in that canyon. Facing down a dozen men with a six-shooter in each hand like some kind of demon."

Josephine's knees nearly buckled. A dozen men? How had Matthew escaped with only two small flesh wounds? Surely God had been watching over him. God and the Horsemen.

"You're a healer, Jo. This . . . this *mercenary* is the opposite of everything you stand for. You can't let that into your life. It changes you."

Those last words carried a haunting quality that stirred Josephine's compassion. He was speaking from experience.

She clasped Charlie's hand. "I know you see him as no different from those men who took you hostage, but you're wrong, Charlie. Matthew is a good man. A former cavalry officer. Someone who fights on behalf of decent people at the mercy of evil men. People like *you*." She squeezed his hand. "Matthew Hanger risks his life for strangers. He's a hero."

Charlie's face paled, and he stumbled back a step. "Did you say Matthew *Hanger*? As in *Hanger's Horsemen*?"

Josephine raised a brow. "That's right. The Horsemen are the ones who rescued you."

Charlie reached for the railing behind him, as if he were having trouble staying on his feet.

"Charlie?" She put a hand to his forehead to check for fever. "Are you all right?"

He pushed her hand away. "Fine," he grumbled. "Let's get in there. Your *beau* doesn't seem the type to put up with delays."

He stomped up the steps and disappeared into the barbershop. Mr. Wallace followed, giving her a shrug of commiseration as he strolled past.

What on earth had gotten into her brother? Wouldn't someone who'd just been rescued from a group of villainous thugs be thankful the famous Hanger's Horsemen were on his side? Yet his reaction left her with the distinct impression that thankful was the opposite of what Charlie felt.

━ CHAPTER ━
TWENTY

Matt made quick work of his bath. One, because he didn't trust Josephine not to march straight into the bathhouse and demand to see his injuries. And two, because Charlie kept shooting him disgruntled looks, and being naked in a tub didn't exactly throw much weight behind Matt's "don't mess with me, whelp" glare. The scowl he used to keep new recruits in line worked much better when he was dressed, armed, and standing toe-to-toe with the kid who needed to be taken down a notch.

Steeling himself for the pain he was about to inflict, Matt lathered the washrag. The wound three inches above his knee already throbbed from the long ride and stung from the soap in the water. But when he scrubbed the rag over it, fire ignited in his leg. Matt didn't so much as blink, though. Just finished as fast as possible, then propped his ankles on the end of the tub to raise the wound out of the water while he dunked his head and cleaned the rest of the sweat and dirt from his skin.

When he emerged, Wallace was standing at the end of the

tub, frowning at the red, oozing spot on Matt's thigh. "Ouch. That looks like more than a crease, Captain. An inch of your hide is missing. She's probably going to have to stitch it."

An unappealing prospect. Not because of the pain involved, but because of the embarrassment inherent in such an exercise. Matt grimaced. Josie was a doctor. A professional. But she was still a woman, and a man just didn't go around exposing his thighs in front of ladies. Especially one he was attracted to. He shot a sidelong glance at Charlie, who had taken off his shirt and was washing his chest and arms at a small tub atop a table. Maybe having a chaperone was a good idea, after all.

"Are you decent in there?" Josephine's voice slipped under the curtain separating the bathing room from the rest of the barbershop.

Matt's legs retracted like a recoiling rifle and splashed back into the water. Wallace grinned in a good-natured tease, but Charlie's guffaw rubbed like salt in Matt's wound.

"Better give him another minute, sis," Charlie called. "He's not quite fit for mixed company."

"I'm not *company*," she grumbled, and Matt could easily picture the disgruntled look on her face. "I'm his doctor."

Thankfully, she didn't press the issue and remained on her side of the curtain.

Matt wasn't taking any chances, though. He lurched out of the tub, uncaring that water sloshed everywhere, and grabbed the towel Wallace handed him. He rubbed the water from his skin and hair with quick strokes, then grabbed a set of clean clothes from his saddlebag. He tugged on his cotton flannel drawers, ignoring the pink stain that seeped into the fabric over his left thigh, and pulled a serviceable gray shirt over his head. He did up the buttons, then reached for his trousers, only to realize he couldn't put those on if Josie was going to examine his leg.

If ever there was a time to think of her as the paunchy, balding Dr. Joe he'd first imagined her to be, this was it. Thankfully, his shirttails added additional cover, but he decided a leather shield would offer more protection and plopped his saddlebag into his lap as he sat on the stool beside the tub.

"All right, Josie. It's safe to come in."

She pushed the curtain aside and strode in, a picture of cool efficiency, as if marching through a male-occupied bathing chamber was something she did on a regular basis. Her face registered no curiosity or shock. She simply drew up a second stool for herself and sat down. Her attention was purely focused on his wound, not him, as she opened her medical bag and set it on the floor. Feeling distinctly less awkward than he had a moment ago, Matt relaxed.

Until she touched him.

The muscles in his leg twitched at the coolness of her fingers against his bath-heated skin. His heart hammered in his chest. Not even the sting of the fabric scraping across his wound offered sufficient distraction as she folded back the hem of his drawers to expose the injury on the outer edge of his thigh. She took hold of his knee and arranged his leg to maximize her view of the torn flesh. His pulse didn't seem to recognize the complete absence of amorous intent on her part. Her touching his bare leg in *any* capacity was enough to set his heart thumping. The fact that she was doing so in a medical, probing-until-it-hurt type of way only dulled his ardor a smidgen.

"Looks like you cleaned the exposed tissue fairly well," she said as she leaned sideways to collect a blue jar from her bag. She unscrewed the lid, and a sickly sweet smell escaped, making his nose twitch. "I'm going to treat it with this carbolated gauze," she explained as she pulled a short length of white material from the jar, "then I'll stitch you up. Two or three sutures should do the trick."

She rubbed the moist gauze across his wound, and he fought the urge to hiss in reaction. Charlie, having finished his wash, was hovering close enough for Matt to hear his breathing. Matt might not mind letting his guard down around Josie and Wallace, but his pride refused to allow any weakness to show around a man he didn't trust.

Josie raised a brow as if she'd read his thoughts, but she made no comment. She replaced the jar of medicated gauze in her bag and pulled out a disc-shaped canister with the word *Catgut* printed in blue around the red cross at the center. She unspooled a length of thread and snipped off the end. After pushing it through a needle's eye, she inhaled, then set the sharp end against his flesh.

For the first time since she'd entered the chamber, she met his eyes. "Ready?"

He held her gaze and gave a slow nod.

Her face softened in apology for the briefest moment before she turned back to her task and poked the needle through his flesh.

A tiny grunt escaped him, but Wallace was doing his best to engage Charlie in conversation, so Matt didn't think either of them heard it. As the tug of the suture pulled through his skin, he fought the urge to wince.

"You don't have to prove anything to me, you know," Josie whispered. "You can groan and contort your face as much as you want." She knotted the thread, then glanced up at him, a tiny smile bending the corner of her mouth. "As long as you don't move your leg, of course. Wouldn't want you to throw off my suturing. I have a reputation to uphold."

He grinned as she cut off the end of the thread. "I'll be still as a post," he vowed in an equally low voice. "Can't have my woman's reputation marred." An ironic statement, considering their current location, but true nonetheless.

Her eyes met his again, her needle poised at the edge of his thigh for a second stitch. "Is that what I am?" Her breath seemed to catch at the edge of her throat. "Your woman?"

Matt swallowed, his heart pounding like Phineas's galloping hooves. Was that what he'd said? Something must've gotten tangled up in his head between *my doctor* and *a woman* and emerged as *my woman*. Yet as he peered into Josie's face, he could no longer downplay his interest as mere attraction or friendly respect. His feelings ran deeper.

Matt's chest squeezed, and before he could call a halt, the truth popped out of his mouth. "I'd like you to be."

She said nothing, but a light came into her green eyes that suggested she might not be completely opposed to the idea.

Then she looked down and stabbed him with her needle.

Matt allowed a small groan to escape him this time. Not so much from the pain, but more as a release. Proving his toughness no longer seemed so vital. Josie had no need for it, and her brother . . . Matt looked over to where Charlie leaned against the edge of the tub, arms crossed, a glowering stare aimed at Matt's head. Matt still couldn't say he liked him, but Charlie might be family someday, and alienating him probably wouldn't win Matt any points with the woman he hoped to make his wife. Perhaps letting his guard down would.

His wife. Was he really contemplating marriage? After losing his family, he'd vowed to be a solitary man, like his uncle.

Shielded from the searing pain of losing people he loved. The army had offered the perfect escape. A man with no family was actually an asset. An unattached soldier could protect the families of others with fearless abandon because his own death, should it come, carried no consequences. No wife or children depended on him for their livelihood. It had been the perfect path. Until Wounded Knee.

And until a bossy doctor with ten-dollar words and gemstones for eyes elbowed her way past his fortified walls to set up shop in his heart. For the first time in his life, his desire to charge forward and lay claim to a woman outranked his instinct to defend and retreat. The strategic shift terrified as much as it exhilarated him.

A muffled whistle from outside filtered through the bathhouse walls.

"Train must be here," Wallace said, dropping his foot from where it had been propped on the tub's edge next to Charlie.

"I'm nearly finished." Josie tied off the second suture, then quickly added a third stitch to Matt's hide. She blew a piece of hair off her forehead, then sat back. "Stand up, please. Legs apart. I need to apply a bandage."

Matt felt his neck warm, but he did as she instructed, catching the saddlebag as it tumbled from his lap. Like an experienced field surgeon, she had a dressing in place and a gauze bandage wrapped around his leg before he could count to twenty. Had he been counting. In truth, he'd been trying to figure out how to hold the saddlebag without looking like an idiot. Not that it mattered. She didn't give the bag so much as a second glance. Once she had the ends of the bandage tucked away, she pushed to her feet and asked to see his arm.

Matt complied, rolling up his right sleeve to expose the crease left from an outlaw's bullet.

She cupped his elbow in her hand and lifted his arm close to her face. "No stitches for this one," she declared. "I'll just dab on some salve, and we'll be ready to go."

The sound of the outside door opening stole Matt's attention from the feel of Josie's fingers on his arm. Before he could voice his concern over being found half-dressed in a bathing chamber with a woman, Wallace and Charlie placed themselves between Josie and the door, blocking the view of whoever might have purchased a bath.

"Passengers have disembarked, Captain." Preach's voice bounced off the rafters, cutting past the tension in the room. "They'll be calling the *all aboard* soon."

"Be there in two," Matt called. He pulled his arm from Josie's light hold, causing her to smear some of her salve down his wrist. "Time for you to skedaddle, darlin'." He placed his hands on her shoulders and twisted her around so that her back was to him. "I'll meet you outside."

Wallace bent to retrieve her doctor's bag and handed it to her. Josie frowned at being rushed, but she accepted the bag and moved toward the exit, her attention diverting to Charlie's hands as she came abreast of him. Giving her brother a little shove, she herded him toward the door with her.

"While I've got the salve out, I might as well see to those sore spots on your hands. Come on."

Charlie grumbled but let her shoo him out of the bathhouse. Wallace followed, leaving Matt a blessed moment of privacy to pull on his trousers, socks, and boots. He tucked in his shirttails, stretched his suspenders over his shoulders, draped his saddlebag over his left arm, and rejoined his men.

As soon as the sunshine hit his eyes, a light brown object hit his hands.

"Got you a new hat, boss." Jonah nodded toward Phineas,

whose saddle was void of both items Matt had been forced to borrow.

Preach led the horse forward. "One of the stable boys took that nasty stuff off our hands. Said he'd clean it up and give it to his brother. Didn't think you'd mind."

"Not at all." Matt fit the new hat to his head. It was stiff compared to his old one, but the size was right, and the cavalry-style shape was exactly what he preferred. He tipped the brim toward Jonah. "Thanks, Brooks."

Jonah nodded.

"Oh! My carpetbag," Josie exclaimed. "I left it by the bench at the boardinghouse. The train tickets are in it."

Before she could rush away, Preach stepped forward. "No worries, Doc. I picked it up. Tied it onto the back of Sandy's saddle for ya."

Sure enough, the palomino sported a red-and-gold-patterned lump atop his rump.

She smiled. "Oh, wonderful! Thank you, Mr. Davenport."

Preach dipped his chin. "My pleasure, ma'am."

"All right. If we've got everything, then," Matt said, feeling a little grumpy over Preach playing Josie's hero, "let's get to the depot and load the horses."

Each man took charge of a lead line, and they moved as a group toward the depot. As they skirted around the platform to gain access to the freight cars, Charlie suddenly grabbed Matt's shoulder.

"Wait."

Matt turned, the sharpness in Charlie's voice sending a jolt of alarm through him. "What is it?"

"Those two men." Charlie pointed to a pair of brawny fellows at the edge of the platform who were talking to the rail hand in charge of livestock. The same hand who had unloaded the Horsemen's mounts the day before. "They're from Taggart's gang."

"Are you sure?" Preach demanded in a low voice.

"Yes."

One of the two men turned, and all doubt fled Matt's mind. He recognized that red beard. And by the way the man's brows rose, he recognized Matt as well.

"We've got to ride!" Matt immediately moved to Josie's side and boosted her up onto Phineas's back before mounting behind her. "Now!"

— CHAPTER —
TWENTY-ONE

Josephine's mind raced as they fled the depot. How had Taggart's men found them? According to Matthew, the outlaws hadn't pursued the Horsemen after the rescue, so they must have taken the train. But how many were aboard? Matthew must have assumed there were more than the two they'd spotted. Either that or he was concerned about innocent bystanders being injured should a gunfight erupt. As far as she could tell, Chatfield had no marshal. For pity's sake, the town didn't even have its own post office.

Hopefully, the smallness of the town would work in their favor. If the outlaws came by train, they might not have horses. The pickings at the livery were slim, more wagon horses than cow ponies. Then again, these men were outlaws. They'd just steal whatever they needed. And any mount they confiscated would be fresher than the ones her group rode. The Horsemen would not be able to keep up this pace for long. Especially with her and Matthew riding double.

She prayed Matthew had a plan. Were there military rules of engagement for times like these? Or did one simply retreat until more cavalry troops could swoop in and deal with the enemy? With no reinforcements available on the ground, Josephine petitioned the Lord for some angelic army support.

She felt Phineas begin to slow beneath her. She twisted and peered around Matthew to check for followers. Nothing yet. Nothing but a small cloud of dust in the distance. A cloud she wanted to attribute to wind or a stagecoach or anything other than what she knew it had to be.

Was Taggart coming for Charlie, still angling for a ransom? Or did he intend to unleash vengeance on all of them for foiling his plans?

Josephine pressed her lips in a tight line as she faced forward again and adjusted her grip on the saddle horn. She supposed she should be afraid, but with Matthew's arms around her and his chest bracing her back, fear wasn't what bubbled up inside her. No. Anger and indignation thrummed through her veins.

These men had no right to hold her brother hostage. To extort money from her father. To threaten the lives of good men. One of whom had her rearranging the picture of her future to include not only a well-run medical clinic, good friends, and the respect of professional colleagues, but the love of an honorable man and perhaps even a child or two if God proved generous.

A family of her own.

She'd known the choice to pursue a medical career would drastically reduce her chances at making a marital match, yet she'd chosen it anyway. It wasn't just a vocational calling, but a spiritual one. She'd sacrifice whatever was necessary to follow the path God had set before her. No regrets. She found joy in her work and satisfaction in knowing her life had meaning even if it wasn't shared with the most intimate of companions.

Yet the instant Matthew looked into her eyes and softly admitted his desire to claim her as his own, her paradigm had shifted. Stretched. The craving for family that had been easy to store away when it was an undefined commodity burst its bonds with unexpected vigor now that it was attached to a particular man. A fierce warrior with a kind heart. *Her* warrior. And no greedy, gunslinging outlaw was going to steal him from her. Not on her watch.

If Matthew could face down a dozen men back in that canyon and come away with only a couple scratches, he could keep their little group safe with tired mounts and open terrain between them and the enemy. He was Matthew Hanger, king of the Horsemen.

Even as the thought charged triumphantly through her brain, the horse beneath them slowed again. Phineas fell back from the pack, the weight of his load taking a toll. The others slowed in response, unwilling to let any separation pull them apart. The Horsemen rode as one.

Charlie, on the other hand, began pulling away.

Josephine made excuses for him. He hadn't spent years riding with these men, so he wasn't able to sense their unspoken needs or gauge their subtle reactions. But even so, his lack of awareness of the people around him hinted at an unflattering level of self-absorption.

"Charlie!" She tried to call him back, but her voice drowned beneath the flood of pounding hooves.

"Don't worry," Matthew said. "He's safe enough. Taggart's men will come from behind. Any distance he gains is just another layer of protection."

For him. But what about for you?

Josephine peered behind them again and found more than dust. Her stomach tightened. "I see riders." Definitely more than two. She'd guess as many as six or seven.

"How far back?"

"Not sure. Half a mile, maybe?" She'd never been good at gauging distances.

"Preach!" Matt yelled, then jerked his chin toward their pursuers.

Mr. Davenport craned his neck to peer behind them, then straightened, his expression showing no surprise. "Yep. They're gaining on us. 'Bout five minutes back."

"That wallow to the north might work." Mr. Wallace tipped his head in the direction of a shallow dip in the earth up ahead, probably a dry creek bed.

Work for what? Josephine tried to peek at Matthew's face, but his attention was focused on his men.

"Jonah?" Matthew pointed. "The wallow."

Mr. Brooks nodded. "I'll fetch the rabbit."

Charlie.

Mr. Brooks gave his mount his head and herded Josephine's brother like a stray calf while Matthew and the others veered toward the creek bed.

Once there, the Horsemen dismounted, collected their weapons and ammunition, and laid on their bellies in the wallow, rifles aimed at the approaching riders. All but Matthew. He waved Charlie over, then took Josephine's hand and dragged her toward the biggest rock in the creek bed. Not that it had much competition from the few pebbles scattered about. The stone wasn't more than a foot high and a foot and a half wide, but it was the best protection the area had to offer.

"Lie flat and keep your head behind this rock," Matthew

ordered, the ferocity of his gaze sending tingles over her skin. "Don't come out for anything, Josie. Promise me."

She nodded. It was all the answer she could manage. The anger that had been suppressing her fear evaporated as the reality of their situation sank in. They were taking a stand. Against an unknown number of outlaws. With nothing but a dry creek bed as protection. Their horses were spent. Their ammunition finite. Their chances of survival hairsbreadth slim.

Matthew turned to Charlie and did something Josephine never would have expected. He pulled his left revolver from its holster and handed it to her brother. "Keep her safe."

Charlie accepted the gun, his mouth set in firm lines. "I will."

"Watch for my signal," Matthew said, his voice like steel. "If things go south, take your sister and ride. We'll buy you as much time as we can."

"No!" Pulse racing, Josephine grabbed Matthew's arm. "I'm not leaving you."

His eyes locked with hers. Hard. Unyielding. "You will."

She shook her head, tears moistening her eyes in denial even as logic confirmed his plan. Two of six was a better survival rate than zero. But to leave him, knowing she'd never see him again? She wasn't sure she could do it.

His eyes softened, and he cupped her face with his hand. "Please, Josie." His thumb caressed her cheek. The captain giving orders disappeared behind the vulnerable man with a tender heart. Her warrior was begging. "Do it for me."

Yes. For him. She would do it for him.

Her lashes dipped as she nodded her consent.

His hold on her tightened, and in a flash, his lips were on hers. The kiss was hard, fast, and left her shaking. When he released her, she swayed on her feet, unsteadied by his sudden absence.

"Get down behind the rock, Josie. Now."

The captain was back, but she didn't mind. The captain was the man they needed. The man, she prayed, who would keep them *all* alive.

Matthew never glanced back as he rejoined his men. He slid into position on his stomach at the edge of the creek bed, propped himself on his elbows, and extended his rifle barrel onto the bank. They'd have the advantage of a protected position, but Taggart's men would be advancing on speeding horses. Even the best marksmen would struggle to hit such fast-moving targets.

"Come on, sis." Charlie's hand cupped her elbow, tugging her out of her thoughts. "You heard the man. We need to get behind the rock."

Wishing she'd worn her trousers instead of the skirt and petticoats that made riding, running, and any other physical exertion inordinately more difficult, Josephine leaned on her brother as he helped her to the ground. She flattened herself on her belly, just as Matthew had, folding her arms beneath her chest, but Charlie kept pushing her head down when she tried to peer over the top of the rock.

"Stop it," he growled as he pushed her down a third time. "If you catch a bullet, all of this will have been for nothing."

Josephine bit her lip and dropped her chin. She was desperate to know what was going on, to offer any assistance that might be required, but Charlie was right. The whole point of taking cover was to conceal oneself. If she kept popping her head up like an overcurious prairie dog, she'd not only be risking her and Charlie's safety, but she'd be breaking her promise to Matthew. *That* she could not do. Surrendering her need to watch, she rolled over onto her back and gazed up at the sky, tuning her ears to Matthew and the Horsemen. She might not be able to see what was happening, but she could listen.

Charlie hunkered down beside her, lying on his left side so he could keep his gun hand free and ready. "Thanks for orchestrating my rescue."

"Of course. You're my brother." And as much as she loved him, she really wanted him to save his thanks for another time. The low murmur of Matthew's voice was hard enough to decipher from this distance without Charlie talking over him.

"I'm our father's son too, but the relationship didn't seem to sway *him*."

Josephine sighed and gave up trying to eavesdrop on the Horsemen in favor of tending to her brother. "I don't know what all has happened between you two, Charlie." She touched his arm. "But I know he loves you."

"He's got an odd way of showing it." The petulance in his tone grated.

She twisted onto her side to face him. "And how do you show your love to *him*?"

His brows formed a deep *V*, as if he couldn't make sense of the question. Then he clenched his jaw. "You're taking *his* side? He left me to rot."

"I'm not taking anybody's side. Now, hush, I think I hear horses coming." A dull cadence sounded from a distance. Josephine tensed.

"I was never good enough for him. He always wanted me to be something I'm not."

Oh, for heaven's sake. Taggart's men were closing the gap. This was not the time to dredge up old hurts.

"*You* are his pride and joy," Charlie droned on. "The child he brags about to his friends, the one he holds up as an example to his disappointment of a son."

"Shh!" The outlaws were almost upon them. The pounding of hooves vibrated the very ground.

"He owes me, Jo. Owes me respect. Owes me my inheritance. I'm tired of being discounted and ignored. You gotta understand." Charlie grabbed her arm and dragged her backward, away from the rock. "This is the only way."

"Charlie? What are you doing?" She struggled against his grip, but her skirts twisted, trapping her legs as he pulled her sideways.

Josephine glanced toward Matthew, intending to call out to him for help, but she held her tongue. The outlaws were the bigger threat. Charlie wouldn't hurt her. Yet even as she reassured herself with that piece of faith, his arm snaked around her waist, digging painfully into her abdomen and pinching her ribs as he roughly hauled her to her feet.

"Don't worry. You'll be safe," he hissed in her ear even as he carted her away from their cover. "I have everything arranged."

He had everything arranged? What did that mean? Was he actually in league with the outlaws?

Josephine pulled against his hold, but when his strength proved vastly superior, she stomped on the top of his foot instead. "Let me go," she demanded, careful to keep her voice low so as not to distract Matthew and the others. She kicked his shin next and swung an ineffectual punch toward his head with the arm not pinned between them.

He easily dodged her blow with a stretch of his neck and ignored her attack on his limbs as if he felt nothing. Thanks to his heavy boots, that probably wasn't far from the truth.

"On my life, Jo, no harm will come to you."

His promise only infuriated her more for its complete lack of intelligence. Did he really think he'd have any control once he handed her over to Taggart?

Digging her feet into the sandy soil, she thrust her full weight against him, trying to knock him off his feet. He stumbled a bit but caught himself, his grip on her tightening.

His face hardened. "Stop fighting me, Jo, or I'll have to do something truly unpleasant." He lifted Matthew's gun and pointed it at the very men trying to save him.

Josephine stilled, anger and disbelief leaving her stiff. "Don't do this, Charlie." Did he have no honor left at all?

"I don't want to," he ground out. "But I have a plan. One that requires your cooperation. If you'll quit fighting me, I might manage to save the lives of those mercenaries you're so fond of." He placed his lips next to her ear. "Trust me."

Trust him? She didn't even know who he was anymore.

"Hold your fire," Matthew called to his men. "They're showing a white flag."

"It's gotta be a trap." Davenport's voice.

"Father might not be willing to give up a year's wages to ransom *me*," Charlie said, "but I'd bet my life he'd sacrifice Gringolet itself to save you."

TWENTY-TWO

Battle lust always surged through Matt when an enemy approached. The need to conquer. To defend. To accomplish his objective. But the war storm raging through him as the outlaw gang drew nearer carried more intensity than anything he'd experienced before. Not because he and his men were outnumbered. Not because they were trapped on low ground. No, he could attribute the painful pounding of blood through his veins to only one cause— Josephine. The need to protect her, to ensure her survival. Never had he been tempted to open fire beneath a white flag of truce, but as he aimed his rifle at the black-clad outlaw at the front of the pack, the desire to eliminate the threat without regard for military protocol and human decency proved hard to deny.

Taggart reined in his horse twenty yards from the creek bed, his gaze diverting to something behind Matt before settling on the prone riflemen ready to fire upon him. The six riders accompanying him spread three to his left and three to his right. Each had a weapon trained on the creek bed, including the man holding the truce flag—a stick with a white handkerchief knotted around the end. Dawson held the flag in his left hand and a revolver in his right.

"I'm not here to attack you, Captain," Taggart called, his arrogance rubbing Matt's hide raw. "I'm here to negotiate."

"Save your breath." Matt didn't lift his head from his rifle sight. If bullets were going to start flying, he intended his to hit their targets first. "Charlie's not going anywhere."

"I beg to differ." Taggart grinned, and the sight triggered an alarm in Matt's gut. The outlaw leader lifted his gaze to whatever had captured his attention when he first arrived. "You got the insurance, Burkett?"

Matt's head whipped around, and his heart turned to stone. Josephine in Charlie's grip. Being carted *toward* the outlaws. In the blink of an eye, he pulled up onto his knees and swung his rifle around to draw a bead on the traitor in their midst.

"Now, now, Captain. That's not how negotiations work." Taggart's voice buzzed in his ear like an annoying fly, trying to distract him from what really mattered—Josie.

Matt didn't care a hoot about the gun pointed at his chest. He doubted Charlie had the guts to pull the trigger. What he cared about was Josie being completely exposed in front of the outlaws.

"I can drop him, boss," Jonah murmured in a soft, calm voice.

Preach and Wallace kept their guns trained on the outlaws, but Jonah had the better angle for taking down Charlie.

The kid must have sensed the danger, for he yanked his sister more fully in front of him. Jonah could still take him down without touching Josie, of that Matt had no doubt, but if her brother died at Matt's command—she'd never forgive him.

"Stand down, Sergeant."

Matt caught Jonah's movement from the corner of his eye as the sharpshooter turned his attention to more acceptable targets. Matt shifted his focus too. From Charlie to Josephine. Her gaze spilled apologies into the air between them even as her mouth pulled tight in anger when Charlie continued dragging her away.

"Don't do this, Charlie," Matt urged in a voice not loud enough to carry to the outlaws. "You're a fool if you think you can keep her safe once you turn her over to Taggart. If something goes wrong, you're one against seven. One against twelve once you're back with the full gang."

"Shut up, Hanger." Charlie glared at Matt, his gun hand shaking slightly. Then he lifted his head and defiantly called out to Taggart. "Send a man for the horses!"

Saddle leather creaked.

"Captain?" Preach was waiting for orders, but Matt didn't have any. Open fire, and Josie could be hit. Do nothing, and the outlaws would take her. *And* their horses. Even if they shot to kill, they'd be hard-pressed to take out all seven without at least one shooting Josie in the process.

Suddenly a shot fired. From his side of the creek bed. Matt spun around as Jonah levered a replacement cartridge into the chamber of his repeater. "Take another step toward them horses, and the next one goes through your heart."

The outlaws' mounts pranced uneasily at the gunfire, and all the men tightened their hold on their weapons, but miraculously, no return fire came.

"Better watch where yer shooting." Taggart's face hardened. His smooth cockiness disappeared beneath icy disdain. "I'll let one go unanswered, but you try me again, and the woman's dead."

Matt watched as all the outlaw weapons shifted to target Josie. A vise squeezed his chest. He and the Horsemen could take out four before the enemy got off a shot, but not even Jonah could get a second shot off fast enough to stop a bullet already on its way from a fifth or sixth gun.

"This is how it's gonna work." Taggart leaned forward in his saddle, his gaze locking again on Matt. "You and your men are gonna leave your weapons in the dirt, then stand up with your hands above your head. My men will tie you up and take your horses, but you'll keep your lives and ensure the little lady over there keeps hers."

Matt itched to shut the man up with a bullet. End the threat once and for all. But Taggart hadn't drawn his gun. Justifications flooded Matt's mind for why that shouldn't matter. Taggart was evil, and evil needed to be destroyed whether it wielded its own weapon or the weapons of others. Yet Matt's honor ran too deep to allow him to shoot a man—any man—in cold blood.

Not only that, but offensive action on his part would endanger Josie. The instant he pulled the trigger, the shot would set off a cascade of return fire. All aimed at the woman he loved. He couldn't take that risk.

Taggart held all the cards, and he knew it.

So Matt did the only thing he could to guarantee Josie's survival. He laid down his rifle, then pulled his second pistol from its holster and tossed it into the dirt as well. Head high, he stood and stretched his arms toward the sky.

As he pushed to his feet, the disbelief of his men weighted the air like the humidity before a storm, seeping into his skin in sticky disapproval. He felt their anger. Their confusion. Their disappointment in him. A cavalryman never surrendered without a fight. Ever.

Then again, cavalry officers were sworn to protect the frontier and the civilians in their care, even at the cost of their own lives. That vow included sacrificing their pride. Matt clenched his jaw. His men might disagree with his decision, might even judge him weak, but he wouldn't apologize. Nor would he change his mind.

"Wise choice, Captain."

One by one, his men followed his example. First Wallace. Then Jonah. Preach held off the longest, kicking at the ground with the toe of his boot in frustration before finally releasing his rifle and dropping his two pistols to the ground. Even then, he hesitated getting to his feet. For a moment, Matt feared he would try something crazy. Grab up his revolvers, maybe, and go on a one-man rampage in an effort to catch the outlaws by surprise. But after crouching on his hands and knees for a long moment, he let out a sigh and stood, his glare hot enough to melt iron as he aimed his defiance at the three outlaws striding toward them.

With Matt's men unarmed, Taggart's gang shifted their sights onto the Horsemen and away from Josie, allowing Matt to draw a full breath for the first time in several minutes. He toyed with the idea of waiting for the outlaws to get within reach, then signaling his men to take them on hand to hand. He felt the coiled energy in his officers. They were ready to strike. To fight for their freedom. For Josie's.

Then he remembered Wallace's injury. The kid was scrappy, but Taggart's men were a rough crew who looked like they thrived on brawling. Down an arm, Wallace wouldn't stand a chance. Preach could compensate. He was a beast with his fists. Matt sized up the men heading their way. Two were burly, tall and broad through the shoulders. The third strutted with a confidence born from experience. Not one to underestimate.

Still, there were only three. If they struck hard and fast and kept the outlaws between them and the guns pointed their way, it just might—

"Oh, Captain?"

Matt turned his attention back to Taggart. The outlaw had dismounted and was waving Charlie toward him. Fire raged through Matt's blood as Charlie forced his sister toward the monster in black. Josephine fought against her brother's hold, resisting him like an anchor dragging along the sea floor, but her efforts were futile.

Taggart grabbed Josie and yanked her up against him. "No heroics, Captain. Agreed?" He drew a wicked-looking knife and pointed the tip against Josie's neck.

She tried to pull away, but he held her fast.

"I'd prefer not to kill her," Taggart said as he lifted his blade and repositioned it at Josie's temple. "But carving her up might be fun. Daddy would still pay the ransom, and I'd get to leave my mark." He shifted his gaze from Josie back to Matt. "I'd like that. Knowing that every time you looked at her, you thought of me."

Bile rose in Matt's throat. His hands had balled into fists the moment Taggart touched her, but they remained paralyzed. Taggart wasn't bluffing. Matt could read the sick delight in his voice and in his movements. He'd enjoy slicing into Josie's fair skin, making her bleed. Torturing not only her but Matt as well.

Taggart might cut her no matter what Matt and the Horsemen did, but if there was a chance Matt could spare her that pain by yielding to Taggart's will, then yield he would.

"I won't resist." Matt forced his fists to unclench. "You have my word. As long as no harm comes to her."

Taggart grinned. "Such gallantry. I knew I could count on you to see the wisdom in compliance." He drew the blade away from Josie's face but kept it positioned beneath her chin, probably to keep her in line as much as Matt.

She was no quivering damsel. She was a hawk—regal even with her wings temporarily clipped. Never had he been more proud of her. And never had he been more determined to make her proud in return.

Josie was going to be out of his reach and under the control of a man driven by greed and retribution. Helplessness clawed at his insides, but he refused to give in to it. He couldn't fight what was out of reach. Couldn't control what was out of his hands. So he'd focus on what he could control: his mind.

As Taggart's man stripped him of his knives, his boots, and his dignity by slamming a fist into Matt's gut and doubling him over, Matt ran escape scenarios. Piling up possibilities. Discarding weaknesses. He flexed his wrists and ankles when they tied him up, creating just a touch of space he could exploit later when he relaxed. He estimated travel speeds based on weary horses. Theorized likely destinations for the gang to rendezvous. Calculated how long it would take to get a message to Thaddeus Burkett, the likelihood Josie's father would seek verification before acting, how many men he might bring with him, where the Horsemen could intercept.

Yet when the weapons were carted off and the horses gathered, when the outlaws were mounted and the Horsemen sat barefoot and bound in the dirt of the creek bed, all thoughts ceased in Matt's mind, save one.

He lifted his gaze to Josephine, who sat mounted in front of Taggart. Chin high. Back straight. Her eyes found his, and for a blessed moment, the connection between them was so strong, he swore he could feel her inside him.

"I'll find you." The vow vibrated from the depths of his soul.

She smiled in answer. "I know."

"I don't think so," Taggart announced. He drew his revolver with lightning speed and fired.

TWENTY-THREE

No!"

Josephine threw her weight against Taggart's gun arm, praying she could divert the trajectory of the bullet, even as her scientific mind recognized the futility. If she was hearing the sound of the gunshot, her movements were too late to do anything more productive than irritate her captor. A fact brought home to her when he cuffed her on the side of the head. The metal of his revolver impacted her skull. Not enough to do any permanent damage. Just enough to hurt like blue blazes.

Tears welled in her eyes, making it frustratingly difficult to focus. She blinked and craned her neck as Taggart nudged his horse into action, but all she could see was Matthew's crumpled form lying in the dust, his men scooting like oversized inchworms to get to their captain.

The first tear fell.

Matthew.

The healer in her started running through all the possible

injuries that a bullet could cause, each more dire than the last.

"Matthew!" Desperate to tend him, she struggled against Taggart's hold, willing to throw herself off the horse if it meant getting back to the man she loved in time to save his life.

"Sit still," Taggart growled, locking an arm around her midsection and trapping her arms at her sides.

No. She wouldn't yield to this man. She'd fight until she had no fight left inside her. She threw her head backward and slammed her skull into Taggart's chin.

He cursed, then head-butted her in return. The blow dazed her momentarily.

"Hey!" Charlie shouted. "You agreed she wouldn't be harmed."

"That was before I knew she was a hissing she-cat. She bloodied my lip."

Josephine blinked as she regained her bearings. Matthew. Matthew needed her. She kicked Taggart's shin with her heel and was preparing for a second, more powerful shot when her captor transferred the reins to the hand holding her in place and drew his weapon.

"Kick me again, and I'll shoot your brother." His voice slashed with lethal accuracy across her soul. "I don't need him for ransom anymore, little girl. All I need is you. So behave yourself, or he'll be the one to pay the price."

Josephine's body stilled, but her heart beat hard and fast in her chest as her gaze flew to her brother.

Charlie looked at Taggart as if not quite sure whether his threat was a ruse.

Josephine knew it was no idle threat. Taggart had no conscience. No honor. Whatever arrangement he'd made with Charlie, he'd cut her brother's throat in a heartbeat if it meant getting what he wanted. Charlie might be too cocky and full of his own agenda to recognize the danger, but Josephine saw it all too clearly. Taggart *didn't* need him.

She lowered her leg. Relaxed her seat. Submitted to the man at her back.

Charlie was still hers to protect. Even if he was a self-absorbed idiot who thought aligning himself with outlaws was the best way to get what he believed he was owed. Foolish, shortsighted, impetuous boy.

When Charlie's gaze moved to her face, Josephine arched a brow as she returned her brother's stare, doing nothing to hide the disgust and disappointment she felt for him in that moment. Yes, she'd stopped fighting Taggart out of concern for his welfare, but she held Charlie responsible in this fiasco. He'd chosen to get involved with Taggart and his gang. To gamble money he didn't have. To extort their father. To betray his sister. To ally himself with a killer who thought nothing of shooting a man for sport—a man bound hand and foot, incapable of defending himself.

Charlie's gaze turned rueful and finally fell, unable to bear the weight of her silent condemnation.

As Taggart relaxed and holstered his weapon, Josephine closed her eyes. A second tear squeezed past her damp lashes.

The Horsemen had nothing. No horses. No supplies. They didn't even have their boots. How would they manage to get Matthew to help in time?

Only you can save him, Lord. Please. Save him.

"Captain!"

Matt barely had time to brace himself before a rolling Preach slammed into his face.

"Where're ya hit?" His corporal nudged him with his shoulder, knocking his hat off and bruising his ear.

"Well, my face has felt better."

"A head wound?" Preach stretched his neck up in an effort to get a better view, clipping Matt's chin as he moved. "I don't see any blood."

Matt groaned. "That's because the bullet creased my side. A rolling mammoth hit my face."

A half-grin sprouted on Luke's face. "'Thou hast stricken them, but they have not grieved . . . they have made their faces harder than a rock.' Jeremiah 5:3."

"A rock sounds about right." Matt grumbled and groaned, but in his soul, he thanked God. Not only for sparing his life just now, but for giving him men—no, *friends*—he could count on to have his back. Or his front, in this case.

Luke grew serious. "You sure it's just a crease, Matt?" He tried to look for himself, but with his arms bound behind him and his shoulder lodged near Matt's throat, he had practically no leverage.

"There's blood," Jonah confirmed, his knees bumping into Matt's feet. His kneeling shuffle might have been slower than Preach's roll technique, but he'd managed to keep his head upright. "It ain't pooling, though. Just soaking his shirt along the bottom of his rib cage. Might be deeper than a crease, but it don't look life-threatening. It's a good thing you dove when you did. I thought you mighta been too lock-eyed with the doc to notice Taggart's draw."

"Nah," Preach denied on Matt's behalf. "The captain's reflexes still work, even if his brain has gone soft." Another nudge with that overlarge shoulder, this time in the windpipe.

Matt scooted backward to create a much-needed buffer

from Preach's shoulder and his assessment. He wasn't wrong. Matt's dodging lunge had been born purely of instinct. All he'd been thinking about in that moment was Josephine and what it would take to find her.

"If you ask me," Wallace said, having inched his way over to the group with some kind of sideways crawl on his good shoulder, "Matt had nothing to do with it. My money's on a guardian angel. Same one that steered bullets away from him in that canyon saved him again by shoving his face into the dirt. Somebody upstairs is keeping you alive for a reason, Captain. Best not disappoint him."

"I don't know about angels, but Wallace is right about one thing." Matt eyed his men. "We still have a mission to accomplish, and the first order of business is to get free of these ropes. I managed to preserve a bit of slack in mine." He began working his wrists back and forth. "I might be able to—"

"Save your skin, Cap," Preach said as he tucked his knees to his chest. "I buried my pocketknife in the creek bed over yonder. Gimme a minute, and I'll fetch it."

Suddenly Preach's frustrated kicking and slow rise during their surrender made a lot more sense. Matt grinned. "You wily old coot."

Preach winked, then set off on a bone-jarring, lopsided roll that made Matt wince. It must be killing Luke's shoulders to have his arms trapped behind him as he rolled, not to mention that he had no way to protect his face.

Yet in less than five minutes, Preach had retrieved the knife and returned. He smiled through the dirt coating him from hair to heel like a boy who'd just uncovered buried treasure, then squirmed around until he got his knees under him. He backed up to meet Jonah hand to hand. As the two non-injured members of the team, it made sense that they worked the problem together, but waiting was excruciating, and not just because the wound in Matt's side had started to throb more noticeably now that he had nothing active to do.

He could deal with the pain. It was the thought of what could be happening to Josie that tortured him.

Taggart yanked Josephine off his horse with all the finesse of a farmhand grabbing a ham sandwich off a platter. Fitting, she supposed, since they'd stopped at an abandoned farmhouse about as far off the beaten path as one could get. She hadn't seen a single house, homestead, or hovel in the last hour. Whoever had settled here had either foolishly believed more settlers would come or had prized his privacy more than was healthy. Whatever its origins, the place had not fared well since its abandonment. The house looked large enough to hold three rooms, maybe four. The size a man with a family would build. Yet with its weathered siding and leaning walls, an enthusiastic knock on the front door would probably topple the entire building.

"I'll take over her care now, Taggart," Charlie said as he swung down from his horse. He took a step toward Josephine, but Taggart's grip on her arm only tightened.

"Dawson!" Taggart barked.

The man with the red beard who'd ridden next to Charlie the entire way lunged at her brother from behind. He wrapped his arm around Charlie's throat while sliding Matt's gun from Charlie's holster.

"Charlie!" Josephine struggled against Taggart's hold, trying to get to her brother, to help him before they killed him right in front of her. "Let him go!"

Surprisingly enough, Dawson did just that. Once he had the gun in his possession, he released his choke hold and shoved Charlie onto the ground.

Charlie sputtered and gasped, but once he caught his breath, he surged to his feet, his face mottled in anger. "How dare you! You work for *me*. I won't stand for this."

"You won't stand at all, rich boy." Dawson twisted sideways, his leg kicking out, his foot smashing into Charlie's knee.

Charlie howled in pain and fell back to the ground, grabbing his right knee.

Taggart dragged Josephine a step closer, close enough for him to lean over Charlie and gloat but not so close that she could reach her brother as he writhed.

"Time to get something straight, Burkett. You've never been in charge. Your ransom scheme was clever, I'll give you that much. Paying back what you owe me with your father's money? Brilliant! Using your sister as insurance in case your daddy didn't feel like paying for you? Even more brilliant! In fact, I gotta admit that when I saw your hat come sailing into the canyon, signaling the move to the second plan, I considered offering you a permanent place in my gang. After all, a man who'd betray his sister to gain his own reward is a man who wouldn't care about casualties during a bank robbery or train heist. But then I remembered you were just a snotty-nosed rich kid used to getting his own way, and the urge passed. Knowing your sister was nearby, though, and that you would lead us to her—well, that perked me right up." Taggart wagged his brows at Josephine. "Bigger paydays always put me in a good mood. And your brother arranged it perfectly. He only forgot one thing."

Taggart turned back to Charlie, his smile twisting into a sneer. "You forgot who you were dealing with. Consider this a renegotiation of our deal, Burkett. I'm no longer satisfied with half the ransom money. Me and my boys are going to take it all. And if you want to live to learn from your mistakes, you'll accept my terms without complaint." He waved Dawson forward again. "Shackle him to the chuck wagon and let Cookie put him to work. If he gets out of line, shoot him."

Dawson yanked Charlie off the ground, locking his arms behind his back. Charlie's right leg buckled when he tried to stand on it.

"Wait. He's hurt." Josephine tried to go to her brother, her healing instincts punching through the horrified numbness freezing her insides at the story she'd just heard. "Let me help him."

"Nope. Got other plans for you, darlin'." He pulled her in the opposite direction.

"Jo!" Charlie called. She heard the fear in his voice. Fear that turned to anger when he called out a second time. "You better make sure nothing happens to her, Taggart. Those mercenaries she hired to free me? They're not just ordinary hired guns. They're Hanger's Horsemen. Harm a hair on her head, and they'll destroy you."

Taggart's step hitched, but he kept walking, dragging her away from Charlie.

Josephine craned her neck around until she could see him. He hobbled alongside his captor, not fighting, but not submitting either. His eyes sought hers.

"Jo, I'm sorry. I didn't think . . ."

That was the problem. He hadn't thought. Not about consequences or dangers or how this scheme of his could possibly go wrong. All he'd thought about was himself. And now the man she loved lay shot and abandoned in the middle of nowhere.

Josephine turned her back, no longer able to stomach the sight of her brother.

One step at a time. That was all she could focus on now. One step, one minute at a time. She wrapped her ravaged heart in the gauze of stoicism. She had to stem the emotional bleeding if she was going to survive. Had to keep her mind engaged, her wits sharp.

They approached a barn. Half the roof had caved in, and the rest seemed glued together by nothing more substantial than a series of mud nests that a family of barn swallows had deserted.

"Your brother tells me you're a doctor." Taggart drew her to a halt. "That true?"

Josephine lifted her chin. "It is."

"Good." He handed her over to a scowling fellow with a mean-looking scar running down his throat. "Your mercenary friends left several of my men injured after that stunt they pulled back in Uvalde. Tending them will keep you occupied while we make arrangements for your ransom. Carver will supervise."

Keeping her back straight and her head erect as she'd trained herself to do when facing powerful men who belittled her abilities, Josephine met the guard's cold stare and gave a brief nod. "Mr. Carver."

Disdain radiated from him. As did a soulless quality that made her insides quail. As much as she wanted to pretend he was just one more in a long line of arrogant men who tried to put her in her place, she knew more than arrogance dwelled beneath his surface. Cruelty lived there. A cruelty she could easily imagine had put more than one man in an early grave.

"Let me know if she causes any trouble, Carver," Taggart said as he flung her toward the guard. "Any disobedience on her part can be meted out on Burkett. I know how much you'd enjoy teaching the whelp a few much-needed lessons."

Carver smiled, the expression knotting Josephine's stomach. "Open season, huh?" He turned that smile on her, and a shiver coursed down her nape. "Just give me an excuse, Doc. Even a little one."

She forced herself to hold the terrifying man's gaze. She'd make Matthew proud. Stare into the face of evil and not flinch. "I think not, Mr. Carver."

As much as she longed to escape and find a way back to Matthew, she wouldn't take the chance of Charlie being beaten or killed in retaliation. An act this man would obviously take great pleasure in.

Using her haughtiest voice to disguise the trepidation surging inside her, she turned her gaze toward the open barn door and took a single step forward. "Now, I believe there are injured men who need tending. If you'd be so good as to have someone fetch my medical bag from the horses you stole?"

She didn't wait for an affirmative response. She simply marched into the barn as if she had no doubt her instructions would be obeyed. Carver allowed her arm to slip through his grasp, but he followed close on her heels. So close that he bumped into her hip when she stopped abruptly.

The smell of dried blood and unwashed male bodies stole her breath. Well, at least she'd have plenty of work to distract her from worrying about Matthew. The men eyeing her from strung hammocks, stump stools, and bedrolls might be outlaws, but they were patients too. Patients who required a physician.

"I'm going to need a plentiful supply of hot water," she said. "And soap."

Lots and lots of soap.

CHAPTER

TWENTY-FOUR

Matt winced as a half-buried rock jabbed the arch of his foot, but he didn't slow his pace. They needed to get back to Chatfield before dark, and to do that, they needed to get to the road and find a local farmer or rancher with a wagon and a hospitable spirit.

God, I don't know if Wallace is off his rocker with that angel talk or not, but if you do have an angel warrior on loan to us, I'd sure appreciate you reassigning him from protection duty to transportation detail. If we don't make it to Chatfield before the last train departs, our chances of finding Josie are all but gone.

They had to get to Gringolet Farms before Thaddeus Burkett left. Taggart would have the ransom demand delivered tonight or tomorrow morning. Which meant Matt had to arrive by midday tomorrow to ensure he didn't miss his window. The banks would be closed on a Saturday, but he couldn't count on that slowing Burkett down. Josie's father could easily have his own stash of cash in a safe at his home. Or he could convince the bank owner to conduct an unscheduled transaction, either by emotional appeal or by threatening to take his business elsewhere. If it were his daughter in peril, Matt would do whatever it took to procure her safety. He couldn't imagine Thaddeus Burkett being any different. Refusing to pay ransom for a wastrel of a son who'd dug his own hole was one thing. Abandoning a faithful daughter was another thing entirely.

"How're ya holding up, Cap?"

Preach dogged his side like a faithful hound, constantly shooting him sidelong glances as if he expected Matt to keel over at any moment.

"Fine." Matt didn't dignify the question with eye contact, just kept trudging forward one step at a time. His side burned like fire and his head ached, but none of that mattered.

"That shirt stain's gettin' wider. All this walking's keeping that wound from closing. You ain't gonna do the lady doctor any good if you bleed yourself to death."

Matt shot his corporal a glare. "I'm not gonna do her much good if I sit down in the middle of nowhere and take a nap either." He tucked his arm close to his throbbing side and let out a sigh. "I know you're looking out for me, Preach, and I appreciate it, but I'm not the one we need to be concerned about. Josie's alone with an entire gang of outlaws." Ruthless men with the morality of snakes. His throat worked as he fought to keep the worst visions of what might be happening to her out of his brain. "Charlie won't be able to protect her. Her father might ransom her, but Taggart can't be trusted to keep his word. There's no telling what he'll do to her before or after he gets his money."

The image of Taggart's knife blade on her face shot raw terror through Matt and energized his tired muscles. This was why he wasn't supposed to let himself care about a woman. It tore a man up inside when he failed to protect her. When circumstances stole her well-being from the realm of his control. Left him feeling helpless and fearful and . . . and none of that mattered. He couldn't undo loving her. Didn't want to. So he'd use that fear as a weapon and let it push him harder. Straightening his stance, he quickened his pace.

"We'll get there, Matt," Wallace said, coming alongside them. "In the meantime, she's in God's hands. We have to trust that he has things under control."

Matt nodded, but the sentiment didn't soothe as much as it should have. Plenty of good men had been martyred doing the Lord's work. And plenty of evil men had thrust their will upon the innocent, leaving nothing but destruction in their wake. A cavalryman didn't work long on the frontier without seeing that truth played out. Death. Rape. Mutilation. He'd seen it all.

Yes, God was capable of protecting Josie, but there was no guarantee that he actually would. And it was that uncertainty that drove Matt step after grueling step.

He supposed a more faithful man would take comfort in knowing that God's will would prevail, and whatever happened would be for the best. But Matt believed there was an evil force with a will of its own at work in the world too. A force that inflicted pain for its own sadistic delight. A force that would steal a five-year-old boy's parents and sister from him and make him bear witness to the atrocities. He didn't believe their murder was God's will. A God who spoke commandments against murder wouldn't condone such an act. Yet this same God had done nothing to stop it.

His uncle had offered what explanation he could, trying to help a hurting boy who harbored anger toward the Almighty.

Sin had consequences, his uncle had said. And God had to allow those consequences to play out even when it meant innocent people got hurt.

Hatred led a Comanche war party to violence against a family of white settlers. A hatred that had been born from white men stealing their land and attacking their villages. And on that day thirty-two years ago, Matt's parents had been the ones to pay the price.

If the cavalry had been there, they could have stopped it. That was why Matt had joined. To get in the way of those consequences taking innocent lives. Soldiers were fair game in war. Civilians weren't. As far as he was concerned, Josie was a civilian in this war with Taggart. Using her for extortion was man's will, not God's. Which meant man could change the outcome. If he could get there in time.

"Road's up yonder," Jonah said, pointing to a level area about a hundred yards away.

Matt's heart stuttered as hope surged to life in his breast. "Good work, Sergeant." He set off at a lope, his wounds forgotten. "Let's go, boys."

They'd covered half the distance when the sound of wagon wheels and a jangling harness broke through the stillness of early evening.

Matt started running in earnest, ignoring the jabs at his feet, intent only on catching the attention of whoever was driving. Despite the pain in his side, he waved his arms above his head like a wild man and shouted.

"Hey! Over here! Stop the wagon!"

The other Horsemen joined in the clamor as they raced for the road. The wagon kept rolling, showing no sign of stopping. Either the driver was hard of hearing or he had no intention of pulling over for a bunch of crazed beggars.

no intention of pulling over for a bunch of crazed beggars. Matt dropped his hands and sprinted forward. This wagon was *not* getting away.

He crossed the plane of the road just behind the wagon and turned to give chase. Thanking God for a sedately paced team of horses, he gained ground. Lungs burning, feet screaming in agony, side cramping, he ran.

He caught up to the back wheel. Then the side of the wagon. Then, finally, the driver's bench.

"Please," he huffed. "Stop."

The driver startled in his seat, then jerked on the reins. "Whoa!"

Matt doubled over, bracing his hands above his knees as he struggled to catch his breath. Never had thirty-seven felt as old as it did at that moment.

"Land sakes, fella," the driver declared as he brought his team to a halt. "You 'bout scared the spit out of me, running into the road like that. Shocks like that take a toll on the old ticker, you know." He thumped his chest, but then his eyes widened as he took in Matt's bedraggled condition. "Goodness, son. What happened to you?"

A clamor behind Matt alerted him to the arrival of the rest of the Horsemen.

"Heavens to Betsy! You hombres look like you been tossed off a train and left to rot. What're y'all doin' out here in the middle of nowhere, and on foot?"

Matt forced himself to straighten his posture even though his side protested. "Attacked by outlaws."

The driver let out a low whistle. "Lord have mercy. They done took your horses?"

Matt nodded. "Guns too. Even our boots."

"Your boots?" He looked more affronted by that indignity

241

than by the stolen horses. He shook his head. "That's down-right despicable."

"We sure could use a ride to town, mister." Matt took a step closer to the wagon. As sympathetic as the driver appeared, they didn't have time for the long version of the story. "The gang who attacked us took a woman hostage. I gotta get to the depot in Chatfield before the last train departs."

"Took a woman? The fiends!" The driver gestured swiftly toward his wagon. "Never let it be said that Paxton Whitaker failed to help a lady in need. Hurry up, now. Climb in. I'll get ya to Chatfield before the 7:40 leaves the station. On my honor."

"You're a lifesaver, Mr. Whitaker. Thank you." Matt tipped his hat as he scrambled around to the back of the wagon. With swift movements, he climbed the wheel spokes and hoisted himself into the bed. The others followed.

As soon as the four Horsemen found seats in the back among an assortment of crates and trunks, Whitaker snapped the reins, and his team surged forward.

"You know, I don't usually make my trip into Chatfield until Saturday morning," the driver called over his shoulder in a voice loud enough to be heard over the hooves and wheels, "but something just kept itching under my skin, telling me to leave early. Guess it's a good thing for you fellas that I decided to scratch it." He chuckled.

"That it is," Matt agreed, deciding Wallace's angel theory might have some basis in reality after all. It seemed the Lord had one assigned to transportation detail after all. "An answer to prayer."

"Oh, I know all about answered prayers," Whitaker said. "My business wouldn't still be afloat if it weren't for the Good Lord opening new doors when old ones closed. Why, just yesterday I had a big sale fall through and was worrying about how I was gonna pay my suppliers. Then you fellows show up."

Matt turned to his companions. None of them looked any less puzzled than he felt. Preach shrugged. Jonah shook his head. Wallace, however, verbalized the question on everyone's minds.

"How exactly are we helping your business, Mr. Whitaker?"

The old man turned just enough that Matt caught his wink. "Take a gander in them boxes."

Preach was the first to take him up on the offer, unfastening the trunk closest to him. Wallace reached around with his good hand to hold the lid as Preach pulled back a layer of cotton batting. His eyes widened. Then laughter burst from his chest as he wagged his head in disbelief.

"What is it?" Matt eyed the crate nearest him.

"Boots." Preach pulled one from the trunk and held it up for inspection. "'But my God shall supply all your need.' Philippians 4:19."

Wallace grinned. "Only God could arrange for a bunch of barefooted Horsemen to be rescued by a bootmaker."

"Go ahead and help yourselves," Whitaker called. "If the outlaws done stole your money too, I can write up an IOU when we get to Chatfield. You fellas seem the type to pay your bills."

As the men started digging through boxes and trying on boots, Matt's mind turned back to Josie.

Thank you for your provision, Father. But please, provide for her too. Watch her back and keep her safe.

Preach slid on a pair and admired the fit. "I think the Horsemen just found a new bootmaker."

Whitaker turned in his seat, his eyes wide. "The *Horsemen?*"

Matt thumped the kind old bootmaker on the shoulder. "I'm Matthew Hanger. This here's Jonah Brooks, Luke Davenport, and Mark Wallace." He nodded to each of his men in turn, and they nodded to Whitaker. "You've just rescued Hanger's Horsemen and earned yourself four customers for life."

"Hanger's Horsemen." Whitaker started to slump in his seat, but Matt gripped his shoulder tightly in support. The team slowed in response to his inattention, but the bootmaker didn't seem to notice. "Julia ain't never gonna believe this," he mumbled.

"Whitaker?" Matt tightened his grip. "You all right?"

Suddenly their driver came back to himself. He shook his head, then sat taller in the seat. "I'm fine, boys. Just fine." He gripped the reins with renewed purpose. "Paxton Whitaker, Bootmaker to Hanger's Horsemen." He glanced back at Matt. "Got an awful nice ring to it." He chuckled softly. "Think I'll make it my new business slogan." Grinning like a kid who'd been gifted the pick of the litter, he snapped the reins and instantly got the flagging horses back up to speed. "Let's go, lads. The Horsemen got a train to catch."

TWENTY-FIVE

Must you hover?" Josephine scowled up at the guard whose breath fogged across her nape like a sticky cloud of humidity. Carver answered by leaning even closer.

Mercy, how she wanted to scrub that discomfiting sensation off her skin, but she'd already sterilized her hands. An outlaw lay sprawled on his belly atop a table someone had pilfered from the farmhouse, his left pant leg rolled up to expose matching entry and exit wounds on his calf.

It amazed her how many of Taggart's men had wounds to their lower extremities. Even in a life-or-death battle against a dozen hardened criminals who had no qualms about taking human life, Matthew and the rest of the Horsemen had held fast to their vow of non-lethal force. Such honorable men. So different from the drunken, foul-mouthed horde surrounding her now.

The men in the barn watched her as if she were the afternoon's entertainment. To some, she seemed to be a curiosity, unaccustomed as they no doubt were to being in the presence of a proper lady. To others, her gender seemed to inspire only lust and crude gestures. She'd quickly learned not to make eye contact with any of them until medical treatment deemed it necessary. After the first hour, some of the novelty wore off, for most had gone back to their card playing or drinking.

Josephine contemplated the hairy calf before her. The outlaw attached to it was half-insensate with alcohol, but the pain of the needle was sure to rouse him.

"Come around the table and hold his ankle down." Josephine gestured to the guard with a lift of her head. "He's not going to like it when I start suturing."

Carver hadn't permitted anesthetization, stating he refused to allow her to incapacitate any of the men. Not that they were in any kind of fighting shape in their current form. Most had anesthetized themselves with liquor and were barely coherent. Even after dosing them with soap and hot water, they still reeked of whiskey and gin. Josephine suspected Carver's real reason for disallowing her use of ether was that he enjoyed watching others suffer. He certainly enjoyed making her life as uncomfortable as possible.

Case in point—instead of walking around to the far side of the table as she had instructed, he reached an arm around her back and latched onto the ankle in question, bringing his foul breath even closer. His front pressed indecently against her back, sending a shiver of fear-tinged disgust over her skin. She held her ground, though. Well, almost. She did take a tiny step closer to the table as she bent her head to her task.

"Your head's blocking my light," she groused, hoping he'd care enough about his compadre to give her a little space.

Carver shifted, erasing the miniscule separation she'd managed to preserve. "Make do, Doc."

Knowing he took pleasure in her discomfort, Josephine

hid it as best she could beneath a stiff spine and a brusque demeanor. The faster she stitched this wound, the faster she could put some space between her and her boorish warden. Closing the edges of the bullet hole with the fingers of her left hand, Josephine jabbed her needle into the hairy calf.

A holler followed by a string of profanity polluted the air as the recipient reared his head back, bringing the top of his torso off the table. Carver reached around her with his other hand and smacked the fellow's shoulder back down, throwing her ribs atop her patient's backside in the process.

"You know, if you'd moved to the other side of the table like I asked," she said as she shoved backward in retaliation for his placing her in such an undignified position, "you wouldn't be impeding my suturing with your ruffian deportment."

For once, Carver had no reply. He probably hadn't understood her insult. Too many ten-dollar words.

Ten-dollar words. Matthew's phrase. Josephine's fingers trembled, and her bottom lip threatened to imitate the motion.

Oh, Matthew. Are you alive? I pray you are. I pray that God is watching over you, providing for you, healing you when I cannot.

Josephine bit down on that quivering lip and forced her fingers to settle as she tied off the first suture. Thinking of Matthew brought too many emotions to the surface. Emotions she didn't have the luxury of indulging, not when any show of weakness would incite the wolves.

Still, she hated knowing that she could help if she were with him. Hated being outside the realm of control. Both for Matthew's situation and her own. The only control she wielded was over the hairy leg in front of her and the needle in her hand.

Matthew's in your hands, Lord. You know what's best. Help me to accept whatever your best means, even if it's not what I want it to be.

Filling her head with quoted verses about how God worked together for the good of those who loved him, and filling her heart with the optimism to believe the promise would translate into the preservation of Matthew's life, Josephine snipped off the suture thread and set her needle to flesh once again.

Inaction was a military man's worst enemy. Matt had been able to power through the pain while he marched across the countryside, driven by his mission to save Josie. But now that they'd made it onto the train and he could do nothing more productive than sit and plot, the fire in his side ignited with new life and refused to be ignored. He shifted in his seat, trying to find a position that lessened the agony, but all he got for his trouble was what felt like a dagger slipping between his ribs. A hiss escaped him along with a flinch he no longer had the energy to hide.

"All right," Preach grumbled as he twisted on the bench he and Matt shared and leveled a frown at his captain. "Vest open. Shirt up. No argument."

Matt scowled. "You fuss worse than an old lady. You know that, right?"

Preach raised a brow as he crossed his arms. "Old ladies don't get to be their age by being stupid. If you're gonna watch my back on the battlefield, I gotta make sure you ain't gonna faint on me because you were too stubborn to tend a wound properly."

"Yeah, well, the person I want tending my wounds got carried off by outlaws, so I'm a little cranky." But he reached for the buttons on his vest anyway. Might as well take a gander at the damage. Had to pass the time somehow. They still had at least an hour before they reached San Antonio.

Thankfully they sat at the rear of a passenger car containing fewer than a dozen people. And most of them were busy trying to catch a few winks of shut-eye.

As he reached for the third button, a hand gripped his shoulder. Matt glanced up at Preach, surprised to find his friend's bossy bearing traded in for an expression of serious intent. "We'll get her back, Matt."

Matt's hands stilled on the buttons as his chin dipped in a lackluster nod. "I know. At least that's what I keep telling myself. I'll go crazy if I let myself consider any other outcome."

"Horsemen never quit," Luke said, his voice quiet yet ringing with intensity. "We find a way to achieve the mission, and we protect our own. The doc's one of us now, Cap. The moment you staked your claim, she became family. There's not a one of us who wouldn't give our life to save her."

Moved to an embarrassing degree, Matt dropped his head and resumed fumbling with his buttons.

"We all like her. In my estimation, any woman who can keep up with a group of hardened cavalry officers on horseback is a woman worth keepin'. Wallace practically worships her, thanks to her saving his life and all. Shoot, even Jonah likes her, and you know how particular he is about folks. Barely tolerates most two-legged creatures."

Matt got the vest undone and gingerly stretched it open on the right side where blood had soaked through. He tugged his shirttails free of his trousers. Dried blood glued the cotton to his skin at the wound site just beneath his rib cage. He eased the fabric away as gently as he could manage, but it still stung like the dickens. And oozed. Blood and a clear discharge. Not a terribly appetizing picture.

"That's definitely deeper than a crease." Preach contorted his big frame to examine the wound more closely. His frown knocked away Matt's last fingerhold on optimism. "I'd be surprised if that bullet didn't nick a rib. Chasing down Whitaker did you no favors neither. That crevice is twice as wide as any bullet would've made. Must've aggravated it with all that scrambling about."

"Yeah, well, that scrambling about got us a ride to town along with new boots, so I'd say it was worth the price." Any sacrifice would be worth the cost if it meant getting Josie away from Taggart.

Preach shrugged. "Prob'ly." His mouth quirked a grin as he jutted one foot into the aisle to admire his boot. "I am rather fond of my new footwear. Couldn't believe that fella had a pair in my size. I usually gotta special-order 'em."

Thankfully Taggart's men had been more concerned with stripping them of weapons than funds. In their effort to speed Josie away, they hadn't taken the time to go through the Horsemen's pockets, which left them enough cash to pay Whitaker for the boots and secure tickets for the train. Of course, the outlaws had stolen the bulk of their money when they stole their saddlebags. Never knowing how much money they might need to complete a job, the Horsemen always rode flush, despite appearances to the contrary. Now, however, all that remained was a collection of spare change. They should have enough to rent some horses from a livery in San Antonio when the train arrived, but after that, they'd be living off pocket lint.

"Hey, Wallace." Preach stretched his boot farther across the aisle and kicked Mark's foot off his crossed ankle.

Wallace lifted the hat that had been covering his face and glowered at Preach, obviously unhappy at having his nap disturbed.

Preach offered no apology. He gestured with a nod to the other passengers sitting in the front section of the car. "See if you can charm one of them fellas into loaning you their whiskey flask. The captain's wound needs tendin'."

Wallace straightened, his eyes widening into full alertness. He leaned forward and eyed Matt around Preach's wide shoulders. "Is it bad? I thought it was just a crease."

"Apparently he confused *crease* with *canyon*."

"It's not that bad." Matt smacked Preach's elbow off its resting place on the back of the seat in front of them, taking great satisfaction in watching his corporal's body jerk forward as he tried to stop his fall. "Just bleeding a bit more than optimal."

"You know what Dr. Burkett would say." Wallace shifted into a schoolmaster tone that would've chafed Matt's hide had it not been for the image his words evoked of Josie and her tendency to boss him around. "Even a small wound can get infected." He turned a searching gaze to the front of the car. "Any idea who the best target might be?"

Jonah spoke up for the first time. "Second bench on the left. Fella with the muttonchop sideburns. Silver flask. Left breast pocket."

Matt shook his head, though he shouldn't have been surprised. Jonah's eagle eyes rarely missed anything.

Wallace gave a nod, got up from his seat, and sauntered forward to work his magic. Preach, on the other hand, tugged his own shirt from his waistband, pulled out his knife, and notched a section about three inches from the hem. Grabbing hold of the split fabric, he tore it all the way around, earning him a handful of turned heads and raised eyebrows from the other passengers.

"I got a handkerchief that's fairly clean," Jonah offered. He passed a white cotton square across the aisle.

Preach dropped it onto the seat between him and Matt. "Thanks."

A minute later, Wallace was back with the whiskey. Matt slouched sideways to expose the red gash, then steeled himself.

Preach met his eyes. Matt nodded. Whiskey poured.

Every muscle hardened into stone as Matt fought to hold back a scream of agony. Preach had the gall to administer a second dose, then finally smashed the handkerchief against Matt's throbbing flesh.

"Hold this."

Matt obeyed, covering the dressing with his hand and pressing it tight against his side as the fire abated just enough for him to catch his breath.

"Next time, I'm voting for cauterization." Matt shifted as Preach reached around his midsection to apply the shirttail bandage. "Probably hurts less."

"You're gettin' soft in your old age, Captain. Whining about scratches."

Matt didn't rise to the bait. In truth, he wasn't sure he could rise to much of anything at the moment. His legs felt about as solid as wet newsprint.

"Captain? You all right?" Wallace slid into the seat in front of them and regarded him with growing concern. "You're looking pale all of a sudden."

He was *feeling* pale all of a sudden. If one could feel pale. He clenched his jaw and fought the fog invading his brain. He was a cavalryman. Withstanding pain was part of the job. He didn't have time for weakness. He had a mission to accomplish. A woman to save. *His* woman.

"I'm fine." He gritted out the lie, knowing he was fooling no one, yet also knowing none of his men would call him on it.

Warriors understood. A soldier completed his mission or died trying.

With Josie's safety hanging in the balance, nothing short of death would drag Matt from the battlefield.

CHAPTER

TWENTY-SIX

Josephine watched the sunset fade with a growing sense of dread. Tending the wounded had kept her busy throughout the afternoon and evening, but as night approached, apprehension found fertile ground in her soul.

She was a woman alone in a camp full of men. Drunk men. Morally bankrupt men. Men held in check by an outlaw whose only motive to protect her lay in her monetary value as a hostage. That and possibly his desire for self-preservation.

Taggart had witnessed the capabilities of the Horsemen with his own eyes. And now that he knew their identities, thanks to Charlie's attempt to throw around the weight of others when he himself had none, Taggart understood who would come after him should any harm befall her while in his care. The number of arrests that could be laid at the Horsemen's feet would give even the cockiest outlaw a moment's pause. Whether or not that pause would last the night, however, was a question Josephine couldn't yet answer.

When the camp cook rang the bell and men started assembling in the yard between the house and the barn, Jo-

254

sephine made a point to look for Charlie. He stood beside the chuck wagon, one arm shackled to a spoke in the back wheel. When he moved to dip water into an outlaw's cup, she noticed his limp, but the leg seemed to be bearing his weight for the most part, so the knee must not be broken. He looked up and caught her eye. She held his gaze for a single heartbeat, then turned away. Some of today's injuries were *not* superficial.

When it came her turn at the chuck wagon, Josephine held out her tin plate to the gray-bearded man with the crooked nose. It looked to have been broken recently and not set very well. Dark bruising colored the bridge of his nose and blackened his eyes as well.

His ladle banged against her plate. "Thank you," she murmured, the politeness automatic.

The cook's face jerked up as if she'd spoken in a foreign tongue. He stared at her long and hard, as if suspicious of her meaning. Then finally he gave a sharp nod. "Yer welcome."

A tiny smile curved her lips, the first such gesture since this whole abduction fiasco began. Heavens, but it felt good. "I can set that break for you after supper, if you like," she said.

The old man's gaze jumped to her watchdog, who was in line behind her, before finding its way back to her. "Thank ya kindly, ma'am, but I reckon it'll heal up good enough for an old coot like me."

"Oh, but I don't mi—"

"The man said no, Doc." Carver emphasized his words with a shove to her backside—one that pinched as well as pushed.

Josephine yelped and nearly dropped her plate in the dirt as she lurched forward. Red-hot anger scorched her throat. She spun around to face him. Her arm twitched with the need to slap his face for such wretched presumption, but awareness of her surroundings kept her in check. Barely.

His eyes flashed with laughter. He knew the war raging inside her. He smirked, his dark gaze daring her to strike him.

Any excuse, he'd said. Any excuse to make Charlie pay the price.

Josephine forced the tension in her arm to relax. "I'll thank you to keep your hands to yourself, Mr. Carver." She dressed him down in her best schoolmarm voice.

Titters broke out among the men. Which was unfortunate, for Mr. Carver didn't appreciate laughter being aimed in his direction.

He grabbed her arm and jerked her against him so hard that her dinner plate fell to the ground, splattering her skirt hem with stew as she stumbled into his chest.

"I'll put my hands wherever I want, Doc, and there ain't *nothin'* you can do about it."

"Hey!" Charlie lurched forward. His chains rattled as he tried to get to her, but his iron leash pulled him up short. "Leave her alone!"

The stone-faced guard refused to comply, of course. "Who's gonna make me, rich boy? You?"

Charlie glared at Carver but kept his mouth shut. The first wise thing he'd managed to do since they'd arrived.

Josephine wedged her hands between her torso and Carver's chest and pushed, surprised when he actually let her go. Not that any sort of latent decency had erupted within his conscience. It was the approaching black-clad outlaw who had no doubt inspired her release.

Once she was free, Josephine took two steps away from Carver and straightened her clothing. The gray-haired cook retrieved her plate from the ground, scraped off the remainder of the splattered stew, and wiped it with a towel. He then ladled up a fresh portion and handed it to her. He never said a word, but the quiet act of kindness bolstered her spirits and her courage.

"You all right, Jo?" her brother asked.

She held her head high and nodded. "Don't worry, Charlie," she said as her gaze zeroed in on the man in black. "The balance of power will change when the cavalry arrives."

"What's that you say?" Taggart asked, his arrogant voice grating across her nerves. "Something about the cavalry? Surely you don't expect them to sweep in and save the day."

Josephine stiffened her spine and faced the gang's leader. "Have no doubt. The cavalry *is* coming."

"I don't think so." He bypassed the three men still in line at the chuck wagon and held his plate out to the cook. "The cavalry's not much of a cavalry without horses. Besides, I shot the captain, if you'll recall. He won't be riding to anyone's rescue."

Josephine refused to flinch even when the dagger of his words sliced into her like a scalpel. "You don't know Matthew Hanger."

He'd survived the battlefield for more than a decade. He could survive an outlaw's ambush. She believed in him. Believed in a God who could save men from lions, fiery furnaces, and giants.

Taggart just shrugged in the face of her faith. "Bullets tend to slow men down, darlin'. Even cavalry officers. If he's not dead already, he soon will be."

Josephine lifted her chin. She'd believe Matthew alive until empirical evidence disproved her hypothesis. "Have no doubt, Mr. Taggart. The cavalry *will* arrive. Hanger's Horsemen never fail."

He shook his head and clicked his tongue in condescension. "They've failed already, Miss Burkett. Or have you forgotten where you are?"

With indignation burning in her chest along with a fierce need to champion the man she loved, she took a step forward and challenged the cad. "Where *I* am is of less importance than where *they* are. They're on your trail, Taggart. And they won't stop until they take you down."

"If you don't stop, Captain, I'm gonna take you down myself." Preach planted himself in Matt's path and glared as if *he* were the commanding officer.

"Step aside, Corporal." They needed horses, and he didn't have the strength to traipse all over San Antonio searching for another livery that might have a night staff. If terrorizing a stable boy was what it took to get him a horse, he'd bellow and threaten until the kid either started bawling or fetched the owner.

Preach, however, disregarded his order. He just stood there, arms folded, legs braced. "This isn't you, Cap," he murmured. "It isn't *us*."

Wallace sidled past the two of them and started smoothing things over with the kid with wide eyes and a stubborn chin who barred their entrance to the livery. A kid Matt had dressed down as if he were a disobedient trooper under his command instead of a child probably no older than twelve or thirteen. One under orders by his boss not to bother him at home unless the place was either on fire or set upon by thieves.

Since Matt wasn't so far gone as to commit actual crimes, that left them at a stalemate, one he'd tried to win through bullying.

Forgive me.

Matt blew out a breath and squinted against the pounding in his head and the agony in his side. He'd thought the pain would improve after Preach's doctoring, but it hadn't. The wound throbbed. Constantly. That, combined with his worry for Josie, had worn his patience thin and his temper thinner.

"Burkett won't be traveling anywhere tonight." The edge of challenge disappeared from Preach's voice. "It's not safe for the horses. He knows that."

And so do you.

Preach didn't actually say the words, but Matt heard them anyway. He *did* know better. He'd let the fear of missing his window with Josie's father drive common sense and common courtesy straight out of him.

"We'll grab a few winks," Preach continued, "get up with the sun, and set out first thing in the morning. Brooks can scout out the livery that opens the earliest, Wallace can ferret out directions to Gringolet Farms, and you can see a doctor for proper treatment."

The kid perked up at the name of the horse farm. "Yer goin' to Gringolet?"

Matt turned to the stable boy. "That's right. You know it?"

The lad still looked wary, but his chin bobbed in a small nod. "My brother got a job there. Said they have the best horseflesh in the West. He gets to bunk with the hands and help the trainers. Mr. Burkett even lets him ride some, since he's so light. He ain't much bigger than me even though he's four years older."

"We're friends of Mr. Burkett's daughter, Josephine." Matt relaxed his stance and carefully modulated his voice.

The boy's eyes widened. "The lady doc?"

"Yep. She's in trouble. That's why we're in such a hurry to get to Gringolet Farms. We've got to talk to her pa."

Wallace placed a hand on the boy's shoulder. "Do you know how to get there?"

"I can do you one better." The boy stood tall. "I can take you the back way. Shave a good twenty minutes off yer travel time."

"I'd be in your debt," Matt said, humbled by the kid's generosity, especially after the way Matt had snapped at him earlier. "And I owe you an apology. I never should've barked at you like I did. I'm sorry."

The kid nodded. "Thaddeus Burkett is a good man. He gave my brother a job with a man's salary after my pa passed on. Don't know how we woulda made it through that first winter without those wages. If Mr. Burkett's girl needs help, I'm helpin'." He looked Matt straight in the eyes, as man-to-man as he could manage while standing a foot shorter. "Meet me at sunup at the livery next to the river, just past the footbridge on Houston. James Portman opens the earliest. He'll get you horses, and I'll lead you to Gringolet."

Matt extended his hand to the boy. The kid hesitated, then clasped Matt's palm with a firm grip.

"What's your name, son?" Matt asked.

"John Spafford."

"Matthew Hanger. How'd you like to be an honorary Horseman?"

The boy's jaw came a tad unhinged for a moment before his arm pumped up and down as he tried to separate Matt's arm from his shoulder. "Yes, sir!"

Matt grinned. John's big brother wouldn't be the only one with bragging rights in the Spafford family after this.

His smile dimmed as they left the livery and his gaze

turned to the inky sky above. Josie was out there somewhere with only her worthless brother as protection against a camp full of undisciplined outlaws. Matt's jaw clenched against the panic rising within him, and with a touch of desperation, he sought the darkened heavens for help. His gaze locked onto the brightest star he could find.

Get her safely through the night, Lord.

For a soldier trained against surrender, he sure was doing it a lot today. Forfeiting control to an almighty God should be easier than giving in to a gang of outlaws, yet he still struggled. He wanted to trust, but he'd lost loved ones before, and the little boy inside the man was terrified that history would repeat itself.

TWENTY-SEVEN

Dawn's glow gently penetrated Josephine's eyelids, stirring her from the exhausted stupor she'd fallen into sometime after midnight. She tried to stretch out of the cramped ball shape she lay in, but her shoes thunked against the bed's wooden footboard. No. Not a footboard. A tailgate. Her eyes cracked open. The tan canvas cover of the chuck wagon glowed with early morning light.

A smile curled her lips as she carefully negotiated her way into a hunched sitting position. She'd made it through the night unscathed. Well, her back ached and she had a terrible crick in her neck—she wouldn't recommend half-filled flour sacks as a mattress substitute any time soon—but her dignity and purity were intact, and those mattered so much more than physical comfort.

Praise and thanksgiving poured out of her soul to her heavenly Protector like floodwater through a spillway. She needed to thank her earthly protectors, as well. Two noble knights in tarnished armor. Rolling forward, she tucked her legs beneath her and crawled to the back of the small wagon, then reached an arm over the tailgate to release the latch.

She lowered the tailgate slowly, but the creaking wood jolted Charlie awake from where he slept beneath it. His head jerked up, and one bleary eye pried itself open.

"Jo? You all right?"

She smiled, and all lingering frustration toward him melted out of her heart. His tousled hair and red eyes circled with dark smudges announced that he'd slept very little during the course of the night. He'd guarded her well. And perhaps even grown up a bit in the process, if the serious cast to his features was an accurate indication.

"I'm fine. A bit sore, but a little walk to the bushes will work out the kinks." She sat on the edge of the wagon bed and swung her legs over the side.

"I'll keep watch." Charlie scrambled to his feet and offered her his hand—the one not chained to the chuck wagon wheel.

After dinner, Taggart had corralled Carver and Dawson and taken them back to the farmhouse. Those two seemed to be his right-hand men, so they had probably secluded themselves to go over their ransom scheme and search for weaknesses in need of shoring up. Taggart's display of confidence in Matthew's inability to threaten his plans hadn't been as impervious as he would have his men believe. Josephine liked to think her insistence that the Horsemen *would* come had planted enough seeds of doubt to rattle him into regrouping. After all, Matthew and his Horsemen had outmaneuvered Taggart's gang once before. They could do so again. Taggart would be a fool not to organize a few contingencies.

Not that she wanted him to make the situation more

difficult for the Horsemen when they arrived, but having
her guard dog temporarily reassigned meant a reprieve from
his constant harassment and lewd taunting. A reprieve that
gave her the chance to shore up her courage and re-starch
her spine as she faced a new day in the outlaw camp.

As Josephine fit her hand into her brother's palm, she
squeezed tight. He really did love her. His sleepless vigil last
night proved it. She had no doubt that he would have fought
tooth and nail to protect her virtue had anyone approached
the wagon. His self-indulgent nature and lack of maturity
might have led him down a terrible path, but the remorse
shining in his bloodshot eyes told her the wisdom that could
only be gained through failure had started to take hold.

"Thank you for watching over me last night," she said as
she gained her feet.

"It's my fault you're in this mess. I never thought . . ."
Charlie hung his head and let the rest of the excuse fall away
unspoken. When he lifted his face again, moisture glistened
in his eyes. "I was a selfish fool. Angry at Father for cutting
me off, for not letting me be the man I wanted to be instead
of one made in his image. I got so caught up in demanding
what I thought was mine by right that I blinded myself to
everything else. Taggart's true motives. The consequences
to you and to the men willing to risk their lives to rescue
me." He blew out a breath. "I was so determined to prove
myself my own man. Yet the man I proved myself to be was
a worthless scoundrel who willingly endangered an innocent
woman—my own kin, no less—for his own gain." He looked
her in the eye. "I'm sorry, sis. So sorry."

"I know." She held tight to his hand when he tried to pull
away. "You can't undo the past, but you can learn from it."
She wouldn't sweep his mistakes under the rug any longer,

but neither would she rub his nose in them. "I believe in you, Charlie. I believe that you can be the man God designed you to be. A man of honor and integrity. You've got a good heart," she said, tapping a fingertip against his chest. "It's just a little rusty, is all. Give it a good scrubbing, scrape away the corrosion, and infuse it with a purpose higher than itself. It will shine again."

He stared at the charred remains of last night's fire, his throat working up and down. He said nothing, just fought the emotions brought to the surface by too little sleep and too many regrets. Josephine patted his chest, then let her hand fall away. She wouldn't press him for promises he wasn't ready to make. This was a battle he had to fight in his own way and in his own time.

Show him the right path, Lord, and give him the courage to follow it.

A tug on her own heart drew her attention. Perhaps it was time to consider moving her medical practice closer to home. The thought jarred her. Immediate disagreement rose to combat the unsolicited idea. She'd worked hard to establish her practice in Purgatory Springs. Had battled prejudice and earned respect. She had relationships there. Patients who needed her.

Her heart twinged again. Charlie needed her too. Not to nurse him to physical health, but to aid in his spiritual recovery. Who else would lend him faith when his ran in short supply? Or build him up when others tore him down? Josephine shuddered to think what their father might say or do after this fiasco. Charlie was going to need someone on his side, and words penned in an occasional letter would not be sufficient. He needed the touch of a hand, a sisterly embrace, and maybe the occasional swat upside the head to get him back on track.

If she neglected Charlie in order to pursue her career, how was that any less selfish than her brother pursuing personal gain at the cost of her safety?

It wasn't.

The truth settled into her soul. *For what shall it profit a man, if he shall gain the whole world, and lose his own soul?* She doubted there'd be much profit for a woman either, who gained her career while her brother lost his soul.

Perhaps Charlie wasn't the only one with lessons to learn this day.

The muted clang of metal on metal drew her out of her cogitations. Arnold Watson, the camp cook, had lost his grip on the striker while he dozed against the back wheel of the chuck wagon, causing it to clatter against the triangular dinner bell in his lap. He snorted his way out of a snore and came awake with a start. In a flash, he had the dinner bell in hand and the striker poised to sound an alarm.

The dear man had not only emptied his wagon of supplies and insisted she sleep in the one place that could ensure her a modicum of privacy, but he'd joined Charlie in standing guard, threatening to raise a clatter fit for a stampede should any man attempt to accost her. Taggart, apparently, hated having his sleep disturbed, so even though the cook would be blamed for raising the racket, whoever instigated the incident would likely share in the punishment. A fact that had proved a sufficient deterrent. Yet what truly moved her was that Mr. Watson had been willing to endure whatever atrocities Taggart meted out in order to keep her safe.

"Miz Burkett? That you?" The cook squinted in her direction, his bushy gray eyebrows nearly hiding his eyes.

"Yes, Mr. Watson. All is well." She gave Charlie's hand one final squeeze, then walked over to her second champion, who was struggling to his feet. She clasped his elbow in a steadying grip. "I can't thank you enough for your kindness. You and Charlie are true heroes for watching over me with such vigilance."

"Ain't nothin' heroic 'bout me, ma'am."

"I beg to differ. You guarded me as well as any knight of old. Even though I'm a perfect stranger to you. You're a man of character, Mr. Watson."

He shook his head slightly, unable to accept her praise. "My character's as poor as my eyesight. It's just . . . well, ya remind me of someone." He turned his back on her and busied himself with repacking his supplies.

"Who?" Josephine prodded as she reached for a canister of salt.

He stilled, a bag of beans cradled in his arms. "Agatha," he murmured. "My wife." His eyes took on a faraway look. "She'd be plumb ashamed of me, degenerate beggar that I am." He lifted his chin. "I used to run an inn. Had four rooms. Provided simple, hearty fare. Agatha kept the rooms tidy. I saw to the vittles. We weren't rich, but we got by well enough. Until she got sick." His chin dropped, and he kicked at the nearby wagon wheel. "Consumption. Took a year to kill her. Nearly killed me too, watching her waste away. Maybe it did. Killed the good parts, at least. I was nothin' but a hollowed-out wreck after she died. Turned to drinkin'. Gamblin'. Anything to dull the pain. Only the pain got worse. Lost the inn. Lost my friends. My faith. Ran up such a big debt that when Taggart offered to buy me out in exchange for cookin' for his men, I didn't even blink. Figured if I died while running with the gang, the pain would be done."

He finally met her gaze. "When you thanked me fer the meal last night, it brought it all back. My inn. Fillin' the bellies of decent folks. Bein' the man I used to be. I never thought I'd feel that way again. Like I mattered.

"I ain't no hero, ma'am, but if Agatha had been the one to live instead of me, and she found herself a prisoner among these hooligans, I'd have wanted someone to watch out fer her."

Josephine blinked away the sheen of moisture that had gathered behind her eyelids, then touched the cook's arm. "When this is all over, come to Gringolet Farms near San Antonio. Ask for me. There'll be a job waiting for you there."

He shook his head and turned back to his supplies, muttering under his breath about softhearted fillies being too kind for their own good. He sidestepped the displaced chuck box, grabbed the large coffeepot, and headed to the water barrel attached to the opposite side of the wagon.

Perhaps he would change his mind. She prayed he would.

"You ready for that walk?" Charlie brushed her shoulder with his hand.

Josephine nodded. Privacy for a woman in an outlaw camp was a precious commodity. She'd never been one to appreciate sleeping outdoors, anyway. Riding, yes. Sleeping? Give her a roof and four solid walls, please. Not to mention wooden floors and sealed windows to keep out the creepy-crawly visitors that roamed free in the wild.

Nevertheless, the collection of bushes southeast of the house had become her sanctuary over the last fifteen hours. She didn't get to visit often, but the moment she slipped behind the thick juniper, it was as if she stepped into a secret passageway in an old castle, where a hinged bookcase closed behind her and shielded her from the oppressive weight of a dozen outlaws' eyes.

She could breathe for those precious minutes. Think of something besides wicked men and what they might be plotting. Tend to ordinary needs and rest her mind. Even medical school hadn't taxed her mental stamina as much as constantly being on guard against Carver, Taggart, and the rest of the drunken horde.

"Here, I filled this with fresh water while you were talking with Cookie." Charlie extracted a silver flask from a pocket inside his coat and handed it to her. Then he dug in his trouser pocket for his handkerchief. "It's mostly clean." There was the charmer's grin she remembered.

Josephine accepted his offerings and the thoughtfulness behind them. "Thank you." She touched his shoulder. He met her gaze, his eyes steeled with a determination that promised to atone for past mistakes. After a charged moment, she nodded, then dropped her hand from his shoulder and headed for the bushes.

As she strolled away from the heart of the camp, Josephine circled her neck and shoulders to work out the soreness accumulated from her cramped sleeping space. A touch of pink lingered in the sky, bringing a smile to her face. Didn't the Bible promise that God's mercies were new every morning? She prayed his mercies would prove bountiful today. Mercies that allowed Matthew to be alive and not irreparably injured. Mercies that would bring swift justice upon their enemies. Mercies that would protect her and Charlie from those who wished them harm.

The juniper bushes might have been only a couple dozen yards away from the cookfire, but the moment those bushes separated her from the rest of the camp, a weight slid off her back—the weight of protecting Charlie, of protecting herself. She inhaled deeply, then exhaled in a long, slow release. Her eyes slid closed, and she concentrated on letting go of the tension in her neck, her arms, back, and legs.

She counted to ten, then opened her eyes and drank in the last bit of pink as it faded from the early morning sky. An unformed plea flew heavenward with her gaze before she turned her attention to more mundane matters.

After taking care of her most urgent need, she unbuttoned the top few buttons of her shirtwaist, dampened Charlie's handkerchief, and set to work refreshing her face and neck. Closing her eyes again, she imagined her bathing tub at home filled with warm water. A bar of rose-scented soap nearby. Oh, what she wouldn't give for her toothbrush. She lifted the flask to her lips and swished a mouthful of water. Not that it made a significant dent in the state of her overall oral cleanliness, but it helped.

Bending her neck forward, she ran the damp cloth over her nape. Maybe they'd let her have her bag today. Let her brush out her hair. How glorious that would feel—

"Where is she?"

The sharp demand brought Josephine's head up with a start. Carver! Her eyes flew open, and her hands automatically clutched at the buttons of her open bodice.

"She's tending to personal matt—*oof!*"

The *thud* of what had to be a fist on flesh cut off Charlie's words.

"No one recalls seeing her last night. Not in the barn."

A grunt interrupted the speech.

"Not in the yard."

Another grunt.

Josephine fumbled with her buttons, her trembling fingers refusing to cooperate.

"If you helped her escape, I'll kill you."

Abandoning the buttons, Josephine rounded the bushes and sprinted back to the chuck wagon, where Carver held Charlie by his shirtfront. Charlie's lip was bleeding, and Carver's fist was raised for another strike.

"Stop!" she cried. "I'm here. I'm here."

"Well, so you are." Carver glanced her way, then set his jaw and pounded Charlie's face hard enough to send him sprawling into the dirt.

Josephine flinched, but she didn't move to help her brother. Charlie wouldn't thank her for babying him in front of Carver, and her smirking guard looked as if he'd take any softness on her part as an excuse to continue the punishment.

"You weren't where I expected you to be, Doc." He turned to face her, his eyes deliberately lingering on the undone buttons at her throat.

Despite the fact that her modesty was completely protected—women showed more skin at country dances than was currently exposed on her person—his gaze left her feeling dirty. Which was surely his intent. As much as she longed to clutch the edges of her collar together to hide herself from his view, she refused to let him shame her when he was the shameful one.

So she kept her hands at her sides and lifted her chin. "Your expectations are not my concern, Mr. Carver."

His smug grin deteriorated into a scowl. "They should be. Unless you don't care if little Charlie loses all his teeth."

She heard her brother rise, heard him spit what she hoped was only blood and saliva and not a tooth onto the dirt. She stared at Carver, letting her disdain radiate without words.

They faced off for a long minute, neither blinking, until finally Carver lurched forward to grab her arm. He started dragging her toward the house, demolishing her momentary sense of victory in their battle of wills.

"Taggart wants to see you," he growled.

This early in the morning? Josephine grimaced. That didn't bode well.

TWENTY-EIGHT

Carver flung Josephine through the open farmhouse door, then released her long enough to shut the door behind them. She stumbled into a narrow hall and had to brace a hand against the wall to keep from falling. Taking advantage of the brief separation from her captor, she scuttled a few steps down the hall, doing up the buttons of her shirtwaist as she went. A much easier task with two hands. Facing Taggart with confidence was hard enough without a set of undone buttons tormenting one's mind. Carver's leering gaze earlier had made her feel as if she were flashing her garters, not a prim trio of buttonholes.

She'd just finished pushing the last button through its loop when Carver clasped her elbow and drove her down the remainder of the hall and into the kitchen.

Apparently undone buttons would be tormenting her after all. Just not hers.

Taggart stood waiting for her, leaning against the dry sink, shirt untucked and unfastened, hair damp as if he'd just washed up. His torso was well-muscled and tanned from the sun, but it didn't maintain her interest. She'd seen better. And on a man who possessed the decency to be embarrassed by his accidental display. Taggart's blatant flaunting was obviously intended to unsettle her. Either as a distraction for a maiden's delicate sensibilities or an attempt to stir a woman's desire. Neither would be forthcoming on her part.

She focused on his smug features and gave the rest of him no more than a flick of a glance. "You wanted to see me?"

He nodded toward the rectangular table to her left. "Sit down, Miss Burkett. You're going to write a letter for me."

"You know," she said as she moved toward the table, where a sheet of paper, a pen, and an inkwell waited, "if you had stayed in school instead of turning to a life of crime, you'd be able to write your own letters."

"Carver." Taggart's tight voice filled the room a heartbeat before a knife sailed past her shoulder to lodge in the tabletop two inches from the edge of the paper.

Josephine sucked in a breath and yanked her arms up against her chest as she watched the hilt vacillate back and forth. The vibrations of the metal blade pulsed inside her head.

Taggart came up behind her. "I've had enough of your sharp tongue."

Josephine swallowed, trying to keep her flapping heart from flying out of her chest.

"Sit down and write exactly what I tell you. Verbatim." His hands clamped onto her shoulders, and he forced her into the chair. "Which, in case you doubt my literacy, is spelled V-E-R-B-A-T-U-M."

Josephine nodded and reached a shaky hand toward the pen, her gaze darting to the blade embedded in the table. She knew how to deal with bullies in academic and professional circles, but wit and bravado had taken her about as far as they were going to with Taggart.

He was on edge. She tried to be encouraged by the notion that he was worried about retaliation from the Horsemen, but it was hard to hold that positive thought in her mind with an eight-inch bowie knife impaling the table beside her hand.

She inked the nib of her pen, then held it above the paper. "I'm ready."

"Your mounts are ready, Captain."

Doing his best to hide his impatience, Matt nodded to James Portman. The Horsemen had been waiting at the livery since sunup. Portman hadn't shown until after seven o'clock. Plenty early for normal business, but forty minutes late by Matt's schedule.

Preach settled the bill while the rest of the Horsemen mounted. It felt odd not to have any gear. Their young guide, John Spafford, was better prepared for their journey than the Horsemen were. He, at least, had a canteen and a .22 caliber youth rifle in his scabbard. Matt felt naked without his guns. He missed the weight of the pistols on his hips. The security of having his repeater within easy reach. Their absence made his skin itch.

Preach swung a leg over a big roan that looked more like a plow horse than a cow pony, but Matt kept his opinion on the horseflesh to himself. Portman had given them the best of his available stock. Solid mounts with deep chests and muscular legs. Shod well, no swaybacks. They wouldn't win any races, but they'd get them to Gringolet.

Matt patted his sorrel's neck, wishing he had Phineas beneath him. He sent a brief prayer heavenward that his gelding was being treated well by Taggart's men, then clicked his tongue and steered his sorrel alongside Wallace, giving a nod to Jonah on the far side. He caught Preach reaching to adjust his non-existent gun belt after he settled into the saddle and shared a look with his second-in-command. None of them were comfortable with the situation, but they'd make do. That was what soldiers did.

"Got a verse for us, Preach?" The familiar question brought some level of normalcy to the start of the mission as the four men drew their horses together behind young Spafford.

"'With him is an arm of flesh; but with us is the Lord our God to help us, and to fight our battles.' Second Chronicles 32:8."

"Amen," Wallace said softly.

Matt held his mount in check for a long moment, letting the words sink into his heart and strengthen his spirit. God's warriors had been outnumbered and outmatched before, and that hadn't stopped them from facing their enemies and emerging victorious. If Gideon could defeat the Midianites with nothing but horns, broken jars, and God, then the Horsemen could trust the Almighty to have their backs as well.

Setting his jaw, Matt leaned forward in his saddle and signaled their guide. "On to Gringolet, John. Fast as you can."

John proved to be an accomplished rider for a youngster. He set a quick pace and carried himself with the confidence of one accustomed to the route. When he veered off the road to a slightly overgrown path, however, Matt called a halt.

John turned in his saddle, his forehead scrunched. "This

is the shortcut I told ya about, Captain Hanger. It'll save us a good twenty minutes."

"I know, son, but there's a chance that Burkett might have already left the ranch. If so, we risk missing him by leaving the road." Matt nodded to his trumpeter. "Wallace, you're the lightest in the saddle and have one of the better horses."

"And you're the one most likely to smooth-talk your way into Burkett's confidence should you meet up on the road," Preach added.

Wallace fingered a small salute. "They won't get past me, Captain."

"I'll ride with him, boss." Jonah tipped the brim of his hat back a couple inches. "A man alone with no weapons could be an easy target."

Brooks didn't mention Wallace's injury, but they all knew it would complicate things should trouble arise. Matt would have assigned Jonah the duty, but a black man traveling alone was just as tempting a target. More so to some. His first thought had been to keep as many Horsemen on the short road as possible, but waiting for one was no different than waiting for two. And Brooks was right. Traveling in pairs was safer, even if the odds of coming across trouble this early in the morning were slim. As his uncle liked to say, an ounce of prevention was worth a pound of cure.

"Good idea, Sergeant." Matt gave a decisive nod. "Watch each other's backs."

"Will do." Jonah reined his mount around and, in a blink, he and Wallace were cantering down the road.

Matt turned back to John. "Lead on, young man." He winked. "And make sure we beat them there."

John grinned. "Yes, sir!"

The kid nudged his mare into an easy lope. Matt and Preach

followed. Despite being overgrown with spring grasses, the ground was hard-packed and easily traveled, free of prairie dog holes and rocky soil that could bring a horse up lame.

They made good time, thanks to their able guide, who seemed to know the path's location even when it disappeared from sight.

Finally, John reined in his mare at the top of a rise and pointed down into a lush valley. "There she is, Captain Hanger. Gringolet."

Large paddocks ran the length of the valley, filled with horses bred for courage, stamina, and speed. A dark bay raced the length of a fence while Matt watched, his stride graceful, his black mane flowing, his head stretched forward as if nothing would stop him from reaching his goal. Matt's breath caught at the sheer beauty of it.

Then another movement drew his gaze. Three, maybe four men in front of a barn. Tacking up their mounts. Prepping supplies. Readying for a journey.

One of the knots in Matt's gut unraveled. They hadn't missed them. Thank the Lord.

A man stood in the center of the commotion. Tall. Commanding. The bark of his voice carried to the top of the rise.

Thaddeus Burkett.

He wouldn't welcome the interference of strangers, but Matt didn't care. Josie was in danger, and her father needed the knowledge the Horsemen possessed about Taggart's gang. And Matt needed the location of the ransom. Whether Burkett liked it or not, he'd just gotten himself a partner.

"Let's go." Not waiting for their young guide to lead the way, Matt touched his heels to his mount's flanks and set off down the hill.

It didn't take long for the men below to notice his approach. Shouts arose, rifles took aim, and a warning shot echoed above Matt's head.

Matt reined in his mount, turning the gelding in a circle to ease his sudden halt. "Hold your fire," he called. "I've got a kid with me. John Spafford."

"Johnny?" One of the men lowered his rifle, exposing his youthful face as he gazed up the hill.

"It's me, Nick. Don't shoot." John's horse pulled up alongside Matt's. Luke flanked the kid on the far side. "These fellas are here to help, Mr. Burkett. They know Dr. Jo."

Thaddeus Burkett yanked his rifle from his shoulder but kept it gripped and ready in front of him as he marched forward. Matt dismounted to meet him on equal footing.

"Keep your hands where I can see 'em," Burkett ordered, pointing his rifle barrel at Matt's midsection.

Matt showed his palms. "I'm unarmed."

Burkett advanced until he stood barely three feet away, his glower fierce. He took Matt's measure, his gaze widening as he noticed his vest. "You a cavalryman?"

"Was, until a couple years ago. Served thirteen years with the 7th."

Burkett's eyes widened. "One of Custer's men?"

Matt shook his head. "Joined up after Little Bighorn." He tipped his head in Preach's direction. "This is my corporal, Luke Davenport. I'm Matt Hanger. I've got two more men on their way via the road. We wanted to make sure we didn't miss you."

Burkett straightened a bit at hearing Matt's name. He recognized it but wasn't overly impressed. Matt wouldn't expect him to be. Newspaper articles sensationalized the Horsemen. A soldier who had seen battle judged a man on his deeds, not the rumors surrounding him.

When he finished raking Matt with his gaze, Burkett turned his critical eye to the animal he'd ridden in on. Matt could feel the judgment. Any cavalry officer worth his salt would have a better horse beneath him.

Burkett's weathered face showed his distaste. "Livery nags?"

Matt nodded. "Yep. Best we could manage after Taggart relieved us of our mounts."

Burkett turned his face and spat on the ground. "I got no use for cavalrymen who'd forfeit their horses to outlaw scum to save their hides."

Matt held his ground. "It wasn't *our* hides we were saving." He waited until Burkett's gaze met his, his green eyes a shade darker than Josie's. "Your daughter's life meant more to me than keeping my horse."

Thaddeus exploded. He lunged at Matt, thankfully swinging his fist and not his rifle butt. Matt blocked the punch with his forearm but took no offensive action.

"My Jo was under your protection, and you let that monster take her?" Burkett accused as one of his men moved to pull him away. "What kind of soldier *are* you?"

Matt understood his anger, his fear, and cast no blame. How could he, when he pummeled himself with the same indictments?

"The kind who will give his life to get her back."

TWENTY-NINE

Preach dismounted and stood at Matt's side, fists clenched, stance wide, ready to even the odds should things escalate, but Burkett deflated before their eyes. He shrugged away from the man who'd grabbed him and handed over his rifle. Probably to remove the temptation of shooting the man who'd failed to keep his daughter from harm. Then he blew out a breath and rubbed a hand over his face.

"Tell me everything. From the beginning."

"You'd best not be plying these men for information without me, Thaddeus Burkett." A small woman, slightly plump, wove around horses and men as if they were no more an impediment than stones were to a free-flowing stream.

Skirts twitching, she marched up to Burkett and planted herself at his side. Her brown eyes sparked as she jammed a hand onto one hip. Suddenly, Matt knew exactly where Josie had gotten her spunk and sass.

"I love those children like they were my own. I will not be excluded. Especially when—" Her voice cracked, but she swallowed and lifted her chin. "Especially when it's my fault our Jo is in this mess. If I hadn't sent that letter . . ."

"Hush, now, Darla. It ain't your fault." Burkett yanked his hat from his head and beat it against his leg a couple times, his face softening. "I should have just paid that stupid ransom the first time. If anyone's to blame, it's me."

She shook her head as he crammed his hat back on and turned away to start pacing. "You did what you thought was right, Thaddeus."

He spun around, his face tight with self-recrimination. "Well, my thinking was wrong, wasn't it? And Jo's paying the price."

Darla—the housekeeper, if Matt remembered correctly from the letter Josie had shown him—moved to Burkett's side and slipped her arm through his. "Casting blame's not gonna help Jo. But if what I heard young Johnny announce when he rode in is true, these men can. Let's hear them out. Together." She looked up at Matt, then shifted her gaze to include Preach. "Come on up to the house, fellas. I've got coffee on."

"We don't got time for coffee," Burkett protested. "Jo's out there—"

"Where, exactly?" Darla's tone sharpened. "Do you know where she is right now, Thaddeus?"

Burkett had a good dozen inches on the little woman, but he was the one looking intimidated. There were definitely more feelings at play with these two than mere respect between employer and employee.

Burkett straightened. "I know where she's gonna be."

"Tomorrow," Darla qualified. "You know where she's going to be tomorrow at three in the afternoon. You have no earthly idea where she is right now. You can afford thirty minutes to hear these men out." She pulled her arm from his and turned to lead the way to the house. "You might even learn something."

A path opened for her as men hopped out of her way.

"Aggravatin' woman." Burkett mumbled the complaint under his breath, but it carried no heat. In fact, were Matt a betting man, he'd lay odds there was affection lacing the remark.

Burkett shot a glare at Matt. "Come on, then."

No affection in that statement. Just iron and grit.

Matt stepped forward in compliance, opting to save his words for what was to come. It would be a tale as hard to hear as to tell.

"Albert. Eddie." Burkett waved at the two older hands. "Y'all come too. Best you know what you're gettin' yourselves into."

The men returned their rifles to the boots on their saddles and made to follow their boss.

Burkett pivoted so that he walked backward, gesturing to Nick. "Spafford boys, give those rented nags some water and rub them down. Johnny can take 'em back to town with him when we're done here. Saddle four of the three-year-olds for these fellas to ride. I ain't about to be slowed down by substandard horseflesh."

Nick moved to take the reins of Preach's mount. "Yes, sir."

Preach shot a half-grin at Matt. "I always wanted to ride a Gringolet mount."

Burkett sidled close to Luke, nearly matching him in height if not in breadth. "Fail to prove yourself worthy of the horse you ride, and you'll be the one put out to pasture when this is over."

The murmured threat only widened Preach's smile. He

elbowed Matt in the side. "I like him. You could do worse for an in-law."

Burkett reared back, his shocked expression quickly hardening to something much more sinister.

Matt bit back a groan. Preach was gonna pay for that. Not that his friend cared. His eyes danced with so much laughter, it was a miracle they stayed in his head.

"One battle at a time," Matt said through a tight jaw, lengthening his stride as if he could outrun the fuse Preach had just lit. "Let's focus on getting Josie back first and deal with the rest later."

"Her name is *Dr. Burkett* to you, soldier." Josie's father's voice rumbled like a thundercloud ready to fling lightning at the mere mortal who dared speak of his daughter in familiar terms.

They didn't have time for this.

Matt spun to face the older man. "Look. My intentions toward your daughter are honorable. That's all you need to know at this point. If you want to come after me with tar and feathers later, fine, but right now there are bigger threats at play."

Before Burkett could reply, Matt swiveled forward and marched up the steps to the house's back porch, where Darla stood grinning at him as she held the door wide. She and Preach could start up a hoedown with all the humor frolicking around on their faces. Making a point to avoid the housekeeper's eyes, Matt set his jaw and strode into the kitchen.

It took only moments for the men to gather around the kitchen table. Burkett sat at the head with his hands flanking him on either side. Matt took a chair at the opposite end, and Preach settled in beside him, leaving a place open for the housekeeper, should she decide to join them after she finished pouring coffee for everyone.

Burkett ignored his freshly filled cup. He planted his forearms on the table, leaned in, and glared straight at Matt. "Darla told me about the letter she wrote to Josephine. Why don't you pick up the tale there and fill in the missing pieces?"

Matt nodded and proceeded to give a bare-bones report of how Josie had tracked them down and hired the Horsemen to rescue her brother. How she'd insisted on accompanying them. How *he'd* insisted she remain out of harm's way in Chatfield while they hunted Taggart's gang. He recounted the rescue of Charlie, emphasizing the strategy they employed, the number of men Taggart had at his disposal, weaknesses they'd observed, and areas where the outlaws had proven competent adversaries. There was no need to describe the danger inherent in the mission. Burkett was a military man. He understood.

After listening intently without interruption, Burkett suddenly flattened his palm against the tabletop. "Hold up, Hanger. If the rescue was successful and Jo was safely in Chatfield, how did she come to be taken?"

Matt shared a look with Preach. How much to say?

"Out with it, man."

Still Matt hesitated, searching for a way to be truthful yet tactful.

Burkett shoved his chair away from the table, the *scrape* echoing loudly in the quiet room. "It was Charlie, wasn't it? He did something stupid." He paced away from the table, as if ashamed to face the men assembled in his kitchen. He blew out an audible breath, then slowly turned and met Matt's gaze. "Tell me. All of it."

"Best I can figure, Charlie suspected you might not pay the initial ransom, so he and Taggart came up with an alternate plan."

The starch drained out of Burkett, aging him before their eyes. He grabbed the chairback in front of him. "Are you . . ." He swallowed and tried again. "Are you telling me my son *willingly* connived with Taggart? That he intentionally put his sister in danger?"

"Charlie would never!" Darla abandoned her post by the stove and moved to Burkett's side. She placed a hand on his arm. "He might be a scamp and a troublemaker, but he'd never do anything to hurt Jo."

Preach scratched at a spot on his whiskered jaw. "A desperate man can do unthinkable things when cornered, ma'am," he said, his voice sober. "Things he'd never consider under normal circumstances."

Tears filled the housekeeper's eyes as she shook her head. "I won't believe it. You don't know him. You don't know how close those two were when they were children. After they lost their mother . . ." Her words broke off in a quiet sob.

Burkett cupped his hand over hers where it lay on his arm. "They haven't been children for years, Darla. The boy's changed. He's been on a destructive path for a while now. I tried to correct his course, but he's as hardheaded as his old man. Determined to go his own way even if the path leads to a jail cell . . . or worse." He looked up from the woman at his side. "But Darla's right about one thing. Charlie might turn his back on me, but he'd never harm Jo."

"I believe he thought he could keep her safe," Matt said, knowing it would be small comfort. Burkett knew as well as he did that once in the outlaw camp, Charlie would have zero bargaining power with Taggart. He was a means to an end—a way to ensure Taggart got his money. Nothing more.

"Fool," Burkett muttered.

"Taggart sent men by train to scout out the nearby towns and spotted us in Chatfield. We made a run for it, but our horses were spent. Taggart's were fresh. We made a stand in a shallow wash. I left Charlie to guard his sister. They both had strict orders to flee if the battle turned against us."

"Jo's never been one to follow orders blindly," Burkett observed, the hint of a sad smile playing at the corner of his mouth. "She tends to make up her own mind about things."

Matt's lips twitched upward. "I know. I made her swear to leave. She gave her word."

Burkett nodded. "Smart move. About the only way to guarantee her cooperation."

"Her cooperation wasn't enough." Matt frowned. This part of the tale still chapped his hide. "Taggart advanced under a flag of truce, and while our attention was fixed on the outlaws, Charlie held a gun on Josie and dragged her into the line of fire, using her as a shield to keep either side from firing."

Darla let out a whimper, and Burkett's expression closed down completely.

"Taggart acted as if taking Josie hostage had been part of the plan from the start. Probably figured they could get more ransom for her than for Charlie."

Burkett grimaced. "Five thousand dollars."

Preach let out a low whistle.

"I don't know how they expect me to pull that kind of money together on such short notice. I only keep about five hundred dollars in the safe here at the ranch. I planned to drag Dorchester out of church this mornin' to withdraw the rest. It'll come near to bankrupting me, but I can't risk Jo's safety. I'll sell off some of my breeding stock if need be. I've got some mares that will fetch a good price at auction. I might lose my army contracts for the next few years while we rebuild, but Gringolet's reputation will survive."

Matt didn't doubt that, nor Burkett's ability to rebuild, but it would take more than a few years if he lost his best mares. Matt shifted in his seat, his stitches pulling tight and making him check his movement. The doc they'd pulled out of bed last night hadn't been too happy about the interruption, but with Preach's encouragement, he had cleaned and closed the wound.

"I can't guarantee to get your money back," Matt said, his voice hardening, "but you should know that as soon as Josie is safe, the Horsemen will be running Taggart to ground."

Burkett raised a brow. "What percentage you askin'?"

Matt shook his head. "No finder's fee." A muscle ticked in his jaw. "This is personal."

Flashes of his last encounter with Taggart rose to torment him. The outlaw's blade against Josie's face. His arm around her waist. His taunting smirk. For a moment, the rage inside Matt ran so hot, he didn't trust himself to speak.

Preach took over the tale. "Using the lady doc as leverage, Taggart stole our horses, our weapons, and even our boots. Tied us up and left us stranded in the middle of nowhere. Then, as he rode off with your daughter in hand, he shot the captain and left him for dead."

Matt worked his jaw and forced air into his lungs, cooling the rage into ice-cold determination.

"He took the woman I love." Matt claimed Josie with a voice that brooked no argument. It was truth. One he wouldn't dance around any longer. One no one in this room could change. He glanced up at Burkett. Not even her father. "He has to pay."

Burkett met his stare, his face hard, his gaze assessing. Then he released his grip on the back of his chair, straightened, and gave a slow nod. "Eddie," he said without turning his focus away from Matt, "get these men some weapons. We've got an outlaw to hunt."

CHAPTER
THIRTY

By the time Wallace and Brooks made it to Gringolet via the main road, the Spafford boys had four new mounts saddled and ready to ride. Matt met his men by the paddock and sent them inside to collect rifles and ammunition. Then, while Preach caught them up on what had transpired with Burkett, Matt took a few minutes alone with the horses to steady his mind.

The instant he'd walked down those back porch steps and seen the four mounts standing at the ready, he'd known which horse he'd select. The dark bay he'd spotted from atop the hill. The one who'd run with such abandon. Proud. Strong. A big heart. There'd be no quit in that one.

Matt approached the gelding slowly, his hand extended, admiring how the sun caught the horse's coat, bringing out the deep gold tones nearly hidden within the blackish-brown hair. The bay tossed his head as Matt neared, yet true to his training, he held his ground. His nostrils flared, but Matt gave him time to grow accustomed to his scent while the two took stock of each other.

As if Matt had passed some equine test, the bay lowered his head and snuffled at his hand. Matt stepped closer and patted the gelding's neck.

"Good boy," he murmured softly, the moment feeling almost sacred. Just him and the horse. Everything else faded away. His surroundings. His stress. Even the strategies knocking around in his brain stilled. All that existed was the horse. Heads close together. Breathing meshing into a common rhythm. Man and horse. Horse and man.

Matt's eyes slid closed. He hadn't experienced a near-instant connection with a horse like this since Phineas. That bond had led to a decade of unparalleled partnership. He'd never expected to find that level of connection a second time, but his gut told him he had today.

"You have an eye for quality, I'll give you that much." Burkett's voice opened Matt's eyes, though he didn't turn. The older man's footfalls were softer than he'd expect from someone who'd wanted to plant his fist in Matt's face a short time ago.

Matt made no reply to Burkett's reluctant praise, just ran his hand over the horse's withers and down his shoulder. He bent to examine leg and hoof. Healthy. Well-defined muscles. Sleek, but not bulky. Bred for speed as much as strength.

"What's his name?"

The footfalls stopped. "Percival."

Matt smiled to himself. "A holy knight. Fitting."

"Percy's dam is one of my best mares. I paid a pretty penny to breed her with a stud carrying Thoroughbred blood. Turned out to be worth the expense. Percy's the best animal on the farm. I tried to buy that stud for myself, but the fella wouldn't sell. Knew I'd keep coming back for more. Which I did. The last colt he sired on one of my mares has lines nearly as good as Percy's. Didn't geld that one. I'm gonna use him as a stud of my own." Burkett's tone changed. "If I don't have to sell him."

Having a stud that could produce colts with Percival's lines would secure demand for Gringolet stock for decades to come.

Matt finally looked at Josie's father. "I'd hang on to that stud, if I were you. Mares are easier to replace." His eyes roamed back to Percival. "Producing stock with these lines will keep the army hungry for your quality even if you can't supply the desired quantity during the lean years."

"Hmm."

Matt wasn't sure what to make of that response. Burkett just stared at him as if searching for an answer to a question only he was privy to. Matt shrugged it off. He had more important puzzles to ponder.

"Where is the rendezvous point for delivering the ransom?" Matt asked as he stroked Percival's neck.

"San Geronimo Creek. Outside the town of Gallagher's Ranch."

Matt raised a brow. "The Ranch is deserted, isn't it?"

"Nearly." Burkett strolled over to one of the other mounts reserved for the Horsemen and fiddled with the tack. "I think there's still a store and a post office, but it's abandoned otherwise."

"Away from the rail lines. No law handy. Close enough for you to deliver the money even if you couldn't get to the bank until Monday morning."

"Taggart threatened to hurt Jo if he got the slightest whiff of a lawman." Burkett scowled. "Told me to deliver the ransom alone too. Which I will, but not before I scout out places to hide my men nearby. It's why I'm so anxious to get a move on. I need time to get everyone into position."

Matt sought the older man's gaze. "That'd be a good strategy if I hadn't employed the same tactic when retrieving Charlie. Taggart will be expecting a move like that."

Burkett grabbed the hat from his head and beat it against his thigh, startling the horse beside him. "What else can I do?" He rammed the hat back on his head, then took hold of the black's reins, easily getting the animal back under control with a calm hand to his nose and a steady exhalation that forced his own shoulders to relax.

Once the horse settled, Burkett stepped away and leaned against the paddock fence. "If I go in there alone, Taggart will kill me, take the money, and likely kill Jo to ensure she can't bring charges against him. Charlie too. Being his puppet is not an option."

"Agreed." Matt worked his way around to Percival's right side so he could eye Burkett over the horse's back. "We'll scout the area and get protection in place like you planned, but I have a feeling Taggart will keep Jo tightly guarded until the scheduled exchange. There'll be no opening for an early rescue. Not that I won't look for one anyway, but Taggart will be on his guard, so I don't expect to find one. The one advantage we have is that he doesn't expect the Horsemen to be there. Especially me."

Burkett tipped his head toward the house, where the other Horsemen were exiting with rifles, pistols, and ammunition belts draping them from shoulder to hip. "You sure we shouldn't leave the gimpy one here? Might be a liability with that bum arm."

Matt narrowed his eyes. "Wallace is worth more in a gunfight with one arm than most men are with two. He's coming."

"If you say so." Burkett raised a hand in surrender. "I'll take all the experience we can get. Albert and Eddie are loyal hands and fair shots, but they're not battle-tested. One can never tell how a man'll react under fire until bullets start flying. As much as I'm praying for a peaceful resolution, I have a feelin' lead is gonna be exchanged."

Matt's gut concurred. "Protecting Josie is my top concern," he said. "The money, your men, *my* men all come second. You good with that?"

"Son," Burkett said with a raise of his brow, "if your priorities were anywhere else, I wouldn't be lettin' you take lead. Now, let's quit yammerin' and get on the road."

It took about an hour to track down the banker and convince him to let Burkett withdraw the bulk of his savings. Charlie must have advised Taggart on the maximum asking price, for Burkett had only $232.17 in his account when they finished. He might make payroll once or twice before his account was completely depleted, but not much more than that. If Taggart escaped with the ransom money, Gringolet would be bankrupted. Burkett, to his credit, didn't hesitate over shoving the banknotes into his satchel, however. Just stuffed the bills deep, buckled the leather straps, and tied the bag to the back of his horse as if it contained nothing more valuable than hardtack and coffee. Matt supposed the comparison might be accurate when held up against Josephine's safety.

Nice to know they could agree on one thing, at least.

All right, two things. They definitely shared the same taste in horses. Matt bent forward and patted Percival's neck as they reached the outskirts of town, then signaled the horse with a squeeze of his knees to open into a lope. The dark bay's gait was so smooth, Matt nearly forgot about his injury altogether, something that had been impossible with the more jarring strides of the cow pony from the livery. A cavalry regiment outfitted with mounts of this quality would be unstoppable.

Thoughts of horses, breeding, and the army couldn't distract him for long, however. Matt's mind continually returned to Josie, wondering how she fared among Taggart's men. He prayed for her protection every couple miles, and when he wasn't running rescue scenarios in his head and trying to anticipate Taggart's strategy, he allowed himself a few blissful visions of what a future might look like with her by his side.

His wife.

The very idea thrilled and terrified him with equal force. He'd never thought himself a settling-down kind of man. His life had been the military, then the Horsemen. Guns and horses were all he knew. All he'd wanted to know. Until he met Josie with her ten-dollar words and her determination to make a place for herself in a man's profession. She was a fighter. But not just for herself. She fought for her patients, her family, her beliefs.

And she believed in him. There hadn't been a shadow of doubt in her eyes when she looked down at him from atop Taggart's horse. Matt had been beaten, bound, and stripped of all means to protect her. Yet when he'd brazenly claimed that he'd find her, she hadn't batted an eye.

"*I know.*"

Those two words resonated in his soul and drove him on despite the pain and the weariness that plagued him. He wouldn't let her down.

They made camp that night along Helotes Creek and set out at first light for Gallagher's Ranch. Burkett and his two hands kept to the road. Matt and the Horsemen fanned out to the west, using the trees as cover in an effort to keep their presence a secret from any of Taggart's men who might be spying out the area.

As they neared the meeting location, an uneasy feeling prickled the back of Matt's neck. It was still several hours before the designated time of the exchange, but Matt hadn't survived fifteen years in the army by ignoring his instincts.

"Brooks, find some high ground. I need a visual of what's ahead."

Jonah guided his mount to a large oak, then used the horse's back as a leg up into the tree. Their field glasses were with the rest of their stolen supplies in Taggart's camp, so the sergeant had to rely on the eyesight the Lord had given him. Thankfully, the Almighty had blessed Brooks with a double portion of that commodity, so Matt had no doubt that if there was something to see, Jonah would see it.

"Preach, watch our flank," Matt said, waving him to the west. "Wallace, signal Burkett that there might be trouble ahead."

Wallace might not have his trumpet, but his voice was as talented as his horn. He'd arranged an owl call with Burkett yesterday while on the trail, practicing until the sound carried and Burkett recognized it from a distance.

As the men spread out, Matt slid his rifle from its scabbard and laid it across his lap. Leaves rustled above his head as Jonah moved into position. Matt turned his gaze upward and watched his friend climb. He lost sight of him a time or two, but he kept his gaze glued to the tree anyway, as if his attention could somehow aid the ascent.

Fifteen minutes passed before Jonah finally made his way back down to the ground.

"What'd you see, Sergeant?" Matt demanded before Jonah even had time to mount his horse.

"There's a path veering off toward San Geronimo Creek." Jonah swung into his saddle and turned his horse so he could face Matt. "It's just ahead, after a small bend in the road. Someone planted a white flag at the junction to make sure Burkett doesn't miss it."

"Any sign of Taggart?" Matt swallowed, his heart suddenly pumping erratically. "Or Josie?"

"I couldn't make out any outlaws from my position, but a small contingent could be hidden, using the trees and brush for cover like we are. The vegetation thins the nearer you get to the road, though, and I didn't spot any buildings that could offer more substantial cover. Didn't spy any horses either, so if Taggart has men out there, it's probably a small number on foot."

Matt chewed on that piece of information, not sure if it was good news or bad. Then he noticed the hesitant lines of Jonah's face. "What is it, Sergeant?"

Jonah shifted in his saddle. "I saw something else, but it was too far away to make out clearly."

"But you're pretty sure you know what it was."

Jonah never reported something unless he was confident in his impressions. He might not have seen every detail, but he knew what was there. *Who* was there. The fact that he hesitated only made Matt's gut churn.

"Spit it out, Brooks."

Jonah met Matt's gaze. "I saw something that looked a lot like Dr. Jo. Her fancy blue jacket, at least. That black slouch hat of hers too."

Matt's pulse pounded, something Percival must have sensed, for the horse snorted and stepped sideways.

"She weren't movin', but she was upright."

What did that mean? Was she dead? Alive? Tied to a stake?

Those scenarios made no sense. How would Taggart collect his ransom if Josie was dead or tied up by the creek for her father to find? There had to be more to this that they couldn't see. But what?

"Meet up with Wallace. Have him signal Burkett to move forward with caution. Keep an eye on his back trail, making sure the outlaws aren't luring us into an ambush. I'll circle around with Preach, cross the road on the far side of the bend, and come at the creek from the north. Hopefully we'll flush any of Taggart's men who might be about."

"You know it's likely a trap, right, Captain?"

Matt tightened his jaw. "Yep. But we're going in anyway."

THIRTY-ONE

Percival vaulted across the road with such speed and grace, Matt wondered if perhaps he should have been named Pegasus instead. Unfortunately, speed and grace couldn't protect him from any spying eyes that might be looking on. Jonah hadn't spotted any of Taggart's men, but Matt's gut told him *someone* was out there. How many someones was yet to be determined.

He and Preach, guns at the ready, took cover among the pecan trees that surrounded San Geronimo Creek. When Matt caught a glimpse of blue through the trees, he stopped, signaling Preach to continue past him to protect their eastern flank.

As soon as Preach moved on, Matt craned his neck right and left, desperate to get a better view through the branches.

Josie?

He recognized the blue fabric. It was definitely her coat. Hat too. But the headgear sat at an unnatural angle. Too close to her shoulders. Too flat. Was she unconscious? Slumped over in a tied position?

Don't get ahead of yourself, soldier. Catalog the evidence.

Matt steeled his nerves and concentrated on what could be observed, not what the observations might mean.

First observation—nothing moved. Except when the wind buffeted the cloth. No arms waved. No head nodded. No feet kicked.

Feet. Matt sharpened his attention. Shouldn't he be able to see the green of Josie's skirt? All he saw was blue and the black of her hat. He supposed she could be wearing her trousers, but even then, *something* of her should be visible below the knees.

It had to be a dummy. Bait to draw them out.

Turning in his saddle, he scanned the area. *Where are you?* Taggart had to have men watching them. But from where?

The fact that gunfire hadn't erupted when he and Preach crossed the road made a full-on ambush unlikely. Which meant this was an intelligence-gathering mission, not an attack. The outlaws would need high ground with a clear view of the path.

Matt scoured the nearby treetops. Nothing.

They wouldn't be to the south. Such a position would risk exposure, with Burkett approaching from that direction. The west failed to offer a clear view to the creek. So that left north and east. East provided the most protection, with the creek serving as a buffer. North offered high ground with a small rise about a quarter mile away. A man would have to have field glasses to see anything from that distance, though.

Matt gritted his teeth as he recalled a particular pair of field glasses that had aided in Charlie Burkett's rescue. A pair Matt had selected himself for their high-quality magnification. A pair now in Taggart's possession, thanks to his theft of the Horsemen's gear. Matt scowled at the rise visible through the trees, wishing he'd left the glasses behind at that canyon and encouraged Phineas to trod them underfoot.

He squinted into the distance, then turned to estimate where the spy's gaze would likely fall. His view would be somewhat obstructed, but there were enough gaps between the trees to confirm Burkett's presence. The view would likely confirm his and Preach's presence too. Though, if they were lucky, whoever watched would only suspect them of being Gringolet hands, not Horsemen.

"Josephine!" Burkett's shout brought Matt's focus back to the blue fabric.

Josie's father rode into view, then jumped from his horse's back. He dashed in and out of Matt's tree-interrupted sight line until stuttering to a halt.

"What kind of game is this, Taggart?" Burkett bellowed loudly enough to rattle the leaves above him. "If you want your money, show yourself. And my daughter."

The affirmation that the misshapen figure *wasn't* Josie poured relief over Matt like the shower of a rushing waterfall and made it easier to hold his position.

"Taggart!"

No response answered Burkett's shout.

While Burkett called Taggart out, Matt signaled Preach to watch the area on the other side of the creek, then turned his own attention to the north ridge.

"Coward. Show yourself!"

There. A flicker of light, like the sun's reflection off glass. Matt strained to make out details, but the distance was too great. Then a form appeared, like a man straightening from a prone position. Another shape emerged behind him. A horse. One trained to lie down in battle and rise to his feet on command.

Phineas.

Matt's knees tightened around Percival. His gut urged him to set out in pursuit, to reclaim what was his and bring an outlaw to justice. Percival perked his ears, ready to respond, but Matt forced his muscles to uncoil. He leaned forward and patted Percival's neck.

"Not this time, boy," he whispered, "but soon."

Very soon.

Pursuing now would only forfeit their one advantage— Taggart's ignorance of the Horsemen's involvement. If there were more men secreted in the area, Matt could play right into their hands.

The rider on the ridge mounted and, in a blink, disappeared over the far side of the rise. No others surfaced to join him, but it was too late to give chase. Phineas had a quarter-mile lead, widening by the second. Percival's legs might be younger, but they weren't fresher. It would be impossible to catch him, especially traveling across country that offered enough hills and trees to conceal the fleeing outlaw's route.

Of all the outlaws Matt had encountered in the canyon, he could think of only one who might have the skills to command Phineas with such ease: the wrangler who had been the first to the remuda when Preach started the stampede. He'd handled himself well. No panicking or yelling at the frightened animals, stirring them into a greater frenzy. Just calm, controlled movements. If there had been more men like him in the camp, the rescue operation wouldn't have worked nearly so well. Such a man could have army experience, enough to understand the capabilities of a cavalry mount. He'd probably watched for Burkett's approach from atop the hill, then dropped both himself and Phineas into the high grass to remain hidden while observing the goings-on below. And now he was on his way to report to Taggart.

But that was a good thing. It would inflate Taggart's confidence. Let him believe all was transpiring according to his plan. That he was in control.

A motion to Matt's right drew his attention away from the ridge. Preach was signaling.

"All clear on the creek side, Cap."

Matt tilted his head toward Burkett and started walking Percival that direction. Preach brought his horse alongside. Both men holstered their pistols but kept their rifles at the ready in their laps.

"There was a man to the north conducting surveillance. Only one, far as I could tell." The next words tasted of bile as Matt forced them through his tight throat. "Pretty sure he was riding Phin."

Preach's gasped *No!* summed up Matt's thoughts pretty well. Disbelief. Outrage. They all had scores to settle, but those would have to wait until Josie was out of harm's way.

Matt ducked to avoid a branch as he steered his horse through the trees to reach Burkett. The older man's head, as well as the revolver in his hand, swiveled to greet him. Matt raised his hands, but recognition quickly dawned in Burkett's eyes. He lowered the weapon in his right hand and waved the sheet of paper he clutched in his left.

"She's not here."

Brooks and Wallace must have concluded that the back trail was clear, for they, along with Burkett's hands, emerged from the trees to take up positions on the path.

Burkett slashed the paper through the air and pointed an accusing finger at the scarecrow standing at the edge of the path. A scarecrow dressed in Josie's coat and hat.

"He's toying with us," Burkett ranted. "Playing some kind of shell game."

A breeze picked up, and the paper snapped in the wind. Matt eyed it. "I take it the exchange is not going to take place here, after all?"

"He drew a map to someplace in Sabinal Canyon, south of Utopia. Exchange is to be made tomorrow afternoon at three."

No railroad between here and there, so they'd have to take the horses. Which meant they'd arrive with tired stock while Taggart had a supply of fresh mounts.

"How far you reckon Utopia is from here, Preach?" Matt looked at his corporal as he stood in the stirrup and dismounted.

The big man shifted in his saddle. "Fifty miles? Maybe more."

Matt approached Burkett, who was spitting-mad and couldn't seem to stop waving the paper in the air. He needed to get Josie's father focused on working the problem instead of railing at it.

"What kind of distance can your stock cover in a day? Forty miles?" The best cavalry mounts could do fifty to sixty, but these horses weren't cavalry mounts yet. They were young. Probably untried.

Some of the redness faded from Burkett's face as he examined the animals around him with a practiced eye. "They'd probably give us forty-five. We've bred them in the hills, so they're used to the terrain, but with the thirty miles they traveled yesterday, I don't want to push them too hard. If a horse comes up lame, we're not just down a horse, we're down a man too."

"Can I see the note?" Matt asked, stretching out his hand.

He had no doubt that Burkett had read it correctly, but a leader didn't make plans without first verifying facts.

Burkett shoved it at him with equal parts reluctance and gratitude. "The blackguard even made her write it herself. I recognize her handwriting."

Matt took the sheet in hand, his gaze immediately attaching itself to the page. To her words. He hadn't seen Josie write anything in the short time they'd known each other. Thirsty to know more of her, he drank in her pen strokes on the page.

He stepped over to Percival and carefully smoothed the page over the saddle, then held the edges down so the wind wouldn't catch them. Preach dismounted and came around to look over his shoulder.

Her penmanship was tidy, free of the loops and flourishes that many females favored. Her letters slanted at a precise angle, close together, like orderly soldiers standing at attention.

Dear Father,

I am well. I have not been mistreated by Taggart or his men. The ransom location has been changed. Follow the map on the reverse side of this note to the new location. Mr. Taggart has postponed the exchange until three o'clock tomorrow. I will see you then.

Your daughter,
Josephine Burkett

Matt turned the paper over and glanced at the crude map drawn there, but noticed nothing of interest. Taggart would have drawn the map himself. Josie had written the note. The writing called to him in a way he couldn't explain. He flipped it back to the front and read the words again, but they left him unsatisfied. There was something else. Something he wasn't seeing. He studied the lettering a second time, ignoring the words themselves in order to examine the actual ink markings. He squinted, then tilted his head to consider it from a different angle.

"Brooks. Come look at this."

Jonah dismounted and approached. Preach shifted to the side to make room.

"Is it my imagination," Matt asked, "or is there a small dot at the top of certain letters?" He pivoted to the left to give his sergeant an unobstructed view.

Jonah said nothing at first, but then, he wasn't one to offer an opinion before it was fully formed.

"See?" Matt pointed to the greeting. "It's there on the D and E of *Dear*, but it doesn't appear again until the crown of the S in *mistreated*."

"What are you talking about, Hanger?" Burkett blustered as he pushed his way into the group. Once he saw what Matt was indicating, he waved his hand in dismissal. "Those are just ink spots. Taggart was probably holding her at gunpoint when he forced her to write that note. Poor girl must have been scared out of her skin. Only makes sense that her penmanship would be jerky instead of smooth."

"I've seen your daughter operate on a man trying to bleed to death," Matt countered. "Never once did her hands shake. She was steady as a rock. Josie's not one to tremble under pressure."

Burkett looked Matt in the eye. "My Jo's strong, yes. Stronger than most men I know. But she's still a woman at the mercy of a gang of outlaws who could do . . . unspeakable . . ." His eyes grew shiny. He turned his head, coughed, then turned back to level a hard stare at Matt. "She's never faced this kind of pressure before."

The truth he'd been doing his best to avoid stabbed Matt in the chest. His Josie was in a den of vipers, any of which could strike without warning or reason. He clenched his jaw until his molars ground together. He couldn't dwell on what *could* happen. He needed his mind for more fruitful pursuits, like deciphering the hunch that had his men analyzing handwriting.

"She might be staring down the barrel of Taggart's revolver," Jonah said, tapping the page with the tip of his finger, "but I don't think she's blinkin'." He twisted his face and offered Matt a half-smile. "I think you're right, Captain. Those dots are too precise to be accidental. I think the doc left us a message."

Beautiful, clever girl!

"Somebody find a pencil," Matt ordered. "We have a message to decipher."

THIRTY-TWO

Matt worked his way through the note a third and fourth time, jotting down all the letters that had dots of ink at their crest. Some were easy to identify, like the O and C in *o'clock*. Others were less obvious. He and Jonah debated the merits of several letters with Preach throwing his opinion into the mix every so often, while the rest of the men paced and waited.

After narrowing down the suspects, Matt composed two horizontal lists along the bottom of Josie's note. The first line contained the letters he and Brooks agreed upon, spaced far enough apart to cover the entire width of the paper. Beneath that were the more questionable letters, aligned with the open spaces of the top line in order to preserve the overall order of appearance.

"Yer wastin' time, Hanger." Having apparently reached the limit of his patience, Burkett stomped over to his mount and collected the black gelding's reins. "We gotta get movin' if we're gonna reach the exchange point ahead of schedule. You can play word games if you want, but me and my men are heading out." He drew abreast of Matt and held out his hand. "Give me the map."

Matt's attention never left the letters. D-E-S-E. Then possibly a T or a G, but neither made much sense with the R-T pairing next on the list of certain letters. If he crossed them out . . .

His pulse jumped as the letters left began to form a word. D-E-S-E-R—

"Hanger!" Burkett snapped.

Matt's head jerked up.

"The map."

No way was he forfeiting this paper until he figured out Josie's message. "Ten minutes," he bargained, praying he'd have it figured out by then. If not, he'd just scratch his line of letters into the dirt and keep working. "Water the horses at the creek. I'll hand the map over when you return."

Burkett scowled. "Fine. Ten minutes." He withdrew his hand and took hold of Percival's bridle. "But I'm taking Percy with me."

"Good. Wallace can take our other horses." Matt tipped his head toward Mark, who immediately collected the reins of both his and Jonah's mounts. "Preach, I'm gonna use your back."

As Burkett led Percival away, Matt swiveled toward his corporal, who was already bending to offer the use of his broad back as their new work surface.

"I think the first word is *desert*," Matt murmured to Jonah, though even as he said it, he realized how little sense it made. There were deserts in Texas, but none nearby. They were all out west. This was hill country. Thick vegetation. Ample water. Wildflowers and trees. This was about as non-desert as Texas got. Matt's throat rumbled with frustration. Maybe

Burkett was right. Maybe he was trying too hard to see clues that simply weren't there.

"Not *desert*, Captain," Jonah said, his finger tracing the next several letters in the list. He paused over an E, then skipped past an L, N, H, and A before tapping a D in the list of possible letters. "*Deserted.*"

A new surge of excitement pumped through Matt's veins. A deserted what? House? Town? Cave? He immediately started scanning the next set of letters. F-A-R. *Farm.* It had to be. He skipped several letters like Jonah had, then jabbed his finger at the M in *Mr. Taggart*. The title had been left off the first time the outlaw was mentioned in the note, so Josie must have purposely added it here to provide the needed M.

Smart girl.

It took longer to figure out the next part of Josie's message. The letters didn't seem to make a real word.

"*Speco* or maybe *Secoc* . . ." Matt tried to sound out the nonsense words. The plodding hoofbeats of horses returning from the creek shot a dose of urgency into his blood. "Nothing fits," he muttered as his eyes traced the same letters over and over.

Preach twisted his neck as if attempting to peer at his own back. "Try skippin' the middle and jump to the end. Maybe you can work it out backwards."

Matt glanced at Jonah, who shrugged.

"Couldn't hurt," Jonah said as he turned back to study the note. "We know for sure the last letter is K. It's probably why she took the time to sign her last name."

"We also know there are two E's next to each other," Matt added. "There could also be an L or an R." *Eek. Leek. Reek.* He glanced at the letters again and pounced on the C. "Creek! Seco Creek!" He grinned like an idiot and squeezed

Jonah's shoulder, wiggling him back and forth as if he were a flag flying in a windstorm. "We found her! Thank God above. We found her."

Burkett dropped the reins to his black and charged forward. "You found my Jo?" He looked from one man to the next, but his gaze zeroed in on Matt. "Where is she?"

"At a deserted farm near Seco Creek."

The fire lighting Burkett's eyes cooled and hardened into coals. "Seco Creek stretches for miles. She could be anywhere."

Matt shook his head, the scent of the hunt still fresh in his nostrils. "Not anywhere." He stepped away from Jonah and clapped a hand on Burkett's shoulder. "She's at a deserted farm. A specific place. A place locals will know."

"Only if you find the right locals." Burkett circled his arm to dislodge Matt's hand. "If we had two or three days, you might find her. But we barely have enough time to get to the exchange point. We can't afford to go on some wild goose chase."

"Not all of us, no." Matt gestured to his men. "I'll take the Horsemen. We'll cut cross-country and ride to Utopia. The town lies between Seco Creek and Sabinal River. Someone is bound to know of an abandoned farm in the area. It makes sense for Taggart to keep her close to the exchange point."

"But that will add several miles to your trip," Burkett warned. "Miles we can't afford."

Matt paced a few steps, frustration mounting. He understood Burkett's reluctance. This was a risky play. But it was the best play they had.

He stopped pacing and faced Burkett head-on. "You said it yourself. If we let Taggart call all the shots, there's a good chance Josie ends up dead. Charlie too. But if we can find their hideout and attack when they're not expecting it, we'll be the ones with the advantage."

"And my children could still end up dead." Burkett's gaze hardened even further. "You go into that camp, guns blazing, and chances are high that my Jo gets caught in the crossfire."

Matt didn't blink. "Retrieving your daughter unharmed is the mission, Burkett. I won't make a move until her position is secure. You have my word."

Josie's father held his gaze for a long minute, then finally dipped his chin in a small nod. When his face lifted, his eyes had softened, the crack in his anger letting some of his fear leak through. "What if you don't find them in time?"

Matt swallowed. It was a possibility. Likely even, as much as he hated to admit it. If they couldn't find a knowledgeable local, there would be too much ground to cover for them to find the farm on their own.

"I'll abandon the search in time to reach the exchange point by the assigned time." He narrowed his gaze. "I'll need you to hold off your approach until three. Don't go in early. Even to position your men. Taggart's bound to have spies watching the place, just as he did here. If they see you coming, they'll send word to Taggart. He'll gather Josie and his men and leave the farm before we have a chance to find them."

Matt knew he was asking a lot. Asking Burkett to give up the one small advantage he held in order to trust a group of men he didn't know to pursue a larger advantage that could either make all the difference or no difference at all.

"Can you give me that time?" Matt asked.

Burkett's eyes closed even as the muscles in his jaw ticked. He stood silent, his face slowly tipping toward the sky as his hands balled into fists. He was a fighter by nature, a man used to being in control. Exactly like Matt. And exactly like Matt, he had to fight his instincts and surrender to the One who held the highest ground. The One who could see beyond the plans of men.

Ever since he'd surrendered his rifle to Taggart, Matt had been surrendering more and more control to the Almighty. He'd had no choice. Never had he been less equipped for a rescue mission than when he'd lain bound, wounded, and stripped of all weapons and belongings. Yet from that moment of deprivation, God had stepped in to take charge. He'd provided boots and transportation. Horses and a guide. Then better horses along with weapons and manpower. Now he'd even provided directions. Ambiguous directions, to be sure, but directions all the same. Matt had to believe that more details would be forthcoming if they followed in faith and allowed the Lord to navigate.

After a long, tense silence, Burkett's chin came down and his lids lifted. His dark green eyes, so like Josie's, met Matt's, a plea tinged with desperation giving them an unnatural sheen. "I'll wait until three."

He extended his hand, and Matt grasped it.

Burkett tightened his grip, his stare boring into Matt's soul. "Bring my children home, Hanger."

Matt gave a brief nod. "I will, sir. Or die trying." After studying the map on the back of the note a final time, he handed the paper over to Josie's father. "God go with you."

Burkett nodded. "And you." With a thump to Matt's back, he returned to his horse, mounted, and set off for the main road at a walk. Albert and Eddie followed close behind.

Knowing daylight was a precious commodity they couldn't afford to waste, Matt signaled his men to mount up.

Preach looked at him as Matt swung onto Percival's back.

"We're gonna have to push these horses harder than Burkett would want to cover the amount of ground necessary to carry out this plan of yours, Cap."

Matt drew the reins around and aimed Percival not west toward the main road, but north to cut off a corner that would place them ahead of Josie's father and his men.

"I know. We'll have to take care. We can't press them past their breaking point, but we're going to have to get as close to that point as possible if we're going to find that farm before Taggart takes Josie to the exchange." He looked at each man in turn. "Keep me updated on the status of your mounts as we go. If we need to rest, we will. It just can't be for long."

"We can dismount and walk with them too, Captain, to lighten their loads," Preach said.

"And use lanterns after dark," Jonah added.

"Whatever it takes to find her." This from Wallace, whose arm must be throbbing but whose face gave no indication of anything but strength and determination.

Matt's chest swelled with pride in his men. His *friends*. Their mission might consist of finding a needle in a field of haystacks, but with God, nothing was impossible.

"Preach?" Matt looked to his corporal for the one thing they lacked before setting off.

The big man grinned. "'If ye have faith as a grain of mustard seed . . . nothing shall be impossible unto you.' Time for some mustard, boys!" With a whoop, he set off at a lope.

Matt leaned over Percival's neck, the thrill of the hunt stirring his blood. "Time to see what you're made of, young knight. Let's go."

THIRTY-THREE

By the time night fell, Matt and the Horsemen had crossed the entirety of Medina County, including fording the Medina River, Hondo Creek, and finally Seco Creek. The hilly terrain had taken a toll on their mounts, leaving the animals' heads hanging low as they plodded toward Utopia.

They'd gambled on the assumption that the best chance to learn the outlaws' location was to ask those living closest to Seco Creek, so they'd sacrificed possible information in favor of speed, stopping only at the Hondo Canyon post office on Williams Creek at about the halfway point of their journey. The postmaster had no knowledge of vacated property in the western part of the county, but he *did* advise them on the best route to take into Utopia, helping them avoid arroyos and canyons that would slow their progress.

Matt slumped slightly to the right, his side throbbing after a long day in the saddle. He hated looking weak in front of his men, but at this point, they were all so weary and bedraggled, preserving energy was more important than preserving pride.

"I see it, Captain." Jonah's voice echoed behind him.

Matt straightened, then swiveled to glance back at Brooks, clutching his side to minimize the pull on his stitches.

Jonah tipped his head and pointed to the right side of the road up ahead. "Buildings. We made it to Utopia."

Matt peered into the darkness ahead of him. It took a minute, but eventually he made out a pair of dark square shadows. Like a horse who sensed the home barn was close, Matt flared his nostrils and lifted his head. Little zings of energy ricocheted through his chest, revitalizing his flagging stamina.

"Look alive, men. Time to start our investigation in earnest."

It was late, yes, but the saloon should be doing a rousing business about now. Wallace could slip in among the locals and ferret out the needed information. Men tended to talk more freely under whiskey's influence anyway.

Only, as the Horsemen wandered down the main street of town, everything was dark. No dance hall music, no light pouring into the street through batwing doors, no horses lined up at the hitching post. By Matt's count, Utopia had two gristmills, three churches, a blacksmith, a general store, and a cotton gin. But no saloon.

Matt sagged in the saddle as they reached the edge of town. No saloon, no café, no hotel. No public building of any kind open for evening travelers. Which meant no source of information available to them tonight. Which would leave them even further behind schedule.

"Look. Up ahead." Preach, riding at Matt's side, pointed to the steepled building Matt had counted as the third church. "Is that a light in the window?"

Matt squinted. The church looked dark to him. Maybe it had been the moon reflecting off the glass. But then he saw it. A yellow light bobbed at the bottom of the window for a heartbeat, then disappeared back into darkness.

"Someone's there," Wallace said. "Might as well knock on the door. See what happens."

"It's God's house, after all," Preach said with a shrug. "Supposed to be open to everyone, right? Whenever there's a need? Well, we got a need."

Matt tugged Percival's reins to the right. Why not? A smidgen of a chance was better than no chance at all. "Let's check it out."

Once at the church, they dismounted, and Matt swore he heard the horses sigh in relief. He patted Percival's neck in apology and whispered praise in his ear as he moved past. "You did well, old boy. As valiant and noble as your namesake."

He wished he could promise that the hardest road was behind them, but he couldn't. There'd be no real rest until Taggart and his men were behind bars.

Matt had his foot on the bottom step leading to the church's door when Jonah's low voice stopped him.

"Hold up, Captain. There's something under the stoop."

Matt bit back his impatience as he pulled his foot from the step. He didn't see why they should care about whatever had fallen under the stairs. They had a mission to complete, and that mission had nothing to do with an item lying forgotten in the dirt. Yet he'd trained his men to heed their instincts. If Jonah's keen eyes had spotted something suspicious under the stoop and his gut told him it was important enough to investigate, Matt wouldn't argue.

"Make it quick, Sergeant." He might not argue, but he would hurry the expedition along.

Jonah got down on hands and knees and crawled under

the stoop, his head and shoulders completely disappearing. How on earth had he even seen that thing? In the dark. In the even *darker* shadows beneath the church stairs. Matt shook his head.

Brooks backed out, ducking his head to keep the floorboards from knocking his hat askew. Once out, he sat back on his heels and dusted off his treasure.

"Looks like a Bible," Preach said.

Wallace leaned close, stealing a peek over Jonah's shoulder. "An old one, by the looks of it. The spine and edges are worn thin."

Jonah rubbed the leather cover against his chest, cleaning off the dirt. "It's a nice one," he said. "Somebody's prob'ly looking for it." He held the top of the book up to his mouth and blew a puff of air across the closed pages. Dust scattered.

"Well, maybe we can do a good deed while we're here." Matt supposed he should be happy about that, but all he could think of was the danger Josie was in and how much his side throbbed. It didn't put him in the most charitable frame of mind. "Let's go." They'd dallied long enough.

Matt forced energy into his tired legs and tromped up the steps. He set his jaw, doing his best to ignore the pain in his side. Taking a determined breath, he knocked on the door, then clasped the handle and gently pushed it open.

"Hello? Anyone here?" His gaze moved to the right, where soft lantern light peeked out between the floor and rear pews. "We're in need of assist—"

A loud *bonk* cut off Matt's words. It was followed by a grunt and a quiet "Ouch."

For the second time that night, Matt watched a man back out of a tight space on his hands and knees. This man had empty hands, however, unless you counted the one vigorously

318

rubbing a spot on his head that would surely sport a lump in the near future.

"Just a minute," he said as he finished crawling out from under the rear pew.

Preach hurried forward and offered him a hand.

"Thank you." The middle-aged man clasped the supportive arm and allowed Preach to lever him to his feet. He turned to face his unexpected company, a sheepish grin on his face. "I suppose it's not a bad thing for a preacher to be found on his knees in church, though it would probably reflect better on me had I been praying instead of crawling under the pews like a mischievous toddler. What can I do—"

He interrupted himself with a gasp as his gaze zeroed in on Jonah. "You found it! Oh, God be praised!" He clapped his hands and rushed to Jonah's side. "Where was it? I've been searching for hours."

Jonah held the book out to him. "Under the stoop outside. Caught sight of it when we was walking up."

The preacher accepted the Bible and clasped it to his chest with one hand while he gripped Jonah's shoulder with the other. "You are a godsend, my brother. Truly. You have no idea what this means." Tears misted his eyes. He inhaled sharply and blinked the moisture away before aiming his gaze toward heaven. He opened his arms wide. "Thank you, Father, for sending these men. For granting them vision to pierce the darkness so they might return to me what was lost."

He chuckled and shook his head. "It's just like the parable of the lost coin. That poor woman lit her lamp and swept her entire house, looking for her coin. I've done the same." He nodded toward the lantern glowing near the side window, then looked down at himself, shook his head, and brushed the dust from his knees. "You'll have to rejoice with me," he said, grabbing Matt's arm and giving it a little shake. "All my other neighbors are tucked away in their homes, preparing for bed." His smile beamed, and for just a moment, the ache in Matt's side lessened.

The preacher laughed, his joy too big to contain, and Matt found his lips twitching in an answering grin.

The preacher released Matt's arm and thumped him on the back. "Guess I have my sermon topic for next Sunday, don't I? Luke 15 might have a lost sheep, a lost coin, and a lost son, but God just gave me a lost Bible parable to share with the congregation."

He held his prize out in front of him, and his palm caressed the leather cover with reverence. His jig-dancing gaze settled into a slow waltz as something deeper than happiness softened his features.

"My wife gave me this Bible." He glanced up and caught Matt's eye. "On our wedding day. She vowed to support me in my calling, wherever God might lead us. I've never preached a sermon without it." A thoughtful look crossed his face as he looked at each of the Horsemen in turn. "I always leave it on the podium at the front of the building after services, but today . . ." Lines crept across his brow as he puzzled through events aloud. "I guess I tucked it under my arm and carried it outside where I shake hands and wish everyone well as they depart. It must have fallen without my noticing, and since I never carry it outside with me, I didn't think to search there."

His attention returned to the holy book in his hands. "When I discovered it was missing, I was so distraught. Then angry at myself for being careless and too scatterbrained to recall where I'd left it." His gaze lifted. "But now I'm wondering if losing this Bible wasn't God's plan all along. Perhaps he wanted me to be here at this time. To meet you."

Matt's pulse picked up its pace. How many providential encounters were they to be blessed with? Never before had he felt God directing his steps so carefully or providing for his needs so completely. It humbled him. What would life be like if he lived from a place of surrender like this all the time?

"I don't know if it was God's plan or not," Matt said, though his heart urged him to believe it, "but we're mighty glad to find you here. We're hoping you can help us locate a piece of property nearby. An abandoned farm near Seco Creek. Do you know it?"

The preacher nodded. "I know of several around here. You got any other information to help narrow it down?"

Several? Matt's side took up throbbing again. How many? Three? Four? Ten? They wouldn't have time to scout them all.

"That's all we know," Preach answered, since Matt's brain was too busy being discouraged to respond. "Except for the fact that an outlaw gang has taken up residence there."

"Outlaws?" The preacher's eyes narrowed, and his jaw tightened. "I hoped they were gone for good this time. I haven't heard of them being in these parts for over a year. Rumor had it they'd moved on to Uvalde."

"Where are they?" Matt took a step toward the preacher, desperation lending an unwelcome sharpness to his tone. The parson's eyes widened. Matt immediately halted and softened his voice. "Please. They're holding a woman captive. A woman I care about a great deal."

The preacher straightened, a glint of purpose lighting his eyes. "Then you need to get her back. If these outlaws are the same band that came through here two years ago, they're no respecters of life. They killed George Hightower and made off with his herd when they discovered him living alone so far from town. He had worked that land for five years. Built a house, a barn, a chicken coop. He planned to send for his family that year, as soon as he drove his cattle to market, but he never got the chance. Now his widow is left with nothing more than a piece of property that won't sell for fear the outlaws will return. And now they have." He shook his head and released a sigh. "George was a good man. Worked hard. Came to church every Sunday. He didn't deserve what happened to him."

"My Josie is an innocent as well," Matt said, his voice trembling slightly. "Taken for ransom, though I imagine they'll kill her as soon as they get their hands on her father's money. That's why we have to get to them first. Rescue her and her brother before the exchange takes place."

The preacher clapped Matt's shoulder. "Well, that decides it, then. You're all coming home with me."

Matt started to protest, but the preacher cut him off.

"No arguments. I'm not about to wish you warm and well fed and wash my hands of you. I aim to play the Good Samaritan in this scene. Might even get another sermon topic out of it." He winked, and Matt abandoned his reluctance. "By the looks of you, you're all worn to nubbins. Tildie loves to cook, and she'll tan my hide if she learns I allowed hungry men on a noble quest to escape unfed. She'll fill your bellies tonight and fuel you up again in the morning before you set out. There's no barn for your horses at the parsonage, but I have plenty of sweet grass and a pump for water. We have a spare room where you can spread your bedrolls, and a rooster next door that will ensure you don't oversleep."

Overwhelmed by his kindness and the continuation of the Lord's provision, Matt dipped his chin and extended his hand. "Thank you."

The preacher clasped his palm. "Least I could do for the men who found my Bible."

"And you'll be able to give us directions to the Hightower farm?" As good as the food and shelter sounded, Matt couldn't afford to lose sight of the main goal.

"Better than that, my friend." The preacher's eyes were back to dancing again, hinting at surprises Matt didn't have the energy to guess at. "I'll draw you a map."

THIRTY-FOUR

I can't believe Parson Andrews drew that map." Wallace exuded admiration as the horses enjoyed a short respite from their travels. "It looks like it was rendered by a professional cartographer."

Matt silently agreed. He held the map at arm's length and examined the incredibly detailed sketch the preacher had given them this morning. The grove of trees to their left matched the leafy markings on the page. Rock formations, creek beds, canyons, hills—they were all depicted with stunning accuracy. If the army had more men like Andrews on the payroll, scouting time could be cut in half.

"His missus told me he was up half the night working on it." Jonah stood in his stirrups and scanned the landscape to the south. "Said he wanted to get it just right. Knew a woman's life depended on it."

Preach took a sip of water from his canteen, then wiped the moisture from his lips. "I suppose every man needs a hobby. We're just lucky his happened to be mapmaking."

Matt folded the sketch and tucked it into his vest pocket.

"Luck had nothing to do with it." He looked at his men, each in turn. "It's God's providence."

He couldn't deny that truth. Nor did he want to. God was leading this expedition, not him. Exactly as it should be. Matt would rather trust Josie's safety to the One who saw all and knew all instead of relying on his own limited vision and understanding. He'd felt God's gentle urging in his life before, but never had it been so overt. It was as if a general had ridden onto the battlefield to direct the operation himself instead of leaving it in the hands of his officers. Before this, Matt might have balked at being relieved of his command. Not anymore. He welcomed the interference and stood ready to obey whatever orders the General saw fit to give.

"We're going to find the outlaws," Matt said. "I have no doubt. The Almighty wouldn't bring us this far only to leave us empty-handed. What I don't know is what will happen when we get there. What price might be demanded of us."

"Same price we've been willing to pay in every other battle we've faced, Cap." Preach gave him a nod.

Wallace echoed the gesture. "Even more so this time, with Miss Josephine in the line of fire. She's one of us."

Matt's chest swelled with gratitude and not a little wonder.

How had Josie become so essential to him in such a short time—to the point that he would ask his men to place her well-being above their own? Had that been orchestrated by God too? Two lives intersecting at just the right moment and under just the right circumstances had proven to be a simple matter for the Almighty lately. After all, the Lord had brought him a wagon driven by a bootmaker when they had no shoes, the finest stock in the state when they had no horses, and a map-drawing preacher when they had no direction. Bringing him a woman to awaken a heart scarred by loss and failure when he thought he was destined to live out his life alone no longer seemed so farfetched.

Strange how spiritual hindsight could change one's view of the future.

"That jutting rock face to the south could be the hill Parson Andrews marked as the northeast corner of the Hightower property." Jonah's comment sharpened Matt's focus on his surroundings.

Matt looked in the direction his sergeant pointed, pulled the map back out, and oriented himself with other landmarks closer at hand. "I think you're right."

Anticipation for the coming battle thrummed through his veins and pumped his pulse into a high tempo. Josie was close. But so were Taggart and a crew who outnumbered the Horsemen three to one.

Matt started to look to Preach for a verse, but a different urge tugged on his spirit. One he couldn't ignore.

He pulled his hat from his head. "Join me, fellas?"

The other Horsemen drew their mounts near, and each man uncovered then bowed his head.

"Lord." Matt wasn't accustomed to addressing the Almighty in front of others, but he couldn't escape the feeling that his men needed the words as much as he did. "Thanks for showin' us the way and providin' what was necessary to mount this rescue. I know we ain't the most righteous of men. We have blood on our hands and failings aplenty, yet if you ride with us, I believe we will prevail. So stick close, Lord. We need you."

I *need you. Don't let me botch your plans with my own ignorance. Don't let this be another Wounded Knee.*

"Grant us courage under fire. Protect us from harm, but more importantly, protect Josie. Let no bullet find her, no injury befall her, no indignity be foisted upon her." Matt swallowed, working hard to keep his head above the murky water that roiled with dark possibilities. "I know vengeance is yours, but we offer ourselves as warriors for justice should you deem us worthy. Make our aim true and our mission a success." He paused for a moment, culling his mind for what he might have missed. Not finding anything, he opened his eyes and tipped his chin toward heaven. "I guess that about covers it. Thanks for listening. In Jesus's name, amen."

A murmured collection of *amens* echoed around him.

"Good words, Captain," Wallace said as he and the rest of the Horsemen fit their hats back onto their heads.

Feeling more settled in his spirit, Matt nodded to Preach.

"'The Lord is my strength and my shield; my heart trusted in him, and I am helped.' Psalm 28:7."

He couldn't think of a better send-off.

Matt gave the signal to ride, then bent over Percival's neck and whispered, "Let's go get our fair maiden, Sir Knight."

As if the horse understood the quest, he sprang forward and surged to the front of the pack, forcing Matt to rein in his enthusiasm lest he tire too quickly. With a grin on his face, and a confidence rooted not in his own expertise but in the God whose presence permeated the air around them, Matt led the way to the rocky outcropping and the outlaws waiting on the other side.

A cool bit of wind brushed Josephine's cheek like the caress of a finger. Her head jerked upward, and a shiver of awareness tingled against her nape. She pushed away from the chuck wagon where she'd been opening the tinned vegetables from her supply bag into Arnold's soup pot, and scanned her surroundings.

She glanced toward the house, then the barn, then to areas beyond, but she spied nothing out of the ordinary. A handful of Taggart's men were readying the horses for the ransom appointment. Others hunkered together playing cards. A few passed around a jug of home-brewed spirits. Taggart remained inside the house. Separate. Apart.

Ever since she'd written that letter, he'd barricaded himself in the house, watching the goings-on through the windows and distributing orders through his lieutenants. Was he weary of his men? Heaven knew *she* was. Or maybe a part of him feared she was right about the cavalry coming and sought the protection of four solid walls.

Carver and Dawson had spent the most time indoors, but yesterday another fellow had spent nearly an hour inside. A man who had ridden Matthew's horse. She'd recognized Phineas the moment the outlaw had ridden in last night, the provoking sight raising her ire. No one should ride that horse but Matthew Hanger. Yet even thieving outlaws recognized prime horseflesh when they saw it. All of the Horsemen's mounts had been claimed in short order, along with their ammunition and weapons. Taggart's top men kept the best items for themselves, of course. Her guard wore Matthew's gun belt and pistol crisscrossed over his own, giving him a gun on each hip.

Carver winked at her as her roaming gaze slid past him. He tucked his thumb into the gun belt and smirked as if to remind her that her man was gone.

But was he?

Another breeze tickled her neck. Stray hairs pulled free from her braid and whipped across her eyes. As she drew them away from her lashes, she couldn't escape the feeling that she was supposed to see something. Something important. Her scientific mind tried to dismiss the thought as irrational. It was just a gust of wind, after all. Nothing more. Yet her instincts continued to flare, prodding her to be ready.

Today was the day the ransom was to take place. The day her fate would be decided. Charlie's too. They had to be ready to take advantage of any opportunity that presented itself. Arnold had slipped Charlie a knife after supper, and her brother had spent the better part of the night whittling the end of the wheel spoke so that he could splinter it and unfetter himself should a chance for escape arise. Or should the threat to their lives reach a critical stage.

She prayed for the first even as she mentally prepared herself for the second.

Her father could have decoded her hidden message. Could even now be closing in on the camp. The Horsemen could be near, as well. Could have picked up Taggart's trail somehow. Matthew would've driven them hard, relentless in his pursuit. He'd promised to find her, and she believed him. Believed he lived and was searching for her.

She had to believe. If she didn't, she'd have nothing to hold back the flood of despair that threatened to sweep her away.

Josephine finished opening the tin of carrots in her hand and dumped the contents into the soup pot. Two tins remained on the tailgate that served as a work surface, but she hid them with a dish towel, then proceeded to haul the large pot over to the cooking fire. Arnold looked up from banking a pile of coals in a separate pit that would soon cover a pair of Dutch ovens filled with biscuit dough.

"Let me get that, Miz Josephine." He scurried forward to

take the large pot from her hands. "That thing's too heavy for you to be luggin' around."

"Thank you." She released her hold on the handle as he took charge. "I thought I'd give Charlie a hand with the potatoes."

"Nice of ya, but I think he's about finished . . ." Arnold hefted the pot over the low fire, fitting the handle onto a hook suspended from an iron crossbar that spanned the length of the fire pit. "That right, Charlie? You got them taters peeled and chopped?"

Her brother hunkered down behind an overturned crate a short distance away, a bowl of prepped potatoes on the ground at his elbow and more on the cutting board on top of the crate. The chain attached to his right wrist had little slack remaining.

"Yep." Charlie answered the cook, but his eyes met his sister's. He felt it too. The anticipation. The need to be ready. "Jo can bring them to you."

Josephine ambled toward Charlie, conscious of the gaze following her every move. Right before she reached her brother, her watchdog pushed away from the tree he'd been leaning against and moved to join them.

Rats. She'd hoped to speak to her brother without Carver's interference. Unfortunately, her guard took his duty seriously. Which made *her* duty more of a challenge. If Matthew was out there, alive and coming after her just as he'd vowed, then the safest place for Charlie was by her side. She doubted the Horsemen felt any kind of loyalty toward her brother after his betrayal, but if she stayed near him, any buffer the Horsemen created for her would extend to him.

Charlie scraped the last of the potatoes from his cutting board into the bowl just as Carver arrived.

"I'll take charge of that knife, Burkett. Set it on the board, then back away."

Charlie did as he was told, raising his hands in the air as he backed toward the chuck wagon. Carver slapped his palm over the handle of the paring knife, then turned and flung it with expert precision at a log jutting from the fire a few scant inches from where Arnold was stirring the stew pot. The cook yelped and jumped back.

Carver chuckled. "Easy, Cookie. I'm just returnin' yer knife."

He was a sadist, and Josephine wanted nothing more than to dump the bowl of potatoes she'd just retrieved over his head. Instead, she made a point of ignoring him completely as she walked the potatoes to the fire and dumped them into the pot.

"I'll wash the bowl for you, Mr. Watson," she said as she headed back to the wagon.

Charlie rose to his feet. "I'll help." He fit his hand to the small of her back and pushed her toward the wagon.

She stumbled a bit at the forcefulness of his shove. What was he doing?

"They're here," he murmured as his hand latched onto her elbow. He hurried her to the side of the wagon where the whittled spoke waited.

"Who?" Her gaze swept the trees at the edge of yard, seeing nothing different.

Then a light hit her face. A concentrated beam that made her blink until Charlie growled a warning at her.

"Don't look."

She turned back toward the wagon, hoping Carver hadn't noticed her suspicious behavior. Her heart thudded in her chest. The light. A signal. A reflection off a mirror.

Matthew. It had to be him. He was here.

"It don't take two of you to wash a bowl," Carver said as he came up behind them.

"Run for the trees." Charlie's urgent whisper screamed through her mind as he snatched the bowl from her hands and kicked the whittled spoke with his boot. The spoke splintered, and the manacle slid free.

"I've had enough of your bullying, Carver." Charlie spun around, swinging the metal bowl at Carver's head.

Carver ducked. The bowl glanced off the side of his skull. He straightened, bringing his fist up as he did so, straight into Charlie's midsection. Charlie doubled over.

"Stop!" she cried.

Run for the trees. That was what Charlie wanted her to do. Save herself while he kept Carver occupied. She looked to the trees. Took a step. But the pounding thuds of fists on flesh tore at her heart. She couldn't leave her brother.

Helpless tears welled in her eyes, blurring her vision. Then a violent punch splayed Charlie at her feet. She bent to help him rise, but as he stood, he grabbed her arms and looked into her face. A cut above his eye dripped blood, a welt on his cheek foretold a nasty bruise, but it was his gaze that arrested her.

Go! He mouthed the word and shoved her away from him. Then, with a roar, he launched himself at Carver once again.

Tears rolling down her cheeks, Josephine ran.

THIRTY-FIVE

Run, Josie." Matt mumbled the plea beneath his breath as he trained his rifle on the man who'd been guarding her. When she stumbled away from her brother, hope leapt in his chest. He hadn't been sure she'd leave Charlie behind, but doing so provided the best chance to get her away un-harmed. Seeing her grab a handful of skirt and sprint for the trees ignited Matt's confidence. "That's right, darlin'. Run."

To me.

She fled straight toward his position, as if she heard his heart calling to hers. But before she'd closed half the dis-tance, a shout went up from the camp.

Faster, Josie. Matt tightened his grip on the rifle. *Faster*.

Jonah was positioned in the branches of a tall oak twenty yards to Matt's left. Wallace and Preach waited on horseback far enough away to be out of sight but close enough to hear when the gunfire started. They had orders to charge into the fray at the first shot.

Matt's shot. The one he planned to hold off on as long

as possible. He wanted Josie clear of the area before lead started flying.

When the cry of alarm rose, the man pummeling Charlie straightened. His arm dropped to his side and his fist unclenched as he reached for his revolver. He tossed Charlie to the ground and set off after Josie. "Don't make me shoot you, Doc," he yelled.

Charlie lunged after him and managed to wrap his arms around the outlaw's feet. The tangle didn't last long, however. The outlaw kicked free, knocking Charlie's head in the process.

The guard raced after Josie, his long stride eating up the small lead she'd gained. Matt judged the remaining distance, and his jaw clenched. She wouldn't make it. Her guard would overtake her before she reached the trees.

A little farther, he urged silently as the rest of the camp came to life. Movement danced in his periphery. Men getting to their feet. Reaching for weapons. Running to the scene. The instant Matt fired, retribution would explode directly toward his position, trapping Josie in the middle.

He needed to draw the fire away from her. Give them a visible target.

After he took down the most pressing threat.

Matt aimed at the guard's chest, his vow not to use lethal force nagging on his conscience. Yet he couldn't afford to miss. Not with Josie's life at stake. He needed to take the high-percentage shot. Praying that the God who'd sent Israel's warriors into battle and fought at their side would understand the extenuating circumstances, he squeezed the trigger.

The shot cracked. The guard dropped. Matt roared a battle cry and charged into the fray.

Josie pulled up short at the sight of him, her beautiful eyes going wide. Matt held her gaze for one precious second, then gestured with his left arm for her to sprint for the trees while he turned his attention to eliminating the threats to her escape.

He zagged to the right. Slowed. Raised his rifle and shot. A man howled, clutching his shoulder. Another shot echoed from above. Another outlaw fell, this time to Jonah's bullet.

Hooves pounded behind Matt. A guttural yell that sounded surprisingly like the bugle call to charge announced Preach and Wallace's arrival. Matt fought the urge to look behind him, to check on Josie's progress. Trusting his men to keep her safe, he focused on his job—protecting her back.

The red-bearded Dawson charged out of the house, gun raised. His barrel aimed not at Matt, but someone behind him.

Matt's blood turned to ice. *Josie.* His position was vulnerable, out in the open, but that didn't matter. He dropped to one knee, raised his rifle, and took the shot. Dawson jerked and fell backward against the house wall. He didn't drop his gun, though. Wincing, the outlaw adjusted his aim. Matt pumped the lever on his repeater to expel the spent cartridge and load another into the chamber. Too long. It was taking too long.

Dawson fired. A horse screamed.

Wallace had ridden straight across the bullet's path, protecting Josie with his horse and his own body. The gelding reared, its front hooves pawing at the air, but the animal didn't go down. Thank the Lord. Wallace drew his weapon and shot Dawson in the chest. The gun fell from the outlaw's hand as his body slid the rest of the way to the ground.

Bullets flew from every direction now. The barn. The

house. The copse of trees to the south. As Wallace withdrew in order to prepare for another pass, Matt sprinted for the only cover near enough to do any good—the chuck wagon. Laying cover fire for himself as he ran, Matt pivoted south and alternated shots left and right. The whine of a bullet zinged by his ear. He tucked his rifle into his body and rolled. After more rotations than he could count, his boot collided with a wagon wheel. He quickly swiveled on his hip to get his head safely behind the wagon.

Only when he stopped twisting did he catch a glimpse of the boots on the other side.

He struggled to unfold. To bring his rifle barrel up. A glint of metal appeared around the corner, warning Matt that he was out of time. He flattened his body against the ground to make himself a smaller target, but instead of the gunshot he expected, a dull metallic *thud* rang in the air.

The camp cook glanced around the wagon, a Dutch oven dangling from his hand and an unconscious outlaw crumpled at his feet. "Get under the wagon. More are on the way. I'll go for the kid."

Matt scrambled on his belly and elbows beneath the chuck wagon, taking a quick glance behind him as he went.

Where was she?

Panic knifed through his gut when he couldn't spot Josie immediately. Had she made it to the trees? No. She'd only been a little over halfway a moment ago when Wallace intervened. Raising up on his elbows, Matt jutted his head out from under the wagon. He caught a glimpse of her white shirt and flapping green skirt, but before he could exhale in relief, a dark horse swooped in from the north.

The rider leaned sideways in the saddle, grabbed her about the waist, and flung her face-first over his lap.

Josie squealed.

Matt grinned.

Preach had her. Thank God.

He'd given his corporal one job: Get Josie away from the battle and keep her safe. Now that she was in Luke's care, Matt could concentrate on finding Taggart and taking him down.

The sound of glass shattering brought Matt's attention back to the house. Crawling to the north end of the wagon to get a less obstructed view of the farmhouse, Matt positioned his rifle and sighted the house. Someone was knocking out window glass with a rifle barrel. A man in black sleeves.

Taggart.

Matt's jaw tightened. Of course the head outlaw had reserved the most easily defended position for himself. They'd have to drive him out. Find a back way in or set the building on fire.

No easy task with Taggart's men swarming through the yard. And not all of them would remain on foot. Matt scowled as his gaze swept the area surrounding the barn. Four or five outlaws had captured horses and were in the process of mounting.

Taggart presented the bigger threat long-term, but riders prepared to give pursuit posed an immediate danger. Josie was the mission, Taggart the secondary objective. Matt shifted his aim to the paddock beside the barn.

A movement beside him, however, had him twisting to the side and yanking his revolver from its holster for close-quarters defense.

"Easy, Hanger. I'm bloody enough already." Charlie raised his palms in surrender, a broken chain dangling from his right wrist. His bottom lip was swollen enough to make his words slur as he halted his lopsided slither under the wagon and waited for Matt to decide his fate.

Matt fought the need to plant his fist on the kid's chin for what his actions had cost Josie and his men, but looking at the battered mess that was Charlie's face, he doubted there was an inch of untrounced territory available for him to leave his mark.

"I saw Preach grab Jo." Charlie didn't shrink from Matt's gaze. "Thank you."

The quiet words softened something inside Matt. Rich with remorse and humility, they were the words of a man ready to admit his wrongs and accept instruction. There might just be an honorable soldier under all that rebellion after all.

Matt turned back to gauge the outlaws' progress with the horses. A man was shouldering open the gate. In less than a minute, criminals on horseback would be after Josie.

"Your sister's not out of danger yet." Matt hesitated for a heartbeat, then flipped the revolver in his hand and extended it grip-first. "Can I trust you not to turn it on me this time?"

"Yes, sir." Charlie took the weapon in hand, his face hardening with determination as he scooted over to take up position beneath the left side of the chuck wagon. "I won't be repeating that mistake."

"Good." Matt aimed his rifle and squeezed the trigger. The first mounted outlaw grabbed his chest and toppled backward off his horse. "Then let's protect your sister's retreat before we lose our advantage."

"Let me go!" Slung ignominiously on her belly across her captor's lap, Josephine kicked her legs and arched her back in an effort to escape.

The big man just shoved her head back down, his arm the size of a small tree. "Keep yer head down, Doc. Too much lead flyin' around here. Matt'll shoot me himself if one of those bullets finds your pretty hide."

"Mr. Davenport?" Instead of arching up this time, she simply craned her neck until she could make out the profile of the man whose knees jarred her rib cage.

Luke Davenport crooked a half-grin and winked, though he never took his gaze from the battle around him. "At yer service, ma'am."

Thank heavens. Josephine relaxed until a new urgency filled her.

Matthew!

She'd seen him for one blessed moment. Vibrant. Strong. Running like a man who hadn't been laid low by a madman's bullet.

Yet. But now there were a dozen madmen taking aim at him.

She twisted her head to look behind her, the scene a chaotic blur as the horse's gait jostled her up and down.

She caught sight of Charlie first. Arnold, the cook, gripped him beneath his arms and dragged him backward toward the chuck wagon, where a man clad in a blue cavalry vest was crawling on his elbows to find cover beneath the wagon bed.

Her heart settled at the sight. Matthew was still alive. For the moment.

Keep him safe, Lord. You preserved his life against Taggart's bullet before. Please protect him again.

Josephine wanted to do more than pray for the man she loved. She wanted to help. But she was a healer, not a warrior. This situation was beyond her control. Beyond her abilities. Her eyes slid closed as she surrendered to the truth. She couldn't fix this. Couldn't shield the ones she loved. Only God could do that.

Yet she must remain vigilant. Her eyes sprang open as certainty blossomed in her soul. *This* moment might call for being still, but a moment was coming soon when she'd be called to take action. She needed to watch. And listen.

The sounds of gunfire grew muffled as the trees thickened. Finally, Preach drew his horse to a halt. He wrapped an arm around her waist and lowered her to the ground.

"Get on Matt's horse," he said, his chin flicking toward a fine dark bay.

One who carried the Gringolet brand. One whose birth she'd witnessed.

"Percival."

The horse nudged her shoulder as she neared, bringing a smile to her face. She stroked his neck, a sense of rightness settling over her.

Matthew had selected Percy. Out of all her father's stock, he'd selected the one closest to her heart. The one she'd been tempted to claim as her own when she left to start her practice in Purgatory Springs. In fact, when she'd offered Matthew her pick of Gringolet mounts in exchange for rescuing Charlie, *this* was the horse she'd imagined him choosing. Somehow, seeing Percival here, now, brought a comfort she hadn't expected. She leaned her face against Percy's neck, closed her eyes, and felt Matthew's presence.

Preach turned his mount to face the battle and drew his revolver. "Mount up, Doc, and be ready to ride. If any of Taggart's men break through our line, my orders are to get you to your father pronto."

He expected her to flee? Not a chance. She was a doctor on a battlefield. Her place was here, tending the wounded.

Especially the wounded she cared about. What if Matthew or Charlie took a bullet? *That* was what she needed to be ready for. Not saving her own skin.

Josephine fit her left foot to the stirrup and swung into the saddle, not caring that her skirt hiked up to expose her ankles and shins. "If we need to retreat temporarily, I'll follow your lead, but I'm not abandoning Matthew and the others." She set her jaw. "I'm a doctor. My place is with the wounded. Whoever they may be."

Preach shot a glare over his shoulder. "You're Matt's woman. Your place is wherever he says it is. And he said it's with me until I deliver you to your father."

Josephine bristled. "I am no man's possession, Luke Davenport. I will defer to your greater knowledge of warfare and do nothing to endanger Matthew or the other Horsemen, but neither will I shirk a fight that is as much mine as it is yours."

She could have sworn she saw his eyes light with respect before his heavy brows slashed down in a frown. "You're the mission, lady. And a cavalryman never compromises his mission. Your feelings are irrelevant. If I have to snatch you off that horse and carry you across my lap to gain your cooperation, that's what I'll do. Got it?"

Josephine gave a stiff nod. "I understand."

But comprehension and compliance were two different things, and she intended to keep her options open.

THIRTY-SIX

I need to reload!" Charlie reached for Matt's gun belt and started slipping bullets from the leather loops into the cylinder of his six-shooter.

"Make your shots count, kid," Matt warned, worried Charlie would run through their supply of ammunition before they ran through their supply of outlaws. "One careful shot is worth ten rushed ones."

As if to demonstrate, Matt took aim at the last rider in the paddock. The same man who'd spied on them at the original ransom location. On the same horse—Phineas.

Matt cleared his mind of the chaos around him, ignored the bullets banging against the wagon bed above his head, and zeroed in on his target. Adjusted for the rider's movement. Anticipated where he would be. Mentally calculated the best angle to avoid hitting his horse. Exhaled. Squeezed the trigger.

His shoulder absorbed the kick of the rifle. The rider absorbed the bullet. He tumbled from the saddle. Phineas held his position as trained.

Matt let out a shrill whistle. Phineas's ears pricked, and

his head turned in Matt's direction. Matt whistled again. Phineas shot through the paddock gate.

The outlaws were concentrating their attack on the two areas dispensing the hottest fire—the chuck wagon and Jonah's tree. Both of their positions were compromised. They needed an exit strategy.

Matt rolled onto his back and fed cartridges into his Winchester repeater. He'd need all fifteen shots for what he had in mind.

"Time to get you to your sister, Charlie." Matt slapped the kid's back, then flipped onto his stomach and crawled out from under the wagon. Staying low, he crouched behind the wagon with his rifle at the ready.

One.

Matt braced his shoulder against the wagon's side.

Two.

He listened. Charlie's scraping. Guns firing. Men yelling. The gunfire seemed thickest to the west, but Taggart was to the north, and the lead outlaw's position would present the clearest shot on Matt and Charlie. Plan formed, Matt turned his body north and braced for the charge.

Three!

He stood. Shot at the house window. Levered a new cartridge into the chamber. "Phin!" He added a whistle to his call as he shot at an outlaw taking cover behind a trough.

Undaunted by the gunfire, Phineas answered his master's call.

"Mount up, Charlie!" Matt yelled in a voice that left no room for question.

He continued firing. At the barn. Then the house. Then at a man running between the two. The man grabbed his right leg, hobbled to the house porch, and crawled beneath it.

Wallace rode up, offering Charlie additional cover in mounting Phineas. "I'm going for Brooks," Wallace yelled. "We'll get him to his mount and put an end to this once and for all."

"Good!"

Matt spotted a new man on horseback in the paddock. He took aim, then hesitated. The outlaw made no move for the gate. In fact, he seemed to be building up speed to . . . Matt dropped his finger from the trigger as the rider jumped the fence on the far side of the paddock where the top rail had fallen down.

"Looks like some are turnin' tail."

And after one broke ranks, others were sure to follow.

"I'll cover your retreat, Captain," Wallace said as he raised his pistol and fired toward the barn. "Get him out of here."

Matt didn't waste time debating. In one smooth motion, he mounted behind Charlie. "Follow the path Preach took," he instructed, keeping his gun hands free while Charlie took the reins. "Don't stop until you see your sister."

Charlie obeyed.

Using nothing but knee strength, balance, and his familiarity with Phineas's gait to keep him on his horse, Matt focused his firepower on the house, keeping Taggart occupied with self-preservation so he couldn't return fire until they presented a more distant target.

Once they'd covered enough ground that Matt could no longer contort his body to fire at the house without falling off the horse, he leaned tight against Charlie's back and urged Phineas to greater speed. A hot sting sizzled across his left upper arm, but he ignored it. All his attention centered on delivering Charlie and getting back to the battle to support his men and take down Taggart.

That attention disintegrated the moment he saw Josie.

"Charlie!" She called her brother's name, slid off Percival's back, and ran to greet them despite Preach's growled order to remain mounted.

Man, she looked good. Healthy. Whole. Her sea-green eyes glowing with relief. Her chin tilted in that no-nonsense way he loved. He couldn't look away. Or catch a full breath.

Charlie separated himself and awkwardly lifted his right leg over Phineas's neck to dismount. Matt dodged to the side to give the kid room to maneuver. That was when Josie saw him.

"Matthew."

His name sounded like a prayer, and the near reverence in her tone made his heart swell to twice its normal size. She halted mid-step, her gaze locked on his.

He wanted nothing more than to drop to the ground and sweep her into his arms. To hold her close and breathe her in. To claim her mouth and tell her everything that was in his heart. But a war raged behind him. A war he couldn't afford to neglect.

Charlie was saying something, but his voice was little more than a dull drone in Matt's ears. Josie seemed unbothered by it as well, her attention never leaving Matt's face.

He raised himself up over the cantle to sit properly in the saddle, then collected Phineas's reins with his left hand, his rifle still clutched in his right. "I have to go."

She bit her bottom lip as she nodded. "I know." She stepped close and placed a hand on his knee. Her chin lifted, and fire ignited her gaze. "You better come back to me, Matthew Hanger."

He knew he could make no promises, so he offered no words at all. Just dropped the reins, bent down, and fit his hand to the back of her neck. He pulled her to him and slanted his lips over hers in a hard, fast kiss born of desperation, love, and all the promises he longed to fulfill.

Then, before the temptation to abandon the fight and carry her away grew too strong to resist, he released her, took up the reins, and rode back into the heart of the battle.

Josephine's lips tingled as she watched the man she loved ride back into danger. She lifted her fingers to her mouth, trying to capture the various sensations, analyzing and cataloging them for future reference. The tickle of his mustache brushing the top of her lip, the bristles of his four-day-old beard abrading her chin, and the sweet pressure of his mouth melding against hers with a passion so fierce, her breath still stuttered.

She told herself she was savoring the feel of Matthew's lips on hers because the intimacy had tasted so strongly of love. But in truth, her desire to cling to the kiss stemmed from the fear that it might have been their last.

Bring him back to me, Lord. Please.

"Can you ride, Burkett?" Preach's brusque voice cut through her prayer and brought Josephine's head around.

Her brother stood before the Horseman, his face a mangled mess. One eye had already swollen shut. The other sported a congealed cut atop its brow. Abrasions lined his cheeks, and who knew how many bruises riddled his body, thanks to Carver's fists. The way he cradled his right side told her he probably had a couple cracked ribs, if not downright broken ones. The last thing he needed was to bounce around on the back of a horse.

"No, he needs to—"

"Yes." Charlie interrupted her, his gaze never leaving the big man before him. He straightened his posture and lifted his chin. "What do you need me to do?"

Josephine bit her tongue and blinked away the moisture gathering in her eyes. The earnestness of his gaze pierced her heart. Of all the times for her brother to opt for maturity and self-sacrifice. He could puncture a lung or be hit by a stray bullet or . . . or he could regain some of the honor he'd lost.

"Ride to the exchange location," Preach said. "Fetch your father and his men. We'll need their help to finish cleaning out these outlaws and to deliver the survivors to the closest law."

"Probably down in Hondo," Charlie offered. Then a thought seemed to sober his helpfulness. "Will, uh, will you be turning *me* in as well?"

Preach, still mounted, glared down at her brother, his expression unreadable. Charlie shifted his weight from one foot to the other as he awaited judgment.

"You chose the right side in the end. I suppose that oughta count for something."

Josephine didn't realize how stiff she'd become until her spine relaxed at his words.

"But if any of us finds you on the wrong side of the law again," Preach warned, his voice so hard it could chip granite, "not even being the doc's brother will save your hide. Got it?"

Charlie nodded. "Yes, sir."

Her brother strode toward Percival, his steps filled with purpose. But Josephine couldn't let him go. Not yet.

She intercepted him. "Wait."

Charlie turned, his mouth set in a firm line. "I'm going, Jo."

"I know."

As much as she wanted to protect him from possible physical

harm, she knew this was something he needed to do. She even admired him for it. Not only was he willing to risk his own safety to fetch reinforcements, but he was voluntarily facing their father. Alone. After betraying the family. That took more courage than riding through a yard of gunslinging outlaws.

"I'm not stopping you," she said, staunchly eradicating all sisterly compassion from her tone just as she would dirt from a wound. "I just want to wrap your ribs before you go. If you puncture a lung, you'll do no one any good."

"Hurry up," Preach grumbled as he turned away from the siblings and focused on the gunfire still echoing from the far side of the trees.

Josephine lifted her skirt, grabbed a handful of petticoat from beneath, and tore off the entire bottom flounce. "Lift your shirt," she ordered. Steeling herself not to react to the damage he revealed, she gave him a cursory examination and gently probed his ribs. "Does it hurt to breathe?"

"Some," he mumbled softly, as if not wanting Preach to overhear the admission, "but no more than it hurts to do anything else."

A rather weak endorsement of health, but considering his current state, it would suffice. She reached for the wide cotton strip she'd slung over her shoulder. "All right, then. Arms up."

He complied, his one visible eye rolling at her big-sister tone.

She wrapped his ribs tightly enough to provide protection and support but not so tight as to impair his breathing. As she tied off the bandage, she looked him in the eye.

"Be careful out there, Charlie. And remember . . ." She squeezed his hand. "No matter how angry Father may be, he loves you."

Charlie gave no response, just pulled his hand from hers,

turned his back, and mounted. A moment later he disappeared from sight.

"Mount up behind me, Doc." Preach waved her forward. "We still gotta be ready to ride if things go south." He pulled his left foot from the stirrup.

Josephine fit her foot into the vacated stirrup, though she needn't have bothered. As soon as the big man's hand clamped over her forearm, she soared through the air like a sack of flour being tossed into a wagon bed. Or onto a horse's rump, in this case.

She held Preach's shoulders for balance as she situated herself, then placed an arm loosely at his waist. He seemed the sort of man to take off at a gallop should he suddenly be called to action, and she doubted he'd provide sufficient warning. Best to have a handhold ready.

Despite the lightness of her touch, she could feel the tension coiled within him. That tension proved contagious, for the longer she sat there listening to the battle, the more her trepidation built. Soon she flinched at every gunshot, worrying over where that bullet might have lodged.

She tried to peer around Preach's broad shoulders, but she saw nothing but trees. "Can you see anything?"

A growled order to be quiet was the only answer she got.

Josephine pressed her lips together. Maybe he could sense what was happening by the sounds filtering through the trees. He had served in countless battles, after all. Surely if he believed Matthew or one of the others was in trouble, he'd do something. Wouldn't he?

She recalled the look on his face when he'd called her his *mission*, the unbending set of his jaw, the cold steel of his eyes. No. He'd be just stubborn enough to follow orders even at the expense of the man who'd given them.

Time crawled by. Minute after excruciating minute.

How could he just sit there? Not knowing Matthew's fate was killing her. Every shot that echoed off the trees slammed into her chest. She needed to see what was happening. Gather data. Assess. Analyze. Find a way to help.

Be still.

She didn't want to be still. She wanted to help. To heal. To—

Be still, and know that I am God.

Her left hand fisted in the fabric of her skirt. Her eyes squeezed shut. A tear slid down her cheek. *I'm afraid, Lord. Afraid to completely surrender. Afraid that if I have no control over the outcome, it won't end the way I desire. Afraid you'll take Matthew from me.*

Lean not unto thine own understanding.

Josephine's heart pricked. That was it, wasn't it? She trusted her own understanding more than she trusted God's unfathomable wisdom.

Another tear leaked between her lashes. *Forgive me.* Slowly, her fingers unfurled, releasing their grip on her skirt. *I surrender.*

Her mind went quiet after that. Or was it the actual air? Josephine's eyes opened. Had the shooting stopped?

The sound of horses approaching stiffened her spine. In a flash, Preach had his rifle aimed and ready.

"It's me!"

Josephine recognized Mark Wallace's voice a heartbeat before his horse cantered between the oaks shielding them from the battle.

Preach dropped his weapon and nudged his mount forward to meet his compatriot. Josephine's right arm tightened about his waist.

"Taggart's on the run," Wallace announced as he reined his horse to a halt. "Over half the outlaws are down. Jonah is working his way through the camp, taking stock of injuries and disarming all enemy combatants."

"And the captain?"

Josephine held her breath, her spirit crying out to God for mercy.

Wallace flicked a glance at her before focusing again on Preach. "He went after Taggart."

"Alone?" The cry tore from Josephine's chest. She grabbed Preach's left arm and made to dismount. "Go after him." She accented her order with a thump to his back as she slid off the horse. "The fight is done here. I'm safe. Mr. Wallace and Mr. Brooks can protect your precious *mission* while I tend the wounded."

Preach hesitated, his gaze searching Wallace's face. She could feel his longing to do exactly as she suggested. Knew he was champing at the bit to get into the fight, to watch his captain's back.

But Wallace shook his head. "Orders are to secure the premises. A handful of outlaws fled. They could circle back. Captain wants us here, guarding the doctor."

Josephine fought the urge to scream as her feet hit the ground. "And who's going to guard him?"

"'One man of you shall chase a thousand: for the Lord your God, he it is that fighteth for you, as he hath promised you.' Joshua 23:10." As the quiet words fell from Preach's lips, hot tears fell from Josephine's eyes.

How quick she was to grab for the reins the instant the path the Lord led her down took a turn she didn't favor. Where was her trust? Her surrender?

Josephine covered her face with her hands. Control was

nothing more than an illusion, a lie to trap the competent in their own capability. One that created such a dependence on self that it clogged the conduit of wisdom and power flowing from the Omnipotent until only a trickle of living water found its way through.

Help me, Lord. Clear out the debris of pride and fear clogging my soul and let your river of living water flow through me unhindered. Help me trust that you are at work. That you will fight for Matthew, for justice. And should the worst happen, that you will fight for me too. That I might believe in your goodness even in the pit of despair.

─ CHAPTER ─
THIRTY-SEVEN

Matt bent low over Phineas's neck, urging him to greater speed as he locked his gaze on the rider in black two hundred yards ahead. Taggart had the fresher mount, and he'd managed to get a jump on Matt by sneaking out the back door of the farmhouse, but Matt's bones burned with the fire of justice, driving him to the edge of recklessness. Taggart would not escape. Not this time.

Little by little, Phineas closed the gap. Taggart twisted to glance behind. Drew his pistol. Fired two shots.

Matt ducked. The shots missed, but not by much. Taggart had skill.

Matt considered returning fire, but his ammunition was low, and rising up to make the shot would give Taggart a bigger target. Plus it would slow him down, and Matt intended to run this outlaw to ground.

Another shot kicked up dirt a few feet in front of Phin's hooves. Phineas didn't even break stride, just ran on, as determined as the man on his back to accomplish the mission.

They closed the distance to a hundred yards. Then fifty.

Matt kept Phineas slightly to Taggart's right, making it nearly impossible for the outlaw to get an accurate shot off, since he had to stretch his arm across and around his body to the left to shoot behind him.

"We got him now, Phin."

Thirty yards to go.

This time when Taggart craned his neck to look behind him, Matt could make out his scowl. Along with the fear in his eyes.

The gun appeared at Taggart's left side again, farther around his back this time. But the curve of his arm was too steep, and when he fired, the bullet flew wildly right.

He only had one shot left, by Matt's count. Not even an experienced outlaw could reload his weapon while racing on horseback.

Twenty yards.

The gun barrel appeared over Taggart's right shoulder, the weapon upside down. A blind shot. A desperate shot.

Gunfire cracked the air.

Phineas stumbled, and his front legs crumpled beneath him. Matt flew forward. Kicked free of the stirrups. Tucked. Braced for impact.

His shoulder slammed into the earth. Then his spine. His hip. Pain exploded everywhere. He rolled. Drew his revolver. Ignored the pain screaming at him to stop.

He came up in a crouch. One shot. Had to make it count.

Forty yards. Fifty.

Matt exhaled. Aimed.

Sixty yards.

He pulled the trigger.

Taggart fell forward, but stayed in the saddle. Slumped, but mounted.

Seventy-five yards.

Matt shot again, but Taggart was out of pistol range. He needed the Winchester.

He lurched to his feet and limped back to Phineas, steeling himself against the agonizing sight of his beloved horse writhing on the ground. Phin would have to wait. Matt snatched the rifle from the scabbard, turned, and took aim.

As he sighted the target, however, it moved. Taggart's horse jumped over something in its path, and the jarring landing unseated the outlaw. Taggart slid sideways. Matt lifted his gaze from the rifle sight and squinted at the black figure nearly a hundred yards out.

Taggart listed farther left, grappling for a hold on the saddle. But his weight was too unevenly distributed. He tumbled from the horse.

Matt dropped his rifle into a one-handed grip and started running. Limping, really, but his pain-filled, ungainly stride smoothed out the more he ran. And he ran for all he was worth. He had to get to Taggart before the outlaw had a chance to reload. He might be down, but he still posed a threat.

Taggart scrambled backward on his rump and heels, his revolver cradled against his belly as he fumbled to pull bullets from his gun belt. His left arm hung useless from its socket, blood staining his black shirt.

Matt ran harder. The stitches in his side tore open, but he refused to relent.

Taggart got one bullet loaded. Then another. He snapped the cylinder into place. Raised his weapon as Matt descended upon him.

Matt swung the stock of his rifle and knocked the gun from the outlaw's hand. Taggart lunged for the fallen weapon, and

Matt dove atop him, pinning him to the ground. He knocked the gun out of reach. Taggart head-butted him, and daggers stabbed the backs of Matt's eyes. He reared up, silver specks dancing through his vision. Then a fist danced into view and slammed against his jaw. The blow snapped Matt's head around but failed to dislodge him.

In a swift motion, Matt brought his rifle around, clasped it lengthwise in both hands, and brought it down across Taggart's collarbone, neatly trapping the outlaw's right arm beneath the stock and pinning it to the ground beside his head.

"It's over, Taggart," Matt gritted out as he pressed his body weight onto the rifle, causing the barrel to dig into Taggart's windpipe.

The outlaw cursed and tried to buck Matt off. In response, Matt planted his knee atop the bloodied fabric covering Taggart's left bicep. Taggart howled, then stilled. Hatred glared from his eyes.

"You'll pay for this, Hanger," he rasped.

Matt shrugged off the threat, recognizing it for what it was—a toothless attempt at intimidation from a man newly stripped of power.

"Probably." He would certainly pay in blood and bruises. But the reward of knowing Josie was safe and the outlaw who'd taken her was behind bars would be well worth the personal cost.

Matt shifted his hold on the rifle and grabbed Taggart's good arm. Lifting up, he flipped the outlaw onto his belly, planted his knee in the small of his back, and twisted his arm behind him. He yanked the injured arm behind him as well, earning another string of curses. Taking a coil of thin rope from inside his vest pocket, he wound the binding around

Taggart's wrists, tied it off, then yanked the outlaw to his feet and dragged him toward the horse that had halted about a dozen yards away after losing its rider.

"Just be glad I'm not shooting you and leaving you for dead," Matt said, a touch of irony lacing his tone.

Taggart, his face mottled with rage, tried to jerk away, but Matt's grip proved too strong. "I should have put you down when I had the chance. Ridden up and put a bullet between your eyes while your woman watched."

"Yep. You should have." Matt grinned. "Though if you think she would have been a passive spectator, you're sadly mistaken. Josie's never passive about anything."

"Jonah Brooks, quit fiddling with that pile of saddlebags and come here so I can tend that wound." Josephine badgered the last Horseman to submit to her doctoring. She'd already seen to the others, after tending the more serious injuries sustained by the outlaws, but Mr. Brooks was proving elusive.

Jonah didn't look up from where he rifled through the outlaw bags piled atop a sawhorse table at the back of the barn. "Leave me be. I'm busy."

"Fine. I'll come to you." Josephine grabbed her medical bag and the last of the bandages Arnold had made for her from the moth-nibbled sheet he'd found in the farmhouse linen closet.

The camp cook had hidden for most of the battle, dashing into neutral territory behind the bushes that guarded the camp latrine after delivering Charlie to the chuck wagon. Once the gunfire ceased, he'd emerged to lend a hand, becoming Josephine's medical assistant. At the moment, he was making the rounds through the barn-turned-infirmary, taking water to the outlaw patients who were conscious.

Amazingly, there had been only two fatalities. The red-bearded Dawson had died where he'd fallen next to the farmhouse, and Carver had succumbed to his wounds despite Josephine's efforts to save him. He'd been the most critically injured and therefore the one she'd tended first. She'd thrust his wickedly large knife into the coals of the cook fire and used it to cauterize the wound in his chest as quickly as she could in order to stem the massive blood loss, but it had been too late.

By Mark's count, five of Taggart's men had escaped, two had perished, and four lay secured to their bunks in various states of injury. Over the last two hours, she'd cleaned wounds, sutured tissue, and pulled lead out of the very men who'd tried to destroy her family. Not that she'd thought of them that way while she worked. They'd simply been patients in need of a doctor.

Looking at them now as she strode past them to get to Jonah, her clinical frame of mind numbed her emotions and allowed her to see them with a level of objectivity. How many had started off as foolish young men running with the wrong crowd, just like Charlie? They'd hardened over time, crime and rough living callousing their consciences until they no longer cared who they hurt in pursuit of gold, drink, and loose women. But they'd been children once, little boys with skinned knees and runny noses. Did they have family praying for them somewhere? Mothers? Sisters?

Take away their hearts of stone, Lord, and replace them with hearts of flesh so that they might repent and turn their lives toward you.

She'd seen the change in Charlie and prayed fervently that he would continue along redemption's path. She prayed her father would not stand in the way, but would offer forgiveness and guidance instead of blame and anger.

At least he hadn't killed her brother outright, Josephine thought with a wry grin. They'd arrived twenty minutes ago, neither very talkative, but both still able to sit a horse.

"Better watch out, Brooks. The doc's grinnin'. No telling what kind of torture she's cooked up for you," Preach called from his position at the north end of the barn where it opened into the paddock. From there he could guard the prisoners as well as watch the terrain for any outlaws who might return. Mark held a similar position at the south end.

"I *would* argue that Mr. Brooks is far too intelligent to believe such a ludicrous charge," Josephine stated as she came up behind Jonah, "but the fact that he keeps avoiding my attempts to tend his wounds has me questioning that assessment."

Jonah failed to rise to her bait. Just turned the saddlebag he'd been searching upside down and shook it until every last crumb of stale hardtack tumbled out.

Josephine set her doctor's bag on the table and crossed her arms. "Your search for outlaw gold can wait, Mr. Brooks. I need to clean that gash on your head."

"It ain't gold I'm hunting, Doc." More than impatience tinged his voice. There was something that sounded like . . . heartbreak.

Josephine uncrossed her arms and placed a hand on the sharpshooter's shoulder. "What is it, Jonah? What are you looking for?"

His hands stopped their frantic shaking of the leather bag,

but his gaze never left the table. "My daddy's compass." His quiet words pierced her heart. "It weren't in my bag. One of the outlaws must've taken it."

A family heirloom, perhaps all he had left of the man who'd fathered him.

She pushed her medical bag aside and grabbed one of the emptied pouches. "I'll help you search."

He shook his head. "It ain't no use. I been through them all. It ain't here." He dropped the bag onto the table. "It probably rode off with one of the men who escaped." His head came up, and a muscle ticked in his jaw. "Doesn't matter. It's just a compass. I can buy a new one." The flatness of his tone stirred her compassion.

"It *does* matter. Let's look through these one more time. Maybe you missed something."

He raised a brow and glared at her.

"Don't get in a huff, now." She rolled her eyes and opened the bag she'd confiscated. "You've suffered a head trauma." Judging by the size of the jagged gash and the extensive bruising around it, he'd sustained a serious contusion while vacating his sniper position in the tree. "It's possible your normally eagle-eyed vision is operating at less than optimal efficacy."

His mouth twitched just a hair at the corner. "Matt's right about them ten-dollar words of yours. They make a man's head hurt."

"Your head hurts because you butted a tree limb with your cranium, Mr. Brooks. It has nothing to do with my choice of vocabulary."

That bit of sass earned her a chuckle as Jonah shook his head and dragged one of the saddlebags he'd discarded earlier back toward him for another examination.

Fifteen minutes later, Josephine's optimism for finding the missing compass had faded, and Jonah's mention of ten-dollar words had reinvigorated her concern for Matthew. As she lifted silent prayers for the safe return of both the compass and the man she loved, somehow the two became intertwined. The longer they went without recovering the compass, the more she fretted over Matthew's failure to return as well.

"That's odd." The statement, the first Jonah had uttered since renewing his search, brought Josephine's head around. "There's a slit in the side seam." He bent his elbow at an odd angle as he dug around in the leather bag. "Could just be the stitching wearing out."

She bounced up on her toes. "Or it could be a hidden pocket. This *is* the bag of an outlaw, after all."

Jonah met her gaze, a flash of excitement, of hope, dancing between them. It was all she could do not to push him aside and take over the exploration herself.

"Get your knife. We can cut away the seam entirely." She'd offer her scalpel, but she didn't want to dull the blade.

He shook his head. "I think I've . . . got it." He pulled his hand from the bag, a tarnished brass pocket compass in his palm.

Josephine beamed at him and clasped his forearm. "You found it! Oh, Jonah, I'm so glad."

Now, if only . . .

Preach let out a sharp whistle. Jonah's smile evaporated, the steely sharpshooter back on high alert.

"Got movement to the north," Preach reported.

"The captain?" Jonah took a step toward Preach as he slid his father's compass into his pocket and reached for the rifle he'd left leaning against the barn wall.

Preach shrugged. "Too far out to tell. Man on foot. One, maybe two horses."

Matthew! It was him. Josephine had not a single doubt. She sprinted past the Horsemen, ignoring their shouts to stop, their warnings that it might not be him.

Dashing into the paddock, she wove between the horses, her eyes set on the one at the far end, nearest her brother.

"Stop her!" Preach yelled.

Her father looked up from the injured Gringolet horse he'd been tending. "Jo?"

She offered no explanation. Just ran. Her pursuers' footsteps pounded behind her.

"Charlie! Leg up!"

Her brother stood at Percival's side, currycomb in hand. The saddle and blanket had been removed. He turned to face her and surely spotted the men on her heels. For a moment she thought he might not comply, but she should have known she could count on the irrepressible scamp to have her back.

Charlie tossed the comb aside as she neared, braced his legs apart, and made a step of interlocked fingers. His eyes sparked with the same loyalty and mischief that had led them to master this maneuver as kids, in defiance of their father's insistence that such a move was too dangerous for a girl.

He gave her a nod. "Ready!"

Three more steps and she was there. She planted her left foot in his palm, gripped his shoulder for balance, then kicked out her right leg as he tossed her up and over. Safely astride Percy's back, she grabbed the reins and set off. With no saddle or stirrups, the jump over the downed fence threw her forward against the horse's neck, but she recovered and kicked Percy into a gallop.

"Go get 'em, Jo!" Charlie's proud call rang in her ears.

The more ground she covered, the more her heart urged her on. It *was* Matthew. She recognized his hat, his vest. But not his stride. He was hurt. Limping. Cradling his side as he led a horse with a man draped over the saddle. Taggart.

Phineas, like his master, limped behind. Head low, steps ginger, a darkened spot above his right shoulder. But like his master, he was alive. Alive and beautiful.

I'm coming, Matthew!

His head came up, as if he'd heard her heart's vow. His posture straightened. The lead line fell from his hand.

"Josie."

She swore she could hear her name on his lips, even though distance combined with Percival's hoofbeats and those of the horse charging from behind made that a scientific impossibility. But then, science didn't know everything.

Matthew started to jog toward her, his steps growing surer the more ground he covered. Josephine calculated the remaining distance. She let Percy run a few more strides then reined him in. The moment he slowed enough for her to dismount without breaking a limb, she slid from his back. Her dismount was not as graceful as she would have wished. Her impatience left her stumbling, but she corrected her balance before sprawling on her face, and that was all she cared about. Staying on her feet so she could get to Matthew.

And then she was in his arms. Crying. Laughing. Her palms splayed across his chest. Her gaze drinking him in.

"You came back to me."

He cupped her face. The pad of his thumb grazed her cheek in a caress so tender, so filled with love, her heart squeezed. After raking her face with his gaze as if he sought to memorize every line and freckle, his hazel eyes finally met hers. "As long as I have breath in my bones, Josie mine, I will *always* come back to you."

Then his lips crashed onto hers, and everything inside her exulted. She returned his kiss with all the passion her worry had tamped down, giving her love free rein. A moan escaped him, and she tried to move away, afraid she'd exacerbated an injury with her enthusiasm. But he tightened his hold, pulling her even closer, deepening the kiss until everything but him faded from her mind.

"I'll, uh, see to Taggart for ya, Cap. Phineas too."

The sound of Preach's voice barely registered in her love-clouded brain. Matthew's kiss gentled but didn't stop. One of his hands left her face, his arm moving sharply for a moment, as if waving his man away, before coming to rest at the small of her back, then pressing up the length of her spine.

A warm chuckle filtered over them, followed by words that had something to do with Preach leaving his horse for Matthew to use. Then, finally, they were alone again.

Matthew didn't ease his hold on her for several long minutes—minutes filled with kisses that heated her blood and curled her toes. When he finally lifted his mouth from hers, her breathing came in ragged little pants. His forehead rested against hers, and his hands curled over her shoulders.

"Marry me, Josie."

Her eyes flew open. Slowly, she leaned back and peered into his face. He met her gaze with such humility, her chest ached.

"I know I'm not much of a catch. I'm a warrior past his prime with blood on his hands and regrets on his soul, but I love you more than I ever loved anyone or anything in my life. After my folks died, I swore I'd never take a wife, never risk the pain of that kind of loss again. But I think it would hurt more to walk away from you now."

A tear rolled down her cheek. He wiped it away with a knuckle roughened and scarred by battle, yet it stroked with such gentleness, she couldn't help leaning her face toward him to seek more of his touch.

"I can't promise you a life free from trouble or hardship," he said, his voice husky with emotion, "but I can promise you that I will love you every moment of every day."

All these years, she'd thought she was destined to minister to other people's families, not one of her own. That no one would want a headstrong woman employed in a man's profession. Since no man had stirred her heart into wanting more, she'd been content with her lot. Until Matthew Hanger burst into her clinic, snapping orders left and right, fighting for the life of his friend. He might be a battle-hardened warrior, dictatorial and stubborn, but he'd treated her like an equal from the day they'd met. He valued her abilities, trusted her instincts, and had risked his life to save hers. Multiple times. How could she not love him? He was everything she'd never thought she'd find.

They might have a lot of details to sort through to successfully combine two radically different lives into one, but if God could join their hearts so completely, she had no doubt that he would find a way to blend their lives as well.

"I love you, Matthew," she said with a smile she could no longer contain, "and nothing would make me happier than to be your wife."

He grinned and bent his head toward hers for another kiss, but she leaned away, her attention darting to the ugly brown stain on the left side of his vest.

"But first, we better tend to that, don't you think?" She

raised a brow, warning him not to argue, then reached for the buttons of his vest and, one by one, pushed them through their holes.

Matthew chuckled softly and opened his arms in surrender, letting her have her way. "Tend to me as much as you want, Doc," he said with a wiggle of his brows that made her fingers stutter on the buttons. "I'm all yours."

EPILOGUE

FOUR MONTHS LATER

Seee you next week, Mrs. Timmons." Josephine held the clinic door wide as the young woman she'd just examined exited the clinic. The October breeze had turned chilly over the course of the afternoon, but Josephine welcomed the fresh air.

Mr. Timmons jumped up from the bench where he'd been waiting outside and immediately took his wife's arm to help her down the boardwalk steps to their wagon.

Heavy with their first child, Elmira Timmons placed a supporting hand beneath her belly as she paused to smile over her shoulder. "Thanks, Dr. Jo. I keep telling Harland that we still got at least a month, but he frets somethin' fierce."

"Well, Harland knows where to find me if that babe of yours decides to get an early start."

The young husband nodded, his face as serious as if he'd been called upon to give a graded recitation in front of the class. "Clinic during the day. Gringolet at night. If you're on another call, I'm to ask Mr. Watson or Miss Darla to get word to you."

"That's right," Josephine praised, trying not to grin too widely. Expectant fathers needed as much soothing as expectant mothers. "And if the baby comes on October 21?"

"I'm to fetch Dr. Peabody or Madge Smith."

"Excellent." Josephine had made arrangements for one of the younger, more open-minded San Antonio physicians to cover any patient emergencies that might arise among her clients on Saturday. And if he were unavailable to assist with a birthing, an older woman from church who had twenty years of midwifery experience had volunteered to assist.

Being roused from bed for delivery duty was a doctor's lot, but she and Matthew had agreed that their wedding night would be an exception to the rule.

As the Timmonses continued on their way, Josephine glanced down the road to the west, unable to stop her heart from giving a little jump. Matthew was due back today. He'd wired her this morning to expect him. The usual place. The usual time. She checked the watch pendant hanging from a chain around her neck. Less than thirty minutes.

She spun back into the clinic and closed the door behind her. She needed to get ready.

Her instruments had already been cleaned and her medical bag restocked before Mrs. Timmons arrived for her appointment, so all that remained was to tidy up the examination room and go through her correspondence.

After her examination table had been wiped down, her clinic stethoscope stored in its drawer, and her medicine cabinet locked for the night, Josephine took a seat at the small desk in the corner and sorted through the stack of mail that had accumulated. A medical journal, the monthly bill from her druggist, an envelope from Purgatory Springs. Seeing the personal missive, Josephine set the rest aside and tore open the letter from Lizzie Carrington.

Dear Jo,

I thought you'd like to know that Daddy's arm is healed up right as rain after his accident with the barbed wire. Dr. Fields has proven to be just as competent as you promised. She's assured me that there is no sign of lockjaw and that the infection I initially panicked over was mild and easily treated.

Josephine sent a quick prayer of gratitude heavenward. Ramona Fields had been one year behind her in school, and the two of them had often been paired together in their laboratory studies. Ramona was exceptionally bright if a bit timid. When Josephine decided to move her practice to San Antonio in order to be closer to Charlie and her father, Dr. Fields had been her first choice to replace her in Purgatory Springs. A competent doctor to tend the people Josephine cared about, and a community accustomed to female physicians for a doctor struggling to find a place to utilize her talents.

Now, about your wedding! Is your dress finished? I can't wait to see it. And Matthew? Has he returned from his latest mission with the Horsemen? I pray he is well. Have you convinced him to accept your father's offer of a partnership in Gringolet yet? A married man should settle down, you know, not go traipsing all over creation putting himself in the path of wayward bullets. I thank God that Paul is content with the mercantile. I don't think I could endure the constant worry—

"Hey, sis." Charlie's call, followed by the closing of the back door, interrupted Lizzie's epistolary chatter. "That package you've been waiting for finally arrived."

Charlie stepped into the room and handed her a long, thin parcel.

Her sign!

She jumped to her feet and grabbed it with all the excitement of a child on Christmas morning. "It came! I worried it wouldn't get here in time." She used a penknife to cut through the binding string, then tore off the brown paper. She laid the black wooden shingle on her desk and ran her hand lovingly across the white stenciled letters.

Dr. Josephine Hanger.

Charlie came up behind her and peered over her shoulder. "That just looks wrong."

Josephine elbowed him in the ribs. "You'll get used to it."

Charlie let out a beleaguered sigh. "I suppose. But you can't *Hanger* it up until next week. You're still a Burkett for a few more days."

Josephine groaned as she turned to face him, her eyes rolling with excessive drama. "'*Hanger* it up'? Really? That was terrible."

Charlie's eyes danced. "That's what happens when you have a brother who's always *Hanger*ing around next door."

"Stop!" She swatted lightly at his chest but couldn't keep laughter from bubbling out of her mouth.

Having the teasing brother back that she remembered so well from her youth made her relocation to San Antonio worth every heartache that came with saying good-bye to friends. Charlie now joined her for church, held down a job, and made a delightful nuisance of himself on a regular basis. She couldn't be more pleased with his turnaround.

Tension still existed between the Burkett men, but there was no outright animosity. After they'd returned home, her father had given Charlie a choice. Either buckle down and learn the business of Gringolet, join the army, or find a job elsewhere to support himself. There'd be no more allowance. He'd only have access to funds earned by the sweat of his brow.

Even in the best of times, Charlie had chafed under his father's management, so working at Gringolet was out of the question. With Matthew's influence, Charlie could have easily found his way into a cavalry unit, but her brother rejected that option as well. Which left finding work locally. A task that proved difficult. Having a reputation for colluding with outlaws didn't inspire a great deal of trust in prospective employers, but God was in the prodigal-redeeming business, and in less than a month, he'd opened a path.

Josephine's father had insisted on bestowing a generous reward on Arnold Watson when he learned the measures the camp cook had taken not only to keep his daughter safe during her captivity, but also to protect Charlie during the gunfight. Arnold had used that money—along with funds whose origins Josephine chose not to question—to open an eatery in the vacant storefront next door to her new clinic on the outskirts of town.

The Chuck Wagon Café made the perfect neighbor for a doctor who could barely boil water. Arnold kept her fed with simple cowboy fare that had proven popular with the locals. So popular, in fact, that he soon needed someone to wait tables and help in the kitchen. Charlie proved the perfect fit. His charisma made him a natural with the customers. Not only that, but Arnold swore her brother had talent in the kitchen. Even more amazing, Charlie actually enjoyed the work. Cooking gave him the freedom to experiment and make his own mark. Something he'd never been able to accomplish under their father at Gringolet.

"You really need to redo the main sign as well," Charlie said. "*Medical Clinic* is so boring. I'd vote for *Bullets & Babies*."

"What? That's awful!" Yet she couldn't stop a giggle from escaping.

Charlie made a comically thoughtful face. "*Babies & Bullets?*"

She planted her hands on her hips. "Just because my practice leans heavily toward expectant mothers and violent injuries does *not* mean I need to advertise that fact to the world."

As was often the case when a female doctor started a medical practice, women comprised the majority of Josephine's clients. However, after word spread about her being the personal physician for Hanger's Horsemen and the future wife of Matthew Hanger himself, she started collecting a new clientele. One a bit rougher around the edges, whose presenting symptoms included bullet holes, penetrating knife wounds, and head trauma usually brought on by collisions with liquor bottles. She never thought she'd miss Mrs. Flanders's carbuncle, but every once in a while, it would be nice to treat an actual illness.

Charlie continued spouting other horrendous monikers for her clinic, but the quiet click of boot heels on the boardwalk outside deafened her to anything he said. Heart fluttering, she checked her pendant watch and confirmed her hypothesis.

It was time.

She tore off her work apron and threw it at her brother, then smoothed her bodice and touched a hand to her hair.

"What am I supposed to do with this?" Charlie waved the white apron at her, but she sidestepped him without an answer and hurried across the room.

The front door opened, and there he was. The man who would be her husband in three days.

Unable to help herself, she scanned him for any sign of injury, then thanked the Lord when she found none. His examination of her apparently followed a more leisurely time-table, for when she raised her gaze back to his face, his was still making a slow, upward climb. When his eyes finally met hers again, she found herself grateful for the cool October breeze blowing into her clinic.

Matthew stepped close and wrapped an arm around her waist, dragging her against his chest. "I missed you, darlin'."

"I missed you too," she said, bringing a hand up to fiddle with the top button on his light blue vest. "A week is a long time."

"Too long." He dipped his head toward hers.

She raised her face.

Charlie pounced. "Matt! Good to have you back."

Matthew lifted his head and scowled at her completely unrepentant brother. Charlie took his chaperoning duties far too seriously.

Heat flushed Josephine's cheeks as she eased away from Matthew's possessive hold. She curled her arm around his, though, and led him the rest of the way inside, leaving Charlie to close the door behind them.

"Did the widow's case go as expected?" she asked. While she'd been setting up her new clinic in San Antonio, the

Horsemen had been investigating the suspicious goings-on in Burnet. Wallace and Preach had spent nearly a month at the ranch before uncovering the truth.

"For the most part," Matt said. "Jury found the foreman guilty of several counts of assault based on the statements given by the men he hired to scare away the Rocking M hands." Men the Horsemen had tracked down and strongly encouraged to testify. "But they couldn't prove murder of the widow's husband. Seems it might have been natural causes after all. The foreman had no actual designs on his boss's widow, just planned to make her desperate enough to sell the ranch to him at a fraction of the price it was worth." He stroked the inside of Josephine's arm, the touch terribly distracting. "Wallace put her in contact with an eastern buyer willing to pay top dollar, though, so she'll be set for life."

"I'm glad to hear it." Once in the waiting room, she turned to face him, slipping her hand down his arm to twine her fingers with his. "How are the rest of the men?"

"Brought 'em back with me."

"To Gringolet?"

Matthew stayed in the bunkhouse at her father's ranch whenever he was in town, which was more and more frequently of late.

"Yep." His face remained stoic, but his eyes smiled in that private way of his that made her heart pound in anticipation. "Figured if I was going to retire the Horsemen, they'd need regular work. Thaddeus promised them jobs once I agreed to the partnership."

"Retire the Horsemen?" Josephine held her breath. She'd been so careful not to make any demands on him over the last months, understanding how important his work was to him. To all of them. But she'd been praying. And apparently her father had been bribing.

"Even got it in writing." Matthew reached inside his coat, pulled out a folded newspaper, and handed it to her. "Francis Kendall was kind enough to give me an early edition before I left Austin this mornin'."

She unfolded the paper and skimmed the page until the article in the bottom right corner snagged her attention. *Hanger's Horsemen Hang Up Their Hats.*

She glanced at Matthew to assure herself that she hadn't misread anything. He nodded, his mouth curving ever so slightly.

Turning back to the article, she scanned the highlights.

With matrimony on the horizon, Matthew Hanger is disbanding his famous foursome of horsemen and turning his attention to more domestic pursuits . . . accepted a partnership in Gringolet Farms with his father-in-law-to-be, Thaddeus Burkett. . . . As of this printing, Mr. Kendall will no longer be accepting requests for assistance on behalf of the Horsemen at the *Weekly Statesman* office.

Joy erupted inside her, yet she knew this decision could not have been easy. She and Matthew had each other, but what about Preach, Mark, and Jonah?

"Are your men . . . ?"

"They're fine." Matthew took the paper back from her and stuffed it in his pocket. "They'll work at Gringolet until they find their own niches elsewhere, but we all agreed it was time to move on. I created the Horsemen as a way to atone for the atrocities of Wounded Knee, but meeting you has shown me—shown all of us, really—that there are ways to do good that don't entail gunfighting and violence. Besides, we made a pact that whenever the Horsemen are needed, we will answer the call. Together. We just won't seek out those opportunities anymore. We'll let the Lord determine which jobs we take. If something crosses our path and stirs our soul, we'll answer the call. Otherwise, we'll keep our pistols holstered and focus on tending to the people closest at hand."

Josephine bit her lip and sidled closer. "People like your future wife?"

Matthew tugged her close. Traced a finger along the edge of her cheek. "Mmm. People *exactly* like my future wife."

"Charlie?" Josephine called without looking away from Matthew's heated gaze.

"Yeah, sis?" Charlie stuck his face annoyingly close to theirs, but neither she nor Matthew paid him any heed.

"Time for you to go back to the Chuck Wagon."

"Fine." Charlie huffed and stomped noisily away. "But I'll be back in ten minutes," he called from the other room. "With a pitcher of cold water."

The moment the back door closed on Charlie and his idle threats, Matthew's lips pressed into hers with a tenderness that sent tiny shivers dancing over her skin. She rose up to meet him, took hold of the back of his neck, and deepened the kiss. He released her hand in order to circle his arm around her back, holding her so close that she could easily believe nothing of consequence would ever come between them.

His mouth left her lips and dropped a kiss on her forehead, the sweetness of the caress reverberating down to her very bones. As her head settled against his chest, she listened to the beat of his heart and knew, without a doubt, that hers would forevermore beat for him.

"You belong to me now, Matthew Hanger," she murmured softly as she held tight to his waist.

"Now and always, Josie mine." He kissed the top of her head, then settled his cheek against her brow. "Now and always."

Christy Award finalist and winner of the ACFW Carol Award, HOLT Medallion, and Inspirational Reader's Choice Award, bestselling author **Karen Witemeyer** writes historical romances because she believes the world needs more happily-ever-afters. She is an avid cross-stitcher and shower singer, and she bakes a mean apple cobbler. Karen makes her home in Abilene, Texas, with her husband and three children.

To learn more about Karen and her books and to sign up for her free newsletter featuring special giveaways and behind-the-scenes information, please visit her online at www.karenwitemeyer.com.

Sign Up for Karen's Newsletter!

Keep up to date with news on Karen's upcoming book releases and events by signing up for her email list at karenwitemeyer.com.

More from Karen Witemeyer

After being railroaded by the city council, Abby needs a man's name on her bakery's deed, and a man she can control—not the stoic lumberman Zacharias, who always seems to exude silent confidence. She can't even control her pulse when she's around him. But as trust grows between them, she finds she wants more than his rescue. She wants his heart.

More Than Words Can Say

BETHANYHOUSE

Stay up to date on your favorite books and authors with our free e-newsletters. Sign up today at bethanyhouse.com.

 facebook.com/bethanyhousepublishers   @bethanyhousefiction

 Free exclusive resources for your book group at bethanyhouseopenbook.com

You May Also Like . . .

When Beatrix Waterbury's train is disrupted by a heist, scientist Norman Nesbit comes to her aid. After another encounter, he is swept up in the havoc she always seems to attract—including the attention of the men trying to steal his research—and they'll soon discover the curious way feelings can grow between two very different people in the midst of chaos.

Storing Up Trouble by Jen Turano
AMERICAN HEIRESSES #3
jenturano.com

Determined to uphold her father's legacy, newly graduated Nora Shipley joins an entomology research expedition to India to prove herself in the field. In this spellbinding new land, Nora is faced with impossible choices—between saving a young Indian girl and saving her career, and between what she's always thought she wanted and the man she's come to love.

A Mosaic of Wings by Kimberly Duffy
kimberlyduffy.com

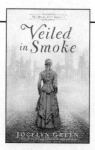

As Chicago's Great Fire destroys their bookshop, Meg and Sylvie Townsend make a harrowing escape from the flames with the help of reporter Nate Pierce. But the trouble doesn't end there—their father is committed to an asylum after being accused of murder, and they must prove his innocence before the asylum truly drives him mad.

Veiled in Smoke by Jocelyn Green
THE WINDY CITY SAGA #1
jocelyngreen.com

BETHANYHOUSE